INDIGO NIGHTS

To Barry, my good friend and mentor, David Greenwood

DAVID GREENWOOD

Michael Terence
Publishing

First published in paperback by
Michael Terence Publishing in 2019
This Second Edition, 2021
http://mtp.agency

ISBN 9781912639878

Dedicated to Christine Martin

'Last night I had a dreary dream.
Beyond the Isle of Skye
I saw a dead man win a fight
and that dead man was I.'

Parts

Introduction

Autumn, 2011

Zac saw Miriam, his ex-wife at the railway station, after a gap of over 15 years. She looked smart and expensively dressed. He thought he had got over her. But his heart seemed to stop.

It was at Shipley, Platform 3, as he stood waiting with a full portfolio for the Ilkley train. He was selling well in a gallery there and the curator, a friendly and supportive man, would most probably pay cash for his new work, so this made him feel fairly cheerful.

She came brusquely onto the platform with a sweet-looking, teenage girl, whom Zac knew to be her daughter, Cathy. She fussed over her as if she was going for some crucial appointment. Motherly and caring, as he knew only too well, she could be. He didn't know whether to try for eye contact or to discreetly ignore her. There had been no unpleasantness between them in the intervening years, much as he had raged against her in his mind. When he looked back towards her, she caught his eye. The Leeds train must have set off with Cathy onboard.

She came over to him, extending a gloved hand, black and supple leather. Her outfit and general appearance looked as clean-cut as ever, well-tailored and still elegantly erotic. As she held his proffered hand firmly, he whiffed a hint of Chanel and class.

Be still my heart, he thought.

They must have exchanged some words. His train now drawing to a halt at the platform. They seemed, from their expressions, to have wished each other well and it wasn't until he was seated inside the Ilkley train and pulling away, that Zac, his throat burning, shuddered, and stifled a sob.

Part One:

HUMILIATION

Chapter 1

London, 1967

"You're a Londoner now, Zac! Best of luck, bonny lad!" called out 'Geordie' Tommy, from the cab of his big Leyland lorry.

You could, in the 'swinging London' of 1967, park right in the centre of the great metropolis. There was warmth in the air that late September and early Autumn, more so than in the West Riding as it was still called then, over 200 miles north.

Zac stood in awe at the straggling and still oppressive-looking semi-ruins of the Bloody Tower to his right and the beautifully engineered and neo-Gothic Tower Bridge directly before him. Also, across the great Thames river and beyond the South Bank, stood Southwark Cathedral and the former haunts of Will Shakespeare and his intriguing and likeable alcoholic actor brother, Edmund. There was no reconstructed Globe Theatre then, or Shard. But Zac relished the moment and thought of Dickens too, who would have visited his father in the old Marshalsea Debtor's Prison and known the evil-smelling 'Clink' and the bleak monotony of his days as a young boy in the blacking factory nearby.

The now-familiar sight of HMS Belfast might still have been in service in what was a formidable Royal Navy. There were many more vessels, lighters and launches as well as naval and commercial ships, as the Pool of London started just to the east of Tower Bridge. There was no Thames barrier to stem the tide and no container ships to rationalise and sterilise one of the biggest Merchant Fleets in the world.

As the tide ebbed, smaller vessels shifted at their anchors and as ever at these times and in all his future strolls along the riverside, he sensed a hush. A slight lowering of the spirits. A lull in the gulls' clamour and the clattering of rigging against masts, as an onshore wind blew fresh from the open sea miles away to the east, beyond Greenwich and Limehouse, as far as Tilbury and the Ocean Liners' depot there. He could even breathe that enticing, though subtle tang of the open sea.

Tommy, one of several drivers at his temporary summer job back up in Bradford, had given Zac a lift down to 'The Smoke'. Zac had a fortnight's wages in his wallet plus holiday pay and a bit of savings. A battered rucksack and a packed portfolio leaned against his young limbs.

Big Tommy vigorously declined the proffered tip and suggested a workman's all-night café as it was still only early morning and they had travelled down from the North overnight. One he knew was over the river to the South in the 'Borough Market', Southwark towards Bermondsey. The other, a short walk to the east, near the docks and Wapping situated among Victorian warehouses and even older, standing precarious, stark and lonely among the blitzed wastes of Deptford and Stepney.

Hopeful and with an empty stomach, Zac headed for Wapping, a full English breakfast and a pint pot of tea. As he swung through the condensation dripping door of Tommy's recommended café, he found a cheery, raucous and steamy canteen, loud with Cockney and Scouse voices.

It reminded him so much of his first blissful day at Art College when he took a tea break at the workman's cafe on Bolton Road, Bradford. A new page in his young life. He remembered Glenda's eager grin, as she glanced up at him with a drop of early autumn rain on the bridge of her nose, that he wanted to lick. A stray wisp of her blond hair from under her dark Cobalt Blue beret and her tentative gesture to recover it, which nearly broke his heart in recollection, as she tucked it back into her baby blue 'Mary Jane' plastic grip. Her mittened hands around a workman's scalding mug of tea.

Chapter 2

He slept the night at Joe's, an old school and art class chum, who lived in Whitechapel, the centre of the Jewish and vibrant East End. The rather dilapidated old terrace stood just around the corner from infamous Sydney Street and not far from Cable Street where Mosley's Blackshirts had been so resoundingly thrashed, in the anti-fascist street battles of the 1930s.

Zac relished the Jewish ambience, its working class, cosmopolitan feel and the real engine of what had become 'Swinging London'. He rolled off to himself the names of the local boys and girls who had made their mark on the British cultural scene. His favourite 20th-century British painter David Bomberg. Mark Gertler and Wolf Mankowitz's 'A Kid For Two Farthings'. Anthony Newley and Lionel Bart. Arnold Wesker and Joan Littlewood.

He noted that the kosher corner butchers' shops around Whitechapel and Brick Lane, looked far poorer than back home. When he took an early morning walk on his first full day in the 'Smoke' for cigs, milk and his 'Guardian' newspaper, he was thrilled to see old men playing chess in the cafes and near the famous Whitechapel Art Gallery and Brick Lane, he saw an abstracted and most unworldly-seeming Rabbi, with his long, straggly beard and yarmulke, looking like he'd just arrived from some grim shtetl in the Pale of old Russia. *This* was Zac's England too. Probably even more so than the others, though he was a Gentile, he felt instantly at home, in not being at home. He had always yearned to join the gipsies and the Circus when it left town.

Chapter 3

The previous evening, he and Joe with his mate along too had gone for a drink in a characteristically English pub, 'The Prospect of Whitby' on the waterfront at Wapping, It had a lively folk-rock scene. It was the rage, now that the Beatles and Stones, were beginning to seem a bit staid. The joke was, that London was not so much 'swinging' any more, but 'dangling'.

The pub went back to Tudor times and was set on several floors. It echoed to the sound of fiddles and whining mandolins. Simon and Garfunkel were BIG, very big that summer and the folk-rock group played one of the latest pieces they had picked up on one of their trips, as unknowns to the older English Folk scene. Zac loved it, as this ambience, he supposed was nearer to traditional England. But the one he experienced at Whitechapel seemed just as real, if not more so. That whole summer had resonated to 'Scarborough Fair' and 'Mrs. Robinson'. Gigantic film posters of a young and gauche Dustin Hoffman, lusting at Ann Bancroft's black-stockinged leg seemed ubiquitous. Magic was in the air that first night in a great city.

They visited the down-market, plebeian Islington, to see Joe's mate's little family. Barry Cole's young wife and baby. He had just had his first novel published: 'A run across the Island' and sharing in the after-glow of his success, we took a couple of bottles of Brown Ale and a cheap Italian red plonk to wet the baby's head.

Life seemed full of hope. 'We working-class lads and lasses and colonial barbarians are coming into our own,' thought Zac.

It was the nearest he got to feeling he was finally making some progress in his life. As a near contemporary of Barry's generation, junior lecturers and painters and pop groups on the up, he had definitely felt that he was in the foothills of fame.

Barry, who had the obligatory cavalier locks, and dungarees, proudly set about changing a nappy, as his cute, teenage-looking wife admonished him for being a 'fascist' over some domestic misdemeanour. Zac would never have heard that 'oop north', even at Art College at the time. They must have been the pioneers of what was to become known much later as the Islington 'Left' intelligentsia. He had the intimation that they were well embarked on the Left, in a 'cultural' war that they could well win.

Later, as he and Joe walked back to Whitechapel, Zac voiced his astonishment that they were still merely on the edge of the old city of London. Shakespeare would have probably had lodgings close by and as they passed Clerkenwell Green, they noticed the slightly battered sign of the British Communist Party. He remembered that Marx had lived here. Italian clock-makers and French refugees had congregated here, at Spitalfields and Bethnal Green, along with early Chartists, this area long having been a hive of political radicalism.

Passing the blitzed ruins of Clerkenwell Priory, Joe pointed out St. John's Gate, heavily restored as it was, one of the few remaining medieval barbican type guardhouses, on what was the old London wall. It looked like the background to one of Hogarth's London street scenes. The Priory ruins lay to their left and on this transcendentally beautiful night, it seemed only minutes before they arrived at Smithfield Market, stocked with baying and terrified animals. Then down Farringdon Road and almost into the old City that Zac's father had seen in flames twenty-seven years before. On to Aldgate and soon they arrived in Shoreditch, not far from Hackney. Even the sound of the names; Bow Street and St. Clements, just half a mile to their right, were so evocative: the gateway to the West End.

Very soon they were back in Whitechapel, where at last Zac eventually went to sleep on Joe's settee next to his treasured, ancient cast-iron litho press. William Blake or even William Mallord Turner might just have left the chambers. London hummed outside nearly all night, the warm, beating heart of the great metropolis. He was home!

Chapter 4

Joe had accompanied Zac with his luggage that last day on the way to the West End taking him on a brief detour around Bermondsey and the edge of 'Dirty' Deptford, a hard-working and hard-bitten dockland area. Bermondsey, atmospheric and exciting as it was with its warren of ancient streets and bomb-sites, wharves and warehouses, seemed impenetrable to them. Heading for the more familiar north bank of the river and the old City, they walked through the ancient centre of the town and up Ludgate Hill to St. Paul's. Burnt umber-stained and pock-marked by shrapnel due to a terrible night in 1940, it stood proud among patches of wasteland and rubble, an icon of London's defiance.

The two old pals shook hands and wished each other the best before going on their separate ways.

From his reading, Zac recognised Fleet Street and the Strand. The Temple Church and the lanes leading down to the Inns of Court that Shakespeare and Dickens would have known, and that later, homeless and destitute, Zac would know only too well. But on that day of promise, he passed out of the old city and St. Clement Danes, paying homage to the RAF squadrons, whose memorials this blitz-gutted church hosted. He passed the Savoy and emerged into the West End. Throwing himself down on one of the steps, with his back to Nelson's Column, he rested before entering the National Gallery.

He had a couple of hours to kill before he headed down Whitehall to Westminster and back along the embankment to Waterloo Bridge. Then to the South Bank again, Waterloo Station and the train to Surbiton. He had been invited to stay with Glenda, an old Bradford Art College friend, for a couple of nights. They had written to each other whilst he was at Sunderland Art College and sometimes met briefly in their holidays, usually in her home town of Halifax, and have a bit to drink and maybe a meal together.

But for now, we need to see that rather naive young man, almost with pity, as he straightens up, brushes himself off and picking up his burden, strides purposefully, with a song in his heart, across Trafalgar Square, to the National Gallery.

He had an appointment with a Dutch lady, Margaretha de Geer. She had been dead about 300 years, but the great Dutch artist Rembrandt had painted her and he had met her once on a fleeting art college trip a couple of years before. He had promised that he would return to renew his acquaintance and here he was, come to fulfil his vow. With excitement and his heart beating, he mounted the great staircase, after depositing, thankfully, his portfolio and rucksack with the porters. Just another drab and inconsequential-looking young man from the provinces, he went up the opulent great staircase and headed for the Rembrandt room.

Sitting down gratefully in one of the madder red plush seats, he stared up into the face of the grand old lady, Margarethe de Geer, her head, skull-like and almost decapitated, rising above her great white lace ruff. But so alive that he could almost smell her. He would return many times in his life to gaze into those wise and fathomless eyes. He drowned his soul in them and even imagined that he could feel the wrench of times past. Could smell the rich and sap-like linseed oils, gums and waxes, in the Dutchman's grey and sepia coloured studio. The dim light streamed serenely from way above the old man's head, prophet-like in his battered velveteen and maroon turban. A light not unlike Zac's native Yorkshire, gloomy but warm. A flick of flake white impasto representing the maestro's under-shirt brought life to the vision. A light that struck the old Matriarch's wrinkled forehead, of the palest Naples yellow over a Venetian/Indian red underpainting, accented by a pale but freshening lemon yellow. Her voice a bit tetchy now, as she twitches her rabbit-skin stole.

"Mynheer Rembrandt-have you no coals-it's freezing in here, and the rain drips down from your skylight, so!"

Chapter 5

After his rendezvous with the Dutch lady, Zac took up his burden again and headed out of the great doors of the National Gallery, south across Trafalgar Square, with a nod of the head to Nelson high above. Then down Whitehall, past the Horse Guards and the grim offices of state, to the lugubrious and overbearing Air Ministry and the incongruously domestic-looking Downing Street. Then to Westminster where he thought about visiting the great French Gothic abbey. But tired now, and overwhelmed, he headed for Westminster Bridge and sat down for a brief rest on an embankment seat.

He rolled a cigarette and gazed wistfully up at Big Ben. He thought of his parents and so many servicemen and women who had been photographed in front of this great icon. For his father, this stone symbol of Imperial Great Britain represented a noble history in which he had played a small part so long ago. Finishing the cig, he picked up his gear again and trudged towards Waterloo Bridge. Then, on to the railway station and the train to Kingston and Surbiton. To Glenda, and humiliation.

Zac tensed up a little at the thought of seeing her again but found himself enjoying this suburban Southern Railway journey. His artist's eye soaked up the cityscape, visible in the distance on the other side of the river. As the train trundled on past run-down factories and the grubby-looking pebble dash of suburban villas, he found he could pick up on the slightly different feel of the older boroughs. Lambeth which William Blake would hardly recognise these days and Vauxhall, that 18th-century pleasure ground. Then Battersea with tantalising glimpses north of a gun-metal river and the gleam of highlighted stucco on faraway Chelsea and Pimlico buildings. Putney had a hint of small-town primness alongside the raffishly squalid Wandsworth which gradually merged into the smug suburbs of Wimbledon and Rayne's Park followed by Barnes Common. Here the river swung south through open-looking heathland, towards Chiswick and the opulent Thames Valley further west, Kingston-upon-Thames and Surbiton.

His stomach tightened as the train took him ever closer to bourgeois Hampton Court, Esher and finally Surbiton. The thought of Glenda and Surbiton frightened him a little.

Chapter 6

She looked the same though they had seen very little of each other in the intervening years, maybe a few drinks in Bradford or Halifax during college vacations. She seemed less Francoise Hardy/Diana Dors now and more Faye Dunaway/Catherine Deneuve. When Zac looked into those unfocused eyes, just before the permitted kiss, he perceived a slightly distant and almost schizoid look as if she was observing some alien life form. Hardly frigid but inhumanly clinical. Chilling in fact. And inexplicably sexy. Maybe it was those lips, soft doors that they were, and unlike her unfathomable eyes, so welcoming. He had to drag himself away and felt slightly repelled by the washed-out, anaemic look on her face. The French expression, 'Une Jolie-laide' came to mind. She seemed a mixture of beauty and brutality.

She introduced him to Frieda, her flatmate and fellow art student, a sprightly brunette, squat and Celtic from Cornwall but with a very 'Home Counties' accent. Glenda had not lost her Halifax accent, a strong and matronly contralto with a more recently acquired veneer of sophistication. Zac could imagine her presenting a formidable yet attractive presence at College. He was sure that the staff there were in awe of her on superficial acquaintance. Like Pip in Dicken's 'Great Expectations', he imagined himself in the presence of the haughty Estella. That his boot soles had suddenly got thicker and his hands coarser.

Surbiton was as suburban as Zac had imagined but not as petit-bourgeois. Its riverside location leant it an almost Bohemian, genteel ambience. From the upstairs lounge, he caught an elegaic view of the river. Large, sloping lawns of the huge villas reached down to the slow-moving Thames. Sylvan and willow-shaded, with here and there, a view of salmon or terracotta pantiled roofs, copper beech trees contrasting with the cool green exclamation marks of poplar and darkest yew. Elm trees graced the river banks as far downstream as Richmond and Kingston.

He couldn't help noticing the shared bed in the girls' room. Nothing remarkable at the time, though up north Zac's fellow students had a bit more space for their rent money. A torn cover from a recent 'Sunday Times' magazine featuring Rudolf Nureyev was pinned above the bed head.

Current pin-up boy for middle-class English girls. Zac couldn't help but smile to himself at what his recent Geordie girlfriends, Joan Duggan and Jooles Carnie from Gateshead and Byker might have exclaimed:

"Howwa, Man-wor no Lezzies!"

He chuckled to himself at the thought of how the girls would have 'got on' and felt more relaxed. Such was the cultural difference between the far north corner of England and the metropolitan, suburban south-east.

Frieda made them all coffee. Zac excitedly opened his portfolio to show examples of his college work. There followed an awkward silence. Glenda, though she could be brutal, was brave and honest. To her, his work seemed old-fashioned and though the word had not been coined yet "heavy." He had discovered for himself at Sunderland an unfamiliar, figurative and neo-romantic strain in the history of English painting, as well as an enthusiasm for the Pre-Raphaelites. He was no longer the 'whizz-kid' that maybe Glenda looked up to at Bradford and though he had become somewhat isolated at Sunderland, it was to the credit of his tutors that they allowed him to continue his lonely path. He had no interest in getting a good Diploma, only to earnestly follow his vision, confused as it was.

To Glenda and Frieda, Zac's sketches of miners, pitheads, ravaged dockland and other devastated northern industrial landscapes seemed 'old hat'. In a subtle way though, he had never thought of himself as a snob, their relative status had been reversed. Glenda was obliged to retake her Foundation year where they met and when he was considered a bit of a star. Now she had become the star and conscientious final year student. He sensed his chuntering on about Ruskin and Marx and his dislike for the currently fashionable American 'Cool' and 'Hard-Edged' abstract international style of the art magazines, made him sound reactionary.

Zac imagined they thought he reeked of sweat and testosterone. They were unfamiliar with pub fights, the end of term piss-ups and bawdy ballad sessions so beloved of Sunderland and Newcastle art colleges. Even with a muscular camaraderie between the sexes, this must have repelled them. He began to understand though, and increasingly so, how Glenda felt and how and why she left the north. She was an ambitious, brave and intelligent young woman, not to mention ruthless.

When it was Glenda's turn to show her work, he had to bite his tongue as it seemed the usual bland, abstract, Americanized fayre. He didn't say so because he didn't share Glenda's honesty or courage. However, he did like the whimsical side she revealed in her studies of the great visionary, William Blake and he said so.

Having already sussed the strength of her ambition, he sympathised, recalling one of their Halifax or Bradford reunions, when she told him her Bradford Tutor had asked: did she want to become another middle-class housewife with two kids and a hefty mortgage? With a rapidly fading ambition to paint once again, once the kids were at College or Uni? Or be a free woman building her own career?' He sensed she was still smarting from that.

He blanched slightly when she said that her Blake studies were only for her own interest. Her ambition was to get a First Class Degree, as a launchpad for her future career. In his neo-romantic way, part of him held that ambition in contempt and there lay the widening void between them. Zac, a romantic and idealist, self-indulgent and irresponsible, erratic, irrational and unfocussed could not have felt more different from Glenda and her ruthless streak.

Chapter 7

They went for drinks in the local pub, an attractive, barge-boarded, riverside place with Edwardian boating group photos on the walls. They sat outside in the fading light, at cast iron and marble-topped tables, as if to complete the Edwardian illusion. It was still warm but a chill threatened from the gently whispering Thames. It would have been inconceivable to sit outside at this time of year in Tyne or Wearside.

Some student contemporaries of the girls joined them and sophisticated conversations followed, mainly about relationships, mortgages and possible teaching prospects. It all sounded very 'grown-up' compared to the frenzied and passionate arguments of Zac's student friends in the 'barbaric' north. For some reason, he had a terrible desire to take hold of each one individually and shake them.

He slept on their sofa that night, reading first, with excitement, Golding's 'Pincher Martin, highly recommended by Glenda. And then even some Leavis, that austere literary critic who was still quite fashionable. When he eventually drifted off to sleep, he had dreams. His body ached for hers as it had for no other woman's. Something as elemental as he had just discovered through his reading. He knew though, that his feelings were not returned by her. Only something understood, something occult, something unnameable.

The next morning, Glenda suggested that he look around town as she was expecting a visit from her tutor, to give her some advice on her dissertation. He sauntered around the pleasant town. It must have been Barnes now, he realised, as Surbiton was a bit further from the river. Again, it was brought home to him, how an attractive and ambitious woman, talented as well, would be drawn to such a charming town, after the apparent grimness of somewhere like Halifax. After such bleakness, the very air must have been liberating to such a noble and free spirit as her.

Zac went to the same riverside pub as the previous evening, enjoyed a couple of pints and read most of the Guardian, giving Glenda plenty of time for her tutorial.

The back door of her place was unlocked, as she had promised. He let himself in and coughed loudly as he started to mount the stairs to her flat. Suddenly he heard Glenda's voice cry out in the ecstasy of sexual abandon. Aghast, he turned and stumbled back down the stairs. She must have shouted down to him, to meet her in the pub. Or maybe it was pre-arranged and in his near grief and shock, he had forgotten.

With his heart pounding, Zac bought a half-bottle of whiskey from a corner off-licence. His first introduction to what would become a future ally. Then he staggered on to the pub. He must have quickly got on to his second pint, by now acquiring quite a taste for the flatter but more hop-flavoured southern brew and was about to pretend to complete the Guardian crossword, when the saloon-style inner door of the lounge bar swung open and Glenda made her entrance. Proud and regal-looking, she was followed by a handsome, and athletic man in his late 20's or early 30's. Very English Home Counties. Good school obviously and probably just old enough to have served a short-term commission in some distinguished and fashionable regiment.

A civil and courteous conversation followed. The man seemed affable enough and had a firm handshake.

"Hello, old boy. Zac, is it not? Heard a lot about you!"

Something deep inside Zac shrivelled. He felt deflated, drained. He let his arms fall at his sides like an exhausted ploughman. His boots heavy with mud, his heart heavy, gnarled like his grubby hands hanging clod-like, defeated. A sudden rage surged and then swiftly died inside him.

They parted on civil terms. Why on earth should he have felt he had any claims on a grown woman whom he had only petted and kissed as teenagers several years ago? Yet it hurt. He was a gauche and provincial boor. What else had he expected from a young woman still in her first bloom, with the world at her feet? Who was he?

And still, it hurt.

Chapter 8

Just being alive and young in the great city at that time gave one an education in life. It was easier to rent a bedsit, too. Zac got one in Chiswick the day after leaving Glenda's in Surbiton. It comprised a largish upper room with a charming dormer window and a cosy little kitchenette. Fully furnished and quite cheap, in a quiet and sedate Edwardian Terrace not far from Chiswick High street. As simple as that. Glenda and he had parted amicably and Zac had more than enough cash to pay a week's rent in advance as well as a deposit for the same amount.

On the evening of his arrival, he strolled around Turnham Green, close to the tube station and a handsome Victorian Gothic church. Then he embarked on a prolonged reconnaissance to suss out a likely local pub. Zac found his way to Strand-on-the-Green, which was something of a local beauty spot and familiar to many Brits of his generation, as the location for many post-war, black and white 'B' moves. On the way there he came across a decaying hostelry, The Lord Raglan, with that delicious melancholy atmosphere, favoured by genteel and alcoholic minor celebrities.

The river and Strand-on-the-Green were closer than he thought and he found it all idyllic. It was still light and warm enough to nurse a pint or two while enjoying the sights and sounds of the river. He often went there on pay nights with a book, sitting outside and revelling in the 'Whistler-like' views downstream towards Chelsea and Battersea.

For a fairly fit and rootless young man, the temporary Employment Agencies provided ideal work opportunities. Later he would meet like-minded spirits: Irish; provincial British; Australians; Kiwis; Canadians and even the occasional American. Though everyone sensed the end of 'Swinging London' they were determined, almost in a spirit of desperation, to join in the fun while they could.

For about six months, he was content to have a temporary job as a Quality Control Inspector at Coty's Perfume Factory on the Great West Road, that sprawl of pre-World War Two industrial ribbon development, north and west of genteel Chiswick and small-town Brentford. The job was excruciatingly boring but his employers, a charming and paternalistic old firm, were pleasant enough to work for.

Coty's occupied an attractive 1930's Art Deco building, with a subsidised canteen. Zac was interviewed by an ex-Oxford Chemistry Don and a butch-looking, ex-WREN Personnel Manageress who was frighteningly kind and gave the impression of someone who had worked on something 'Hush-Hush' at the 'War Office.

Dull though the job was, the people in the factory seemed pleasant, if a bit tame and sometimes Zac wished he had stayed on longer. Chiswick was a genteel enough place to live, albeit decaying. Even though his wage was poor, he enjoyed a drink at weekends and spent most Sundays hiking the huge expanse of London, exploring his capital city. He felt mildly patriotic then, for all his leftish political views.

He started the bad habit of taking the occasional day off, just to relieve the monotony of his work which reduced his income somewhat. But he revelled in the decadence of it. However, because of this self-indulgence, he often struggled to pay the rent and even occasionally felt the pangs of hunger, as he would rather forego supper than an evening drink in the drab and austere 'Lord Raglan', amongst the decaying thespians and genteel derelicts in the Saloon Bar. Gradually, the pang of loneliness became as tangible as his occasional hunger. He felt a kind of metaphysical unease. A miasma of quiet despair enveloped him, that was almost impossible to describe. One aspect of this unease was that he felt lost in time, or that he had too much time. He was merely passing through this strange planet and as an avid, if undisciplined reader, the particular author he was immersed in at any one time, took over his emotional life. Zac became a 'time traveller.' He was uncentred, his moorings lost as if an ebb-tide had sheared his anchor.

London too appeared to be 'dangling' and the whole world holding its breath. The political atmosphere everywhere had turned mildly toxic. His alienated existence didn't shield him from the double shock of Martin Luther King's assassination and that of Bobby Kennedy. Enoch Powell's turgid 'rivers of blood' speech had an abysmal effect on the attitudes of some of the sulky, white working-class Londoners with whom Zac worked.

"Well, he did go on a bit," complained one of his West London workmates.

Yet little vignettes of the magic of those days stood out. Out of time, almost.

Chapter 9

After he left Coty's employ, he was walking back to Shepherds Bush one Sunday evening in the early Summer of '68. He had a room there and was working for 'Manpower' an employment Agency in seedy and more Caribbean Notting Hill. He felt hungry and with payday not yet due, he didn't even have the tube fare home.

It had been a long walk from Kingsbury where his assignment had been in a plastics factory. But he was not far from Baker Street and then only two miles or so, slightly downhill through Bayswater and North Kensington to Wood Lane and his little room. After passing through Marylebone, he knew the longest part of his trek was over but his feet were dragging and he felt as if he had entered a dream where he found himself walking through a city suddenly devoid of people, just their shadows remaining like a de Chirico painting. London could be like that, suddenly quiet then still.

Just as he was feeling really forlorn, he saw Paul McCartney who by his body language appeared to be as dejected as Zac. Extremely good-looking and elegantly-dressed, he had his head down and being the only two people around and about to pass each other on the same pavement, Paul raised his hand in a perfunctory salute and even nodded his head, returning Zac's eye contact with a 'sotto voce' greeting. Zac knew the Beatles were embroiled in some kind of battle concerning their record label, Apple, whose offices were in nearby Baker Street.

Chapter 10

During this period, Zac was not lost, just overwhelmed. But he was young and still sanguine and determined. The great buzz of the metropolis sustained as well as oppressed him. Because of his increasingly radical politics, he was a regular visitor to Hyde Park Corner and Tower Green. He became a huge fan of both the Reverend Lord Soper and the vibrant young firebrand, Tariq Ali, without completely losing his admiration for the country's history and Empire.

One day, as he was mooching around the back of St. James's Palace and The Mall on one of his 'rest' days, a platoon of Guardsmen swung into view. They marched in step, fixed bayonets and boots gleaming, bearskins shining an iridescent indigo blue and deep Lampblack. Their commanding officer to their side, with sword raised, marched straight out of Wellington's army and into the London of parked Minis and 'E'-Type Jaguars.

He stood in awe, feeling like a country bumpkin, as he tried to discern from the hackles on their busbies, which brigade they were from. Green and white for the Welsh Guards. Red or white for the Coldstream or Grenadiers. A Coldstreamer, he decided, from the grouping of his tunic buttons, remembering what his Dad had taught him. A particularly fine-looking guardsman caught his eye and gave him a sly wink and a flash of ivory white teeth above his shining brass chin strap.

There were plenty of city types in London too, with the obligatory bowler hats, emerging from the bowels of the underground with the same martial spirit of his fellow countrymen. A small part of bohemian Zac thrilled to the swank and manliness, the spit and polish, the 'esprit de Corps'.

Chapter 11

On his wanderings or time stealing excursions, Zac felt the footfall of history. St Mary Woolnoth, Old Jewry and St Clement Danes still resonated to the sound of half-remembered childhood nursery rhymes: "You owe me three farthings rang the bells of St Martins"; "Orange and Lemons, rang the bells of St Clements."

Dad was there one terrible night in December 1940 when half the old City was on fire and south across the river the great Tate and Lyle sugar refinery in Bermondsey had been hit. A huge wave of white-hot caramelised sugar had surged through the dockside wharves and into a boiling Thames at Southwark and Tower Bridge.

He would have seen the Temple church on fire, St Clement Danes rising above a sea of flames in the Strand and St Paul's Cathedral, standing iconic and proud over Fleet Street, miraculously untouched. Another burning cauldron from Cheapside and Bow to the Old Bailey ("When will you pay me?") Holy Sepulchre at Newgate, a flaming Guildhall and St. Lawrence Jewry in the centre of the old medieval city.

He heard the thwuuum-thwuuuum of the Heinkels and Dorniers overhead, watched the interweaving, threading searchlights and heard too the constant thwack-thwack from the anti-aircraft batteries in the great London parks. Then the plaintive howl of the All Clear, echoing from the Medway ports, downriver to Gravesend and Rochester and the Victoria and Albert Docks. Then upriver to Chelsea Reach and Hammersmith and further upstream to the western and plush suburbs of Richmond, Esher, Epsom and Virginia Water.

Zac wandered those streets, following his father's ghost.

Chapter 12

Even though Glenda was busy with her Final Year's course work, as promised, she occasionally kept in contact.

At Wood Lane, in his quaint little bedsit, dear old Mrs Smith, his landlady, 'coo-eed' to him from her back room on the ground floor and said there was mail for him. When she handed him a scarlet and scented letter, he knew it was from Glenda.

Inside, he found a fiver and an invitation to come and visit her. The Goddess had smiled upon him.

Chapter 13

30th September 1963

It was his first day at Bradford Art College. The bright, fresh faces of his contemporaries. The sassy glamour of the older girls up at the main building. The fashion and textiles students, all of them budding Mary Quants, with their yard-deep mascara, primary coloured acrylic jewellery and crazy, hooped earrings. It wasn't quite mini-skirt time but too late for the drabness of the 'Beats' half a generation before. Though a few sad-looking types lurked like Marabou Storks about the corridors and the vast, sky-lighted studios of Bradford College of Art.

The Art College was a Victorian masterpiece. The polluting indigo on the stonework failed to camouflage the almost Parisian magnificence of its structure, the mansard roof which represented something of a Bradford speciality and exquisitely set and moulded Oriel windows. There was a noble staircase up to the main entrance and in contrast a temporary-looking potting shed. A yard abutted the sculpture basement and ample studio space on the first floor above. The main feature of this elevation was a magnificent life room, with windows extending from a ground floor/mezzanine up to the third floor.

Despite the Baroque facade, Victorian Bradford loved it's Gothic and this was revealed in the main interior staircase, the central feature of which extended up four or five floors to the lavishly sky-lighted roof, opening up a vertiginous stairwell, up and down which rushed colourful vocational students, vivacious and tremendously sexy!

Zac's year and his particular group had excitedly absconded to the Art College pub, The Manville Arms, known as a den of iniquity by the more respectable citizens and where youngsters thronged, drank and bonded in the saloon bar. Both sexes sported newly-bought duffel coats, the odd college scarf, fresh and new or even school ties, as these were still rather socially constrained times. He was almost embarrassed to be wearing clerical grey M&S trousers, a school blazer and vigorously polished black leather shoes.

The base for their year was in a Victorian annexe across town which made for an almost Oxbridge Collegial atmosphere of intimacy and, dare one say, happiness? Maybe a contributing factor was that they had all escaped from either school Sixth Forms or in Zac's case, a dreary and snooty Grammar School where flannel trousers and social conformism were the rule. Then there was that which his more proletarian new comrades had escaped from, almost certain recruitment into the mill or the armed forces. The girls amongst them had the choice of the mill, secretarial school or shop work. Maybe that explained the 'Demob Happy' feeling amongst them. Maybe it was also because only a year before, President Kennedy had stopped them all being roasted alive in a thermonuclear war, during the Cuban Missile Crisis. Or maybe they just were young and bursting with energy and hormones.

Chapter 14

Glenda Sugden was one in the group, huddled together at the beer-soaked table. Of all the excited and roistering freshers, she seemed to like Zac, or maybe chance just threw them together. Zac felt a bit surprised as he was very virginal at the time and as one of his charismatic artist tutors apostrophised him later: 'The very image of a first-year Divinity Student.' Glenda herself was a bit of a Dolly Bird. Long blonde hair and a nice figure. Swedish or Finnish looking, with the bone structure and colouring, suggestive of Scandinavian heritage. She reminded him a bit of Françoise Hardy, with voluptuous lips and an unaffected, rather handsome smile, warm, brave, and open-hearted. A Halifax lass, down to earth, he thought, rather patronisingly, and a 'D.H Lawrence Woman'.

The backroom, or what was laughingly called then 'the Saloon Bar', had waiter service. Something that was to continue in the North for many more years. There were bell pushes for service but these were hardly needed as Fred, their waiter, toothless and with a dish towel over his shoulder, a beer gut held in by a broad, leather belt and a tray packed with brimming glasses, seemed ubiquitous. In those optimistic days, there was full employment, or very nearly. But working conditions in many places were archaic. Over the years, every time Zac came back to Bradford and homed in on the 'Manville', Fred was there, with his toothless whistle, extending a stubby arm, pints of foaming beer swilling around on his tray.

Many youngsters joined them, then departed home or to the Art Shop to buy from a list of materials ordered by their tutors. Some, Taffy, Derek, and a couple of jolly lasses, Lilla and Beryl who was also strangely old-fashioned and rather prim, all came from secondary modern schools. Glenda and Zac found themselves cocooned in their own space, almost an item, in contemporary parlance.

All of them bonded like old comrades. It seemed whatever their social origins, they felt liberated. No longer pariahs and outcasts. It was like a foretaste of heaven. Zac wondered if, in far darker times, their parents might have felt like this on joining up, after they had been assigned to their regiments or billets, meeting contemporaries from all over the Empire as well as Britain.

Zac sat at a small saloon table opposite Glenda. But he basked in an aura of calm expectancy between them. He picked up on a Halifax accent, warmer, more rounded and Lancastrian than the harsher Bradfordian. She had no airs and graces with forthrightness and courage in her gaze. Her 18-year-old forehead had the subtlest lines and faint blemishes, which unaccountably, he wanted to kiss. He dearly wanted to kiss it, tenderly. Oh, so tenderly!

Her eyes appeared slightly unfocused and vague, with a night-time intelligence. Introverted and enigmatic, as if she was looking inwards. She had a skilfully applied 'bravura' slash of dark grey/black indigo mascara, lending an oriental look to her gaze. She knew how to use a cursive single stroke of eyeliner to each eyelid, making them look more alluring, with little or no eyeshadow. Her long, blond hair framed a well-proportioned and longish oval Scandinavian face. Her jaw was strong without being brutal and her lips sensual. Her teeth regular and dazzling, her smile that of a brave and dashing World War Two Soviet airwoman.

A loose lock of her hair caught the late afternoon light. Then she smiled, and a sparkle in her eyes lit up his soul. Zac must have fallen in love with her there and then.

Her whole aura was both womanly, with a hint of Diana Dors and yet slightly girlish. Narrow-hipped but otherwise curvaceous, she wore a navy gabardine raincoat, its belt tied tightly but casually. Had she lost its buckle or was it a concession to adult fashion, a touch of French chic? She snuggled occasionally into her old Grammar school gold and indigo-striped scarf and shivered slightly, in the early autumn chill. He could see her now, lifting mittened paws to blow on the delicate exposed flesh of her wrists. He thought he could smell the outside air, fresh rain and ozone and something else, a moorland air coming from her. Her rather ugly but strangely touching, 'brave boy' nose, made him anxious again to kiss it. She settled her dark cobalt beret at a self-consciously chic, Parisian angle and chuckled.

"You never" she retorted to an anonymous joker in the company and Zac's heart seemed to stand still.

He must have leant forward and caught a quick appraising look from her, not at all hostile. He found that he liked her very much and the stillness between them deepened. Ever so slightly, his heart ached. But deliciously so.

The magic was dissipated by a hairy arm, jutting around his right ear, holding a foaming pint. He relieved Fred of his burden and caught a wink from his new friend, Roy, one of the lads in their party who raised his glass.

"Cheers, Zac, lad! Thought we'd lost you, there!"

Chapter 15

Life Class was a joy, none of the slapdash, easy-going regime of school or the Art Club.

"Silence in the Life-Room!" shouted Bill Major, one of our charismatic and young tutors. "Right. Begin."

It was how Zac imagined it would be.

Moya Krause, another tutor, a sultry brunette with Cleopatra eye make-up, held up her pencil to make a sight-line on the model, Zac's first naked woman.

"Lovely tonality, Zac," she said in a charmingly husky voice. "But more structure required."

Her musky fragrance, her Salome-like aura made her appear sultry and exotic. Was she Viennese Jewish, perhaps? Mused Zac. The enticing shimmer of her black stockings, so sheer, her high heels. Her thigh and a breast pressing ever so gently into his.

"Oh, my God. Don't give me a hard-on," prayed Zac, silently.

Awakening him from his reverie, John Carter who was already getting a name in London as an up and coming abstract painter, and her athletic, charismatic husband, burst into their space just as the model took a break.

"Look what I got from town? A Royal Marine Commando Combat jacket, and the latest desert boots. All from the town Army and Navy surplus store. Five quid the lot, boys and girls!" he yelled. "Ce-Zanne!" his familiar war cry.

Dutch cockney, Andy Hoogenboom, a sculptor, was another of their highly talented part-time lecturers. Sexy and every inch the flamboyant continental artist, he sported an ex-US marine WWII flying jacket, probably original. Something he casually mentioned buying on a trip to Paris for the weekend, in Les Halles.

"Should have seen the place, mate!"

He was a real ladies' man, with twinkling cornflower blue eyes his boyish

Cockney manner. They all had the fashionable craze, for their set, of anything from the States or the continent, apart from Germany. A Gitane always dangling from his lips, he had an easy and comfortable way with women. Zac admired the gentle and non-lubricious way he put their life models at ease when they were obviously slightly nervous of baring themselves to young men, who had probably never seen a naked woman before, never mind drawn one.

You could really sense youngsters setting their own fashion at that time and not just students. There was always some lad, even in these early sixties, sporting very long hair. Some lass experimenting with near mini-skirts, or faded and home-shrunk Levis. Patrick Hughes, Zac's favourite tutor, was every inch the formidable-looking intellectual but with a wild, anarchic and friendly mien, coupled with a Shavian wit.

How could he stay long in a stifling Police family, after such dazzlingly generous and 'turned-on' company? Thought Zac.

They worked hard too and having survived Christmas at home, he looked forward to what the new term would bring, as well as a new pop classic out nearly every week.

At home, Zac sensed a darkening in his Father's mood. He disapproved of the liberal attitudes Zac was adopting. He had got into university and even had an offer for Oxbridge but turned the opportunity down for Art College and was not regretting the choice. His father was incensed.

"What a waste!" he grumbled.

A war-time hero and now a Policeman, a man's man in a macho men's world. He was typically Victorian, almost Teutonic in his attitudes. He was a terror at times and kept Zac's sweet and submissive mother in his thrall.

Chapter 16

One night, during Zac's second term, he dragged him out of bed and warned him to clean up his room, which was full of art materials, or he could find another 'billet'. Then he threw off his police uniform jacket, removed his leather belt and ordered him onto the bed, face down and 'in position'. Though he was tall and strong now, having worked in the market at weekends for a few years, lugging and even throwing huge sacks of potatoes about, Zac was still afraid of his father. The Sergeant still carried an air of authority about him, from his dark blue jacket with Police Sergeant's stripes and his WWII RAF medals.

Something snapped in Zac's psyche, although, for now, the Sergeant had a physical advantage. Zac suddenly saw his father for the Nazi thug he really was and braced himself for a beating. He had an old bed with a cast iron head and he clutched the bars and gritted his teeth as the blows rained down. After a bit, he discovered that he didn't feel the pain and in fact could ride with it. Zac had not realised that he had an erection and as the sergeant dragged him to attention, he was humiliated to see his tumescent penis and he felt degraded and ashamed, naked and debased, debauched almost.

Zac stared into his father's eyes. Beneath the ageing flab and jowls, he could still see the young and rather handsome Teutonic face but above all Zac saw the 'dark face of England' as his Irish friends in London later described it: a John-Bull Bastard, a Hangman and a slave driver. The brutal face of a typical British Army NCO. Bull-necked with a double chin smeared in bacon grease. At that moment, all that he had left in the way of awe of the sergeant and the power and class that he served, was a slight physical fear.

Zac despised England then, at the fag-end of an increasingly discredited Tory regime and the whole corrupt superstructure, built on a hundred million African slaves. He remembered Grandma Greenwood, his stepmother, already semi-senile when in the 50s, only half a dozen years before, another execution was announced in the morning on the pompous and overbearing BBC: "The condemned ate a hearty breakfast."

"Eeeh, ah DO like a good hanging!" she said.

This was Dad. The saluting base. The Trooping of the Colour. England's bloody glory. The Queen's Birthday gun salute, echoing around Kremlin-like Whitehall and he was near physically sick. Somehow the stench of stale urine and faeces overcame him. He had seen up Britannia's skirts and he did not like what he saw.

Zac felt a cold fury for the Sergeant and that uniform and the stinking Empire, that had been beaten onto his body. Etched into his soul. As his father stormed out, warning him to have the room spick and span by nightfall, Zac resolved never to go back.

His mother had been sobbing behind the door and as the Sergeant stormed out, she fell on Zac and hugged him.

"Harry, the boy needs a Doctor, look at the wheals!" she cried, in her Scottish accent.

"No blood," said the Sergeant as he thudded down the stairs.

"Don't go, son. Don't go, son!" she implored.

"I can't stay here, Mum!" said Zac and he decided to abandon her.

He felt that he was in an untenable position. If he left, he feared that it would break his mother's heart. He was her firstborn and, he liked to think, her favourite. If he stayed, there would never be any peace. The Sergeant was still a strong man and though Zac was fit, he knew that in a barbaric fight, he would have to take a weapon to him.

He closed the door, vowing that no man would ever humiliate him again.

When Zac reported what happened to his tutor at Art College, he learned a valuable lesson. Conservative values being the best was a myth. His tutors rallied around him and his Head of Department, Eric Rimington, lost no time in organizing help. Two postgraduate students and a young tutor, Martin, offered Zac a room in their flat.

Now, he was really among the grown-ups. Noisy games of Monopoly and Poker in Tony's room, whilst toddler Ellie gurgled next door in her cot. Cinnie, dusting the flour from her hands, joined them, along with Martin for a game. The conversation was witty, with reminiscences of the Royal College and Goldsmiths, Cinnie's college, Martin's tales of Paris and National Service in the Cavalry and Tony's of the hard life of his Cumbrian mining family. Martin's experience was one of being an officer, even for just a short-term commission, he was 'freighted' with an unconscious sense of the privilege of rank. But at least it made for a more tolerant and assured attitude to life. As opposed to the Sergeant who, even when reaching RAF officer rank by the end of his WWII service, remained an NCO to the core. Reactionary, brutish, and stoic, Cromwellian.

Massive change was in the air, as they listened with excitement in the early hours, to the great Clay/Liston fight from Madison Gardens, New York. Then, not too much later, with a glow of class and regional pride, Tony and Zac and all his college year, rejoiced at the reception of four Liverpool lads in New York. England was swinging! The party had started and they wanted to go!!

Chapter 17

Suddenly, he found himself at the heart of Bradford's Bohemia. The University was still unfinished as a building but the Art College had become the centre of Bradford's Rive Gauche, or the closest the dirty old city could get to such a thing. Zac already felt in his mind, that he had one foot firmly in the Metropolis as if there was a branch of the Northern Line or Piccadilly just round the corner from him in Bradford.

Glenda and one or two other girls would come back to Zac's room, located alone among offices and warehouses near the centre of town. It had a single element electric cooker, a battered armchair and a camp bed. Zac was almost a 'social catch' with visiting London artists and models and was invited upstairs to their wild parties.

Chapter 18

One blissful afternoon, Zac found Glenda lying on top of him. Her arms up the back of his ubiquitous battle-dress shirt, feeling his healing wealds and scars, tonguing his throat and with her splendid breasts thrusting into his chest. Her hair smelled like heather and a sudden Spring shower as she caressed his face.

Zac had received a small grant from the Council and earlier, Glenda had taken him shopping in the markets for pots and pans. She had tucked his arm under hers, a strangely proprietorial and conjugal gesture, as she took him also to the newly-opened C&A's where he bought under her guidance, some shirts.

"No jeans for you, Zac, you need a pair of chinos," she laughed. "Plus three pairs of Y-fronts and several of socks."

He felt unaccountably thrilled at these, her 'commands'!

It was the nearest he ever got to being, superficially, at least, a young man 'on the way'. His old mates from school, rebels, and to him always seeming much more precocious and certainly enjoying more freedom, suddenly began to look up to him.

The ball was at his feet.

Chapter 19

So, for a short time, Zac was Cool, Cavalier, no more the clumsy and dour Cromwellian. He had his own 'Gaff' and he smoked funny cigarettes there with fast ladies and Afro-Caribbean session men up from London.

One day, after an early finish at College, he mentioned to Glenda how he had thrilled at the first sight of Julie Christie in the movie 'Billy Liar'. Swinging her tote bag, a symbol, he thought of his fantasy 'new' woman, a 'mate', as well as just a girlfriend or wife. She was a free spirit' as well as a huntress, with her loping stride and devil-may-care aura. He remembered seeing it when he'd just finished sitting his 'A' levels, only 12 months, and what seemed a lifetime ago. In a half-imagined way, he was beginning to see Glenda as the fulfilment of his dream of a liberated woman.

The sort of girls Zac knew in Sixth Form, and slightly despised, seemed snobbish and facile. The girls at church and Youth Club, though nice, appeared bovine and unchallenging. Those in the Young Communist League, intelligent but prudish. Those at the Mecca Dance Hall where he went hunting after drinking a skinful of ale with Pete and Malc, struck him as either whores or viragos.

Zac joked to Glenda that he would have got on the train to London with Julie at the end of the movie, unlike the hapless Tom Courtney character in the film.

They went to see the new "Doctor Zhivago" film, starring Julie Christie and Omar Sharif. Zac adored Julie Christie. She reminded him of a Cinemascope and sanitised Glenda and his heart sang to the movie's theme, "'Lara's Song" tinged with the magic of old Russia, a deep melancholy and sweeping grandeur, a Tolstoyan warmth and panache.

Afterwards, he walked her to the bus station. Saying goodbye to her stabbed him to the heart. But he didn't know why.

Though he often had exciting company during these times, situated where he was, he could also feel desperately isolated, alienated even, in this, his native city. His flatmates were not always around out of term time and he was not a habitual pub drinker at that time. Nor could he afford to be so.

He had his part-time work in the market. But even during what he now saw as only a brief hiatus before going to Sunderland Art College in the coming October, he began to feel some of the anomie, a subtle and corrosive acid that fracks the soul.

Part Two:

BRIDESHEAD

Chapter 20

Zac was fed up with Surbiton even though he felt nearer to Glenda. He had become tired of his itinerant labouring throughout West London, temporary jobs in Kingston and the somnolent, suburban, affluent areas of the Upper Thames Valley. He worked nights in a bakery near Chessington Industrial Estate and even for a time in a precious metal factory. Glenda finished her last year and though Zac lived in her old room, in a students' house, he felt alienated from this generation and nostalgic for his student days. He was becoming one of those ageing, perpetual students, those Peter Pans who couldn't escape their youth. His obsession with Glenda had something narcotic, hence unreal, about it, and his alienated life seemed like a dream.

He was lost but sometimes his Goddess turned a kind side towards him, barging through his flimsy door and after kicking his bed almost affectionately, would order him to do some errand, even to accompany her to the pictures in Kingston, or when she got her first flat on her own, to her place in Putney. They sketched each other, sometimes reading to each other desultorily. She was not one for going to the pub, at least not with him! Sometimes they danced slowly around her room, giving him a chance to hold her. Glenda on one occasion let him fondle her black Hessian boots as he stumbled to express his dying devotion to her. Sometimes she would turn on him aggressively, sometimes even in public. Zac was embarrassed by her attitude to barmen and shop assistants. However superficially, Zac always kept up a comradely repartee with such people, his own people anyway.

Zac didn't really like her.

And yet he would have died for her.

At this time, it baffled and crucified him.

Chapter 21

She was a burgeoning feminist before it became fashionable. After one of her rages, when he was back in his room in Surbiton, he dreamed all night long about taking the overground train back to Putney and kicking her door down. When to his horror, he fantasised about doing actual violence to her and knowing that he couldn't act this out, he resorted to his trusty ally, whiskey. He kept a half bottle handy and it seemed to do the trick. It calmed him down and eventually he drifted off to sleep.

His swansong in Surbiton had been an end-of-term party that Glenda threw at her place, where Zac was to meet his future pal Stan, a fellow northerner from Birkenhead. Handsome in his WWII Yankee sailor's whites, blonde locks and full beard, he looked every inch a Merseyside Adonis. They each indulged in a bit of manly banter and bonded immediately, like puppies. They were of the same class and generation and from two of the most infamously 'un-cool' rat-holes in England. Boys from their background made their first and lasting friendships after a challenge to a fight.

"I want tae fight yis," was both an invitation and a threat, from Merseyside to Clydebank.

Lifelong friendships were often contracted like that and with no lingering malice. He was in the year below Glenda and they both retired to the kitchen to bond and drink a libation to the Gods of soccer, Liverpool for Stan, Newcastle 'Toon' for Zac. Zac liked Stan a lot. Both of them worshipped Liverpool manager, Bill Shankly, that great socialist Glaswegian.

"You'll never walk alone!" they caroused together until shut down by a petulant and embarrassed-looking Glenda.

Though he was dishonest about wanting to teach, Zac knew that he would qualify for a grant and that there might still be some hope, albeit a forlorn one, of his teaching higher education to young adults. He felt too bohemian now to pretend to be a responsible member of society and at least he was doing some intensive and deeply influential reading, more so than painting, which he only did fitfully and in an undisciplined way. The south country and metropolis had alerted him to the magic of language, even of ideas and now with pressing urgency, politics.

Chapter 22

Then, Zac ended up in Brighton. On a day trip at first. One of those sultry but oppressive August days when London felt like some great Necropolis, the populace having become the walking dead, strangers everyone to each other, a surrealist, De Chirico-like dreamscape resembling that of the mystical moment when he and Paul McCartney had exchanged glances.

He knew why it was called 'London-by-the-Sea' and he felt instantly at home there. He found that he needed to teach (a lie really) but to do that he needed to study for an Art Teachers' Certificate. Brighton College accepted him and the Tory Surrey County Council even offered him a grant.

His first rooms, again in a student house, were near Seven Dials. Montpelier, an elegant yet unpretentious mid-Victorian Crescent with white stuccoed apartments, the Brighton hallmark, was situated on a steep but sensuously curving hill atop the Downs and above the shining sea.

He met many other congenial souls there and decided to stay on in the town even though he had no interest in acquiring a regular teaching job. By now, he had become an incorrigible drifter, or Bohemian. Zac didn't think he was a 'bum' but as he wasn't painting seriously and was mainly lurching from one financial crisis to another, he believed his life was taking a deviant, if not a dangerous course. Most of his fellow post-graduate students had taken up teaching posts and moved on, while he was left on his own, frankly- a bit lost. Adrift.

Chapter 23

If you have read Graham Greene's 'Brighton Rock' or Patrick Hamilton's 'Hangover Square' you would recognise under the cheerful yet tawdry sexiness of Brighton, a more sleazy and sinister side.

Zac was going through one of those periods in late winter, broke and between jobs and people. Brighton had a quasi-metaphysical feel to it as if you were about to slip into another dimension or age. The muffled footsteps behind you during a Channel fog, morphing into the sudden jangle of harness and reins, a stifled cry, hoofbeats on ancient cobbles retreating into the alleys and lanes of the old town.

Stumbling upon a shop doorway around the seedier area at the back of the West Pier, close to Norfolk Square and its tiny but jolly pubs and cheap lodgings, Zac took the opportunity of lighting a cig and taking his bearings before mooching uptown to James Street and his tiny bedsit.

By the light of his near-spent match, just before it guttered in a puddle by the kerb, he glimpsed in the murky side window, a collage of beige and sepia calling cards for Swedish lessons for naughty boys and various arcane societies. Brighton, judging by his brief experience so far, seemed to be full of those. Oscar Wilde's nemesis, Lord Alfred Douglas had ended his days in dingy chambers there, editing an anti-Semitic magazine, as an enthusiastic supporter of Sir Oswald Mosley's British Union of Fascists.

One card stood out: a Celtic cross against a faded Union Jack logo with a barely discernible legend advertising a new Camelot. A sucker for anything Arthurian, Zac struck match after match and scribbled down on the back page of his latest Casteneda volume, a contact telephone number with an address in nearby Hove, the land of the retired and forgotten.

He wasn't so broke that he couldn't afford a drink and knowing the Backstage Bar near the Old Steine and Pavilion had a public telephone booth, he thought it a good idea to have a pint there and call the number he'd written down. If there was no answer then he could enjoy a chapter of his book and a pint, or maybe two, and a smoke.

Zac was on the point of hanging up when a slightly breathless and cultivated voice took the call, sounding something like the Poet Laureate Sir John Betjeman.

"Hello," he said. "A bit of a climb up the old stairs, sorry about the delay!"

Zac told him quickly about the shop and his interest in Arthurian Britain. It was something he had picked up from his fellow teaching students in the past year, many of whom were from the West Country where a genuine revival in English 20th century neo-romanticism was evident. He went on. He thought, curiously that his northern version was tiny in comparison and in his case took more of the form of east European and Soviet social realism or interest in the Border Ballads, and Irish folklore. In his opinion, there was a stronger interest up there in Ewan McColl, the Seegers and even long-dead US socialists like Woodie Guthrie. Many of his fellow northern diehards were among the ones who had booed Bob Dylan when his show came to Newcastle and he first played the electric guitar. Zac and his mates saw Dylan as a sell-out. They were THAT 'uncool'-and heavy! There seemed a lot of irrational and whimsy stuff still going down south among the generation only 2 or 3 years younger than himself about the 'Golden Dawn' and Rosicrucian groups, many of which had flourished in Edwardian London and seemed to wash-up in the south coast towns.

"Call me Gerard, old man," said the gracious voice.

He enthused about people like Crowley and the members of the pre-first world war mystics like Gurdjieff and Ouspensky, whom he had met.

Zac said that he had a special thing for a 'second reality' and a kind of muddled earth worship, and as he'd just read Robert Graves' 'White Goddess' anything along the lines of matriarchy and the ancient Druid culture.

"Mr dear boy," said Gerard. "What are you doing tomorrow night?"

"Nothing, more likely, than going for a lonely pub crawl with my Mexican Shaman book," said Zac.

He was anticipating some wages from the agency for whom he was working part-time.

"Well look, myself and a few of the chaps are having a meeting in the upper room of the Red Lion on James Street. We're called the 'Albion

Society'. Some are a bit political but you're not to mind. They're a fine bunch of chaps and dare I say the odd chappess?"

Zac knew the pub well. It was just around the corner from his place so after saying a cheery goodbye he hung up and sat down to finish his pint.

He pondered to himself about the archaic-sounding language of the old gent. He thought of one or two Guardian articles he'd read about Brighton and conversations overheard between slightly seedy-looking, ex-public-school types, hints by old Communist Party friends up in London or Bradford and then he slapped his thigh at his naivety.

Fascists! He thought. But maybe he could infiltrate them for the good of the Cause?

The next day, he swung through the saloon-style doors of the Red Lion on James street about 25 minutes early, knowing that, like a true Special Agent, he would need to cover his rear and locate a quick exit route!

There was only an old bloke with his dog in the far corner it being 'early doors' and he asked the friendly barmaid, Suki, for a pint of Guinness. Zac disliked the local brew, one of the fashionable canister beers of the time. As the glorious malt settled slowly, he mused about the enormity of what he was doing.

What would Stan up in London think? Or his Dad, hard and conservative as he was? At last, lifting the pint from the bar and delighting in its glorious heft and laughing head, Zac found himself a strategically placed seat by the entrance. He sat down with his back to the door and mused about the delightful drink to come and possible unpleasantness upstairs. His stomach rumbled and tensed until the porter worked its magic. Involuntarily, his skull theatre started, placing him in his Dad's Lancaster bomber, just 25 or 26 years ago.

The Flight Sergeant, Dad, standing clear of his jump seat, starboard of the pilot and Skipper Bert, as he finishes the litany of the take-off drill. Already the noise is terrifying, the old crate groaning and straining at the leash. Dad now forgetting his gut-wrenching fear as he switches and changes tanks of lethal high-octane spirit, counting off the revs from his panel and ready to lend his weight to Bert at the stick and his hand to the throttles once the great beast starts rolling. Zac could almost smell the acrid and fear-drenched sweat of fit young men after a seemingly endless take-off run. Bert hauling the brute away from the Lincolnshire earth, Dad heaving forward on the throttles. Then 'clunk',

"Starboard undercarriage locked, Skipper," says Dad.

"Port," clunk, "too. Steady as we go," says Bert and then they are lumbering into the black and fathomless sky.

Back in the Saloon Bar of the Red Lion, Zac shook his head. 'Christ, this is a good brew!' he thought, smacking his lips and looking around. 'No Gerard yet, but I want to get this down and maybe another before I join the master race upstairs,' he thought to himself.

Spring,1944, back in his imagination, Bert, at last, exhales loudly on his intercom. While Dad sets the props and Merlin engines to constant speed and pitch, Bert eases forward to level out, a friendly bear in his Irving suit and leathers, hunched over the controls. Relaxing, he stretches a bit.

"Ok Boys, Skipper here, we're on our way. Roll-call if you please and try to cut the chatter. Test guns in 20, air gunners and Nav, I'll want a compass heading in 25. Ok, boys? You there, Rear-Gunner?"

"Roger, Skip," replies Gungha Dean, my Dad's oppo, a tough little Aussie

"You there up there, Ron? Not playing with yourself?"

Ron was the mid-upper gunner and had a tendency to snooze! And so on: Peter, the Navigator; Lobby, the Bomb-aimer; 'Tiny Tim' the Wireless Operator.

"Enemy coast coming up in 10…"

Shuddering with shame, Zac spied the door to his right leading to the toilets and the back exit to a side street down to the esplanade. His fathers' spirit beckoned him on and he continued in shame with the drone of imaginary Merlin engines and the 'Dam-busters March' ringing in his ears.

Shivering, he went on his way and it wasn't until he'd marched past his lodgings and up to Kemptown that his heart stopped beating and he sought refreshment in the Bristol Hotel on Marine Parade.

Chapter 24

Gradually he was becoming a Southerner and with some qualifications. He grew to love the South Country. It was 'Cavalier' country. Glenda had been wise.

It was quite easy to hitch-hike and of course cheaper than the train and he fancied, English people liked each other more then. Zac used to love meeting people from different walks of life and for all the lingering racist and neo-colonial attitudes common at the time, there was that feeling of things opening up, which had begun in the late '50s. The war was long over and the future looked good.

Chapter 25

Though not as easy as the northern hitch-hiking route from Apex Corner near the M1 at Edgeware, it was still pretty easy for a fairly presentable young man to get a lift, usually as far as Gatwick, at that time a rather charming looking aerodrome. It was about halfway to Brighton and Zac usually got a lift there from friendly lorry drivers, in Leyland and Bedford trucks. He loved to lean across the engine housing, throbbing noisily between himself and the driver, offering cigs or a light and exchanging opinions on soccer and even sometimes, cricket. If it was a fellow northerner they bonded like old comrades and usually when stopping at the many 'greasy spoon' transport cafes, Zac bought a meal: a great dirty mug of stewed tea and a chunky bacon sandwich with lashings of HP sauce. A bit different with Londoners and even more so with those from Kent and Surrey, already, to his northern eyes, petit-bourgeois and Americanised.

Sometimes he got lifts with junior Army officers and RAF aircrew which to Zac was especially exciting. Despite his anger, Zac deep down was still his father's son. Tory probably, these chaps were from comfortable backgrounds and as long as he kept his politics discreetly to himself, amiable blokes and tolerant. The Army men, refreshingly, liked their German postings which reflected the general feeling of Zac's generation, that the war was definitely over. Such was the optimism in the air, he remembered one Lightning fighter pilot telling him how he and his comrades strived for eye contact with their Soviet oppos in the rear turrets of their huge Tupolev bombers which routinely tested UK coastal defences. Usually, ribald hand signals were exchanged or open pages of the latest 'Playboy' magazine displayed, splayed against the Lightning cockpit canopies. Soviet airmen held up fingers, 7 out of 10 for example in approval; aircrew on both sides came to recognise each other.

Usually, after telling his 'lift' his life story, not very long at that time, they parted in good humour, sometimes even with a handshake. There was still the lingering feeling of a kinder and more friendly England at that time.

The place names seemed so Home Counties, that Zac felt strangely alienated, being forced with a shock to accept his 'Northernness'. Henfield,

Birchgrove, Pangdean, all so twee and the glimpses of over-tamed countryside between the thatched, smug little cottages seemed paltry and at best reminiscent of hackneyed old illustrations in the Rupert books and 'Boys Own' comics of his childhood. It made him think, by contrast, of his Celtic Norse ancestry and the wide-open and rain-lashed moors and fells of Zac's beloved North Country. Up there even the place names sang of the clash of steel, the battered shield wall of Viking ancestors. Eric Bloodaxe in Stanmore, Langstrothdale, Stanwick, Arkengarthdale, Gunner-side, Wild Boar Fell and Mallerstang, Viking redoubts and the gateways to marauding Scots armies. That passionate skyline, whether limestone crag and fell, or gaunt and skeletal pit heads, those Gothic forests of smoke-belching mill chimneys.

Pease Pottage and Plumpton, I mean to say! Zac sighed to himself, so Mary Poppins! It was with an almost sensuous pleasure though that he emerged, usually on the Old Steine from his last lift and heard the clamour of gulls and sensed the surge and salt of Sussex by the sea. The gentility of the times persisted in the exquisite Flanders and Swan 'The Slow Train' so evocative of that England, of market towns, cathedral close and old Rectories, cream teas and eccentric vicars.

Chapter 26

One of the high points of this period was when Stan stayed with Zac for a couple of weeks, while he was in the elegant Eton Place and working at the Royal Sussex Hospital.

Zac had a job as a part-time nursing auxiliary in the Royal Sussex County Hospital, in Kemptown, a bohemian, but formerly aristocratic and genteel part of town which sat upon the gently sloping Downs to the east and looked down to the esplanade and seafront. He lived in one of the once-elegant, though jerry-built Regency streets leading down to the sea. Kemp was the name of the builder and he pioneered the use of steel and iron scaffolding over which he lavished stucco on rough soft-core cladding. It rather mirrored his occasionally more negative feelings about the town. What with wartime 'hit and run' Luftwaffe bombing and post-war austerity, the often gloriously cream painted stucco at that time looked past its best, less like the Corniche at Nice and more like a gloomier, northern Naples. Zac loved it for that and no wonder Graham Greene set one of his best novels there. Landlords, fearing the increasing losses their properties would bring, let many rooms off to the more indigent. So, for writers and artists, this was a promised land. Underneath the faded elegance there was something more than raffish, something vicious. It was no accident that as well as having one of the most radical socialist groups in Britain there was a thriving fascist enclave.

The job could be demanding, even though it was at the bottom of the healthcare ladder. On one shift, for example, he had to help resuscitate a couple of blokes in the early hours and then help lay out some poor old man just before breakfast. On that particular occasion, he came back to the flat, with summer dawn blazing through the tatty regency windows of his room, to wake a bleary-eyed Stan and make them both coffee only to find himself collapsed in a near coma with Stan's beaming and benevolent face looming concernedly over him.

It was not always 'wine and roses' nor even 'Brideshead Revisited', a book he'd only discovered the year before in Surbiton, whilst penniless and shivering in his miserable rabbit hutch of a bedsit. Its winsome, escapist charm had captivated him and Zac had discovered a love/hate affair with the author, Evelyn Waugh.

Chapter 27

Another tough night shift at the Royal Sussex up the road. The little night nurse and Zac had managed to get an hour's respite and were psyching themselves up for the frenetic last two hours of their shift, changing urine bottles and emptying catheter bags, the first morning tea for the patients, then temperatures and the making of beds, which usually meant his running up and down the ward and back and forth to the kitchen, to check that patients' eggs were boiled for just the right time.

They were just about ready for a quick check around and a second cup of tea and medication with the Staff nurse, when Mr Hargreaves, a kindly old duffer, went into cardiac arrest. Zac knew the routine and was able to drag the old boy down the bed and start inserting hard boards under his mattress while racing feet thundered into the ward. He had been forewarned to expect no niceties from the resuscitation team and wasn't discomfited when he was thrust aside by Sister Parker and one of the Duty Doctors. The latter was already astride the recumbent patient and Zac had run to get the cardiac pack as Doc pumped violently on Mr Hargreave's chest.

He walked briskly around the rest of the ward reassuring the other patients. As the day staff started to drift in, he was able to wind down. Screens having been drawn around the old boy's bed, he was able to do a quick sweep around. Nervous and poorly older men could quickly panic and an almost comical chain reaction of arrests could be set off. Thankfully they had saved their patient and though stressed and ragged, Zac was able to brush and clean off and feeling 10 foot-tall, walk out of the ward and into the fresh sea air wafting up Eton Place. A fresh early summer day beckoned and he felt worn out but, exalted.

He wearily trod the stairs up to his room to wake a bleary-eyed Stan and made them both a coffee, Nescafe instant of course with Carnation milk, fridges being a luxury at that time for his class.

Zac must have slept over twelve hours. Twice, Stan had come over to his bedside to see if he was ok. They must have both eaten but Zac was oblivious to anything until 30 minutes before his shift was due to start and he trudged back up the hill to the Royal Sussex.

Chapter 28

Yet again it had been a heavy night on the ward. Zac crawled wearily back up the stairs to his Eton Place 'chambers', thankful that it had been all downhill to the flat. It was one of those slightly misty Brighton dawns which seemed to muffle the sounds of the stirring town. Even the early-morning milk floats and seagulls appeared subdued. It suited his mood. What felt like minute pieces of gravel had invaded the backs of his eyeballs and a tightness in his throat made him long for a huge mug of tea in the peace and quiet of his flat.

Stan was still in bed as Zac knew he would be. He stared at his tousled blonde hair and beard, thinking he would leave him for an hour and maybe surprise him with a cooked breakfast later. This also meant he wouldn't have to engage in conversation. He didn't want to tell Stan about his night even though Zac knew he would be completely sympathetic. He left him to sleep, threw off his nurse's jacket and tossed it straight into the basket in the bathroom, trying to ignore the faint smell of faeces and urine. It had been a bad night.

Young Ron Prentice had died of his Hodgkin's disease before supper. A gentle and sensitive young man, whom Zac likened to Keats. Ron had been a postman with a young wife and a little girl. He died in time for Zac to lay him out respectfully. By midnight, Sally, the student nurse and he were sipping some well-earned Horlicks at the night desk. The long ward disappeared in perspective; the peace broken only by low groans coming from the dimly-lit patients.

As Zac was serving the first cups of tea to the patients, many of them nervous and on edge after that frantic night, a little light relief came from Reg Balcombe, a veteran WW2 Coastal Command pilot with whom Zac had an easy and bantering rapport. He had early-stage lung cancer.

"Heavy night, old boy? What's the score?' he said, turning his oxygen mask aside and looking the very image of the Sunderland Flying Boat Pilot of his youth.

"One chopped, three probables and one leaving, trailing smoke!"

replied Zac whilst rushing and sliding to the next bedside.

A stifled guffaw came from the old sod.

"Bad show, old boy," he said. "Shame about the young lad, Ron. I liked him."

"I hate to think of young Ron down there among all those stiffs," said Sally a bit later, choking back her tears.

Then she suddenly but quietly pushed her chair back, saying she was going to the loo for a smoke.

"I done the p/u's, Zac," she said, her voice trembling. "'Won't be long. I'm in the lavatory if Sister comes."

Sometimes, in the intimacy afforded by the night-light and in the peace and quiet of the 'Graveyard shift' a young nurse would confide in Zac about her boyfriend troubles, even her bodily frailties. He felt honoured to be included in their worries about period pains and 'ladies' problems'. Zac liked the idea of being accepted as an honorary woman, one of the girls. Also, maybe it was the dormant artist in him but he loved looking outside the cone of the night light, where the shadows of the ward deepened into a kind of Gothic and Monastic space, an aura of quiet grief. The dedication implicit in that vision reminded Zac of war-time propaganda photos of RAF aircrew and Russian tankmen poring over their maps. Even though he was in a woman's world, he felt privileged to experience some of that 'crystal spirit' of his parents' generation, their idealism, comradeship and dedication.

That evening, Zac and Stan decided to spend a couple of hours focusing on literature, before visiting the pub. Stan did his usual Shakespeare parody of the News: 'in Parliament, in lofty Hall of Speech!'

"Oh," he said, suddenly. "I nearly forgot Tony's letter!"

He ripped it open, read avidly with a benevolent grin on his face then finally burst out laughing.

"Good old Tony! Could only happen to him. And what a coincidence, just like Perelman!"

Zac had met Tony briefly at Glenda's end-of-term party, as well as Stan, and a few months ago when he and Stan had shared rooms near Norfolk Square, just up the hill from the West Pier. Zac liked him a lot, a most engaging character and another Gurdieff fan, quirky and kind. He was no fan of Glenda's though. Tony was all of 9 stone and dressed in the almost obligatory WW2 RAF uniform common among students and anarcho-leftists at the time. An amiable and slightly bemused-looking southerner, quite middle class and from a Quaker Public School, he exuded kindly calm as well as humorous eccentricity. In that hiatus between their finishing college and going to their respective homes, Zac had been offered a little room in their flat, an attic set of rooms with views down to the sea. They had access to the roof and the three of them, Zac, Stan and Tony would share a joint and a few beers up there, Tony enthusing about Gurdieff which seemed a Kingston thing. It says a lot about the Britain of that time and the art school network that Stan, a working-class lad could be bosom pal with someone of Tony's genteel background. They were both more like the free-wheeling and thinking students of pre-degree days and formed a formidable comedy duo. They occasionally sent scripts to the BBC's 'Ha-Ha' department as Tony addressed them, but with no results as yet.

So, Stan proclaimed a digest of his letter. Apparently, back up in London, or in Bristol, his home town, he related the latest mishap in his love life. He'd made a date to take a girl to a theatre to see a show, probably 'Hair' or 'Jesus Christ-Super Star' which were doing the rounds at the time. She didn't turn up and assuming the worst, Tony went in to see the show on his own. The next day he phoned her to ask what had happened. Turns out she had been performing in the very show, front line of the chorus, a dancer!

"Only Tony could fuck up like that," cried Stan, shaking the curls on his head, of which he had an abundance at that time.

After a cup of tea and a smoke, they were back to reading and declaiming the words of good, if flawed scholars. Zac felt relieved not to be working at the hospital that night, especially after the horrors of the previous few weeks which he felt unable to share with Stan. He would have understood though, he was that kind of a man. His Buddhist reserve was not of the cold southern English type which he disliked.

"Fail again (paraphrasing his mate, Beckett) but fail better!" said Stan who loved his work.

"Ah well, brother but hey it's payday in the morning!" exclaimed Zac, who was more of a Pinter man.

"Then drinks will have to be taken then, me old mate!" said Stan.

Zac loved his Birkenhead 'twang'.

"And why not indeed!" he returned.

That night, Stan must have been busy. When Zac returned home in the morning following another gruelling graveyard shift at the hospital, he found something quite extraordinary and completely unexpected. There on the table by the great Regency bay window stood a large scale Airfix model of a Spitfire. It had been painted with great skill, aided no doubt by the soothing smoking of a few joints.

"Zac?" said Stan, sliding the model Spit across the table towards him.

Zac was beside himself with admiration, praising Stan's craftsmanship as he lifted it up wonderingly, then imitated a diving pass towards his pal's head. Stan laughed then suddenly turned serious.

"Zac," he said. "Have you heard of this bloke, John Pudney?"

They had a stash of poetry anthologies, bought in dozens from sales throughout Brighton's junk shops. Zac, a devout reader of prose, was about to discover the joy of poetry.

"Listen to this Zac mate," said Stan. "The two early stanzas are foxed, here goes. It's one of the best World War two poems I've ever read, and it's by John Pudney."

Stan's Merseyside twang was even more evident in his excitement as he read:

Shed no tears

For Johnny-Head-in-air

He sleeps as sound

As Johnny Underground.

Fetch out no shroud

For 'Johnny-In-The-Cloud

And keep your tears

For him in after years.

Better by far

For Johnny-the-Bright-Star

To keep your head

And see his children fed.

Zac remembered this gem of a poem so resonant of the period, being quoted in the wartime movie 'Way to the Stars'. It was all frightfully stiff-upper-lip and very British but idealistic and probably seen by both their parents during those dark times, years before they were born.

"Wow, follow that!" cried Zac. "Very 1940's. I can't imagine the in-crowd going for that."

This was the time of Monty Python's Britain after all. Even though the poem seemed stilted and repressed and very British, both of them agreed it was rather splendid.

"Er, yes'," drawled Stan. "Poor show about old Ginger!'

They were old enough to imagine the harsh reality of war, the screaming Hurricane pilots trapped in their flaming coffins, the piss and vomit, the boiling blood and the sheer gut-wrenching horror in the skies just above them and over into Kent and Surrey, the stench of roasting human flesh, the bone-weary exhaustion of young men so tired that they landed their Spits and Hurris asleep sometimes. The vacant spaces in the Mess, the raw young recruits, those faces you would never see again.

Zac explained what he liked about it and Stan enthusiastically agreed.

"It's all content, subject-matter, heart stuff, no stuffy formalism," said Zac.

"Yes, yes old boy. Roger that!" replied Stan.

"Mmmm," said Zac. "Johnny bought it over Brighton."

Then he quoted aloud from half-remembered films he'd seen as a kid, while Stan took a pull on his pipe, a recent affectation, looking very much the part of Wing Commander Engel, DFC.

"'A brew, Stan," said Zac. "And let's have some more poetry. Never knew there was any decent stuff from World War Two!"

"Oh, indeed there was old son! Put t'kettle on, old lad. I've got just the thing here!"

Stan parked his rather malodorous briar in the ashtray.

"Bass is Best, purloined a few nights ago in a town centre pub," said Stan, then coughed before intoning: "The Naming Of Parts."

Zac brought their tea tray over. Lipton's Tips, provenance uncertain but somewhere on the Sussex Coast for sure.

"Today we have naming of parts," repeated Stan, adopting a mock-cockney accent. "It's an NCO, ya see, Zac. It's a poem about class, time shifts, irony, class-against militarism and stuff…"

"I'm all for that," said Zac. "Pray continue. Different registers, so to speak?"

"Spot on," replied Stan and recited:

"Yesterday, we had daily cleaning and tomorrow morning

We shall what to do after firing. But today,

Today we have naming of parts; JAPONICA," he put on his posh voice.

"Glistens like coral in all of the neighbouring gardens.

"Tell you what, Zac. You take the posh voice - they alternate - and I'll take the Sergeant's, but continued in Officer's Register…

"And today we have naming of parts."

He took a quick sup of tea.

"This is the lower sling swivel. And this

is the upper sling swivel, whose use you will see

When you have been given your sling. And this is the piling swivel

which in your case you have not got."

Stan quickly passed the battered and foxed missal over to Zac.

"Best posh voice, mate!" he said.

Getting the idea, Zac put on his best 'talking to the Bank Manager' accent.

"The branches

hold in the gardens their silent, elegant gestures,

which in our case we have not got."

Filled with the magic of irony and thrilled at the wit and pathos, Zac handed over to Stan, quaffing a mouthful of cooling and now tepid tea. And so they continued, passing Henry Reed's great poem to and fro, delighting in the sheer splendour of linguistics. Towards the end of the short but magnificent stanzas they recited spontaneously in unison:

"They call it easing the Spring; it is perfectly easy if you have any strength in your thumb; like the bolt, and the breech

And the cocking-piece, and the point of balance,

Which in our case we have not got."

Simultaneously they raised their voices:

"And the almond blossom,

Silent in all of the gardens and the bees going backwards and forwards

For today we have naming of parts!"

A sea mist had crept up on Kemptown and the late afternoon seemed infused with a serene, amber light, distancing the cries of the gulls and the roar of an occasional vehicle. They both lapsed into what seemed a totally appropriate silence.

They continued their companionable studies and word games until supper-time and looked forward to an evening in 'The Bristol', a haven for burgeoning bards and alcoholics.

A Mughals' meal, a couple of shared spliffs, a game of words and jaw-breaking guffaws, then washed and shaved, Zac being beardless at the time, and at a fair lick, they strode forth to the pub, the fancied light of burning galleons in the high sky towards France and thence to 'The Bristol'.

So, here they were in 1971, two of the first 'Young Fogies', northerners and working class at that. Stan and Zac settled into their seats at a table by the window. Zac looked south by west a little to fair France in the offing and a hundred leagues away. Stan, as usual, was finishing the Guardian crossword, as they got to grips with the first pint. In a nautical, as well as a literary mood, Zac was perusing a book of Jane Austen's letters. Coming across this gem, to her sister, Cassandra, he quoted aloud:

"Dearest Cassy, I give you joy of Frank's return, which happens in the true sailor way, just after our being told not to expect him for some weeks. The Wind has been much against him…"

"Such evocative, elegant-and yes, joyous and CRISP English, Stan! Writing about one of her sailor brothers, obviously, and Nelson was on the sea at that time-and the French-Goddamn their eyes!" exclaimed Zac.

Stan looked slightly concerned but relaxed into his usual kindly Buddhist smile. Zac went on to enthuse how one could almost smell the salt sea of those times, Jane Austen lived not far from Portsmouth, after all, and he went on to rant about 'Persuasion' being her best novel, the sense of maritime history going on but off-stage somehow; the mundane practicalities of a sailor's life, prize money and promotion prospects and God knows what it was like for a sailor's wife!

"And unthinkable for the lower deck," said Stan. "She never even mentions the common sailors and those men o' war must have been floating concentration camps!"

Zac went on to imagine how they smelled and gazing wistfully towards France, he could almost picture the lemon light, modulating to yellow ochres and rusty raw sienna on the topsails of some '74, hull down and beating up-channel towards Dover and the Downs. He was about to speculate on what Ms Austen, a recent enthusiasm, smelled like, so vividly did he feel that great novelist's presence. Perhaps of witch-hazel and a natural feminine fragrance? He imagined her being of a certain class and a country gentlewoman. Stan, seemingly discomfited, rustled the pages of the Guardian.

"Er, quite," he muttered, then suddenly looked up.

"Ah! Company and good!"

Zac thrilled to the gentle squeeze of Robin's hand on his shoulder.

"Now, Zac," said Robin, leaning in towards him. "Before we get too merry, I must ask - and George agrees - that you come back to our place later for a coffee."

Zac agreed heartily, as they both liked these two charming men immensely and were beyond the 'macho' prejudice of the time that they were out to seduce them. 'Play with your bums' as the somewhat crude 'Manchester John' had warned them.

A shocking English habit but Zac couldn't quite place Robin socially, an explanation perhaps of why educated Irishmen had more success at being upwardly mobile than Grammar school types like him and Stan. Zac found George easier to pin down because he was English. Indeed, later in the evening before they got too drunk, George confirmed their suspicions that he was from the Hampshire/Dorset border, very South Country and comfortably Tory, although his politics proved anything but! He had probably attended a very liberal and progressive public school, such as Stowe, but elitist, no less and had then gone on to Cambridge to study civil engineering and architecture. He had a string of well-respected designs for nuclear power stations in Europe to his name. Though very English in demeanour, his dress style was quite continental, unlike Robin's, the Irish Rebel who dressed, ironically in the height of English classical fashion.

Zac returned to the mystery of Robin and his social formation, snob and Marxist that he was and he confusedly ran through what pinned Robin down socially.

One particular evening, Zac's reading before the booze began to hit, was a Keith Douglas' classic "From Alamein to Zem-Zem" a memoir of his time as a young Subaltern in a crack and very posh regiment at the battle of El Alamein. It was a classic and despite his pacifist tendencies, and Stan's, they both admired its panache and style. This particular night, Robin, who always liked to see what they were reading before the revels began, exclaimed in a way very untypical of him.

"Oh, dear old Keith!"

Did he know him? It was highly plausible but as was Robin's way, he gently clammed up, asking us both what was our pleasure. Another blissful and highly civilised evening ensued.

He was just about old enough to have served in the last war, probably as a very young officer which would make him a youthful-looking man in his early fifties. 11th Hussars? Zac wondered. He had the dash and charm of an 8th Army cavalry officer. Both pals could remember similar men as teachers at their respective grammar schools; eccentric, knowledgeable, witty, and very liberal, even in many cases very left-wing. Zac knew that Rommel joked to two captured 8th Army 'Desert Rats' that if Montgomery wanted to know where he was, to check out where the armoured cars of the 11th Hussars were, that crack reconnaissance regiment, always just over the horizon from him.

Or Foot-guards, I'll be bound, thought Zac to himself. He had beautifully crafted brown brogues and an expensive tweed sports jacket with very un-weathered looking leather elbow patches and cuff linings. Had to be Irish Guards though, at the very least the Enniskillens, or maybe a posh cavalry outfit like the Blues or Lifeguards, in which case he had served on tanks probably, hellish death traps or Tommy Cookers as the Germans cynically called them. He was tall, taller than Zac and well-built, obviously an athlete at one time, a sportsman. However, Zac doubted somehow that he rode, so he thought he might have mustered under the Foot Guards, later joining some shady special outfit at which the British Army excelled, deviant homosexuals, artists and Irishmen in particular. Maybe SAS, or Long Range Desert Patrols?

"Now, Zac, another?" asked Robin, gently interrupting his reverie and he apologised to the company while George in his diffident way, went to the bar.

Stan was reminiscing about his time at Kingston Art College and Ian Robinson, his tutor. They had a lively theatre group of extroverts like Stan, Ian and his fellow humourist and inseparable friend, Tony Hodge. Somehow, Zac mused, Glenda, Stan's near-contemporary would not have joined them. As George came back with the drinks, Stan was in full flood and even stood up to demonstrate the gestures Ian had taught them for 'Pere Ubu', Jarry's Masterpiece. Robin, throwing his head back the while, in careless and youthful rapture.

Looking at him, Zac suddenly thought, Newman! Newman, or John Henry, as he was called, was a poet and Oxford Tractarian, later the great Cardinal of 'Gerontius' fame. Zac saw in Robin's tender yet normally ironic gaze, something of the younger Newman, the still evangelical undergraduate. There was something strangely holy yet wicked about him.

With Robin staring avidly and gleefully at him, Stan went on to talk about Bruce Lacey and the Argonauts, an outfit of eccentrics who hung out near Richmond. Zac remembered seeing them on one rather alienating evening at the Round House in North London.

"Bejesus I knew the youth!" laughed Robin. "And that George Melly knew him as a sailor boy on leave in Soho, dontcha know!"

Zac remembered them all dressed as WW1 aviators. Those were the still genial times of the very early '70s and the crazy 'Bonzo-Dog-Doo Dah Band'. Was there anybody Robin didn't know? Thought Zac thought to himself yet again.

Back at Robin's and George's place in Kemptown, one of those elegant and heavily stuccoed pale cream Regency apartments. It must have been on the top floor as it had an almost square window. The palest indigo light shone into a sumptuously masculine chamber, rich, vellum-covered old books, touches of brass from nautical instruments, some Regency political cartoons. Zac thought Robin could have been and maybe even still was, a lawyer or barrister. Stan was listening to the gentle and courteous George. They had got around to discussing architecture, their passion for the Gothic, in particular. There were many energetic interventions from Robin, a fellow enthusiast, as he hustled to his kitchen for wine, home-made elderberry, and canapés.

With a gentle nod of his head, Robin indicated Zac to follow him into the kitchen, a clinically clean and yet very feminine space, with something of the still fashionable Elizabeth David about it. It had lots of well-scrubbed pine and imported Italian marble, with chains of garlic and red onions festooned from the pulley racks, hanging like a sloping roof. Another small Regency window, darkened now, gave a glimpse of the Channel below and a few dimly discerned grey-white breakers.

"So, young Zac, I can see you are intrigued as to my military career?" twinkled Robin. "I was in Italy with the 8th Army. You can see what a sensitive soul George is but for me - and God knows I hate war - it was the time of my life. Heard of His Majesty's, The King's Own Dancing Girls? Actually, the King's Own Dragoon Guards, my outfit, armoured cars and light tanks. Fine young men filled with the joy and idealism of the time. Schtumm, though. George doesn't want to know, the silly old Queen."

And his laughing Irish eyes twinkled again.

But you're a bloody-minded young bastard, Zac! Here take the tray and I'll tell you some other time about the SAS!"

Back in the lounge, Robin gleefully showed them Ruskin's great 'Seven Lamps of Architecture' as well as a volume that was to set Zac's Muse on fire for the next 50 years, his 'Stones of Venice.'

Zac noticed the contrast between Robin's puckish grin and the most tender look in his eyes. Not prurient, but strangely spiritual and he was reminded vividly again of Cardinal Newman - a wistful tenderness and a sweet and gentle melancholy. Zac thought suddenly, confused and deliciously pissed on Elderberry wine, that he must have mentioned the great Cardinal to Robin. He felt himself blushing as Robin turned to him.

"Now, young Zac, something for you to read one day but not yet."

A languid hand reached to one of the shelves, found a little old pre-war Pelican paperback and slid it into my jacket pocket.

"That went everywhere with me in Italy when I was your age. You will be ready for it, I think in, let me see, 1992?"

Zac recalled a relatively sober interlude on one of their evenings at the two men's flat, when Robin mentioned Robert Southwell, Shakespeare's Jesuit and martyred contemporary. George was tasked by Robin to recite Southwell's superb 'A Burning Babe'. Afterwards, during a desultory and ramblingly civilized conversation, dear George still kept his kindly reserve when Robin let slip that he was a believer, something unfashionable at the time. He was a Catholic. Then Robin managed as usual to swerve the conversation in a different direction.

"Come on mother!" he said to George and they were all ushered out into the balmy and softly salty night.

As they stepped out onto the moonlit esplanade, he remembered Robin had mentioned going to tea dances early in the war in Rottingdean. Somehow, they had got on to Kipling who had lived near there for a time. That was around the time of Dunkirk, in1940. He must have been in the army then, a survivor of that debacle. Irish Guards, I'll bet, thought Zac. Could he even have been a Jesuit?

Many, many years later on one of his jaunts to London, Zac saw a clerical figure, with a biretta, the three-cornered hat as worn by Roman Catholic clergymen. The man stooped slightly as he ran through the puddles of Soho Square close to where so long ago, he had witnessed the early morning milk floats and the homeward-bound strippers negotiating Gerrard Street and the corner of the square. Zac shivered as he sheltered under the lintel of the nearby French Pub and shook out his umbrella. His heart was racing at the thought of retracing his steps and greeting him but he couldn't and he hated himself for his coldness. He was almost sure it had been Robin and he even imagined a quick look of recognition and embarrassment in his eyes. Zac later discovered that nearby Farm Street had a catholic church which was very friendly to gay, trans-gendered and lesbian people. Queers, as he used to call them.

Chapter 29

It had been a bad night on the wards. Zac still felt the presence of absence, every time he passed Mr Byrd's old bed. He had also been required to spend a few frenetic hours chasing up and down to the ward above, where a young man lay partially crippled and screaming. He had tried to jump off the cliffs at Rottingdean during a bad acid trip. There had been two arrests and the death of an elderly man at four in the morning.

Zac couldn't eat and he didn't want to talk to Stan about it. He needed some fresh air and was gasping for something alcoholic. Not for the first time in his life he set out to buy a small bottle of vodka from the Asian-run off-license on James Street. He downed it all and took his time getting home, strolling around Sussex Square with its gorgeously elegant Regency houses and along the far leg of the even more opulent Lewes Crescent and its beautiful private gardens. The sun from France was breaking through the gentle morning mists, promising a halcyon Brighton day. Sussex-by-the-Sea indeed!

Zac spotted a corner shop open and decided it might be a good idea to 'play mother' this morning and buy the ingredients for a nice traditional English breakfast. His appetite was coming back, he wasn't yet ready for bed and wanted to let Stan sleep in for a bit. He knew that the high he still had from alcohol could be treacherous but for the moment he thought he could still trust his ally and had used it well. He also knew that in an hour the 'down' would come, though fortunately he had a couple of nights off from the hospital and he didn't need to think so much about Mr Byrd, nor of boring Stan with his near trauma of the previous night.

Back in the bedsit, he delayed waking Stan, until he was delivering some delicious aromas of fried mushrooms and bacon. Hearing him stir, Zac quickly made them both a coffee. Having done so, he continued their banter from yesterday's literary session. Thinking of Stan's love and connection with Beckett and still slightly high but hopefully not smelling of raw alcohol, Zac bellowed in his best German accent a quote from Pinter:

"Who wet the wicket at Melbourne, Weber? What of the ontological argument? Was Heidegger right about falling into the quotidian? What did he do about it and when did it happen?"

"Oh, my God, Zac!" complained Stan blearily.

Just then Zac detected a wisp of dirty blond hair on the other side of his pillow and a startlingly cornflower-blue eye.

"Ooops, sorry Stan I didn't know you had company! Starving. Bacon and eggs do you, mate?"

"Er, Zac meet Helga. Helga, meet Zac. She's just HAD her breakfast!"

Helga wiped her mouth with a muscular-looking fist.

"Ach, Herr Bomber Pilot!" she said, wiping her mouth again and grinning lasciviously.

"Want some HP sauce with that, Kraut!" said Stan, playfully pretending to strangle her.

Helga grinned and guffawed loudly. Zac caught a whiff of something warm and cosily female, as she extended an arm like a coal-heaver's towards him, which he didn't feel it appropriate to kiss. This promised to be an interesting day.

"I'll set us another place," said Zac. "I presume Helga still has an appetite?"

The following morning, after Helga had set off for her language school in Hove, Zac asked Stan about the literary situation. The night before they had had a rather whimsical conversation, while Helga snored between them, about books that tended to read us. 'Wuthering Heights' for example was almost impossible to read but always seemed to weigh down their bookshelves with the heft and promise that one day it would scream at them to be read. Zac also mentioned Graham Greene's 'The End of the Affair which he had only dipped into but seem to hold the threat of his destiny. Even now Zac had the premonition of a fraught love life.

Stan was one of the last real Art College eccentrics, that generation who were never career artists but rather default provincial teachers, anarchists, rock musicians, stand-up comedians and general subversives and hipsters. With his short sight, benevolent gaze and Trotsky glasses he symbolised that benign insurgency of the times of the 'Kens' and 'Micks' within the burgeoning poetry and rock societies up and down England, the latest

Penguin Camus or Fannon in their pockets. In the same way, the slightly previous generation of 'Angry young men' had prided themselves in wearing open-necked ex-RAF service shirts and leather patched elbows, quaffing pints at the University Labour Party societies in the then-new Red-Brick Universities spreading across the land like some benign rash.

Even outside academia, for instance, in Zac's beloved art college local, the Manville Arms, there always seemed to be some emaciated and dishevelled street kid from his school days just landed from Marrakesh, Katmandu or Kabul, invariably called Tex or Hank, in a flurry of beads, John-the-Baptist hair, sandals and threadbare, bleached denims.

Though a bit more cerebral, Stan had the fashionable working-class autodidact aura but with a settled vibe which proclaimed he had arrived. The lad from Birkenhead had perfected the inheritance of a new Britain which our fathers had fought for. He had been in contact with Sam Beckett and even toyed with the idea of becoming, as the great man suggested, his amanuensis.

With a hollow exhalation and phoney tank-commanders' voice Zac continued his musing aloud:

"You could recommend a play about two blokes deep in shit pontificating in a Regency bedsit in Brighton!" he said, spluttering, having taken a quick draught of his cooling tea. "'Strewth, Stan, this is some brew!"

Both of them collapsed, laughing and writhing on the straw-matted floor.

"Told you so, Zac!" said Stan.

The two mates were stoned out of their skulls. Laughing Cavaliers.

Somehow, an eternity and 45 minutes later, Zac staggered to his feet and launched himself towards the galley kitchen.

"Coffee is in order, I think?" he suggested.

"Uggghhhh," gurgled Stan. "Good idea!"

Zac managed to stagger to the bathroom for a shower. Feeling fresher and ready for some of Stan's cooking and maybe a pint or three in the Bristol, he pranced semi-naked back into his now golden chambers, shivering but ready for whatever was on for tonight: a couple of Danish or

Finnish girls, his particular favourites, from the language school; some wit and repartee with Robin and George and certainly a game of name-dropping with Gareth, one of the literary poseurs at the rather genteel bar.

"Hey, Zac!" called Stan, with his nose pressed to their big bay window where the rays of an early evening sun refracted from Eaton Place and back onto the cream and pistachio coloured row opposite. "There's a lady waving to us!"

Zac peeked around the galley partition and saw Molly hanging over the rail of a Juliet window on a higher floor opposite. He waved to her.

"Don't you remember her from the other night, Stan? At the Bristol?"

Molly was jumping up and down excitedly, all 60 odd years of her, but little-girl-like and Zac loved her.

"That's Molly, Stan!"

She must have been with one of her clients, or 'gentlemen' friends, as she coyly referred to them. Zac signalled down to the esplanade and vaguely westward. She raised a right thumb, nodding vigorously then pointed to her wristwatch. Zac signalled back '20' with two shows of his hands.

Zac and Stan sat down. After pouring them both a glass of white wine, Zac explained about poor Molly, her controlled alcoholism and 'Death Kiss Kate.' Stan went pale.

"Poor lass," he stuttered.

Chapter 30

England's 'shining sword', the mighty Avro Lancaster, was Zac's dad's kite, though he had trained on both Wellingtons and Stirlings. Indeed, his baptism of fire had been on the infamous Stirling.

Lancaster JO-E for 'Ecstasy' was fourth in the queue of Lancs trundling around the perimeter track for the night's 'show', propellers wind-milling, thousands of horse-power straining and snarling, primordial shapes in the half-light of a deeply rural Lincolnshire in the faint moonlight of an early Spring evening in 1944.

Alongside the assembly point, up to the take-off position at the far end of the runway and dimly discernible from the ground crew's igloo', stood some figures forming a farewell party. They included not only lowly ERCs but some Top Brass, NCO's and junior officers and among them a few off-duty WAAFS, possibly the girlfriends of aircrew members assembling for battle. One among them, a single and anonymous-looking figure, stood alone at the farthest edge of the runway, near to the perimeter track, dark indigo, almost black against the descending dusk.

Dad's crew must have felt a huge release of tension after the gut-wrenching interval since their briefing, a few hours before. Dad himself was frantically busy up in the cockpit next to Bert the pilot and skipper, half-standing up from his jump-seat in the flight engineer's station. Harry, Zac's Dad, was twirling the fuel cocks on his panel enabling hundreds of gallons of fuel to fill the commodious wing tanks while calculating its balance to keep the aircraft in trim, a highly skilled and crucial task. At the same time, he would have been reading out loud the pre-flight checks to Bert and as the Lanc lumbered slowly forward, checks were done:

"Magnetos on," confirmed Dad.

"Roger that, engineer!" said Bert.

Finally, Dad would lend his sturdy strength to Bert's gauntleted grip on the throbbing throttle levers and if need be, to the control stick to 'yank' the Lanc from the deck. Take-offs were always the most fraught of occasions, what with the hundreds of gallons of highly-flammable high octane aviation spirit and the hundreds of pounds of high explosive and incendiary bombs, not to mention the ammunition for 8 Browning machine guns. Cold sweat must have soaked his uniform shirt under his flying overalls and Irvine Leather Jacket, as he lent a hand to 'Lobby' Lobsinger, the bomb aimer who wisely hauled himself up from his prone position in the nose, as any slip-up and he would be the first casualty. A burst tyre or a collapsing undercarriage leg would see the kite slew viciously and dangerously to port or starboard, probably fatally if other aircraft were in the way. There was room, anyway, to join my Dad Harry in the cockpit and Lobby alone in the 'front office' had time for a quick glimpse of the well-wishers on the runway's edge, see an occasional cap raised in joyful salute as eventually, each in its turn, the single Lancs would roar past. The good-natured dog profile, characteristic of the Lanc's nose provided a surreal contrast to the contained and brute machine force of its engines.

There was no time and little room, however, for the Wireless Operator, 'Sparks' Jock' Tweedie and Navigator Peter Barlow, Dad's best mate, who sat hidden behind their curtains, cramped, respectively by electronic equipment and a small table, covered with instruments and maps. They were jammed up close to that dread main spar, intersecting the mighty port and starboard wings of Avro's Behemoth, where so many aircrewmen, trapped against it by massive G- force, were to perish, spiralling into a blazing inferno below, incandescent beams below, too, from searchlights caressing with malevolent, non-human fingers, the fuselage interior, then blackest night, then vermillion and crimson, clinical manganese blue-green, searing, blazing heat, aircrews' voiceless screams and howling crescendos of Merlin engines shattering the indigo night.

Ron, the mid-upper gunner was positioned behind the main spar, halfway along the roof of the fuselage and leading to 'Gungha' Dean's rear-gunner position, lonely and dangerously exposed. A tough little Aussie, Ron was Dad's 'oppo' and on leave Dad often brought him to Bradford or they did the night clubs of London together. Ron had a bit of time and from his perch a good view of the well-wishers outside. He would waggle his two Browning heavy machine guns, adjust his foot stirrups and give a trial rotation of his turret, before a cursory wave to the 'Bods' on the tarmac as the Lancaster picked up revs and swept past them.

At 'Ecstasy's' time for take-off, the brakes released with a surge and she swept forward, the spectators' faces turning vermilion in the navigation lights of Britain's 'Shining Sword'. As first the port and then the starboard wheels came unstuck from the runway, did Ron have time to see the forlorn figure below him as they roared past the perimeter track, with the 'clunk-thunk' of the wheels coming inboard? Or did Gungha in the rear turret, with the best view and little to do but cock his guns and run checks to his harness and 'chute notice? Did the giddy feeling of being hauled upwards and backwards into the gloaming, stop them from seeing that upturned female face, pale now, in the deepening indigo night and maybe the suggestion of a slow salute of a gloved hand up to a peaked WAAF cap?

Molly waited a few more minutes, saluted a now-empty sky and with a deft and downward flick of her gloved hand, smartly about-turned and marched back to her WAAF Quarters.

Later, in his igloo, ERC chief, 'Dusty' Rhodes was about to watch another hour creep by. Hearing that there was no news from 'Group' about 'E-X for Ecstasy', Dad's wingman, he went out of the igloo and stared up at a no longer indigo night sky, hoping to see a dot in the pale grey and the tremulous wink of navigation lights, or to hear a distant sound of Merlin engines. One by one, the other Lancs landed, taxied onto the hard standing and shut down their engines. The silence that followed felt heavy with pain and loss, heartache and remorse.

It might be a long wait, she thought. 'Dusty' Rhodes and 'Sooty' Sutcliffe, lowly ERCs, now back in their igloo by the runway's edge, either hadn't noticed her or chose to ignore her out of hatred. 'Death-Kiss-Kate' was more than a legend in Bomber Command that last full year of the air war in Europe, 1944.

Chapter 31

In 1971 Brighton, Stan and Zac were enjoying their literary explorations. One memorable evening they strode into The Bristol.

"Ah, my people!" said Stan, waving a benediction to all in the general lounge.

As they both beamed munificently around the light-drenched room, the gleaming sunset pouring in shades of golden ochre, a hint of magenta and alizarin, crimson rose, they found to their horror, their corner occupied by The Gareth. Stan's upper lip curled into a sneer.

Zac left Stan rooted to the spot and approached the class enemy who seemed to have company and was sporting his maroon velvet trilby, now crimsoned from the westering sun, cheroot waving about his head as he played the 'raconteur'. Molly was at the bar with her back to Zac and in the company of ex-RNVR WW2 Commodores and retired Indian Army brigadiers. In that most endearing way that Zac thought some women have, she snatched at his elbow.

"This is my Zac!" she announced to the old gents, who to their credit inclined their heads and one even proffered his hand.

Not knowing whether to kiss it or shake it, Zac turned to Molly instead and asked what was her pleasure. She was desperate for people to like her, he knew since he first caught a glance from her and detected the devastating lack of love and her neediness, something he recognised in himself. She had a Maggie Smith kind of vulnerability, with a guileless, slightly ravaged face and if it wasn't for her obvious niceness, would look like any Home Counties matron at a Royal garden party, or village fete in West Sussex. A firm and still sensuous figure of a woman, though well into her sixties and with an almost athletic bearing.

She clutched Zac's hand to the small of her back. He knew it wasn't sexual, she was just socially stranded and desperate. Her dress, short but tasteful, glowed with the subtlest apricot and cherry colours.

"Zac is a friend and neighbour of mine, on Eaton Place, aren't you, dear?" she said.

Zac wanted to crush her to himself and let her bury her sweet and suffering head in his chest, knowing full well that she lived in a dreary and tiny bedsit in Hove and saved what loose change she had for a taxi up to Kemptown and her 'Gentleman Friends'.

A couple of evenings later, The Gareth, in his patronising but well-meaning way gently pulled Zac aside at the bar.

"Zac, old boy," he said. "I thought you were frightfully kind to poor Molly the other night!"

He lingered a moment, pocketing his change and waiting as Zac gave his order of four pints. He and Stan were particularly thirsty.

"Well," he continued. "You know her story of course?"

He then went on to tell Zac about 'Death-Kiss-Kate'. She had first come to the Bristol during that torrid and historic summer of 1940, with some young fighter boys from RAF Tangmere, just up the coast towards Portsmouth. Zac swallowed hard, thinking of 'Poem for Johnny', that he and Stan had been discussing but half an hour before.

But back to the evening with The Gareth occupying their hallowed position in the pub. He took a generous swig from his pint, wiped his rather false-looking and wispy beard with a claret-coloured handkerchief extracted from his blazer top pocket.

"Stan and Zac," he announced loudly. "Sir Ralph here is about to reminisce a bit about his days before the Great War. I'm making a show for ITV about vanishing piers," with a nod and a grin to Sir Ralph. "Not those of the Realm of course and Sir Ralph has agreed to give some amusing anecdotes. Is that right, Sir Ralph?"

The old boy nodded a bit brusquely.

"Ralph, please… er, lads?" he said with a courteous but in the subtlest way, nod to Stan and Zac as if acknowledging them as most worthy and deserving peasants, troopers all, of course!

Turning on a tape recorder and placing a mike between him and the knight, Gareth gave the usual preamble:

"We are here in Brighton at the blah blah Hotel, on the occasion -blah- - and Sir Ralph used to come here a bit of time ago-blah-blah-over to you, Sir Ralph Richardson!"

"Well," drawled the old boy, his distinctive voice had Stan and Zac enthralled and they leaned in closer over the table. "It was just before the Great War, late summer 1914, the First World War to most of you, I expect?" said Sir Ralph, coughing slightly.

Gareth took the opportunity to intervene obsequiously.

"Of course, you served in the Second World War, in the Royal Marines, that right, Sir Ralph?"

At this, Sir Ralph peremptorily waved a hand and pulled the mike nearer to him.

"W-w-well, my aunt and I used to come down here for a long weekend or a B-b-b-Bank Holiday and stayed at this rather fine Hotel. I had a sports blazer like you, young Gareth and a rather dapper straw boater which I was anxious to s-s-s-show off to the girls. So, after breakfast, I asked permission of my aunt, a formidable lady, straight out of Oscar Wilde," he chuckled and paused for a genteel sup of Bass best bitter. "W-w-ell, Aunt wishing to stay in K-k-Kemptown and maybe read after a short walk, let me go for a stroll down to the P-p-p-Palace Pier along Marine Parade and knowing I wanted to look out for young ladies and the like, admonished me gently, warning me not to be l-l-late for lunch. The gong sounds for lunch at One pm, Rafe!" he said giving a perfect impersonation of Wilde's Lady Bracknell. "And don't linger over those young gels!"

His audience, including Zac and Stan, laughed spontaneously.

"Well, w-w-what with one thing and another," he continued, with a stage wink. "I was delayed and c-c-came back just as they were serving the soup and to an r-r-rather ir-r-rate Aunt!"

Pausing for effect, he took another sip of his now flat-looking beer.

"A-a-a-nd," he stuttered in is best Lady Bracknell voice. "F-f-f-Furthermore… W-w-w-war is d-d-declared!"

There followed a roar of approval.

"Any-one w-w-would think it was m-m-my f-f-fault!" cried the aged knight.

The assembled party collapsed around him, with Stan and Zac clutching their sides with laughter.

Zac noticed poor Molly looking wistfully over at them and he subtly and slowly backed his chair away from the company. Stan was doing well, keeping the old Knight amused, with Gareth playing the obsequious straight man. Tactfully Zac managed to lever a chair next to his own at Sir Ralph's table and gently beckoned to Molly. Seeing her face light up with joy, he walked over to her and gently took her arm.

"May I?" asked Zac as he kissed her sweet face and led her to his table.

Sir Ralph, rocking with laughter at the Stan and Gareth double act was in no mood to refuse an introduction, not that he was the sort of man to do so anyway. As the laughter subsided, Zac seized the opportunity and pressed Molly gently forward, his left hand in the small of her back, his right hand in hand in hers.

"Sir Ralph," he said. "May I present to you, my good friend Molly?"

The wonderful old actor leapt to his feet with an eager and fond expression in his eyes and his two hands extended.

"'By God, M-M-M-Molly!" he exclaimed. "Utterly charmed!"

With a deft twitch of his hand, Zac placed a chair for Molly next to the good and gentle knight. They looked for all the world, like two old friends, reunited. And thus continued one of the most enchanting evenings of Zac's young life.

He didn't remember much, apart from Stan clearing some floor space of chairs and tables while he and Marie-Joelle, who had suddenly appeared, together with Molly danced the Mazurka. They twirled around the space between the old Radiogram and the aspidistras in the middle of the huge picture window, looked on by a bemused Mrs Reynolds. Their vacated corner by the parrot cage and bar billiard table was filled with the screeching of birds, as their cages rocked to and fro.

Zac came off-shift the following morning to detect a struggling shape under Stan's blankets. Stan was at the kitchenette and from the smell of it, infusing a fresh brew of coffee. Zac pointed to the not so blameless looking bed and raised his eyebrows to Stan in a voiceless enquiry.

"Come on, lazy-Marie-Joelle!" shouted Stan, by way of an answer.

"Ahm not lazzeee!" came a reply from the squirming blankets. "Ahm seek!"

Zac approached and discerning a Gallic eye in the sweetly aromatic depths of the bed, he extended a hand, M Hulot-like, and bowing, quickly introduced himself.

"'Monsieur Greenwood, Mademoiselle!"

A hand emerged and shook his vigorously.

"Allo, Zizou-Zac! Monsieur L'Aviateuuuuurrrrr!"

"Clean 'er up, Zac," shouted Stan. "And she's yours for the day!"

A very French-sounding screech and a well-aimed flip-flop hurtled towards Stan.

***

"Listen to this, Zac!" shouted Stan, sitting back from placing the small EP disc on the turntable of the Dansette Hi-Fi.

Having breakfasted after a sleep and a quiet night on the wards, Zac was wondering what they might do that day. Stan had been out shopping and as he was the self-appointed and superb cook, Zac had made no objections. Stan must have picked up a few discs and the odd paperback probably from one of the Charity Shops that were now beginning to proliferate on the high streets of most British cities. Dylan Thomas' voice rang out, sonorous, rather posh for a Welshman and quite theatrical.

"As I went out one morning

walking down Bristol Street

the crowds upon the pavement

were fields of harvest wheat'

"Jesus Christ?" mouthed Zac, aghast.

"Sssh!" said Stan, touching his lips with an admonishing finger.

"But wow-who?" asked Zac.

"Auden!" replied Stan, reaching for his stash and rolling a joint on the 'Velvet Underground' sleeve, available for such nefarious activities.

Zac sat back in amazement. He had been waiting for this all his life, a shock of recognition, something understood, ancient, familiar and yet as exotic as a Bird of Paradise or the Russian Firebird of ancient Slavic myth.

'And down by the brimming river

I heard a maiden sing

Under the arch of a railways,

Love has no ending.'

Stan gave him a thumbs up and an interrogative glance then handed him an expertly crafted joint. Zac took a hearty toke and paused to digest the pungent-smelling herb, whilst listening avidly to those wing/ed words:

'I'll love you dear, I'll love you

Till China and Africa meet,

And the river jumps over the mountain,

And the salmon squawk in the street.'

"What the f-f-f-f-f!" spluttered Zac as Stan smiled at him, benignly.

'I'll love you till the ocean

Is folded and hung up to dry,

And the seven stars go squawking

Like Geese above the sky.'

Stan fell out of his battered armchair in ecstasy.

"Some straw, this what?" he muttered.

The Welsh drunk continued.

'The years shall pass like rabbits

For in my arms I hold

The flowers of the ages

And the first love of the world.'

On and on went this ravishing pastiche, this mythic and magical masterpiece.

"Let's just take it in chunks, Stan?" said Zac. "You must know this, of course?"

"Oh, yes, Zac, but never a recording like this. Though it's quite well-known and recorded in about 1950 in New York and just before his death."

They both scrabbled for pen and paper and started taking the great poem down in chunks as they stopped and restarted the EP.

"Let's take it with us to the Bristol tonight and have a kind of duet, a game of words?" suggested Zac.

"Good idea, mate, my creative juices are stirring!"

They thought a bit of enhanced declamation might be in order so, giving each other a couple of verses to learn by rote, they had a session at Zac's dart-board, a fixture for most students or bohemian types like them. They agreed that the first to get double top had to recite two verses and if they went on, without getting bored, for a bull's eye, the winner had to recite the whole magnificent poem. Stan squared off for first turn. Zac looked down at his notes, reading and concentrating on the magic words, internalising the cthonic rhythms;

'But all the clocks in the city

Began to whirr and chime'

Out of context surely, thought Zac.

'O let not time disturb you,

You cannot conquer time.'

Stan whooped having scored and passed over the darts as they both recited the two verses in unison. Zac went on to miss the dartboard, he was so stoned, so he had to miss a turn while Stan intoned after scoring again:

'In the burrows of the nightmare

where justice naked is,

Time watches from the shadows

And coughs where you would kiss'

When Stan handed the darts to him, Zac blurted:

"Ah, post-war Apocalyptic and all that stuff?"

"Oh, fuck that eng. lit stuff, just WALLOW in the words, the WORDS- poetry is made of WORDS!" replied the increasingly passionate Stan.

So, it went on but they quickly got bored. They were fairly athletic young men after all and spying a rather battered rugby ball, another 'must' in bachelor pads at that time, they decided on a run down the Esplanade to the broad path by the coarse shingle. So sprinting like wingers for the All Blacks, they headed down to the esplanade and then seashore, declaiming what they'd learned by rote, each of them correcting the other, resting for 5 after Stan had taken a terrific punt and nearly drop-kicked the ball into the sea. They sat down for some serious scanning and rote learning, a joint deemed a useful mnemonic and continued down to the sea's edge, stumbling and spluttering:

'In headache and in worry, vaguely life,'

"Catch!"

'drifts away

And time will have its fancy

tomorrow and today.'

And so on and so forth until with a mighty kick, Stan punted the ball into one of the cast iron supports of the Palace Pier. After a further rest and a joint, they loped back at a more sedate pace and then fully conversant, shouted in unison while intermittently over-arming the ball to each other:

'Into many a green valley

drifts the appalling snow

Time breaks the threaded dances

and the diver's brilliant bow!'

Near the highest point of Marine Parade and before they scaled the two flights of stairs below Zac's flat at Eaton Place, they paused stoned, bushed and exhilarated. Knowing the most amazing stanzas were yet to come, Stan suggested an interval while they washed and prepared supper.

They were well-prepared later at the sink for the following:

'Oh, plunge your hands in the water,

Plunge them up to your wrists

then stare in the basin

And wonder what you'd missed.

Stan bathetically produced a soapy carrot and as he rolled a couple of 'post postprandial Specials', he intoned:

'The Glacier knocks in the cupboard

The desert sighs in the bed,

and the crack in the tea-cup opens

A lane to the land of the dead.'

Then in unison, as Stan made an artful twist in the joint's nose:

'Oh look, look, in the mirror

look in your distress

Life remains a blessing

Although you cannot bless.'

"Jeez, you can tell old Auden had a good time writing that!" interjected Zac, even knowing they were near the end.

"Not as good a time as we're having, old son," said Stan. "Or are going to have!"

They both collapsed into insane giggles.

They came round eventually at their favourite table at the Bristol but not before they had passed Manchester John, looking even more debauched than usual, at his usual pitch on the corner of James Street and Marine Parade. He said they both looked as if they'd just come back from Aden after 40 years and found out that they'd won the pools.

Zac didn't remember much apart from them both finishing off the poem over their first pints:

'O stand, stand in the window,

As the tears scald and start'

Suddenly a tearful Zac thought of poor Molly.

'You shall love your crooked neighbour

With your wicked, cruel heart.'

Zac felt a familiarly insistent but gentle grip on his shoulder and saw Stan beaming beatifically up at George who pulled up a couple more chairs.

"Well, what have we here?' asked Robin, an overture to what they had come to expect as another one of the most magical evenings of their lives.

Leaning back and in near ecstasy, Robin gave in to Zac's questioning and confessed that he had indeed known Auden.

"The old Queen," he added, quietly.

After a few more pints, the conversation heated up.

"If that was how he looked," said Robin, lowering his voice and with a mischievous twinkle in his eyes. "Can you picture his balls?"

The assembled company collapsed into riotous hysteria.

"Hear him, hear him, Mother of God!" cried Stan through tears of laughter.

"My round, I think?" said Zac said as he loped off to the bar.

Occasionally, Stan and he made up a Menage-a-Quatre, with either Marie-Joelle or Helga. They were both great fun but M-J was a riot, a rarity, a French hippy and at that time, an Anglophile. She liked Zac anyhow and the three of them used to perform a 'Jules et Jim' routine, Marie-Joelle, doing her 'chemin-de-fer' parody, puffing and blowing a reversed joint in her commodious mouth.

"Regardez-Moi, mes gars, Zizou, Zac, oh, mon Dieu! Ahm going to eat you, two boys, when we get back 'chez-Zac!"

As the three of them stumbled along the bank of pebbles, just east of the Palace Pier, they were caught by a sudden surge of the incoming tide, sending them tumbling like seals into each other's arms. Marie-Joelle's magnificent braless tits, Baronial, the heft of them standing proud in her soaked blouse, as they stumbled, stoned and laughing, then raced each other, tripping and falling up the strand to Marine Parade and into the Bristol.

"God save all here!" proclaimed Stan, which brought a round of applause, even from the poseurs at the bar.

Chapter 32

London Trots

Zac had a bit of fun that year as an itinerant labourer in the big city, or 'The Smoke' as he called it, like all Londoners. In the provinces, it would have been dire but he found himself working next to an irrepressible Aussie who had driven through Asia and had a beat-up Volkswagen campervan for sale as he struggled to survive, living in Earls Court, or Kangaroo Valley as most of Zac's contemporaries called it. Aussie and South African voices could be heard in every pub, great blokes so long as you kept off the politics. Being bookish as well as a boozer, Zac tended to bond with the more introverted Canadians and New Zealanders. Again, great blokes, like the Aussies but gentler and they always made Zac feel at home. This was strange, given that London was his capital city. It's just that he didn't believe it was. He also had a couple of American friends, interesting men always on their way to Sweden or back. On the run, so doubly interesting and heroic young men, black and white. The Vietnam war was coming to its ferocious and sickening climax.

This made Zac a bit more political and he participated in the occasional 'Stop the Bombing' march to Trafalgar Square. Even Glenda who had appeared back on the scene accompanied him on a Demo. Zac remembered a wet Saturday going up to Hornsey Art College in North London to hear Tariq Ali speak. He'd missed the student demonstrations and so much had changed in the space of two years that he was rather unsympathetic to them and the 'Evenements' in Paris had largely left him cold.

Zac had a soft spot for De Gaulle so much immersed was he in WW2 history. Something of the purloined atmosphere of the old Left of the 1930s lingered and fascinated him. The passion and chagrin of the Spanish Civil War; the sorrow and the pity of Nazi-occupied Europe; the raised and clenched fist and militant look suddenly seemed theatrical to his working-class soul. He disapproved of the Afghan sheepskins and expensive, thigh-length, genuine leather boots, pretentious French art-house films at the chillingly hip and unwelcoming ICA, not to mention the aristocratic Hampstead intellectuals and Mayfair Marxists. Zac felt more the genuine thing. He almost always had a copy of Orwell in his pocket or one of the great US writers of that pre-war period: Steinbeck; Hemingway or Henry Miller.

He was too irresponsible to be really politically active, although he did detect something in the wind. He did not share the blithe and synthetic optimism of the slightly younger generation. Something darker motivated his apolitical mindset at this time. It was more of a moral thing concerning the re-emergence of Fascism and the dying of the great British Labour Party. This was also the time of the Prague Spring so he felt disillusioned with the Soviet Union. Although he'd lost contact with his old Communist Party GB pals from his pre-Art school days, he suddenly felt Trotsky was the man!

He found himself one autumn evening in Fulham, West London, sitting in a packed Trotskyite meeting. The tough, incisive speeches were a bit over his head but he appreciated their rational, professional and civilised tone. There was a new Tory government in the offing, which appeared harsh and threatening and a general feeling pervaded that things were getting serious, the party times were over. Zac noted a large number of black guys present, bearded and intelligent, no-nonsense people. It reminded him of a church meeting back home but with brains and contained anger.

Zac raised an academic question about Trotsky's part in the repression of communist Soviets in the Civil War. He'd just finished reading 'Conquests, The Great Terror' now highly discredited. A dark and sinewy hand from behind his seat thrust a note into his hand: 'Hue and Cry about Kronstadt' by Leon Trotsky, including the publisher's name and ISBN. Such was the serious timbre of these meetings.

Zac had a sickening feeling that this was never going to work in Britain. Humbled, he made his way home from Fulham, through Hammersmith and the short distance to his bedsit, now in Addison Road. He offered to walk a young woman home to her room in Barons Court, only a mile or so away. She seemed timid and mousy but as Zac now realised, she probably had a lion's heart, a Simone Weil 'de nos jours'. As he gave her a chaste and comradely kiss outside her place in Baron's Court, his heart sang, as he saw that brave and earnest little face gazing up to stars, shining on a thousand streets below. He knew he would remember that sweet and earnest face, that 'Crystal' spirit. However, sadly no stars were visible in London in 1971, nor had they been for over 150 years.

Chapter 33

The Saffron Lady. A Russian Princess

Late summer 1971, Zac had a couple of friends, both ex-art school students, he'd met on a teachers' training course in Brighton the year before. Montpelier Crescent, where he'd shared a flat with them, was a slightly seamier and smaller version of Lewes Crescent in Kemptown and Belgrave Crescent in Hove. At the top of one of the many chalk hills leading up from the Brighton and Hove seafront and up to the Sussex Downs, it was just to the side of Seven Dials, calling to mind why Brighton was called 'Little London by the sea'.

One of his flatmates in those days was Sarah. She had a single room and the landlady being a rather conservative but genteel soul had furnished it beautifully. Though, as Stan said, Sarah was one of those deliciously feminine girls who seemed to just magic up her own boudoir in any new flat or bedsit. It was exactly the type of room Zac imagined Virginia Woolf or her Mrs Dalloway would have loved; whether in pre-war Bloomsbury or Brighton in the early nineteen-twenties.

Sarah was the quintessential 'Lady' and even subscribed to that anachronistic and quaint periodical! She always seemed pleased to see Zac. Stan used to joke that even if the Gestapo paid a call, she would earnestly and obsequiously clasp her hands, enquiring if the 'gentlemen' had had their tea and whether they took milk and sugar?

Zac felt at a loose end and anyway he always loved her company, so a year later he decided to pay her a visit. He thought her ex-boyfriend, Tim, might have temporarily taken over the tenancy with his Canadian girlfriend in tow and Sarah still occupying her single room. Tim was an alumnus of Kingston and knew both Stan and Glenda but he didn't mention her much. Zac liked Tim, even loved him. He thought of him as a benign Frank Zappa, if that doesn't sound like an oxymoron. He was a Lancastrian and one of those 'sun-children' who seemed permanently happy. He liked a bit of grass too and was always painting with a joint on the go. "Hi, Head!" he used to say to Zac, using the slang of the time. He was just a joy to be with and epitomised the more positive side of the times.

He stood outside the front door, ringing the bell in the hope of rousing someone. He always knew Sarah to be a home bird but no-one responded. Zac thought Tim and his girlfriend, who loved Acid, might be spaced out so he turned to leave. It was an early January day but with that Olympian light that you get on the south coast, a morning sun in a cloudless and freezing clear sky bouncing back off the Channel and up the hill among the white and cream, spun sugar villas climbing the hill and up to Montpelier Crescent.

Suddenly he heard a gentle groan coming from the other side of the privet hedge by Sarah's driveway. He peered over and saw a lumpy, brown shape with tangled, hennaed hair and elderly lady's limbs, splayed at strange angles. He leapt over the hedge.

"Hullo, what have we here?" said Zac, kindly. "A young lady in distress!"

He soon had her shakily standing upright and joked that this paving was expensive to replace. She chuckled and Zac realised that, like many old girls of her generation, she was a good sport. Her forehead and nose had taken a bit of a knock and he asked how she felt.

"Felt worse, young man!" she laughed.

Zac bowed to her in mock ceremony and offered her his arm. He loved her immediately.

"Step this way, young man, while I…" she broke off as she fumbled for her key.

Fuck it, he thought. I'm not going anywhere and I like her. Again, he offered her his arm, as she found her key and raised it with a trembling hand to the Yale lock. Once the door was open, she turned to face him with the dignity that only elderly ladies of her generation familiar with corsets and tea dances could manage.

"I didn't catch your name, young man?"

"Zac," he said.

"I fear my butler is away in Worthing at his aunt's," she said, her eyes twinkling. "Be pleased to step this way."

"Yes, m' lady!" said Zac. "And let's get that nose seen to."

She leaned her surprisingly lithe but heavy body into his and he wondered what she would have been like as a young woman, first World War generation. Probably lost a few boyfriends in France, too, he imagined.

Zac picked up a whiff of urine and very briefly the snotty Grammar Schoolboy in him recoiled but he quickly corrected himself. He'd worked in enough hospitals and care centres to realise this is what happens and the poor old girl had just taken a massive hit. She should be concussed right now. He stood with her, almost enjoying her fragrance and her heft, her strong spiritual vibe and what he could see in her eyes now, a massive kindness and grace.

"You didn't tell me your name, Milady?" he said.

"Nina, or in 'me prime'," she answered, mocking herself. "When I was at Court, Ninotchka!" and made a stiff little curtsy.

Thanks to Stan, Zac was a Nabokov fan and had recently read his delicious memoir: "Speak Memory" much of it evoking the old Russia of his father's day. He also noticed Edwardian-looking photos of lovely girls and boys from a more prosperous age but also photos from the Soviet era. Zac recognised, thanks to his aviation interests some female Soviet fighter aces and pointed to one that he knew, Lily Litvak, 'The Rose of Stalingrad'.

Zac looked enquiringly at her, not wishing to linger as he could tell she was probably looking forward to a stiff drink and a nap. Zac had a good ear and he recognised an accent.

"Rus?" he asked.

"Da, da!" she replied, with a twinkle in her gentle eyes.

He gave her a wink and inclining his head towards a glazed and white painted inner door, which he thought VERY Brighton, he started to lead her by the arm towards it. He couldn't help playing the wag and started to sing:

"Stately as a.."

"Galleon," she finished for him, Nina, Zac's Russian Princess, with a frail but fruity laugh.

Anticipating a chaos of old lady's knick-knacks, an Edwardian rout of Benares ware and tacky, sepia-framed, formal family photos, he opened the door and stood back to let her enter first. She leaned back against the door jamb and gazed at him. Those eyes, he thought those eyes.

"Look, Zac," she said.

A blaze of saffron and amber light from old St. Petersburg shone, of Naples Yellow, Golden Ochre, of Madder Browns, Burnt Umbers, Raw Siennas, Indian reds and Alizarin Crimsons, assaulted his eyes.

Part Three:

DOWN AND NEARLY OUT IN LONDON

Chapter 34

Stan had long gone to London and Zac received a letter from Glenda, now back from Pakistan. She was currently in quarantine, having caught malaria and was living somewhere west of London. Although he wouldn't be able to visit her, Zac took it for granted that she would need him. Or maybe he was deluding himself, as the magic of Brighton was beginning to wear off. He felt that he couldn't continue as a mere auxiliary nurse at the hospital and he should somehow rise to another challenge.

His recent past periods in London and Brighton had been intense, confusing and almost traumatic. Though later, Zac went slightly mad, he had hints of glory and yet he almost certainly degenerated. Perhaps, more to the truth, he had become a drifter, homeless and alienated, possibly something of a loser in what was becoming, though an American import, a term of disparagement. Swinging London had been 'dangling' for a bit and Brighton had lost its transgressive charm. Its image as an English San Francisco seemed pathetic and in much of the rest of England, he had sensed a malaise in the air. Zac mentioned, in passing to a charming Jewish American student/hippy couple, whom he met and befriended in the Bristol pub, that he had a feeling England might not make it. They were among the best friends he made on the south coast, real intellectuals and almost socialist.

Zac worked in the bakery in Hove for a while, always useful for casual work for the unsettled and lost, as he was fast becoming. Somehow, the 'wand of youth' had passed from over his head. Zac had become a bit sad, a bit lost. He found himself in a kind of limbo. He didn't want to go back up north yet and felt he wasn't finished with London either.

He had walked the streets for a couple of nights, literally because he couldn't remember trying to find a place to sleep. He had some cash and it might have been more than just a couple of nights. He remembered being able to wash and brush up for ten pence, in Liverpool Street Station; coffees in pre-Murdoch Fleet Street cafes; lingering over half pints in Bloomsbury pubs, redolent of the 'Fitzrovia' poets of the 1940s. You could imagine Dylan Thomas and Caitlin staggering into the pub, clutching each other or that gentle and good man, Patrick Hamilton, scribbling over his future masterpiece, 'West Pier', lighting yet another Players' Navy cut.

As Zac stumbled around Soho, tripping over with tiredness, he realised that London was not a town that never slept. He headed down to the river for some respite and rest under the railway arches of Blackfriars' and London Bridge. Nearly falling into the road with fatigue, he realised that there really was a Mary Woolnoth and he stumbled gratefully into the blitzed and now grassed over nave to lie down and await the dawn, shivering from that first false one, presaging a last drawing chill.

One was less likely to be kicked or urinated on by a Copper in those more civilized times and a civil reply to the constabulary's enquiries was usually met in kind. Zac's tank commander voice was good for this, Coppers being such snobs.

He soon began to realise that despite his railway station ablutions, he had begun to smell. Constant walking made sweat permeate the seams of his trousers and his shoes seemed saturated with it. He knew in his bones the feeling of being 'dead beat' and a sudden glimpse of himself in a shop window, meant he knew the look of it, too. Zac was now a shambling ghost. He had rediscovered the trick of poorer kids in his schooldays and inserted cardboard into his shoes as an extra sole. This particular morning, down at the great river's edge where the receding tide had left a small beach from where he could paddle, he washed his feet. Then daringly, despite the autumn chill, he washed his more intimate parts.

Shrinking into himself, as an early-morning train thundered across Hungerford Bridge, Zac understood how an army survives on its feet. After he had breakfasted on a stale roll and a mug of stewed tea, at a taxi-drivers' café, with its warm green paintwork and friendly banter, he managed a rough shave in Waterloo Station. Another old army adage sprang to mind, that a shave is as good as two hours' sleep.

Feeling better but now completely without money, he staggered up west where he knew there were better job prospects and more salubrious and cheaper lodgings. If he could get a job soon, he had a good chance of eventually renting a bedsit or even a flat.

Still staggering but enjoying the brightening day, light-headed with hunger and leaden-footed, Zac moved back onto the embankment where he thought of resting later in the day, up Charing Cross Road and onto the bustling Strand, towards Piccadilly Circus. When he reached Trafalgar Square, he knew he could rest among the temporarily homeless like himself and the student back-packers. Suddenly, the Goddess smiled upon him.

He had hardly noticed the tough-looking but vaguely pretty girl, who in answer to his choking request, handed him a copy of 'Soviet Weekly'. As he waited, dizzy and almost fainting, at the crossing to Northumberland Avenue, he felt a moist peck on his cheek. It wasn't until he had stumbled across the road, through the thronging and honking taxis, that he realised he had been kissed. Looking around, he saw a pert and small blonde girl, peering over dark Granny sunglasses, clenched fist raised and a cheeky but comradely grin breaking up her sweet face.

A nightingale sang in Trafalgar Square.

Though his eyes felt as if they'd been temporarily removed and rolled in sand, Zac managed to drag himself west to Hammersmith where he knew there were one or two employment agencies, where he could find temporary casual work. As he'd learned from his previous London sojourn, he could also meet congenial spirits; Aussies and Kiwis, Irish and Scots, Canadians, even fellow northerners and the odd, forlorn Yank.

First of all, he signed on at the old Labour Exchange at Barons Court, hard by the Tube station; a rather grey and grimy part of London reminding Zac of Leeds. Tall, red-grey brick tenements and decaying solicitors' and accountants' offices, some still scarred by wartime shrapnel. The light-hearted spirit of the sixties stayed in the air though. Two Essex university students were chaffing and laughing and Zac joined in the fun.

He was still on what was called 'The Professional and Executive Register' so he hadn't descended completely into the proletariat. Also, the 'wand of youth' still waved over him and the two students and they joined each other in excoriating the Wilson government. The 'spirit of 1968 was evident too in these upper-middle-class types but it was genuine and Zac got involved in talking about writing. They mentioned two North Americans; Ed Dorn and Ed Warrant. The latter had been born in England and the former was a poet whom Zac heard later on the BBC. He liked his emphasis on breathing and the oral tradition in poetry. It rhymed with Zac's frustration of what he saw as the over-intellectualisation of 'eng.lit.' taught in universities. It also chimed with his culturally conservative love of the 'primitive' or 'ballad' form.

When Zac's turn came for an interview, the nice lady seemed willing to help and expressed surprise that he was unemployed.

"You look so motivated!" she exclaimed.

She offered a couple of management positions and a trainee job as a technician/designer at a tank factory near Maidenhead! Virtually picking himself up from the floor at this prospective employment, he marvelled that she should express astonishment that he was destitute.

"Well," she said, lowering her voice. "There's what we call a 'Rowton House' down by the bus station at Hammersmith Broadway."

Zac knew it. It was not far from the river and the distinctive Hammersmith Road Bridge, he had got to know so well a couple of years ago when he used to take the Greenline single-decker bus to Surbiton and Kingston for that brief time that he was still seeing Glenda. He remembered the journey through the south London suburbs, stretching endlessly in dreary petit-bourgeois dullness followed by leafy common land and the splendid villas of rustic Surrey.

Thinking of the building she had mentioned, Zac remembered a huge, Scottish baronial-hall style monstrosity, a cross between a prison and his beloved but near-ruined St. Pancras Station.

"Well," the nice lady whispered. "It's called Butterwick House and we pay for our clients to stay there. It's rather a rough clientele, VERY Victorian, but clean and only 10 shillings a night. We arrange a pay-out of your Dole money there every Thursday."

As he was going through a crash-reading course of Oscar Wilde and George Orwell, Zac enthusiastically agreed to parade there as soon as possible. What an adventure! A bit of slumming and 'class collaboration'!

"Righto, that's the spirit!" said the nice woman shaking his hand.

He stalked out, turning right into Shepherds Bush Road and to a new adventure! He'd give it a few days and maybe get a job – well yes, get a job straight away, remembering that he had no money. Today was Monday and Dole day not until Thursday. Oh well, well, he thought. At least I'll have a roof over my head, tonight.

He went down to Butterwick House which was as bizarre inside as outside. He felt remarkably cheerful. Funny how a few nights without a roof put things in perspective. The first thing the place reminded him of was a Victorian Mental Institution that his school choir sang in every year at Christmas but not quite as depressing. Endless, white London-tiled corridors stretched to all points of the compass and Zac noticed a wide, flagged, gently spiralling staircase ascending to one of the turrets to his immediate left.

An ancient and toothless Lowland Scot sat on a high stool by a turnstile gate, like the entrance to a dog track Zac remembered in Sunderland and equally as anachronistic. Tough and rough but without any menace, his Scots 'Charron', wearing gym pumps, pointed to a tiny kiosk, after asking if he was on National Assistance, or was he British, Irish or Scots? The kiosk struck a surreal note, given that there were vast and echoing vaults soaring, cathedral-like into the roof, via imagined clerestory stories and flying buttresses, Piranesi-style mezzanine floors, semi-circular and barred windows looking down on mysterious, Dickensian spaces below.

A face with a querulous Welsh accent sat behind the kiosk window and asked Zac whether he'd be on nights or days. It wasn't a Doss-House because a lot of lorry drivers used it but it seemed a permanent home for old men and some long-term indigents. Zac's Welsh friend with a friendly smile told him to wait as he had already said that he had to find work quickly and though he desperately wanted to get his head down, he would have to see to that first. His Scots friend was then asked to show Zac to his chamber where he could leave his paper bags.

Zac was ushered up just a couple of flights of the spiral staircase and down a long corridor with what looked like cages along each side. They were enclosed by boarding which stood way beyond head height and then grilled further with ancient metal mesh. Everything was encased in a nacreous, dirty yellow light. Yet despite this, there was no heaviness and whether it was because these were pre-Thatcher days or that the men were older than Zac, many of them WW2 vintage, he felt comfortable with them. In fact, he went on to meet some of the finest men he had ever known. It was a living symbol to him, of England, made up of many 'Englands', under a Gothic and quirky superstructure, transcending his own petty lifetime.

Zac called in at the Job Centre again to look for casual or temporary labouring work. Even hotel work, the lowest paid, at least got you a meal and a few quid at the end of the week. It was a cash economy then and you could usually get a 'sub' to pay for a few beers and smokes. He received an introduction and headed back down towards the Broadway, turned left and before reaching the great river, strode along the road to Fulham and the posher Chelsea, which was light-years away in terms of finances and social class.

Shortly, Zac found himself faced by another gigantic industrial building, a cross between the Spike and Kafka's Castle, Cadby Hall, home of Lyons' Bakery and what he was to learn later was a clearinghouse for most English-speaking and budding writers. He worked his way through echoing vaults, transepts and chancels and past hurrying white-clad minions until he eventually found an Irishman wearing a tie. Zac's social antennae found this a strange combination at the time. The Irishman pointed up some metal stairs. He felt he had been trudging up clanging metal treads, throughout his youth. An ecclesiastical and almost nautical leitmotif, he thought.

"Till where ye'll see a wee black fella wi' a clipboard," called the Irishman.

Zac put his hand on the steep rail and set off up the stairs, finally emerging on a gantry with gangways receding in all directions. Here he met his next cicerone, a friendly Jamaican.

"Call me Winston, man!"

Winston signed Zac up and told him that he could start in a couple of hours if he so wished. Then he pointed along the gantry to another office where he would find a charge hand to take him for kitting out with his 'whites'. Zac did so and was met by a fresh-faced young Irishman, a new recruit, like himself, as well as a most elegant, handsome Afro-American.

"Nat," he said. "Pleased to meet you guys. Follow me!"

They clattered down yet another gangway and series of ladders to a basement. Nat looked them up and down and reckoned Dominic, the young Irishman and Zac were the same height.

"You wait here guys," said Nat and disappeared into what looked like a Quartermasters Stores.

Zac liked the Irish lad immediately. Dominic from Mullingar hadn't had a bite to eat, nor a wink of sleep since leaving Holyhead two days ago. They conferred urgently on whether or when they could get their next meal and how in hell would they be able to stay awake until their twelve-hour night shift began in a couple of hours?

Nat was to prove their saviour and Zac vowed to never forget him. He showed them where to undress and change, then led them up more clanging stairs and pointed to another room in this crazy Kafka's Castle.

"Get your heads down here and I'll wake you guys up in coupla hours with a coffee and a bite."

They pulled a few benches together and that was that.

After a couple of hours, Nat's aristocratic features loomed over them.

"Tea is served, gentlemen!" he said.

Nat sat opposite them, in a gracious and comradely gesture, obviously enjoying their pleasure. He told them his story. He was ex-US Air Force who did not want to go to Vietnam. Like a few Yanks, Zac was to meet, he was a refugee and hoped to study Aircraft Engineering either here in London, or more likely in Sweden.

Zac signed on again at the old Labour Exchange at Barons Court, just to make sure he had the back-up of another job if the bakery one didn't suit and to keep up his National Insurance payments. He got into the rhythm of the long hours and enjoyed the congenial company with many breaks, with time for reading and bonding with other young exiled men from all over the English-speaking world, including the engaging and vibrant West Indians.

Chapter 35

Spem in alium, Latin for "Hope in any other", composed by Thomas Tallis in 1570, one of the greatest examples of early English.

It was probably the contrast between his recent circumstances and the magnificent setting of St. Paul's' Cathedral, that gave Zac his most aesthetically and moving spiritual experience of this period of his life. Something of extreme contrast and out of time. Thomas Tallis had lived through the reign of Elizabeth, so he wasn't solely a catholic and in fact, he was famous in Henry VIII's reign. Zac and Dominic, along with the rest of the congregation, sat in the near-circular checker paved marble floor beneath the dome, the choir singing in Wren's great Quire beyond. Zac stirred slightly, as did the surprisingly small congregation, while the famous cathedral choir cleared their throats in anticipation of their efforts to come.

As a rule, Zac preferred Westminster Abbey with its Gothic appeal and more ancient ambience. However, he looked up in wonder at the inner, painted dome, a triumph of English Protestant and Renaissance architecture. Despite his doubts, he couldn't help but admire the magnificence. It remained the other national shrine of England. Zac looked back down the nave at the similar pomp and pride which evoked ancient Rome; Britain's national heroes, sculpted in marble and porphyry and the exquisite Baroque wooden carvings of Grinling Gibbons. For all his apparent alienation, Zac still felt like an Englishman and at ease with his country.

The music moved him profoundly, more so than the plays of Tallis' contemporary, one Will Shakespeare. Catholic Tallis and later in the service, William Byrd, another catholic, seemed connected to him. They were doomed men, like another Mr Byrd back in the Royal Sussex County Hospital, whose cancer-riddled body, bandaged to the cot sides of his bed reminded Zac of the graphically sculptured 'Vanitas' effigies of former clerics in the tombs gracing the side chapels of the two great cathedrals. Zac wondered if his boyhood piety still stirred. He saw the ecstasy on Dominic's transfigured features.

Something understood, Zac felt deep inside his soul but something catholic also bridled at the Protestant and Whiggish usurpation of the old religion by upstart protestants. He suddenly felt, looking at gentle Dominic's face again, that maybe he reflected the light that shone in the great Irish saints' faces in Zac's ancestral Northumbria: Saints Aidan and Columba; Colman and the Anglo-Northumbrian Bede. As they stood to leave, both Zac and Dominic spontaneously crossed themselves. Zac suddenly thought of brave Southwell's 'Burning Babe'.

The following night, their limbs and muscles aching, Dominic and Zac found themselves on the same shift. They made some new friends, one of the benefits of being young and in London at that time. They found at least four blokes, mainly older than them, who were domiciled at the Spike. They exchanged information. One of them, a sardonic Glaswegian, told them in the many breaks that they hadn't seen the 'wooden fella' yet, the coffin, a broad and deep crate that they used for bringing down the dead, mainly older men, who obviously in the past must have been dropping like flies.

"What about the Bellman?" asked Zac. "Have I been hallucinating?"

"No," said Jock.

It really was Victorian, medieval even, when the Bellman came down the spiral staircase, with two men bearing candles aloft. There were so many power cuts, the wiring in the old place being so ancient.

Jock had a constant companion, an Englishman called Reg and though there was never a hint at either being homosexual, Zac was amazed at the companionship these men showed to each other and their displays of comradeship. Zac wondered if it went back to days of National Service because these blokes were that much older than himself. He asked Jock outright, and he agreed. He was proud to have served in the 'Pioneer Corps', which Zac had thought of as the most despised outfit in the British Armed Forces, like the RAF regiment in that respect. But Zac began to see that older men, however poor, shared something 'Royal', something of the Imperial Purple. They had stood together on the parapet of old Britannia. They had served. Zac and his contemporaries were mere civvies.

Zac was to find something even more interesting when Jock and Reg suggested that the next time they had a power cut at the 'Big House' they stayed downstairs for breakfast. They weren't allowed upstairs at such times and anyway there was a very basic canteen service. With one winking to the other, they concurred that it was an experience not to be missed! They also went on to say there were some really interesting old guys there as indeed was proved to be the case. Zac's real Post Graduate education was about to get even more intense.

***

"Largo Caballero!"

"The Guadarrama."

"Teruel."

"Pablo Negrin."

The first Russian fighter planes over Madrid and the Siege of Barcelona, the bloody fascist holocaust at Guernica were all exalted. Dominic and Zac sat in awe of the three old blokes at the table in the Spike, bearded, two of them, and all three in voluminous Basque berets, celebrities of the socialist and communist British Left.

Zac kneed Dominic gently, as he knew he was educated by the Christian Brothers and knew from so many Irish mates what spiritual and intellectual damage a Maynooth priest could do.

"Ssh!" Zac mouthed at him.

But his Irish mate knew the score. Carl, Pablo and Ron gurned great, beaming smiles and clenched their right fists. In the background, candles guttered on some scene out of Daumier's Paris or Gustav Dore's London.

"Aye, I was at the Guadalajara and the Ebro. Near captured at Teruel, so ah was," said Pablo in his strong Belfast accent.

"Aye, it wor rough like, bonny lad," said Ron.

Carl nodded in a polite and deferential way.

"Yes, it was, rather," he said in his middle-class, deferential North London tone.

Zac presumed he was a nice only child brought up by two first-wave Trotsky-ite lesbians in Hampstead.

A bit of an argument ensued as to the worth and significance of Orwell.

Pablo thought him a 'bourgeois Trotskyist cunt', giving a wink to Carl. Ron thought the anarchists were to blame for dividing the left. Carl named the brutality of the KGB sent in by Stalin to purge the P.O.U.M, Orwell's' outfit.

Zac didn't mention his beloved Simone Weil who he knew had been there, if only in her role as a cook. He didn't want his transcendental yearnings trod on by what he looked up to, three fine but embittered atheists.

Simone, before this time had been a dedicated communist then had a spiritual experience which took her on her journey into faith, while not budging her faith in socialism. This seemed a precious combination of ideologies and was a font of great treasure to Zac, which he scarcely understood at the time.

Eventually, they were allowed upstairs. He and Dominic went up to the first floor and their separate cells, leaving the three noble compadres to their day. God bless them!

***

Like many Yanks Zac had met, Nat was on the run from the US Air Force heading for freedom in Sweden.

"I ain't got no quarrel with them Vietnamese and I ain't no coward!" he said, parodying Mohammed Ali, who had recently said the same.

Nat spoke with an educated accent and in his courtly way he went on to tell them about his education and speciality in aircraft engineering. He was hoping to get a job at SAAB, the great Swedish auto and aircraft manufacturing firm.

On Friday night they got 'The Sub' from the dapper Irishman, Zac had met a couple of nights before. With small change and 'crispies' aka banknotes, burning holes in their pockets they headed out of Kafka's Castle up Shepherds Bush Road to one of the many workmen's cafes, frequented by Irish boys on the building sites. Zac signed Dominic in at the Spike and they looked forward to a stripped wash, a shave and a long, long sleep.

When the job at Cadby Hall and Lyons Bakery petered out, Zac stayed on at the Spike. An Orwellian part of him was enjoying a bit of slumming and in his relative youth, Zac had forgotten how desperate his position had been when he first entered those gloomy, Gothic portals. Dominic felt the same. They only bumped into each other occasionally now, because his workplace was upstairs in the Vienna department, in a mysteriously inaccessible bakehouse, behind the north-facing mock battlements.

One day, when they met in the depressingly white, enamelled tiled foyer, Zac thought it might be a good time to say their goodbyes. Zac was on his way back from his nocturnal rambles in the City and wanted to get his head down for a bit before taking a stroll around The Manor and maybe getting signed on at the Job Centre, or at Manpower, an agency in Hammersmith that he had used a couple of years ago, which seemed like an aeon away now.

Dominic looked a little febrile and knowing that for an Irishman, he was not much of a drinker, Zac suggested a stroll outside. Fresh air seemed a good idea so they headed for a little park by some Peabody apartments around the back of Barons Court. Zac told Dominic he would escort him to his tube station afterwards. They found a park bench to sit on, surrounded by discarded syringes and empty cider bottles.

"Well, then, Dominic mate. What's the plan?" asked Zac.

"Zac, Oi've an aunt up in Kilburn and some family. That's up north, isn't it?"

"Yes!" replied Zac. "Somewhere off the Northern or Bakerloo Line though I think the new Victoria Line might go there and the Metropolitan Line. We've used that on our trips to the West End at weekends."

"Oh, I thought it was up in Newcastle around there," said Dominic, handing Zac a scrap of crumpled paper, with a pencil-written address on it.

Zac looked at it and distinctly saw the Underground stations listed on it. Suddenly, it struck him, Dominic couldn't read. Zac's heart went out to him. Somehow, he got over it and made light of the misunderstanding. He immediately promised to escort him to the right station. Looking again at the scrap of paper, Zac noticed a Church name written down. He knew and loved the Irish boys enough to realise that it was standard procedure for poor and illiterate young Irishmen, destined for the 'building', to report to a priest who would have a list of lady parishioners only too willing to be landladies to such men. His pure and angelic face suggested that and he showed no lack of intelligence.

Zac quizzed him about home back in Mullingar. He felt a lump forming in his throat as Dominic told him about sleeping three to a bed. His mother worked at the Priest's house for their rashers. He described how he had run away from the Christian Brothers. Zac asked how long he had spent without food, since leaving County Mullingar? He had noticed, unlike his own mild discomfort at not eating, Dominic showed signs of real malnutrition. He suffered from lack of concentration, vagueness and fainting fits. Once Nat and Zac had stopped him from falling on the way to the main bakehouse.

"Oh, Zac. 'Twas a wee bit longer, maybe a few days, da Mudder she ran out of rashers and went to da priest and he said for me to go to England."

Zac hugged him close to his chest with tears in his eyes. They both stood up and hugged each other again and Dominic burst into tears.

"Jeez, Zac, 'twas a long toime oi nivver been hungry loike dat!"

As they hugged, they rocked each other from side to side, like children. Later Zac walked him up west. They needed to dry their tears and enjoy some more fresh air so they headed along Holland Park and Bayswater Road, through another world of posh villas. When they got near to Marble Arch, Zac bought them both an ice cream. They had recovered their good cheer and Zac was able to draw a map on a cafe napkin, with directions from Marble Arch underground station to Kilburn.

"See you around, mate," said Zac and they shook hands.

Dominic turned on his heel and Zac never saw him again

Sometime later, during one of their many breaks at the bakery, a Canadian 'head' or student passing through, paused to speak to the group. Zac recognised him as a leftist, they had discussed Orwell together in the past.

"You guys hear about the trouble in town with the Irish boys?" he asked.

Prime Minister Heath had recently sent the Army into Northern Ireland and a massive riot had kicked off in Kilburn, extending down into the West End. Nobody had heard anything about it on the BBC. The Lefties among the lads, Zac included, resolved to get downtown as soon as their shift ended. He arrived in time to see Park Lane, St James and from Piccadilly to Tottenham Court Road awash with water from fire hoses. He witnessed upturned police cars and smashed and boarded-up shop windows. Neither the TV news nor the papers were covering it.

"Move along there, nothing to see here!" shouted a police officer.

Chapter 36

Strangely, and to use a cricketing term of the time, 'against the rub of the green', Zac found himself in good company. Although he continued in his dead-end jobs and quasi-Bohemian lifestyle, he met one or two interesting young lads at Kafka's Castle as he nicknamed Lyons Bakery in Hammersmith.

Dick O'Donnell and his brother Frank had lodgings in Addison Road in Shepherds Bush, a solidly working-class and cosmopolitan part of London. It was not too far away from work, nor the West End for their young limbs and restless libidos. Zac shared a comfortable room in Dick's Uncle's house with two amiable Scots lads who also worked at Cadby Hall.

Zac was beginning to find Irish people more congenial than his fellow Brits. For a while, they were a group of youngsters, even though Zac was nearly 30 and he looked on himself as an inward exile with the rest of their gang as a kind of Anglo-Irish-US diaspora. Zac enjoyed their company for some of his forays uptown, providing a change from his solitary and dour drinking habits. Though he didn't remember much sex, Zac recalled it being easy and a very pleasant thing to chat up girls in the pubs of Chelsea, Kensington, Baker Street and Notting Hill.

Maybe because of the onset of the new wave of feminism, the ubiquity of the 'pill' and his set being a fairly presentable bunch, they seemed to have no trouble making friends with the girls, even just for a dance. If some of them had the luck to go further it was an unwritten rule that they'd take it in turns to give up their bed for a comrade and double up with another, or sleep on a spare sofa. They even went to the trouble of having spare flat keys cut.

Zac felt that he was no great gift to women but was fairly presentable and found to his surprise that it was quite easy to make girls laugh, so at least he was useful in breaking the ice. Zac was still at the borderline misogynistic state of wanting to be a good comrade and a team-player, rather than a lover. Still, they were good times and he began to swagger a little, feeling more at home.

However, a wild spirit started calling Zac from the moors and crags of the north. Had he lived in Melville's or Conrad's time, he would have headed for the docks at Limehouse and crewed a ship heading for the Indies.

Zac's new friend, Dick, had connections, a clan and a family in the States. Zac felt sure Dick was a Catholic but those were the dark days of 'the troubles' and sectarianism among his own set would have been taboo. Dick had the look of the Boston Irish and they often discussed American writing as well as English and Irish.

Zac had just discovered F. Scott Fitzgerald and his nickname for Dick was 'Diver'. They had great fun one night, drunkenly reciting lines from MacNeice's 'Carrickfergus', on the District Line home from Earl's Court,

They also shared a disgraceful bender in Soho, at one of London's most iconic and degenerate venues, The colony Rooms. Zac found himself in the company of the most decadent people he had ever imagined, ageing alcoholics, faded writers, slumming artists and Thespians. An evil-looking hag, perched like a vulture at the bar turned to face him.

"Hello, Cuntie. What yer got in yer beanbag, drinkypoos for Mother?" she sneered, giving him a vaguely discernible wink and pulling on her cigarette holder. "Mine's a brandy, Lottie, a double!"

Zac's anger made him think that he was his father's son after all. They didn't stay long.

Around the same time, they were 'eyed up' by Francis Bacon, at Gloucester Road tube station. Zac also remembered lots of 'pussy' or 'hot Totty' around at that time. They went to a party in Earls Court and Dick swore that the big girl surrounded by 'Bruces' at the bar, was Germaine Greer. They managed to avoid a fight with a couple of Aussies, a regular event at the time.

One day at Shepherds Bush tube station, when neither of them had remembered to buy a ticket, Dick donned his guitar and serenaded the Jamaican ticket collector with a calypso.

"Ok, boys," said the man wearily. "That was great but hang on to yo' day job!"

Such was London at that time for Zac. There was joy followed by searing loneliness. He saw Dick as a kind of Gatsby or Dick Diver figure, charismatic, his Irish charm brimming with the promise of great things to come, maybe even just around the corner! But brief friendships ended with the job, comrades moved on or returned home and Zac was left in one of the loneliest cities in the world.

Zac's second London period was coming to an end. It had seemed quite congenial at the time and on the surface, he felt lucky to have been friends with Dick and his charming family. His toothy smile reminded Zac of the Boston-Irish Kennedy family and he wondered whether he belonged to a cadet branch of that family. It wasn't long since the world had been shocked by Robert Kennedy's assassination. Knowing Zac was interested in the States, Dick suggested he go there. He advised him to take a short course at Trinity College Dublin or Kings College, Belfast, just to get a student card and an absurdly cheap and subsidised flight to the States. So, there was promise in the air and the letter from Glenda that morning was almost affectionate.

In the meantime, they were both watching Parkinson on TV in Dick's flat, something of a cult at the time and laughing at his 'down-to-earth' Yorkshire manner.

"Bejayzus!" said Dick. "I love this guy. See the way he just poked his nose, while grinning to himself?"

It was the infamous Helen Mirren interview, where Parkie was trapped into looking like a typical northern, macho slob. Her sheer 'chutzpah' and insolence angered them at the time. Then they got around to talking about the Aussie party in Holland Park the previous night.

"Did 'ya see, Ken Tynan there, Zac?" asked Dick.

"Jeez, no!" he replied.

"A whole crew of them were there, Zac. Jeez, you're so unworldly sometimes! Clive James and Richard Neville and didn't you notice Germaine give you the eye?"

"You're kidding!" exclaimed Zac.

"Sure, Zac. You hide your light under a bushel and you weren't even too pissed!"

Zac did remember seeing Germaine Greer in a corridor. He noticed the

Hockneys on the wall as he cringed into it to let the Aussie Amazon go by. Her eyes had blazed ferociously but he thought he saw her wink at him as she passed.

"I remember an Aussie geezer, one of the mob we had an altercation with later, squeezing my arse as I went into one of the bathrooms," said Zac.

Dick guffawed.

"Did you not know, ya eedjit. It was Germaine herself. It's one of her party tricks. She wrote about it in last week's Observer!"

The Observer was their favourite Sunday paper at the time.

"Oh, the one where she said she was turned off by Englishmen because we wear Y-fronts?" said Zac.

Dick leaned back in his chair, laughing loudly and slapping his long thighs.

"Zac, she meant Irishmen as well and I can assure you, that she was lying. A word to the wise-wink-wink!"

The next day, Glenda turned up. She had been in quarantine for malaria somewhere in Surrey, not far from where she met her Pakistani husband, Hassan. Glenda had shown her noble and generous side at that time. Zac was living in the students' house in Surbiton that Glenda had vacated. He found that on one of his days off he was welcome to take the Greenline bus through the very salubrious upper Thames Valley suburbs of Virginia Water and Esher to her place of work.

She was a waitress and that's how she met Hassan, a very bright and accomplished engineer. When she finished her shift, she took Zac to Hassan's bachelor pad in Walton-on-Thames, very posh, in a rather clinical way, though Glenda had that aspect to her. Zac thought she was genuinely being kind, or maybe a dark part of him was correct in suspecting that she wanted to further humiliate him.

Hassan was very westernised as most educated Muslims were at that time and when Zac asked him, he said he preferred to be called 'Jim' and that he was Indian. He found him a thoroughly pleasant chap and that dark part of him guessed that Glenda had made it clear that Zac was in no way a rival.

They entertained him a couple of times in a civil if slightly soulless fashion. Jim would drive them in his Jag to Heathrow Airport where they lingered over a few drinks in the airport lounge, enjoying that slick and international jet-set style, if only at second hand. Zac felt there had always been something displaced and alienated about Glenda. He seemed a merry and rooted peasant in comparison. He fell more and more under her spell. Yet it was almost a narcotic and unreal sensation. 'The sedge has withered from the lake' he thought to himself. At that time, he was coming very much under the sway of the south country, even if this part of Surrey, a vastly wealthy county anyway, still held something of the heavy sweetness of Keats and even sometimes nearer the city, a feel of Blake's visions.

'La Belle Dame sans merci hath thee in thrall,' he continued quoting to himself. Before sending Zac courteously on his way with a lift to Esher station in the Jag, Jim gave him a lovely and modernistic sharkskin business suit and they both wished each other well. Later Glenda went to Pakistan as his bride, a very brave thing to do at that time.

So, now Glenda was back, in his bedsit in Shepherds Bush, still with her chilling and almost studied poise. But why was he being so negative? She was a Goddess and though she hardly possessed an easy charm, she had deigned to care for him, to enter his drab male existence and even sometimes to return his kisses. What's going on? He thought. A goose-girl and now an international jet-setting sophisticate, like Catherine Deneuve in one of her more schizoid roles.

He held that precious image in his heart for a moment, while she sat at his unusually clean and cheerful, yellow Formica table in his recently refurbished bedsit with its stripped pine bunk beds, Habitat armchair and oatmeal-coloured carpet. She looked clean in her chilling Nordic way, navy blue sweater and Levis, her hair tied in that plaited single band at the back of her head, in a way that made Zac want to weep for joy. Her arms, one elbow resting on the back of his pine dining chair, her face turned towards him, a Catherine Deneuve air about her, eyes expressionless but enigmatic. slight Halifax accent;

"So, Zac," she said in her slight Halifax accent. "What are you going to do?"

Chapter 37

Those few crazily congenial weeks of his burgeoning friendship with Dick O'Donnell had seen them both half-starving at one time and embarking on a shoplifting spree down the Goldhawk and Shepherds Bush roads. Both of them were too honest or middle class to complete the heist and the Asian shop proprietor seemed to sense what they were up to. Then either Zac or Dick would get a tax rebate and they were out on the town.

Whether Dick was gently leading Zac, or maybe he was, at last, taking the reviews in the 'Observer' seriously for a change but they both saw two films which profoundly affected them: 'The Wanderer', a French adaptation of Alain Fournier's 'Le Grande Meaulnes' and 'Death in Venice'. They went for a drink afterwards and stumbled on a lovely pub near Baker Street that seemed full of lesbians, The Gay Hussar. Zac made a mental note to take Glenda to see those films when she came out of quarantine. He felt that Dick had helped bring a bit of class into his life. He was almost an angel.

Glenda had stayed at Zac's place a couple of days and while she was up west, shopping and seeing the sights, he found himself rolling on Dick's floor with his elfin and red-haired sister, just over from Belfast. As he was biting and sucking her sweet nipples, Brunagh said:

"You know, there's something special about you and Glenda, Zac. I hope it works out for you both."

It must have been slow in coming to fruition because Zac had taken the top bunk the past two days of Glenda's visit.

Straightening themselves up, Brunagh and he got ready for Dick to come back from shopping.

Zac felt nervous and still almost a virgin, whereas Glenda was the raving and rank opposite. He gulped and went downstairs for a shower in their communal bathroom.

Both couples went to see 'Death in Venice' that night. For Zac, the magic of the film was still there and Glenda revelled in it, reminding him that they had both been to the films, in their chaste way many times over the years. Glenda compared it in its excellence to Pasolini's 'St. Matthew's Passion', which Zac was yet to see, though both Dick and he loved Italian movies and they often talked about Antonioni's 'Blow-Up' which revealed the hollow and sinister reality under swinging London, even portraying the Hammersmith Spike, that he knew so well.

That night, Glenda and he found themselves in each other's arms and despite his fears, they were moving together very well, in the tenderest way ever, unlike their clumsy gropings of before. Zac felt confident of their reaching mutual satisfaction, when… damn, a key struggled in the lock. Remembering the unwritten code, Zac left certain bliss to obey the old soldiers' rule never to leave a comrade out in the cold. It was Dave, ex-RAF and fellow drinking chum from 'The Bristol' and he needed a roof for the night. That was the code and Zac obeyed it. He did not think Glenda was amused.

"So, what are you going to do, Zac?" she asked again, staring at him with those enigmatic eyes.

I don't know! he wanted to scream. Zac thought he had fallen beneath her level, years before, but something must have been in the air. Had the Goddess granted him a second chance? He apologised for the previous night and surprisingly and graciously, she accepted. Maybe she felt relieved and was just horny after so long in quarantine? Maybe her stay in hospital had been for something else, such as a 'Ladies' Problem'. She was reluctant to talk about it, or Zac was just too prudish or innocent to ask.

Zac knew she was offering some kind of a promise but he suddenly realised how little he had come to care about his future in worldly terms. However, in another 'world' he seemed to be growing and bristling with energy. The gulf between his making a career and the position he now found himself in seemed insurmountable.

He said as much and suggested a woman might expect something a bit more substantial than that? The thought suspended in the air between them for a moment then she went on hurriedly to tell him she was headed home, up north for a bit, before probably taking an art teachers' course in Brighton, as Stan and he had. He must have impressed her with his tales about the place. And so, once again they went their separate ways but not for long. The 'sedge had withered on the lake.'

Zac went slightly mad over the next few weeks. La Belle Dame Sans Mercy had him in her thrall! He even stalked a most beautiful Guards officer near Chelsea Barracks and only felt better about this venture into homosexuality when later he read that Tolstoy had done exactly the same in the Petersburg of his youth!

He heard a voice, on one of his frantic walkabouts near the river, like Stan but with a faint American accent.

"Hey, Stetson, you who were with me and the ships at Mylae. That skull you planted in your garden, has it not sprouted yet?"

The hair on the back of Zac's head seemed to stand up and shivering, he almost ran to London Bridge, seemingly another fugitive of the great city, undone, thrawn, insane.

Zac remembered a skirl of pipe music, an altercation with a couple of snotty ex-Etonians in The 'Queen's Elm, a South Kensington pub. He had recently discovered the elegant delights of south Kensington and Chelsea but now he rushed for the District Line and the short hop to Shepherd's Bush which had the hottest Tottie in town according to Dick. Then he sprinted back to Addison Road for a few hours' sleep.

"I'm off to Brighton, Dick!" he shouted up the stairs. "I'll write!"

Zac grabbed his rucksack and headed for Victoria Railway Station to catch the early morning train to Brighton.

He walked out of the station to a breezy Brighton and he was near enough to the English Channel at the foot of the hill, to see choppy white tops on a gun-metal sea, the gulls clamouring around him above, as he headed down to the seafront. Zac had no idea, it being a working day, where or whom, he was going to see, so he decided on a trip down memory lane and turned left at the Palace Pier.

He felt it against his religion to take a bus and started to walk. He had a couple of weeks' wages and some holiday pay from old Jo Lyon's Bakery back in the Smoke, which helped to give him a spring in his step. He walked briskly up the esplanade, halyards singing on the metallic flag posts, bunting and pennants fluttering, like his now exulting spirits and past the Dolphinarium, promising himself a long overdue visit there and then on to Marine Parade. With that morning's 'Guardian' in hand, he progressed to

Kemptown, enjoying the brisk and breezy day and the prospect of a couple of drinks and a wait to see who might turn up.

Nobody Zac knew well was in the Bristol pub but he enjoyed a pint of Worthington bitter, briefly nodding to a dozing Mrs Reynolds at her table in the far corner, where, like a King returned from exile, he relished a first sup of his beer and before snapping his newspaper open, cast an appraising and even proprietorial look over the sea towards France. He saw just a couple of coasters out towards Dieppe, butting through the waves and making a bit of smoke.

He ordered an 'Oggie, the Bristol's signature Cornish Pasty and another pint, the previous one having gone down without touching the sides of his throat. He picked up a copy of the Brighton Argus from one of the tables, a right-wing Tory rag but useful for jobs. The good thing about these south coastal towns was they provided many part-time, casual and temporary hotel and nursing home jobs where drifters like himself could find anonymity, some cash and food and even at times, a roof over their heads, no questions asked.

Zac took a ball-point pen and circled a couple of kitchen-portering jobs, in Hove to the west of Brighton. He even gave a cursory look at bedsitter accommodation around there. Hove was sedate and he wanted to keep a low profile for a bit. Zac didn't know what Glenda's intentions were, or whether she wished to pursue their relationship. He only knew that he felt a deep bond of service to her and wanted to make himself available, even at a distance. In the meantime, he needed something a bit more fleshly and wondered if Helga was still about. They'd enjoyed a cosy and physically intimate if casual relationship and a day or even an hour in her company seemed like a good idea.

Zac headed out of the Bristol after enjoying another pint and went to the bar of the Hervey, a haunt of the university radical left and the more intelligent drug addict. If she wasn't working, Helga was likely to be there, her alcoholism being a bit more advanced than his, though still at the social level.

No Helga but he did find Charles, the most incongruous of landlords of a bohemian bar, still displaying his WW2 officer's cap in a glass case behind the saloon bar.

"Ha, Comrade Zac!" said Charles with customary irony. "The usual?"

He poured Zac a pint of draught Bass plus a drink for himself.

"Just a snifter for me, old boy!" he said.

Zac laughed to himself. Raving alkie that he was, the old sot, he had a sense of humour and referred to Zac and his layabout mates in the bar as the 'Revolutionaries'. Vera, his plump and seductively charming Viennese wife, came around the corner of the Saloon bar, pursing her voluptuous lips and blew a kiss.

"Ach, Zac, mein liebling!" she said. "You just missed Helga!"

Windowless, in daytime and without comrades, the Hervey wasn't a place to linger. So, he quickly perused the Argus for more vacancies and likely-looking flats and bedsits. After ringing a few, he finished his pint, saluted Charles and cried "Wieder-Sehen!" to Vera, before heading down a very pleasant James street and back into town. A sojourn in the Pavilion Gardens seemed a pleasant idea, a turn around the elegant 'Lanes' shopping area and then along the Western parade and past the Palace Pier to the West Pier and onwards to Hove. He planned a brief reconnaissance of likely accommodation, a promising pub and a few telephone calls for jobs. Life wasn't so bad after all, he thought, sensing the beginning of a new adventure. However, Zac felt a little uneasy, something of Mahler's subtle changes in mood that he had relished in that superb Visconti film, he had seen with Dick and Glenda not so long ago. An end of season feel was settling on the south coast resort, always a bit melancholy, though highly evocative to Zac who felt it was his season.

He landed a job as a kitchen porter job in The Sackville Hotel, in Hove. It was really only a glorified dish-washing job, with part-time and split shifts so he would have enough time for stooging around and feeding himself without having to dip too much into the 'wedge' of capital he had earned at old Jo Lyons.

He soon found a tiny, ground floor bedsit in Cromwell Road near the Sussex County Cricket ground, in a quiet and respectable suburb set back from the elegant square on the frontage of stuffily respectable Hove. He recalled Robin saying something, in one of their long conversations about their hero, Oscar Wilde, that Lord Alfred Douglas had ended his days, the year Zac was born, in a seedy basement in Hove, scribbling anti-Semitic articles for the 'Fash', last of the 'Black Douglas' family and excoriated as such in Wilde's 'De Profundis' letter from Reading Gaol so long before. Curiously, Zac still felt as if he was under orders from Glenda. La Belle Dame Sans Merci most definitely had him in thrall!

There were always great characters to be met at these places. Itinerants from all over the UK, a fraternity really as you were likely to bump into them at Butlins in nearby Bognor, or as far north as 'Skeggy' in Lincolnshire, Skegness to the uninitiated, a place as a youngster Zac heard was great for the 'birds' and for losing your virginity. He guessed they were the late 20th-century version of the sturdy beggars and strolling players of Tudor times! The two blokes who commanded their dishwasher in shifts were Bill, a Leeds man of impeccable working-class origins, a bit younger than Zac's Dad and almost a Beckett Character. Zac delighted in seeing him ushering his ex butcher's delivery bike into the kitchen and parking it against one of the Victorian fixtures while he deliberately removed his bicycle clips.

"Never thought it'd come to this, Zac, lad, rear-gunner on a dishwashing machine!" he said.

He had huge and ancient, highly-polished boots too! A 'Stan Laurel' type character and with similar humility and droll humour.

One of the few locals Zac got to know was Seymour, deferential and rather servile he was an amusing comrade.

He had a strong country;

"Mornin', Zac, me 'ansome! What laaarrkks last noit!'" he said in his strong, Sussex accent, like an innocent and whimsical Dickens character, a smaller Joe Gargary or Kit Nubbles. There still seemed to be more Dickensian characters among the working-class folk in the south; a bit sneaky and tame though, as Dr Johnson so ruefully observed but gentle and humorous, kindly sometimes, as well.

Two assistant chefs, itinerants as well, were adorable. There was Polish Chester; 'Don't ask me how I got that name!' He looked tubercular and his sunken chest and hunched shoulders seemed to endear him to the waitresses.

"He be a natural gennelman, ee be!" said Vera from nearby Shoreham.

In between his tubercular coughs, Chester was given to very wise sayings, which Zac made him write down on slips of paper; these he zealously saved but sadly lost later.

Mikhail, his Russian mate in the kitchen, was a picture of Slavic innocence and toughness, with a permanent beatific smile. A Tolstoyan peasant, you could imagine him cheerfully stalking with his little dog through a burning Moscow of 1812.

"Zac, plizz," he said. "You got any pills? Tonight, you drink many wodka with Mikhail? Yes? Da! You like Vorskhi?"

"What?" Zac replied, then twigged. "Ah, Mikhail, you mean Whiskey?"

"Da, da, da!" he said, thumbs up, beaming face and resplendent in his sous-chef whites.

It was a joy to have such lovely men for company even if the job was so dull and menial. Every day passed like an innocent dream. It had to end; Glenda was on her way. She had applied for the same teaching course that Stan and he had studied a couple of years ago.

Zac found a flat a bit more central, though still in Hove. He knew that with most jobs to the east of Brighton, Kemptown would be now an address beyond his finances but he could still have the occasional foray to his beloved Bristol Hotel. Zac had a ground floor room, divided by a central corridor from a sunny kitchen and with a shared toilet and bathroom. It was nearly next door to a pub, the Norfolk and just below Norfolk Square, still inside Hove and directly opposite the West Pier, a more antiquated, and to him, a more tasteful one than the rather flashy Palace Pier to the east. Being a bookish boy, Zac remembered George's and Robin's recommendation of Patrick Hamilton, author of 'West Pier' and 'Hangover Square' and little known, if at all, by Zac's generation. "Lovely soul," had been Robin's verdict on him. A sad and lonely man but as Zac was to discover, a hero of the anti-fascist, pre-war British Left and even before Greene, he had expressed that lingering melancholy, even evil, in this part of Brighton.

A good-natured bunch of prostitutes, mainly Yorkshire girls haunted the street beyond the elegant railings outside his bedroom window. It was amusing on hot summer nights to listen to their banter with each other and their calls to likely customers outside his open windows. Once, he leaned out to give a light to one of the girl's cigs, so close to the street was he. The bijou bowed windows proved very useful for this. They were intimate, as well as elegant, like a film set for a Jane Austen novel.

There was something of Italy or Spain about Brighton. One day he was joking with one of the lasses from Sheffield, or one of those South Yorkshire Pit Towns, he thought by her accent. He asked her why they never asked him for business.

"Cause you're young and handsome, ducks!" she said. "We're a bit lairy of reasonable-looking young blokes wanting business!"

Zac said goodbye to his lovely workmates in the kitchen, needing more money to pay for his new flat and he got a job at Clark's Bakery in Hove. It was only a 25-minute walk from home and he worked on shifts, the night ones finishing in the early hours, so a good job for somebody who still thought of himself as a young man about town, with prospects, if not great expectations!

He soon reconnected with former mates: his favourite Jewish New York hippy friends; an ex-tutor and New Zealander - Zac had yet to meet a bad Kiwi! - Martin Lewis who had more formally introduced Stan and him about 18 months ago.

"I kept on hearing from Martin about this amazing bloke and that I would love him, and I fucking hated you even before we met!" said Stan, later.

"Ah but Stan, we met at Glenda's Party a few years before in Kingston, remember?" said Zac.

Stan grimaced. He did not share Zac's obsession with her.

Zac looked Martin up again in Kemptown, or to be more precise, closer to Rottingdean. It spoke much for those more egalitarian times that it would be taken for granted, amongst Art College people anyway, that friendships were acceptable between students and members of staff and that these could extend beyond college years. Martin, felt the same about Zac, that Ian Robinson at Kingston had felt and admired about Stan. Zac felt closer to being accepted in intellectual company, than any time since. He mixed with educators from all over the world and in particular, the Southern Hemisphere. Maybe that said more for overseas academics like Martin.

On reaching his Rottingdean apartment, Zac was introduced to an Argentinian academic and art historian, stunningly attractive in her Latin

American way. Martin poured them a generous Scotch each and they launched into a lively discussion on everything from Germaine Greer's latest book to Ivan Illyich's eccentric notions about education.

"Wrong!" proclaimed Zac. "Borges and Lacan, incomprehensible!"

Martin in his inimitably charming manner took Zac's elbow.

"Francesca," he interjected. "Zac here is a future and great British novelist! Enjoy his company while you can."

Zac received a dazzling smile and a shaking of exotic curls and bangles.

When he could, he mentioned Glenda and Martin made Zac promise to make a date for drinks in the next ten days before term started and to bring her along for introductions.

As Zac wasn't due to start at the bakery for a week, he thought of contacting Glenda with the invitation to Martin's Party and also to visit Charleston, the cottage the Bloomsbury Group used as a retreat in the 1920s. They half-fascinated and half-repelled him but a part of Zac now really loved Sussex, for all his northern and socialist 'chippiness'.

Zac tried to remember where she lived. He thought she had rented a room on the esplanade, between the Grand Hotel and the Palace Pier. You could do that in those days, before the property boom of the 1980s. Brighton still had its raffish and seedy side, which he loved. Anyway, Glenda turned up and in her, Catherine Deneuve style stole the show. It left Zac feeling rather cross with her. He realised she had a knack, no doubt helped by her good, if clinical and hygienic looks, of holding the attention of a group. He noticed a kind of chill and negativity about this, had always done so in fact, which explained his unease about their strange relationship.

Zac knew in his bones Glenda was playing the 'Lawrence Woman' gambit, which always went down well with southern middle-class blokes, indeed Martin seemed to be encouraging it. She always could read her audience.

"And what brought you to Brighton, Glenda?" he asked.

"Oh well, I fell in love with this Pakistani bloke," she announced, stressing her Yorkshire accent more than usual. "And went back to his country to marry him. Came back here, as it didn't work out. Wanted to move on, so ended up here."

Only then and absent-mindedly did she say that she was there to start on an Art Teacher's Course and knew me. She seemed to dominate the conversation by killing it. Zac did notice a silence and thought to himself, that Glenda was one of those people who added a sense of absence to a company. He truly disliked that aspect of her and he thought Francesca and another couple of women sensed that as well. Martin sweetly passed over the embarrassed silence and changed the subject.

"So, Zac, hear anything of your mate, Stan?"

He had recently read an autobiography by Francoise Gillot, one of Picasso's later wives. Glenda reminded him of that kind of extremely irritating Frenchwoman. La Gillot's Parthian shot at Picasso was that she wanted to find new challenges; young men who were shooting fresh arrows into the future. Zac thought that Picasso's parting remarks were somewhat more graphic, and most probably in a demotic Catalan.

Anyway, Zac was angry with Glenda and didn't see her again for a bit. He also passed over the chance of the visit to Charleston, the Bloomsbury Group's Sussex retreat. Another day, he thought, maybe with a nice girlfriend.

Funnily enough, Zac received a letter from his mother the next morning, containing an old photo of her and him on the cliffs just beyond Rottingdean, outside St Dunstan's Red Cross Rest Home for war veterans. She also included the address of Zac's vicar uncle in Ditchling. The visit from his mother and his Dad's snooty but kind sister had been on the way to cousin Christine's wedding. Christine was Uncle Tony and Aunt Betty's daughter, always a favourite with Zac. He had assumed that he had not been invited to the wedding because he was a pariah but in fact, Zac was soon to realise that this was not the case. He had for some time suspected that the posher branch of the family had been distanced from him because he was too much the black sheep or bohemian, perhaps even because he was a Red?

He didn't think the snobbery originated from Sussex, that 'Cavalier' county and he was sophisticated enough of a Marxist to know that the worse snobs were the 'Warrant Officers' of the British class system, in his father's case almost literally. It was his class that constituted the 'gatekeepers' of the class war, its police force, ideologically in the case of Dad's fascist sister and in his case literally. A Policeman's or Vicar's son is taught very early about the class system. He knew that his brother had visited often and Zac suspected that his breach with his father had been something deeper and more elemental than the political. It had been ideological, 'written in his body'. As near to 'original sin' as the great Cardinal Newman hinted at so graphically only a hundred years before, or less?

Zac decided on a trip to Ditchling, a place famous in the 'Arts and Crafts' movement of the turn of the century. He knew it to be a very pleasant and very bourgeois place nestling under the exquisitely pretty South Downs and not far inland, near the county town of Lewes.

He took the Greenline single-decker coach which was almost a vintage vehicle at that time. The journey, brief though it was, felt straight out of the innocent, staid and genteel Fifties: up and down, prettily rolling and picturesque little chalk hills and through twee little villages, filled with thatched-roofed cottages, the ubiquitous Norman Church and quaint village green, duck pond and ancient inn.

He had phoned for directions in advance.

"Zac, dear boy," replied Uncle Tony, the only posh member of the family. "Just ask ANYWHERE for the vicarage. It's right next to the church anyway and across the green, though some of the villagers call it the Rectory. Will be LOVELY to see you! AND, Zac, pack a sponge bag and toothbrush. You MUST stay the weekend!" Always the perfect gentleman.

Dinner came a bit late though as Uncle Tony had a christening to see to. It was quite a family affair and so English and traditional upper-middle class, in the nicest possible way. Hardly surprising that Jane Austen and so many of her ilk came of such a milieu.

Zac had already made his introductions. Christine was now an actress and her husband, Henry, also an actor and obviously from a similar social background and class to Christine. He knew Christine well and along with cousin Brenda, was his contemporary. On the few occasions they had met at family gatherings at Granddad Greenwood's, they had always got on.

Christine was highly strung but always smiling and loved to organise them into concert parties and the like. She was an enthusiastic joiner-in of the sort of games post-war generation kids enjoyed. Zac loved to kiss her and Brenda, his other cousin and they lightened his heavily testosterone-driven boyhood enormously. Brenda, a glorious redhead, Zac always had a massive crush on.

Henry, though without the northern working-class or Celtic knack of making one feel at ease, was a natural and Zac suspected, a Christian gentleman; something straight out of Jane Austen, a Mr Bingley or a Colonel Brandon, perhaps?

Looking through the serving hatch from the kitchen, where he had been helping the Housekeeper Mrs Baines before Dinner had been served, Henry tipped Zac a kindly and manly, if rehearsed, wink. He knew something was wrong and with his innate civility and his faith, he looked set to rectify it.

Michael was the next eldest to Christine and born with spina bifida. He spent most of his life when not at this nurturing and prosperous Christian home, at Cheyley Heritage, a Home for badly disabled children. Though it had been hushed up, Zac knew he had tried to take his own life a couple of times. It was Michael, together with a talk on 'Thought for the Day', a spiritually-inclined radio programme on the BBC, who persuaded Uncle Tony to join the church.

He had plenty of money, was from a wealthy if landless Sussex family and on leaving the army in 1944 had set up his own and very successful business as an architect. His Conversion, then, could not be described as opportunistic. He had always shown an interest in Zac and his ambitions to be an artist.

"Zac, sit here if you please," said Uncle Tony, indicating an empty place at the top of the huge dining table, which Zac imagined must be Georgian at least. "So happy to have you in our home. Forgive the working togs!" he smiled, gesturing to his dog collar and leather belt bound cassock. "No time to change, old man!"

He then rattled off a prayer at a fairish lick.

"For food and fellowship, thank God!" he ended. "Righto, you lot dive in!"

Zac suddenly realised that his own belt had slipped off. Still feeling a bit 'bolshie', but simultaneously class conscious, he blushed heavily, downed his fork and wrestled surreptitiously, he hoped, with his left hand and despairingly, struggling, apologising the while, with his right. The buckle had come completely loose. He hadn't chosen to wear Hassan's gift of the shark-skin suit as he thought it would be inappropriate for the occasion. He had managed to buy a passable dark clerical grey suit second hand, an easy thing to achieve in Brighton at that time.

"Zac, are you all right?" asked Auntie Betty, a look of concern shining in her face. "You seem to have lost a lot of weight? Is it…"

Zac felt Uncle Tony's left leg move in the direction of Aunt Betty, sitting opposite. He had never been one to put much weight on anyway, even with his intake of beer. Zac had assumed so much work in a hot bakehouse had kept his weight down and apart from a small pill habit, drugs, even grass, it was no big issue with him.

"Zac, I want to tell you one of the reasons you weren't invited to Christine's and Henry's wedding," said Uncle Tony suddenly.

Zac looked down the table and saw Christine lowering her head and touching her face with her napkin. Next to her, Henry also looked distinctly uncomfortable.

"We were told," continued Uncle Tony, wincing visibly. "That you were getting into some bad company and, er the heavy drug scene. We know of course about your politics, somewhere left of Lenin, we believe?" he added with a conspiratorial grin. "But really, though we can perfectly understand your position, the situation with your father and now, by extension, your brother, is uncomfortable for us socially and for me particularly, as a good churchman."

Zac screwed his napkin viciously, wishing he had not bothered coming to this place, Ms Austen's England and the HQ of the class enemy. Then he felt a squeeze on his shoulder as Henry walked past him and he saw Christine wipe a tear from her cheek.

"Uncle Zac," blurted dear Michael. "I love you anyway!"

Aunt Betty was now in tears. Uncle Tony showed his true Christian spirit, shoved his Sheraton chair back, threw down his napkin and leapt to his feet.

"Zac," he cried. "I apologise from the bottom of my heart. You will always be welcome in our home!"

"Bless you, Uncle Zac. I'll bet you've had lots of adventures!" said Lizzie, Christine's younger sister, clapping her hands excitedly.

When Zac was on his way to the bathroom, Christine impulsively hugged him and Henry now back at her side, gave him a brotherly handshake and a kindly wink, squeezing his hand warmly.

Zac took the Sussex Greenline coach from Ditchling, through an Eric Ravilious landscape; dry brush strokes of malachite green down-land and lightest ochre and iridescent chalk scars, cliffs, beech stands and glimpses of a pewter sea and Samuel Palmer-style hamlets and corn stooks aflame with an early summer evening sun. Time to head back up north, thought Zac to himself, yearning for the high moors and a more rugged people.

He found himself profoundly refreshed by his Ditchling visit, feeling that something deep down in him had been reconciled. He sensed the beginning of a new chapter in his life.

Back in Hove, he threw a few things into his rucksack and just two books for his journey; something deep by George Steiner and his favourite anthology of Gerard Manly Hopkin's verses and letters. Suddenly, he glimpsed Robin's gift by his bedside: Newman's 'Apologia' as yet, unread and took that also.

He left a note for Glenda on his door, collected two weeks wages and some holiday pay from Clark's Bakery down by the Sussex County Cricket Ground and without looking back, headed up the hill to the railway station, for London and eventually back home to Yorkshire and the North Country. His heart ached until he glimpsed the slag heaps and pitheads of South Yorkshire, near Doncaster and then his heart sang. He was back in the real England.

Part Four:

BACK HOME

1973

Chapter 38

I shall now take over the story of Zac and use my baptismal name, David and write in the first person. Goodbye Zac and my first youth. Welcome to the next stage of my life, as the Reluctant Revolutionary.

With my tail between my legs then, I arrived back in Bradford, all I had accumulated contained in a WW2 respirator rucksack and two carrier bags. With my fashionable, ex-WW2 RAF greatcoat I must have looked like any one of hundreds of thousands of displaced youngish men wandering across Europe, in both the mid-late 1940s and fashionably, the early-mid 1970s.

Mum rushed from the kitchen to hug me, drying her eyes on her apron.

"I'll put the kettle on and how many eggs do you want, son?" she said.

Dad disdained my proffered hand, his cynical and hard-bitten copper's face breaking into a well-oiled sneer.

"And how long will you be gracing us with your presence, Number One son?" he said.

I turned, still stung after all these years and even after such an expected greeting, walked through the hallway, and hung up my coat. I came back to the kitchen and put my arms around Mum's slightly thickening waist. I snuggled her ears and smelt the familiar smell of flour and baking.

"Lovely to see you, Mum. I missed you so much."

She squeezed my arms in reply as I nodded towards the living room.

"And how's the Sergeant?" I asked.

"He's no sae bad son just don't work him up!" she said, pushing me away gently. "Get back to him, Davy. You know how jealous he is, just try to humour him?"

She brushed a lock of her still brunette hair from her forehead and I sensed the fear, the submissiveness, the servility almost and I realised nothing had changed. I entered the 'presence', the sitting room, his lair and the old brute signalled to the settee's edge at a precise right angle to him. I clenched my fist and gazed in revulsion at his bull neck, the collarless Police shirt, tieless, with a strangely threatening stud catching the evening light, his only eccentric streak and his newly cut hair, short back and sides, military-fashion.

"So, what's the plan? Your mother's missed you. Some of your letters…" he broke off and waved his right hand almost effetely, dismissively, like some arrogant and sadistic British aristo in a third-rate Hollywood movie. I told him, being careful not to mumble, or sound too positive.

"I thought you might have a nice little job teaching in a Grammar school somewhere in Surrey or Sussex. You know, nice little house like your brother?" he said.

Like everybody else? I felt like retorting but remembering Mum's warning, I bit my lip and cursed the old snob in my heart. The muscles in my still young stomach clenched.

I cast my eyes around, everything looked spotless as usual, though I suspected they'd been able to afford a cleaner now. There was a music centre and what looked like a colour telly in the far corner opposite Dad's 'pew' but nothing to depart from the stifling petit-bourgeois conformity of the room. I could predict unerringly that in the bookcase, in the front room next door, along with a set of Edwardian and lavishly illustrated volumes of the 'History of England' on the lower shelves, there would be on the top one, above the bound 'Readers' Digest' volumes, a copy of 'John Halifax, Gentleman', something by Winston Churchill (Sir' to you!) and 'Moriarty's Police Law', next to some bound copies of 'Wisden' the cricket fan's Bible.

An enlarged photo of 463/7 Squadron, Bomber Command, a faceless throng of 'Bods' in uniform all stacked before and on the wings of a gigantic Lancaster, head-on, would be on display above the bookcase, precisely perpendicular and midway between both ends of the top shelf which would have a framed photo of me to the right and to the left, Stuart, my beautiful and successful, blond brother, known as Number Two Son.

I warmed up for a bit of heavy banter, Father having the look now of somebody prepared to be entertained. I could lay on the charm and I rattled on about some of my experiences in London and on the south coast, giving him an opening to reminisce about his Blitz experiences, which he did and entertainingly so. He was a complicated man and could be charming and extremely amusing himself, almost the dashing young man he used to be, in a certain light.

Eventually, Mum entered with a tray of food, kneeing the door shut behind her. I knew that it would be good: two mugs of tea for Dad and me and three lovingly fried eggs and toasted and buttered tea cakes for me. She always seemed to baste fat over the yolks so artistically, something she would say proudly she had picked up in Service.

"Eat this, son," she said. "And it'll fill a hole till supper. I've got a good joint of Gammon ferrr yis!"

After a bath and then the gammon supper, Mum remarked on how thin I looked. Dad added wryly, that's what drugs and loose women did for one. While I was upstairs waiting for the bathtub to fill, I peered wistfully into the big back bedroom that Stuart and I used to share. I felt a bit of a pang because we had been constant playmates us and our dog, Bruce, a delightful and loyal Border Collie/Labrador cross, now long passed over the Golden Bridge. Somehow, I felt that I had let Stuart down as an elder brother. I didn't notice for a few minutes that Mum had made up a bed for me there. Though Stuart's old bed was tightly and clinically covered by a candlewick bedspread and recently folded and ironed laundry, I felt a pang. The presence of an absence, Stuart's Rugby trophies mocked me from a corner display case. A tiny plaque inscribed with the legend: "Haste ye back to Bonnie Scotland" made me feel sad.

I felt even sadder knowing Dad had given her a hard life but I was mature enough now to realise they had been young once, like me, younger in fact and very much in love, hence the arrival of Stuart and me. I had no offspring. Stuart, on the other hand, had become a model family man, with a little boy first, followed just recently by a baby girl.

I was surprised that father hadn't started to rub it in yet what a disappointment I had been to him and what a failure. His mood had inexplicably changed to being almost avuncular. I heard him singing when it was his turn to use the bathroom: 'Davy's come home again' and it occurred to me that Mum often wrote in her letters that he had even been known to ask: 'I wonder where my wandering boy is tonight?'

His good mood persisted and he rang his old Police pal, Bill, to suggest we go out for a drink. I liked Bill, although authoritarian and right-wing like a lot of his profession and more of a racist even than Dad, he had always shown an interest in me and tried to stand up for me against Dad when he was in one of his terrible rages.

Bill came willingly. He was a high-ranking detective now and despite being cops, neither of them were big drinkers, so it was decided we would go to a quieter part of town, away from the locals and up on the edge of Bronte-land to the sort of pub where bosses liked to take their secretaries, discreet, rural and beyond the city limits; 'Bad Lassing pubs' as they were known in these parts! I am sure they also had 'snouts' they liked to meet there, a policeman never relaxing entirely from his vocation and on the few times I'd been allowed this honour on visits home from college, there was always some old guy who would address both as 'Sergeant' and offered us a drink. Bill and Dad referred to them later by their court names, such as 'William George Illingworth', even at their own homes, when we shared hospitality. It always delighted me as a boy to listen to their men's talk, while the women, like gatekeepers' wives, bovine and tame, chatted and clattered dishes mindlessly in the kitchen.

So, my first night home passed surprisingly peacefully. Suspending my critical mind, I could almost, like my more conservative brother, relish the secure feeling of being in the company of solid and honourable men, WW2 veterans and pillars of society. Bill had an even more distinguished war than Dad; a wounded veteran at war's end, he had seen some heavy fighting in Belgium after 'D' Day and met the Russians outside Vienna in '45.

I slept in starched and ultra-clean sheets that night for the first time since leaving home five years and what seemed like a lifetime ago. Before my head touched the pillow and for some time after, I planned how to restart my life.

Up early and before father, I enjoyed a quick Scots breakfast-porridge without sugar and a bacon sarnie and headed off on the trolley bus down the hill to Bradford. From the upper deck, I relished the painterly qualities of the grey and blackened stone terrace houses and where the rain still lingered from an overnight squall, the indigo and gun-metal highlights of a watery mid-morning sun. Already I felt that lugubrious sensation in the air of heavier soil and the damper climate of the North, so unlike the lightness and dryness of the Sussex chalk country. I can smell even now the stale nicotine and bronchitic breath of the other passengers, the stoic grunts that passed for Yorkshiremen's conversation; 'Aye, lad! Appen! A' wa' forced to laugh!'

The gender apartheid persisted with mainly blokes upstairs and the women downstairs. I watched the occasional tubercular and insubstantial looking Mirpuri textile worker, puffing on his first cig of the morning, hands cupped devoutly around its tip. Condensation streamed down the bus windows as we progressed past vast Victorian woollen mills, many of them half empty but with a touch of former Imperial grandeur. My heart exulted a bit as we came to the terminus and I saw the town hall as J.B. Priestley had seen it so long before me, in all its Italian Quattrocento majesty. I wondered if the town hall clock still chimed 'Tom Bowling' at Midday, and Midnight, as Priestley had described it in his good-hearted and uplifting 'The Good Companions'.

I had decided to visit the Job Centre, still in a gloomy, pre-war, fascist decor style edifice on Nelson Street just past the city abattoir. It being a weekday the vile smells of 'rendering' were beginning to cast a nauseous pall over the area. I planned to get a list of jobs, unemployment at that time being pretty low but not expecting some of the eccentric service sector ones that I would be offered in London or Brighton.

I found the staff brusque in the West Yorkshire manner but efficient. After that, I headed back and up to Bradford's 'Rive Gauche' the nearest thing there to the Left Bank of Paris or London's Notting Hill, yet a long, long way from either! I headed for the Manville Arms, after buying a local daily paper for further cover and sad old sod that I must have looked, I loped up Great Horton Road to the environs of the University, big and still brash looking and just opposite the elegant Victorian Art College. Below that stood the pub where I had bonded with Glenda and my other young contemporaries, so full of youth and hope, such a long time ago.

Once in the Manville Arms, I nursed a pint while perusing the jobs' section of the paper and reviewing the vacancies' list the Job Centre had provided me with. Some obvious art students were lunching raucously and I felt an affinity, yet curious estrangement from them. It was almost painful trying to recapture youth, futile even and I started to realise how much of a southerner I had become. The girls seemed loud and abrasive, the men slightly thuggish and well… boring looking.

Finishing my pint, I decided to have another one in the centre of town at Spinks American Bar, which reminded me more of the alienation of London. The session men, scene-shifters and lighting men, I had thought, with their metropolitan but proletarian worldly cool: 'Hya, Chief!' delighted me, urban gipsies and strolling players all! In the Manville, I had felt like an exile in reverse.

I telephoned one of the Job Centre numbers from a wall-mounted and ancient device near the Gents and almost relieved at getting an 'engaged' tone I headed out of the doors, leaving behind memories of 1963 and started down the hill past the Alhambra Theatre to the American Bar on Morley Street below the Markets. I hoped there might be a couple of scene shifters or even actors down there. I adored their company and I couldn't help thinking of the film 'Billy Liar' that I had seen with Glenda so long ago. Smiling to myself I thought: 'But I would have got on that train with Julie Christie. I could have been a contender!' Part of my yearning for London was to find her, or someone like her. I remember going to see the film with Glenda at art college, new then in its grittiness and realism and my telling her that. I had received a disobliging and characteristic reply, I remembered, a more feminine version of 'Aye,'appen' and her baleful stare. She had her Cromwellian side, dour and severe.

I also looked forward to meeting some session men, Londoners usually and either black or Jewish guys, cool and great fun to be with. I remembered a couple of my old mates in Bradford were such. Malc, a butcher in the market, had been a professional drummer for Mecca Dance Halls and Pete Lancaster, my old school best friend, last I heard was a session man for the long-running, hippy musical, 'Hair', down in London.

I headed up the hill to the Rawson Indoor Market, the Butchers' part to renew my friendship with Malc, now with his own stall there. He was the drummer in our Jazz band/Skiffle Group. Pete Lancaster, 'Lanky', an old school pal, had been our charismatic trumpeter and I was the indifferent banjo player.

When I stepped up to the bar and ordered a pint, Webster's and a whiskey chaser, session man style, I was shocked to see a polished brass plaque attached to the bar warning unaccompanied women not to approach! I was astonished! I was definitely 'back home' now! After a couple of pints and weary of the pompous daytime clientele, arrogant sounding wool men and bland accountants, I drained a third pint and headed up Market Street, past a half-demolished Kirkgate Market and into Rawson Meat Market. Assailed by the cheerful calls and banter from the many stalls, I was pleased to see Malc, fit-looking and bearded, not the chubby newly-wed session man who came to see me when I was away at college in Sunderland years ago. He had contracted as a drummer at the Sunderland Mecca.

He seemed delighted to see me and introduced me to a friendly and gentlemanly fellow butcher in the opposite stall, Pete Taplin, from a well-established market family, like the Morrisons. Pete invited me to dinner at his home in Baildon. Very Posh, I thought. Malc said he and his wife would come along too. I was to enjoy their butchers' banter and devoted and manly friendship. At last, I felt that I had arrived back home.

I had provisionally decided on two jobs: one as a casual in Newbould's Bakery the south side of Bradford but accessible by bus. Knowing Dad's contrary moods, I didn't know how long my welcome would last and at least a night job would give me daylight to find accommodation. The other one I settled on was a small craft and engineering workshop right in the heart of Manningham, an area I knew well as my childhood haunt and heart of bedsitter land.

I called at the Royal Standard on Manningham Lane, a Tetley's House and similar to the North London Gin Palaces I used to go to for jazz music and loved for George Melley and his Bessie Smith renditions! Suddenly I felt like an exile in reverse. A nostalgic pang seized me and seeing a phone there, I rang the Manningham works, in the hope of getting an interview and fixing myself up with a job before getting the bus home. Any Excuse.

I must have had a couple of pints and thought I'd better clear my head a bit first, so decided to walk most of the way to Manningham and to Garfield Avenue, where the job was situated. I remembered it suddenly as being just opposite the rough end of Leamington Street, my childhood home and across Oak Lane, now the beating heart of the Pakistani area and the best curry houses in Europe. I remember it as being faintly respectable: buildings with leaded windows, which was a Bradford speciality; darkened grit stone and dingy lace curtains. In my youth it had been the haunt of old ladies, alien-looking Poles and Ukrainians, Catholics, I recalled. I used to throw stones at them and in intervals of truce, we played football and swapped cigarette cards and WW2 military souvenirs. Two bob for a Red

Army belt buckle, I remembered, was way beyond my pocket money at that time. My parents ordered me not to play with the boys wearing lederhosen, the only bit of political awareness from them to emerge, but Poles were acceptable. There were viciously pretty little Ukrainian girls called Svetlana or Mara and I had a punch-up with a tall and sullen youth in lederhosen, Volk-Deutsch, I think. I head-butted him, an arrogant and sneering boy disliked by the other kids.

Clearing my head just a bit I decided to walk all the way up to The Airedale Brush Company, intrigued and not knowing quite what to expect. It was above a garage and as I climbed up a clanging metal staircase, I almost fell through a rickety door into what looked like a Dickensian 'Blacking Factory'. It had an ambience not unlike my first art college days, down to the rabbit-skin glue pot simmering on an ancient gas ring in the corner and the individual benches equipped with vices and arrays of hand tools, pliers, mole grips and the like. A motley crew of simple and good-natured faces looked up at me, young men and a couple of oldsters, all a bit strange seeming but friendly enough. A transistor radio boomed out the latest acid rock and Bowie numbers.

A man emerged from a tiny glazed office in the corner and offered me a strong and meaty hand.

"Mr Earnshaw?" I asked.

"Mr Greenwood, I presume?" he replied and I shook the hand of my new boss.

"Step this way, lad," he said, eyes twinkling as he ushered me into the small office. "Sit thee down, lad," he continued, glancing at my proffered JobCentre card. "May I call you Dave?"

We sat facing each other across his cramped desk, which overflowed with paperwork.

"You might have noticed most of the lads here are a bit- well, shall we say, Dave, none of these lads is going to be a rocket scientist," he said.

He filled me in on the job saying he knew it was only temporary and that the post was mind-numbingly simple but they were overloaded with work. Most of the lads were educationally subnormal, some ex-soldiers with head wounds who couldn't hold down a normal job and one or two beautifully amiable blokes I noticed were Downs Syndrome boys.

The work involved wrenching old bristles out of broom-heads and other more industrial looking appliances and glueing new bristles in their place. I felt an immense sadness about the place but decided to take the job on, starting Monday. We discussed wages which were reasonable for the North and he introduced me to the gang. After being fondled affectionately by the Downs Syndrome boys, I headed back outside, almost shedding a tear, as I clattered down the old fire escape, a feature in hilly Manningham and out onto the street. I trudged up the steep hill of Oak Lane, so redolent of childhood memories and further up, between the great chasm formed by the grandiose Listers Mill, acknowledged as the greatest in the Empire in Grandad's day, with its massively tall chimney dominating the city skyline. I went on past the recently established Police Station, a kind of a Bastille, brutal and bunker-like. I kept climbing the hill of Oak Lane to Lilycroft road, my old infant school on the left, past the Royal Infirmary, down the hill to the famous Girls' Grammar school, where Barbara Castle had been an alumna, onwards to the suburban respectability of Bullroyd Estate and my father's house.

Back home I went into the kitchen to tell Mum about my progress. Though near retirement, Dad was still at work but expected home soon. Mum was pleased I had a job and I went upstairs to wash and change for dinner parade. I heard a car climbing up our short drive, Dad obviously and wondered what he was driving these days. For an advanced driver and road safety expert, ex-traffic cop and ex-bomber aircrew, lecturing the public regularly, for no money, just a cup of lukewarm tea and an Abernethy biscuit, he was surprisingly cautious in his choice of cars. Neither of my parents had ever been rich but like most people of our class and their generation who were in work, material conditions had improved dramatically since the '50s and '60s.

As we seemed to be as near mates as ever possible at this stage of his emotional cycle, I thought I'd nip out for a bit of manly banter about motors.

"Nice motor, John!" I called as he hauled himself out of the driving seat of a chunky Morris 1500 hatchback.

He responded with a glare. Oh, dear, I thought.

"Father would do, lad!" he retorted but suddenly showed his lighter side. "Or you might call me, Dad!"

With an exultantly ironic expression on his face and now drawn to his full height, he approached me menacingly, muttering under his breath.

"I have a treat for you, Number One Son! Instead of belabouring you with my knout, I have decided that mother, you and I are going to have a musical evening tonight!" He turned back to the clumsy looking Morris and gestured to the rear seat. "Be you be pleased to uplift those!"

I was able to pick out a couple of carrier bags of what looked like vinyl LP's and ancient '78's. Then we chaffed each other a bit about the motor.

"It's bad on juice and the gearbox is a stinker," he said. "But your mother likes it and it is comfortable for me, my back, you know."

The old sod never admitted any weakness, so I reckoned it must have been an important consideration because the 1500 probably was one of the worse British-built vehicles since the Wellington bombers he trained on in WW2. It had a long, well-upholstered and luxurious pig-skin front seat. Judging that he was in a strange but relatively light-hearted mood, for him, I followed him, burdened with the carrier bags, through our cramped and mean hallway into the living room.

"Be seated," commanded Father.

He pointed to the far corner by the right-hand side of the window, its ledge freighted with Benares ware, looted or 'liberated' from a brief trip by his squadron to Rangoon and Asia Command in the war against the Japanese. I slumped into the stated place, the standard lamp to my right, a battered pre-war leather pouffe to the front and opposite the music centre and my old wind-up gramophone. The Standard lamp was the first article of furniture Dad and Mum had bought after moving out of our grisly rented terraced house back in 1950's Manningham. I could still see the pride of possession on Father's face when the delivery van from Busby's, Bradford's famous department store, delivered it, an outward and visible sign of bourgeois respectability in pre-war days for Dad's generation.

Mum readjusted the gate-legged table. It originated from Heals of London but Grandad had bought it second hand from a bombed-out Lingard's store in Bradford, in 1940.

"Supper's nearly ready," said Mum, seeming to curtsy, unironically, to Father.

"Thank you, Mother," said Dad.

After a short interrogation as to my employment prospects from him and some sardonic remarks concerning my eligibility and employability, we repaired to the table. Mum fussed around with our condiment set and best silver, which was plated actually and a wedding present from his RAF crew, Stirling 1943. Suddenly he addressed me with disarming frankness and a twinkle in his eye.

"I don't know, Number One Son, whether to take you out with Bill later for a drink, OR hang you from the Main Top!!"

Then he guffawed and picked up his knife and fork, with a permissive nod, indicating 'you may eat' to me and a glance at my hands, tentatively touching the edge of the dining table.

We set to on a plate of stovies and mashed turnip, a Scots speciality of Mum's and I waited for the great Patriarch to set the tone of the conversation or depending on his mood, no conversation at all. Mum's brittle and fear-drenched banalities didn't count at such times and every Sabbath, as I recalled. Often my throat would dry and my stomach clench as I prepared for an icy and clinical silence. Such intervals many years ago could be terminated by unexpected, astonishing rages and violence, with a packed table upended, my father shouting with rage, mother shaking with fear, our dog, Bruce, cowering in a corner and my little brother Stuart on the verge of tears, nearly wetting his short pants. Not tonight, however, Dad was in a strange but almost for him, flippant mood.

Afterwards while Mum cleaned up in the kitchen, I felt the hint from her that I should stay in the Presence and humour him until he divulged what form the evening's entertainment would take. I sensed something darkly comic, Gothic almost, knowing his humour.

"Well then, Number One Son, what news on the employment front? Brain Surgeon, Admiral of the Blue, Chief Brothel Keeper?"

I told him and he graciously replied that at least it was gainful employment. He asked me about Brighton again.

"Your Mother and I thought you had found your vocation as a nurse!"

he said with a knowing smirk.

I chatted quite a bit about the 'Royal Sussex' and nursing generally and managed to raise a few laughs, particularly when I mentioned Stan. Mum, probably relieved at the laughter, sidled gently into the room and took her seat near but opposite my father. I had written about Stan to my mother and she always asked about him. She seemed to understand my taste for the company of sensitive, learned young men. Father less so but he seemed to accept that my celibacy was no indication of latent homosexuality.

"So, Stan, his father a plumber or something?" said Dad.

I bridled at this and was prepared to jump in but Mum, surprisingly, showed some courage and leapt to Stan's defence. Dad gave a mischievous twinkle, then started to warm to him when I sang his praises and explained that his dad had been in the British, Polish and possibly even the German armies.

"He's from Birkenhead, too," I added.

"What a terrible place to come from!" said Dad.

Getting his drift, I was now beginning to accept that Dad and Stan, should they ever meet, would probably get on like a house on fire. I wondered what depths of cynicism Dad spoke from. To paraphrase the great Cardinal Newman: 'From what aboriginal catastrophe, what fall from grace was he was protecting himself?'

Chapter 39

The Musical Evening

I hadn't noticed the new piano at the back of the room until now. It was a compact modern Yamaha, pre-electronic. I suddenly realised I had missed our old upright from Manningham days, the one that in 1944 must have been stacked with beer mugs, as Dad and Gungha, Mum and Mabel, her WAAF comrade back with her on leave, sang their hearts out, Dad lustily pounding the keys. Dad leapt up almost athletically for a portly, middle-aged man and saddled the seat, loosening his tie, a young airman again and ran a thrilling arpeggio up and down the plastic-looking keyboard.

"You, Number One Son," he announced, swiftly and deftly turning around. "Will be in charge of the 'wind-up' and of course, the entertainment from your end. You may have an inspection," he continued, pointing to one of the carrier bags.

I did so, spotting ancient 78's and two or three battered vinyl LP's and some tatty-looking EP's. I noticed with an antiquarian's thrill: 78's of Finlandia, in most people of our class's collections at that time; The Warsaw Concerto and Coleridge Taylor's Hiawatha, another favourite among Dad's contemporaries, particularly in West Yorkshire the home of the great Oratorio tradition. There were also several other 78's from the immediate pre-WW2, standard lamp owning class.

"Don't forget the fish-knives, Norman!" I cried, patting the standard lamp proprietorially.

Dad, surprisingly, looked around at me with a roguish 'That's my boy!' sort of a grin. I noticed him explaining the trope to Mum, even hearing the word, Betjeman, and my heart sang. This was SOME homecoming.

Picking out some records to play, I was delighted to see the classic Huddersfield Choral Society's rendition of The Messiah with Sir Malcolm Sergeant,1962.

"Let these our revels now commence!" cried Dad. "And oh, Number One Son," he added handing me two pound notes. "Go to the off licence for three bottles of Newcastle Brown."

He remembered this was my favourite from my college days in Geordieland.

"And, oh!" he added. "Here's another pound, almost forgot, an ounce of St Bruno Flake and a packet of pipe cleaners."

"Ya won't forget my Kenneth McKellar, son?" Mum called after me as I leapt for my coat in the hallway.

I nodded my assent. I had noticed the LP and loved him anyway and also some prehistoric 78's of the Glasgow Orpheus Choir, something that all three of us loved.

It turned out to be the most 'un-hip' but enjoyable evening since my boyhood. Dad and I sang the duet from The Two Gendarmes, Dad superbly so, followed by the Two Grenadiers and I sang a passable rendition of Handel's great Silent Worship. All of us joined in some Burns and listening to my scratched LPs, the glorious Baroque of Handel and the gentle speaking voice tones of Sir Hugh Robertson, with his lilting West Highland accent introducing The Eriskay Love Lilt, recorded in some pre-war studio in Glasgow more than a lifetime ago.

When I stood up to go to bed, I thought I had never had a more enjoyable evening at 'Dotheboys Hall'. As I hugged Mum goodnight, I noticed tears in her brown and gentle eyes and even Dad's smile was less arctic.

Dad, sardonically, whilst conducting some serious and surgical excavation in the bowl of his pipe with a penknife, man-breasts and jowls a-quiver, muttered lugubriously:

"I think I'm in touch with my feminine side at last. It's all Number One Son's doing, I suppose," and he smiled up at me glacially, fanatically gripping his pipe in his still handsome teeth.

I saw very briefly, a dashing and brave young airman before me, a hero. It seemed OK. I was wrong, of course, but he was a complicated man.

Chapter 40

Thinking that it was too good to be true and I wouldn't be able to maintain this good relationship, I set about looking seriously for accommodation. Mum agreed at breakfast knowing all too well what the old man was like, though she seemed torn because she was overjoyed to see me home. Stuart was over in Lancashire, a very busy and hard-working accountant. I'm sure he was ambitious too and with a little toddler, they were content to meet up once a month, usually in a nice country pub nearer Skipton, on the edge of the Dales. Stuart had a nice executive home in rural north Lancashire.

Dad had gone to work and after gulping down another cup of Mum's tea, which had to be the best in the world, I dressed and headed for town intent on perusing the accommodation lists in the estate agents and newspapers. It was a good excuse too to savour the Yorkshire brews. I was beginning to get used to the local bitter beer again!

I don't know why but I ended up at the Manville Arms again, even knowing that the art students would be away for another two or three weeks until the start of the new term in late September. A few diehards would still be around though. Bradford Art College had few overseas, or out of area students though, having missed the chance of degree status in the mid-1960s.

There he was, Irish Jimmy, not much changed since I first met him as a pre-diploma student early in '64, an art student with his own place and at 19 years of age, at the precocious focus of what was Bohemia, at that!

"Well, you old bugger, Sean MacDurex himself!" I cried and leapt up to smack him on the back.

Jim with his ubiquitous conspiratorial grin - he always seemed to be divulging classified information - half strode towards me with a sailor's roll, heroically swinging out his crippled right leg.

"Well, Dave, you old fucker!"

He was handsome in the way of a disgraced Franciscan, like certain kinds of Irishman resembling a police informer, professional snout, purveyor of soft drugs and porn, a loveable rogue. I had always carried a copy of The Ginger Man and The Naked Lunch, Olympia Press, VERY daring in those halcyon days of 1964. And, I recollect, in those pre-Pill days, my first Durex, hence the nickname. The Ginger Man gave me unending pleasure over the next ten years and The Naked Lunch, with its sense of genius, something dark and transgressive, went on to haunt the rest of my youth. The Durex, on the other hand, only brought me self-loathing, disappointment and a recollection of an artefact, both sordid, archaically quaint and in-utile. I had made clumsy and unsuccessful love to Glenda back then. I winced briefly at the memory and of a shameful walk with her to catch her bus home to Halifax.

We rattled on for ten minutes and then with a subtle wink, Jim bade his farewell.

"Got a man to see about a dog," he said. "But here, this is Wes. Dave, not long up from the Smoke."

He beckoned to a looming but benign-looking figure who gently and tentatively approached me. He was tall, a cavalier obviously and had the darkly handsome Iberian looks of a certain kind of Irishman, London Irish in Wes's case. Jim turned and limped away out onto Great Horton Road, off to his special assignment. I instantly liked- no, loved Wes. I pointed towards the bar, showing my empty pint glass.

"Want one, mate?" I asked.

With a look of the weariest sadness, gentility and an almost Sussex courtesy, Wes agreed to a pint of Tetley's bitter.

After another couple, he confessed to a smack habit. I shuddered, being fairly straight in that department but a part of me loved that he was one of life's walking wounded. I had just read The Wound Dresser before I left Brighton, Whitman's poems to the US civil war wounded. Coincidentally, Robin from the Bristol had lent me a copy and told me to look out for Britten's interpretation in music. Afterwards, I was able to hear John Adam's version on a BBC high-brow radio show, a more recent and haunting recording.

Catching a gleam of the late summer's afternoon light in Wes's ravishing black hair and swooning at the ultramarine/indigo highlights and the massive sorrow in his handsome and aquiline face, a touch of the Duke of

Wellington, mixed with that of a heroically melancholy Spanish Bullfighter, I yearned to hold him in my arms and to cradle his noble head. I had never felt so immediately intimate with a man and I was mildly perturbed. I wanted to nurse him and as I had often fantasised about the dead Christ, to bind and dress his bleeding body and salve his bleeding soul.

I had not expected to find love that early afternoon, at least not in that form, but I had rediscovered a sort of tenderness. I was not homosexual but Wes and I seemed to 'rap' in the slang of the time, in a way that I had not achieved with any other human. We shared our confused feelings about the north and our nostalgia for the Smoke. Wes being a North London lad, we talked about the jazz pubs around there and just jived and gelled like an old couple reunited.

He talked about the Round-Head feel of Bradford.

"What about the 5th Monarchy men, Lilburne and Winstanley?" I said in disagreement.

It was the only cloud on the lightness of our bonding.

"Hey, I'm Irish, remember?" said Wes. "And anyway, you know what happened to those two blokes!"

Indeed, I did. I remembered taking Glenda around Putney Parish Church and my cursing Cromwell, as we studied inside that fine old church, the memorial to the great Declaration of liberty by some men of the New Model Army. I shuddered at the thought of Glenda, her dourness and lack of charm and I wished I was gay. I wondered where on earth my heart was because I had come here to pursue her ghost and in vain, the memory of a fresh young girl, a Cromwellian, despite her joyous and Cavalier body, her delicious pussy and her startling, and Royal breasts.

We decided to move on to another and quieter pub as I didn't want to get drunk and I still had some flat-hunting to do. Wes told me not to worry, he knew the best area, though he was staying with friends, smack-heads I surmised and we took a taxi up to Manningham, my childhood home and now my new place of work. Repairing to a roughish Tetley's pub, The Carlisle, popular with whores, Pakistanis and Sikh bus drivers, and the odd Irish navvy, telly blaring the latest racing results and form from Haydock and Kempton Park, we had another couple of pints. I underlined a couple of likely looking addresses. Wes gave me the name and phone number of a possible landlord. Eliot Ness was his nickname among the gay and drug community, and in these days before the more manicured 'Housing Associations', the best bet for those of us living in the Twilight Zone.

I went on to share over 'one for the road' something of my mixed feelings about my homecoming and we agreed that we were both exiles, in my case, in reverse. I talked about Glenda, my liking for nice men, that rare commodity and my revulsion for sexual contact, my obsession and yet loathing for certain women, and my seemingly perverse obsession with them.

"David, we're both women, get used to it!" said Wes. "There are more than two sexes, you know. You've got a lot to learn!"

Then, bravely for that time and that pub, he leaned in and kissed me.

"We'll keep seeing each other, I know that Dave but right now I HAVE to score!"

We went our separate ways.

Chapter 41

I got back home just before tea and Dad coming home from work. I'd made a provisional time for an inspection of a possible flat after a brief telephone chat with 'Eliot Ness'. If a Roundhead could be a roguish character then he fits the bill!

"Yes, Lad," he said. "See you, number 51 on St Paul's Road Saturday morning."

I knew it well, the heart of bedsitter land and just down the road from my job which started on Monday. I felt my homecoming hadn't been too bad, although I still felt an underlying unease.

Dad was fairly civil and we ate in something approaching a companionable silence, fish, chips and mushy peas that he had picked up on his way home from work, the Friday ritual. Dad was going out with Bill for a drink at the usual joint in Thornton, with maybe a detour into the town centre. I suspected a bit of sleuthing on their part, snouts to see, contacts to refresh. I thought it might be good to stay in with Mum and talk to her, catch up with her and just be a considerate son for a change. We both knew it wouldn't be long before I would be leaving.

As soon as Dad left, Mum pulled out all the old photos which I enjoyed seeing and the recent ones of her grandson and my new nephew, Christopher. I felt a pang of jealousy which shamed me. Inexplicably, it hurt me to think of her as a Granny and I felt slightly jealous that every fortnight or month they met up with Stuart and their daughter-in-law, Jean, in a posh roadhouse near Grassington, in the Dales. They could then dote on their new granddaughter, Amanda, quite reasonably and again I was shocked at my meanness of spirit.

Mum gave me a couple of glasses of the best Laphroaig whiskey and we both basked in a bit of Jacobite nostalgia as we ran through her Kenneth McKellar records.

Dad and Bill turned up not long after the pub closed, slightly fresh but more exhilarated really. I gathered there had been a murder; some wretched woman, a 'prostitute' Dad hissed under his breath and both men rushed to the telly. By some freak, we were able to pick up very shortwave intercom conversations from Bradford City Police Patrol cars. This had been Dad's previous job before he became more desk-bound.

Drawing a blank, because Bradford had not yet been totally amalgamated with West Riding Police, they both sat down and unwound with a cup of tea served by Mum and we anticipated some manly and non-frivolous police talk.

The usual formalised names came: Nora Emily McC?; no fixed abode; previous convictions for soliciting; looking for a man with possibly size 7 boots, ridiculously small and maybe a lorry driver, and most probably a 'punter'. It was the kind of litany that would foul the West Yorkshire air over the next few years, that of Manningham in particular.

"The poor lass!" muttered mother, sympathetically, affected by the patriarchal censoriousness exuding from the two coppers,

"No better than she ought to be," interjected Dad, adding that she was just an old woman and with daughters probably on the game also.

Bill at least, definitely a Roundhead too, had the grace to shift uncomfortably saying that he thought he knew the family and while the main investigation proceeded, he'd put out a few feelers in his large, originally Irish catholic family. Poor Norma had indeed, worshipped as a child, along with the infant William Augustine Henry, at St. Joseph's, the huge Catholic church in Girlington next door to Manningham. Bradford had an ecumenical spirit, one of the very many fine things about it. Though Bill had lost his faith years before, he kept it up out of his required respectability and for the sake of his pious wife and family.

Dad, I think was a believer but not a regular attendee at the local Anglican church. I think he worshipped England actually and the Anglican Church was his 'Shinto' temple. Test Cricket and The Trooping of the Colour were probably the nearest he got to committed worship. It was interesting though to hear Bill, who was christened William Augustine and Dad reminisce about the great Father O'Connor, the original of Chesterton's Father Brown who often visited Protestants as well, in the Manningham Parish.

As soon as Bill had left, Dad reverted to his old custom of referring to me indirectly.

"Has SHE got a job yet? Has the youth been to town, behaved herself?" he asked and so on and so forth.

I mused to myself, it being Saturday the next day, how I was going to keep out of his way because I could well see the trajectory of his mood veering to the dark and menacing. Monday, I started work, so hopefully, I would have some respite from him.

Fortunately, he had a couple of advanced driving students for Saturday. Apart from bringing them back for tea, I knew I would see little of him. To his credit, he took no money for these lessons and also seemed to enjoy giving his lectures to the public on road safety and good driving. It looked like I would have time with Mum and I could work out some kind of a plan. I really missed Brighton though and my heart ached for Glenda. Perversely, I know, she was beginning to feel like my Nemesis.

I met Eliot Ness the next morning and liked him. Sinners were more congenial to my spirits as they were less likely to be judgemental. I was able to pay him a week's rent, plus a deposit of the same amount and was pleased to find it a small but clean garret room with a gas ring and reasonably, if sparsely furnished. I only had the rucksack to bring and the two carrier bags I had arrived with, so moving in should prove no problem if I had to leave 'Dotheboys Hall' precipitately.

I decided to keep the alcohol intake down until I had a week's work behind me. So, pocketing my new flat key, I headed back home. I knew Dad would be out until early evening, after an advanced driving student tutorial and then a lecture to the Townswomen's Guild. He would be at his insufferably Aldermainic worst after that, I knew. Mum was out with colleagues from her work, two lovely ladies Dorothy and Eileen whom I would get to know well over the years. They were comradely and kind like that generation of working-class women. Dorothy had a car and they gave Mum that little bit of liberty she was otherwise denied.

It was definitely getting worse at home and in such a short time. Dad had taken to referring to me not only in the third person but as Barbara, his name for me had I been a girl. Mum and her mates were off to shop at Ponden Mill. Some people thought it was the inspiration for Emily Bronte's Thrushcross Grange in Wuthering Heights. It was in fact, a newly-restored old wool mill deep in Bronte country, specialising in wholesale upmarket linens and other soft household goods. There was a nicely-appointed cafe there too and the girls loved to enjoy a pot of tea and freshly made scones and butter. I would have the place to myself so maybe I could start on some sort of a plan, a relaunch!

First, though and for the first time since being a teenager, I went upstairs to what was now Mum's room. I sat at her dressing table, staring in the mirror, making a 'moue' with my lips, thinking to kiss my reflection and imagining Glenda's lips searching my mouth and mine hers until suddenly she dissolved into Wes. I stared into the mirror, stared at my despair, then shuddering, I gently opened the bottom drawer. I relished and was ravished by the sweet feminine fragrance issuing from its contents. Then came a hot and dry feeling, a sensation of tears about to sting my cheeks as I caressed them, left and then right with my mother's silken nighties, my right hand then searching in the bottom of the drawer for her best stockings, so satin-smooth, so sheer!

I was most definitely a Cavalier and Wes and I were comrades of some new Sexual Order, Stendhal's Scarlet and Black? I drew one of my mother's headscarves around my head. I leaned in and the dressing table mirror revealed an echo of my mother, younger and not as pretty.

"I wonder, I wonder?" I said to myself.

Then I closed the drawer on the headscarf and lingerie and rushed out of her room, her boudoir, past the framed prints of the Duke of Wellington and Lord Nelson on the landing walls. Voicelessly screaming with a subversive joy, I ran pell-mell down the stairs to the hallway and threw myself into the chintz and kitsch of the front room. I seized a sheet of A4 paper from the bureau by the chest of drawers and a ballpoint pen and set to, making several lists and a plan of action, for a 'come-back' and what was to become a lifetime's habit. Also, a lifetime's habit of staring in the mirror and sketching myself as different characters and increasingly, something that horrified me and at the same time, obsessed me, my awe and fear of women.

I heard a noise at the door and Mum came in, having been dropped off by her mates. I rushed frantically up the stairs.

"I'm in the bath, Mum!" I shouted down to her.

I made a big to-do with flushing taps and swishing bathwater and the quickest undressing session in Music Hall history.

Later, I brewed some tea and sat ready to hear of her good time. She looked flushed and happy, ten years knocked off her face. This all disappeared and the anxiety returned when she realised what the time was.

"'Dad'll be home, Davy. I'd better be getting tea ready, son."

"What's the matter, Mum?" I asked. "Don't you like me leaving the family home so soon?"

She seemed scared.

"In some ways, he's getting worse," she said. "It's best you leave. But I think he's annoyed you've decided to go so soon."

"I found him a bit more genial this time," I said.

"You have no idea," she snapped.

I noticed her crushing her hankie and saw tears in her soft brown eyes.

"I'm sorry, son," she said and I sensed for the first time, a deep well of misery in her.

I was going to ask her for a dance, an old ritual we used to have but realised it would be inappropriate. I knew she was on the point of breakdown. On my visits home from college years ago, it had been our custom when Dad was out, to have a twirl about the living room. Mum had been an expert dancer and loved anything Russian or Polish. She had even been known to fraternise with young men from the Communist Party on the Red Clyde, in her first months of the war when she was a rookie WAAF near Glasgow. One of her boyfriends had been a Polish rear gunner in a Wellington bomber but he was shot down over Germany and reported as missing. 'Rasputin' was her earliest endearments to me, I could just about remember before my brother, Stuart, came along. I could see her now on the few times that I was ill, beaming down on me and holding out a cup of hot Oxo, saying: 'Come on now, little Rasputin, coorie doon,' as she tucked me in.

As a young student on leave, I would twirl her around the room in a clumsy Mazurka, shouting: 'Come on, little Mother!' and she would laugh aloud with joy as we capered around the sterile and cheerless front room.

'Rasputin!' she would cry, as I twirled her around and I would correct her: 'Raskolnikov… R-R-R-R-ASKOLNIKOV!!!!'

I knew that the kitchen, despite what certain feminists were beginning to say, was a sacred place and I didn't even bother to help her clean up unless asked to do so.

"Dearest," she said now. "I'll set the table and leave you to it."

I felt for her and knew that, like me, she had no appetite. I heard the sound of a car coming up the drive and thought, oh Christ, he'll be insufferable tonight having been in the company of people 'with wool on their backs'. He had been invited to give a lecture on Road Safety and Advanced Driving by the Bradford Town's Women's Guild. He was the most supine and servile Tory, of course. My whole body tensed and my stomach clenched taught.

"Is there a young man by the name of Copperfield in the house?" Dad called out to the chill hallway.

His mood changes were sometimes unpredictable, often the gloom-lifting ones turned out to be worse. This seemed one of these times. I went into the hall to greet him and Mum emerged too from her fastness, to find Dad doing his W.C. Fields bit. I loved his impersonations.

"Ooooohhh," he cried, fluttering his hands on his chest and his finest Gannex car coat. "Who is this callow youth, Mother?"

He was high as a kite and I preferred him with a drink inside him. He breezed in, allowing me to hang his Gannex coat up. It was about the only thing he had in common with the then Leader of the Parliamentary Opposition. Christ! I thought. The old brute is impenetrable!

Things became a bit calmer and we enjoyed a fairly normal tea.

"Where has SHE been today then?" said Dad, suddenly. "Has SHE moved her things into HER new flat yet? Honestly, you would think this, our family home was some Hotel, some kind of a BORDELLO!"

I humoured the old brute, more fearful for Mum than myself. I had liberty at hand, Mum was imprisoned both physically and as I now realised, mentally. She would never leave Dad. The sadness was almost palpable, the pretence of normality almost obscene.

I decided the next day, it being dry and a Sunday anyway, to pack my rucksack and leave. Dad was still in bed when I left but I shouted a cheery farewell up the stairs, getting a grunt as an answer. Mum stood by the front door, wringing her hands inside her apron.

"See you again, son," she said. "Bring your washing. Ye're welcome for Sunday lunch anytime, just give us a call and here," she thrust some notes into my anorak pocket, to which I only offered token resistance. "I hope this helps to your payday. Goodbye, son, been great having you!"

Impulsively, I hugged her to me.

"Ach, away ye go, Rasputin-ya wee skunner!"

She was wiping a tear from her eye with her apron, as I turned swiftly on my heel, stifling my sobs. I shook myself, as I pretended to stride 'manfully' down the drive, past the privet, the wisteria, and the Portugal laurel.

"For today, today we have naming of parts," I chanted to myself, not knowing quite what it meant but finding its ritualistic sound, in some way consoling. "But tomorrow, tomorrow we have what to do after firing!"

Part Five:

THE VALLEY OF BONES

Chapter 42

It didn't take me long to settle into my room. There was a single bed, clean-looking and well made up, a washstand, single gas ring and a tiny sink unit. I panicked slightly until I opened a drawer in the dressing table/chest of drawers and found an ancient electric kettle with its lead wrapped neatly around it. Monkish and Spartan but it all suited my plan, my mission. I stacked a few books on the small cabinet by my bed and on the tiny mantle shelf over the blocked-up fireplace. A cheap and slightly tatty Formica coffee table, survivor of the late '50s sat on spidery legs by the single easy chair. Two Utility style WW2 dining chairs graced a flimsy but serviceable dining table.

There was only one main window starting at floor level and rising to the join of the slope and return of the mansard and the main roof. This must have been part of the original garret or servants' quarters. I had to kneel down on the reasonably clean, threadbare carpet to see out and down onto leafy sycamores and the once elegant St Paul's Road, now gone to seed.

My neighbours all seemed to be workers and there was a quiet buzz in the street below, so unlike the geriatric calm of Hove, down in West Sussex. The area had not quite become the Red-Light district it was soon to be. Though even through my naïve eyes, I could spot a number of Working Girls patrolling the immediate area down from Oak Lane and on through St Mary's' Road and the notorious Lumb Lane. There was still something of a village atmosphere with a hint of bohemia about the area. Maybe Montmartre or Montparnasse was like this once, I mused? Anyway, I preferred it to the stifling purlieus of petit-bourgeois suburbia where my parents lived.

Weeks' later, one evening, on my back from the offie, or Off-Licence, I was accosted by a cheery-looking lady of West African appearance.

"Eh, what you looking at lad?" she called out. "You live here, you're a local!"

Now, I opened my kitbag and took out the food Mum had given me. Ever thoughtful, she had packed food that only needed reheating or was processed, sensing I probably only had one gas ring and a kettle. I smiled as I stashed the packets of Vesta Chow Mein and Curry in my tiny chest of drawers, remembering there were some of the best fish and chip shops in Britain around here, albeit halal and Asian-owned, and of course some of the best and cheapest curry joints in Europe.

I had what I needed for the start of my comeback and sat down with a brew of coffee in my new flat. This had become a sacred ritual now, I had seen so many new flats in my career as a fugitive and in my imagination, a Special Agent. I took out my Oxford pad, rolled a ciggie with Old Holborn and studied my plan.

In my imagination, I unpacked a Makarov 9mm Automatic pistol, KGB model, checked its magazine and looking down its sight thought of Glenda. I hefted it in my right hand, thrilling at the surge of power and transgression it gave me, then thrust it in its shoulder holster and hung it on the back of the bedsit door, behind my best blazer. Not a good idea to pack 'heat', I fantasised, on what was beginning to look like a lovely late summer's Sabbath afternoon.

I had almost forgotten the Newman autobiography that Robin gave me in Brighton, though he had warned me that I wouldn't understand it for many years more. Bearing in mind what he, Stan and I had theorised, that books could read you, I thought it was worth a perusal all the same. It promised the spiritual and intellectual weight that would give my soul a bit of structure. Restless as I was, I was no Hippie, no 'go with the flow' merchant.

I had also managed to pack a selection of the works of my favourite poet and cleric, Gerard Manly Hopkins. My collected Simone Weil I cherished absolutely and placed it by my bedside, thinking that I'd buy the latest Rowan Williams when I got my first wage. He was at that time a rising man in the Anglican Church in Wales and I liked what I knew and read of him.

After coffee, like all Special Agents, I needed to recce the locality. Even though I had been brought up around here, I was only a child then. I wanted to find a good library or bookshop and other shops, basic stuff. I could suss out the social scene; I wasn't a churchgoer at that time but I thought maybe I could go later, after supper, when I'd sussed out the local pub scene. My job was only up the road about 15 minutes' walk away so I thought I should also check out the local, elegant park I remembered from my childhood. There was a superb gallery there with a fantastic and quirky Victorian permanent collection and an eccentric, genteel cafe.

I shivered slightly, sensing something brutal and menacing in the Manningham air. It was less bohemian up near the mill here and lumpen, almost criminal compared to cavalier and sleazily genteel Brighton. I still yearned for the unfinished business of Glenda down south. I shuddered as I unaccountably remembered my resentment at some outrage of hers. At a crack from my Makarov, she was sent flying across my garret in a haze of vaporized arterial blood and as she ricocheted off the far wall, her blood cascaded in torrents and spurted from her ruined chest, as like a rag doll, she flopped and metamorphosed into my anorak strewn carelessly over my unused bed.

I awoke from this hallucination in a cold sweat and after a shake of my head, stumbled to the kitchenette sink and splashed my face with cold water. I needed some fresh air and a drink, several.

A stroll around the park then, I thought as being Sunday the pubs wouldn't be open until 7 pm. Maybe some tea and a read, a concert on the radio? I'd brought my battered old transistor from Brighton as I had no love for the telly.

As I entered the great ornamental gates by the Keighley Roads and the bottom of Oak Lane, I thought how Romantic and mostly pastoral the park appeared, even though it was a typical, imperial-looking municipal park of its time. Here I was, so near to the great Mill in Oak Lane, in the shadow of which I was brought up and when I was a little older, played Red Indians among the rhododendrons of the park.

I got what I thought was the 'look' from a couple of Asian youths, as I neared the great mock Baroque Cartwright Hall but I didn't return it and feeling somehow blessed, I walked on with no harm. The atmosphere, though certainly heavier than Brighton, lacked the 'edge' of London and I was able to walk, unmolested, a single, youngish man, down to the elegant and romantic lake. I savoured a kind of an old-fashioned Sabbath smell and spontaneously turned to see one of the two Pakistani youths raising a hand and I discerned the flash of a friendly smile. I raised my right hand, smiling in return. For absolutely no reason at all, I suddenly felt indescribably happy.

After about 50 paces, I noticed Wes across the lake, looking rather forlorn and miserable.

"Wes!" I shouted, raising my arm, feeling sorry for him.

He had a companion, about my build, with a John Lennon cap and a miniature terrier in his arms. Our paths were converging, so I hurried and was able to cut off their retreat, should they be thinking of one. In those days I positively reeked of heterosexuality. Wes introduced me to Ronnie, bespectacled and with ironic and clinically intellectual eyes, who replied with a London accented greeting and an accompanying limp hand. Ron struck me as a most charming person but I feared for Wes, almost regretting not bringing my imaginary Makarov 9mm automatic. We parted, each of us promising to see each other around.

The Sabbath gloom was beginning to envelop the Park as I headed to the North Gate. The huge tower of Manningham Mill's chimney was pure Lowry, dominating Victor Road which climbed up the hill. Over halfway up and on the left, Leamington Street was where I had been brought up and further up on the left, on Victor Terrace stood the Greenwood Patriarchal home, an undistinguished end of terrace dwelling.

I trudged back to my new flat, depression deepening, thinking of poor Mum and the similarly gentle and so obviously distressed Wes. I made a Vesta Chow Mein and sat down with a cup of tea, wondering when my spirits would lift and the miasma of sorrow enveloping Manningham would dissipate. I thought about going out for a drink and another recce or just listening to a play on Radio 3 and then having an early night.

I did go out for a drink of course and found two hostelries nearby, close to the great St. Paul's Church. It had become a mainly Muslim area and seemed a little forlorn but still redolent of Edwardian respectability. I noticed plenty of leaded windows and tiny front gardens, the urban equivalent of the increasing gentrification going on in the surrounding country villages which involved the introduction of hanging baskets and Ploughmen's Lunches, in a countryside that had rarely seen a plough, being mainly pasture and moorland. There was more of an atmosphere of mild criminality, with a hint of Bohemia in the two pubs I visited. I found myself amongst a couple of fraught-looking working girls, some misfit and mature student types like me, 'Trots' and Street Theatre Activists and members of the slowly-emerging, radical gay enclave.

I gasped at the beauty of a crop-haired brunette, a darker version and taller, of Jean Seberg and I caught a hint of a dazzling and unfashionably shy smile. She was sitting with some pretentious, androgynous-looking theatrical types. I couldn't keep my eyes from her, discreet as I tried to be. I pretended to be concentrating on my paperback whilst in reality, I was basking in the beauty of the brunette and fantasising about a Goddess. I thought I caught her name: Bobby, or Rob, something suitably Sapphic and mysterious. Then briefly I heard her voice, gentle and with no discernible accent, refined and reserved. I felt that I could like her very much.

The atmosphere generally though, unlike north London and Kemptown in Brighton, was more assertively working class. A few genuinely working men, in their Sunday suits, Catholics obviously, played a desultory game of dominoes while others played darts.

Incongruously, Manningham could be exotic. One Friday morning I heard the muezzin call to prayer from a converted Victorian Baptist church and I felt the same tremor of recognition, of something understood that I had felt at the friendly glance from the Pakistani boys.

Here in the pub, I knew I could sit and read without looking like a complete freak, as I would have done in Barnsley or the heavy industrial steel towns and outlying estates of South and West Yorkshire. Here, folk seemed free with eye contact. A cheery looking couple of Dykes, Tom Boyish and happy-go-lucky, were chaffing with a group of working girls and sensing she wanted to chat, I asked the more extrovert one if I could join them for a game of darts, or Arrows as we say here. A very gay-looking guy made up a foursome, extremely short-sighted and looking as if he knitted his own clothes, he introduced himself as Googie.

"Aw right, 'ar kid!" said the Dyke/Tom Boy, slapping me on the back. "I'm Ellie, that's my mate Pansy," she added pointing to a strapping, good-natured Mancunian.

"Hya, bicycle-face!" said Pansy, raising her glass and winking at me.

I dog-eared my book and joined them. Pansy and I took on Googie and Ellie and got severely thrashed.

Feeling much better about the North now, I drank up and after cheery farewells, marched the short distance home. I made sandwiches for my first day at my new job, washed, made a cocoa and retired to my monkish bed. I had my favourite bedside reading: Simone Weil's Gravity and Grace and the Hopkins' anthology, of course. But I opened my Levi book, The Light-Garden of the Infant King, at the dog-eared page and continued from where I left off in the pub. I marvelled again, as I had done in London and Brighton, how sometimes a book could read you. With my heart beating, I came across a passage where Peter, a delightful man and a closet-catholic like myself and his travelling companion Bruce Chatwin were silently encouraged by an Afghan Imam to sit and share the peace of an Islamic saint's garden and shrine. Softly and graciously, the kind old man brought them a posy of flowers and later some cardamom-spiced tea. I delighted at reading how men might be and read on ten more pages to the end of the chapter, then dog-eared my page once again, hit the pillow and closed my eyes for a blameless sleep.

I loved the unworldliness of the Muslim Kashmiris and Mirpuris who formed the majority of my new neighbours. Meanwhile, in the morgue in Bradford, lay the murdered body of poor Norma, defiled, corrupting and despised.

Chapter 43

Some of my new workmates were already assembled at the foot of the iron stairs in Garfield Avenue. I introduced myself and received friendly greetings in return, especially from the Downs Syndrome boys.

“I'm Derek!”

“Peter!” chimed the other. “We’re brothers!”

“'I'm Dave!” I replied, with as hearty a smile as I could muster.

A couple of older blokes, though it was difficult to tell what age Derek and Peter were, cringed back from me. One of them bore the scars of grievous facial injuries and the other appeared so badly disabled that I was amazed he could stand. Fuck off and leave me alone was the look I got from these two. Mr Earnshaw, my employer had forewarned me that a couple of blind blokes were on the team as well. I had liked the way he had said that and it fulfilled my best hopes of the sort of society we were becoming. There was a small Remploy sign on the exposed brickwork, halfway up the outer staircase, indicating the use of the government’s re-employment scheme for disabled people, which explained my new boss's apparent philosophy but no matter, I thought. The lads and I chatted a bit until just before 8.30 when a maroon SS Jaguar pulled up.

“Not seen one of those for a bit!” I exclaimed and gave Mr Earnshaw a positively appraising look as he emerged from the vintage dream.

“Morning, lads!” he said, genially. “Who’s first to put' kettle on?” and obviously a routine, he then threw his keys to an enthusiastic Derek, who clattered at a cacophonous rush up the stairs, with Peter in tow.

I followed at a discreet distance, intending to help the crippled blokes but my tentative efforts were brusquely brushed aside.

“You first, Mister,” growled the disfigured one. “We can manage!”

I quickly mounted the cast-iron stairs.

Thankfully there were no power tools and I was pointed to one of the benches by Derek, a self-elected chargehand.

"You're my mate, you are, David!" he said, grinning.

I filled up a bit and caught a wink from Mr Earnshaw, standing just inside the door of his office.

"Be with you!" he mouthed, shrugging on his brown work coat.

What a nice man, I thought. I was grateful, on what turned out to be the most dreadful day, that I liked my new boss.

I had heard while shaving that morning, something on Radio 3 about Air Force jets and troops bombarding the Presidential Palace, in Santiago, Chile. It was a bracing cold-water shave. Bloody Eliot Ness and bent plumbing, I thought, what do you expect? Towelling myself briskly and finishing the rest of my ablutions, I had hurriedly dressed, picked up my sandwiches and bolted out of the door, throwing my jacket over my shoulder, it being a halcyon late summer/early Autumn day.

As promised, Mr Earnshaw came to our workbench and showed us some ancient, domestic brush heads, then pointed to some alarming-looking, industrial ones being stacked up by the two older blokes. I never knew such things existed.

"Call me Jack, Dave!" said my new boss.

He explained that the job for Derek and I entailed pulling out the old bristles with a pair of pliers while gripping the brush handle in a vice on the side of the bench.

"I'll catch you later, lads," said Jack. "I'm going to check on Ron and Bill!" I assumed these were the two crippled guys.

Derek set to, smoothly and efficiently. I struggled. Fit as I thought I was, I found the hard work almost beyond me.

"Oh, David," said Derek smiling angelically. "You'll get used to it. See there's a knack."

He gently rearranged what I thought was my wiry grip on the pliers, pointing out that maybe an adjustable mole grip spanner might be better? I was amused at how my Downs Syndrome friend seemed to speak with a kind of Home Counties or London suburban accent. While Derek beamed benignly at me, I struggled on with my task. It seemed to work, though I found it hard-going and by lunchtime I was humming along with my new comrade to Radio One, even enjoying Jimmy Young, the British Housewives' heartthrob and favourite DJ at that time.

Lunch was only half an hour but as a new boy, I would have the option of leaving at 4.30 while the rest of the gang, Derek and Peter enthusiastically worked a couple of hours overtime. We sat or lounged around the iron staircase, eating our 'snap' and lighting up our cigs. Though Derek and Peter recoiled from our smoke, we chuntered amongst each other contentedly. Peter came over to slap me on the back manfully and ask how I liked my new job. I had to say that I liked it and thought to myself privately that the mind-numbing nature of it was just what I wanted!

After lunch, as I was placing another broom head in the vice, Jack called over to me that he wanted a chat, round about 3 o'clock, nothing important. I set to, happy to be in the company of Derek, who winked at me conspiratorially, a man happy in his work. At 3 o'clock, I turned up outside Jack's office door.

"Come in, David," he said. "Sit thissen down."

He pointed to a high and battered wool sorter's stool near the filing cabinet, next to an astonishingly tidy sink. He filled me in on the nature of the job. Some of it was government-funded, though Jack confided that his little workforce were not just charity cases and thanks to them he was making a tidy profit. He knew I was only filling in between jobs and asked me to help him by just being a 'mother hen' to the lads. I was amazed, this was not the harsh world my father had conditioned me to, nor was it my previous work experience, even in the softer south. We shook hands and leaving this kind man's company, I returned with some enthusiasm to my mate and the task in hand.

On the way home, I bought a Guardian newspaper. I headed off via Carlisle road, the other main artery through Manningham, which reminded me, endearingly of Shepherds Bush and the Goldhawk Road, with the same ethnic mix which I loved and a working-class ambience which could be Brick Lane or Whitechapel in my socialist Pantheon!

I reached my flat and threw myself into my battered chair. Then I shuddered with fear and shame and almost wept as I read about the developments in Chile, hoping that as coups went, it might either fail or being in Latin America, it would blow over within the week.

The following morning, the BBC news proved depressing and I bought a Guardian on the way to work. The job was almost easy now and I kept an ear open for news flashes on the works radio. There wasn't much that day or on the evening news but over the next few days, the Chilean obscenity broke in all its horror. By Friday I was almost openly weeping and in a brief foray out to the pubs on Thursday night, I was pleased to see Ellie with some of her friends eagerly discussing the tragedy. I tried to catch her eye, got a solemn wink from her and the feeling that my joining the conversation might not be welcome. Such was the emerging gender politics of the time but I felt heartened that at least some people were concerned. Nothing was mentioned at work but I noticed Jack had a rolled-up copy of the Guardian in his hand as he emerged from the Jag on Friday morning.

I discovered he had a charming habit of inviting the 'boys' individually into the office for a chat, which I found amazingly civilized. When my turn came, Jack said he'd been dying to talk but feared making me look like a 'trusty' or boss's toadie.

"So, what d'ya think, Dave?" he asked, looking in the direction of his Guardian, in those days a leftist newspaper. "Should I say, comrade?"

"How did you know, Jack?" I replied, with a grin.

"Takes one to know one, Comrade!" He said, laughing and shaking my hand in a manly grip. "I left the Party in '56."

"Hungary?" I asked.

The term 'Tankie' had not yet been coined but I more or less expounded my orthodox Stalinist position. We conferred on what was looking like a historical setback for the working class and both solemnly cursed the Yanks and our complicit Tory Government. I expressed my almost trenchant pessimism.

"Looks like we might have a new government within a year," said Jack.

"What, Harold Wilson?" I responded and though I liked him, I felt I couldn't share his optimism.

He went on to praise my work and said he thought well of my attitude to Derek and Peter in particular. We agreed on bringing these meetings forward and having more 'heart-to-hearts'. I rejoiced to myself at meeting another true patriot at last.

I think that he understood that I wouldn't be staying long. My restlessness was becoming frenetic but at the same time, my depression was almost engulfing me. I had taken to having a stiff whiskey as soon as I came through my flat door at the end of the day's work. I even gave up the alfresco lunchtime breaks I had enjoyed so much, for a bottle of cider at home instead, something I had never done before. The Devil, at last, was out of his lair.

One Saturday I went to the Central Library in the town and photocopied a portrait of Stalin in his prime, on A6 sized paper, to paste on some mounting card I had bought, with a drawing block and charcoal, during a visit to the Art Shop by the college, a good excuse for a brief visit to the Manville Arms. It was the very same art shop where Glenda and I had stocked up on materials on that magical first day at college, a lifetime ago.

In the Manville that day, Chile was on everyone's lips and a sense of outrage and horror pervaded. I felt proud of my fellow arty types and as soon as I got back home, I constructed my Stalin Icon and placed it proudly on the small mantelpiece. I intended it never to leave me and I gave a stiff salute, a clenched fist and gritted my teeth as I stood back and faced the old boy, my hero and saviour. At the time, I felt a void opening up beneath me but not just for me. I wondered if my parents felt this at the time of Munich and subsequently, the Molotov-Ribbentrop pact?

The following Friday and pay night, I decided to drop anchor on the booze for a bit and have another look at my Plan, refine it and maybe do some reading and drawing. I was still feeling restless but if things worked out, I could still make it to 'last orders' up the road, if I studied till 9.30.

I had noticed in the pubs some interesting, older and probably post-grad students, serious-minded and if a bit charmless, a refreshing change from the freaks' circus I remembered in Kemptown, Brighton. I would need to look into doing something in Further or Higher Education. I knew I was a born teacher though not committed enough to teaching in a school. To be honest, kids bored me. I also thought that if I could wangle a grant, it would at least keep me occupied and away from the soul-destroying factory jobs I'd had since leaving Art College in 1967. Also, to be honest, I knew that I was something of a Peter Pan and found straight life immensely tedious. I also liked the cut of some of the women, though not all of them.

Who knows, I might even get back to painting? Though it seemed a long shot at this time. I knew I would need a wedge of money to make a career out of it and had yet to even think of how to go about it.

I opened my new sketchbook and charcoal box bought at Daley's Art Shop the previous day and pulled from my rucksack one of my family's Dickens' volumes I had 'borrowed'. I set to, sketching tentatively but energetically from my beloved Phizz illustrations, something I had not done since my teens. I wondered if Dickens knew a lot of alcoholics, as on a quick flick through the Victorian pages - what delicious smells! - I gazed adoringly at the lovingly-imagined pen drawings of Mr Dick, Newman Noggs, Mr Makepiece Jaggers, Mr Micawber and Mr Wackford Squeers.

Two hours' later, I reckoned I hadn't done badly, though I was honest enough to realise that any genius I perceived in my work was thanks to two great and long-dead men. It was fun though and I rustled up a quick meal from Mum's emergency store. Fed, washed and brushed up with an added splash of cologne, which was my one luxury at the time, I leapt for my coat, crashed out through my flat door and rushed down the stairs intent on finding some company and a couple of pints. I seemed to have discovered a ravenous thirst!

Again, I saw Ellie and a group of dykes with some university types. Knowing the score now, I kept a respectful distance until summoned, thankful I'd brought a book with me: West Pier by that sad and good man, Patrick Hamilton. It was about Brighton and the location of my last quarters there, West Street, below Norfolk Square and I prepared to indulge in a bit of virtual wanderlust and nostalgia. The beer would be welcome too. Even though I was unlikely to be asked to join the company, the girls fascinated me, where, for all my vaunted socialism, straight working-class women wouldn't have. I heard Chile mentioned a few times but also something about some kind of assault on working girls. I hoped it didn't involve the lass who, with Googie, had thrashed Ellie and me at darts the other night.

At closing time, with just a discrete wink from Ellie, I headed back to St Paul's road and an early night, with what was becoming a bachelor's routine: wash, cocoa and bed; an hour's read then lights out. With a sigh, my head hit the pillow and before sleep, I mused about the evil swamping the world.

The weekend was coming up and I felt the urge for some kind of action, any kind. I was growing stir-crazy again, after only a couple of weeks back up north. Next morning was Saturday. I breakfasted, shaved, dressed and rushed down the stairs desperate to get out of my claustrophobic room. Just as I reached the front door, I noticed a red envelope on the shelving above the meters. I knew straight away it was from Glenda, her calling card. I picked it up, my heart palpitating and recognised her sensuously looping script and when I turned it over, a hand-drawn heart with a G at its centre.

I was hooked again, landed, my soul threshed and struggled as I rushed back up the stairs to open it and as she anticipated, study it for every nuance of meaning. I sniffed at its scented sheath, her spoor, her web.

My heart raced as I threw myself into my battered armchair and ripped open the envelope.

Dear David,

Sorry I wasn't there to say goodbye to you when you left for the North but I came over all 'woozy' - been having rather a lively time of it lately-Ha! Ha! I suppose that you think I am all sorts of horrors!!

I posted this to your Mum and Dad's address and if you're reading this it's because it's been posted on.

I noticed it was unfranked, so Dad must have mailed it through my door.

Well, what a year! I suppose I might meet you in Halifax at Xmas, if I come 'oop north', though thinking about it, I might be doing some travelling again. Paris appeals and you know how I WORSHIPPED Simone De Beauvoir, and thanks to her encouragement, I have always been an independent woman. As such, and as I've put money by, a 'Room of One's Own' might not be beyond my purse in 'The City of Light'.

As you know, I yearn to meet new people always(women included of course!)who are shooting arrows into the future! A pity you couldn't take it down south any more. As soon as I came to College here, I knew that the North was no longer a place for me, though I love my brief trips back! Halifax is so QUAINT, and the people such dears! If a bit dull.

My Buddhist classes are going well, and I guess now I am almost VEGAN. Just as well, as I might be going to an Ashram in Switzerland-met some lovely people in Glastonbury last year who go there often. It's expensive but will help the career I've got mapped out. Oh, by the way, do you still like fish and chips? You know, of course, of my fascination with Jung? I could see opportunities opening for me as a Jungian Art-Therapist and with the resurging interest in Feminism, that could be a new angle. Of course, you knew, David, that I was always a feminist!

My fascination with the 'I Ching' might come in handy as well-and hey, I am a bit of a 'Dolly' as you always kept telling me-so I might become a quite 'marketable' Commodity? Ha! Ha!

I suppose that you're dead keen on rebuilding your shattered life now, in the north. I told you that I always loved you in a sort of way-but NEVER fancied you! When you came to my graduation party in Kingston that time, I thought it so sweet that you smelled of engine oil from your engineering job, but don't you think that your proletarian fantasies are a bit 'old hat' now, dear Dave?

That time in Shepherds Bush, I thought you really HAD SOMETHING! Even though obviously dirt-poor you seemed REALLY fired up, even a bit sexy! But here's me being silly! I had just come back from Pakistan and a wrecked marriage and a month in Quarantine here, so was in a strange state.

Are you still seeing Stanley? You DO love your men friends, don't you! Ha! Ha!

Look after yourself, Dave-until our paths cross again. They DO seem to-don't they? I enclose a £10 note. Knowing how restless you are, I have a feeling I might see you again-and soon? Don't spend it all on beer! My 'I Ching' reading just now sees you as a 'Forlorn Prince of the North'. I always saw you as a 'Highlander' in my mind's eye-some sort of a wretched and doomed Jacobite. But again, silly me!

Love, Glenda XXXXXXXX

Chapter 44

Brighton

I sat in my pre-booked seat on the Leeds train connection to London, looking forward to next the next leg of my journey, Victoria Station to Brighton. My heart thumped as I thought of 'Billy Liar' so many years ago and I smiled to myself, silly fellow. I knew that at least I was chasing my Julie Christie, my Goddess and Nemesis! I tensed, urging the train to get moving, my body surging with adrenalin.

I took a pull from my Dewars of Perth half-bottle of whiskey, rapidly proving a loyal friend and ally to me. I sat back and relaxed, dozing fitfully through the dull scenery of British Rail's East Coast line. I mused about my plot to make an ally too of Eliot Ness, whom I had correctly sussed as an amiable but biddable rogue. I had left his rent in an envelope with a short note saying I might be away for a bit, as I had business down south. He usually liked to collect the rent personally and see how I was getting on.

I had left the rent close to my partially drunk, half-bottle of Glenfiddich whisky. When I left for work each day, I made a barely discernible mark with an HB pencil on the label, showing the level I had drunk to. I was always amused to see when I returned from work, a slight drop below my mark, showing that about the quantity of a 'double' was missing. There had also appeared a crudely-drawn eyepatch on my Stalin Icon. It was done in the charcoal I'd left on the mangey coffee table by my easy chair, along with my Dickens books and other sketch materials.

I reckoned he owed me one and we could have a joke about this if I got back late and I owed him rent. I don't know what I was expecting but it turned out to be a wise move as I discovered later.

I arrived in Brighton late in the afternoon and as I had enough money for an overnight stay, I booked into a cheap guest house off James Street. I tortured myself for half an hour, walking to the back of the Regency tenement where she had a bedsit, just up from the seafront and near to the Grand Hotel. It was one of those typical south coastal Indian Summer, halcyon evenings, the cream stucco of the seafront hotels bathed in a bronzed and almost golden light, elegiac in its late-season melancholy.

Knowing she lived around the back, high up on the third floor and that a window would be open, I stationed myself in the gathering dusk to see if I could catch a glimpse of her drying her hair perhaps (down boy!) or just leaning over the window sashes, hanging out her panties. I shuddered at the prurience of such a thought. Or, it being chillier now, maybe I would see her lower it. I thrilled suddenly to hear her laugh, a surprisingly hearty one and wondered if she had company. I smoked two cigarettes, unusually heavy smoking for me and stood transfixed, in delicious pain and awe, waiting for darkness.

I warned her that I was coming, not just to see her, of course, that would be an impertinence but to see Tony C, who was looking after some of my books and stuff. She had been a lover of Tony's, who had attended the same year as Stan at Brighton. Tony, like Stan, proved a loyal friend and knew of my obsession with her. I think he pitied me. Stan thought me totally insane.

"She's a cunt but I'd love to fuck her!" he had observed, crudely but with some venom for him.

Thinking it was time to make my move, I walked around to the front, a clamour of gulls accompanying my knock on the door. I was friends with the lass on the ground floor and knew a few others in the house, so anticipated no problems gaining admittance. Ros, the cheery single parent, saw me from the first floor flat and beaming broadly, rushed to let me in. I had been friendly with her little son on occasions and Ros, seeming to expect me, led me up the stairs to Glenda's door where only a few weeks before I had felt so crestfallen and defeated.

"Is that Mr Greenwood?" came Glenda's rather brassy voice.

After I assented, she let me in, smiling inscrutably and greeting me after her fashion.

Corny, I heard in my imagination, soft and sickly Hollywood-style music, you know, where the female lead turns her head, gently with a flick of satin hair and then the camera pans to the eyes, close up, of Lesley Howard or Gregory Peck, then back to the melting eyes of a Bergman or Vivienne Leigh.

I lowered my arms, surplus to requirement it would seem and sat in the same easy chair I had occupied a few times before, during this last and strange year. Looking to roll a cig and asking permission, I noticed a tampon, still wrapped near the table's edge.

"Oh, I see you've rolled yourself a joint already?" I said, to make light of it.

Glenda was a sport about such things and laughed out loud.

"Well, what to say, Glenda," I persisted. "Tampax or Lilletts? Which would you recommend?"

She laughed again. So, pushing my luck but sensing a change in the atmosphere, to something much warmer, I suggested my preference for Tampax.

"I know! Brand X and it's running down me legs!" she screamed in broad Yorkshire.

I had been scared of her reactions. She could be contrary. She showed her affection for me in inverse proportion to how she really felt about me. We had always kept our room doors open in our shared accommodation even up to a couple of years ago, a relic of the easy camaraderie of our student days. In Surbiton, or even later in Brighton, I was to be awoken by a comradely kick from her, or my blankets being ripped off of my still slumbering body.

Phew, I thought. Thank Christ for that!

"Sorry you're indisposed, lass!" I said and knowing her Francophilia, I pushed it a bit further. "Ah, les Anglais sont disembark-ay! Hein?"

I was pleased to get a further spurt of laughter from her. It was going to be all right, whatever 'it' consisted of, I just decided to go with the flow.

"Dave, stop digging!" she said with a hearty grin.

We could almost be back in my royal but dingy room off Lumb Lane, Bradford, in 1964.

I expressed genuine concern for her state and when she went into her tiny kitchen to brew a pot of tea, I felt secure in following her, without a stream of imprecations falling down upon me. I hadn't packed my Makarov anyway. I forget what we actually said but somehow, I felt I had got some kind of a grip, or purchase on whatever might be precious between us and just enjoyed being with her, not expecting romance. Funnily enough, I felt part way to accepting that there was something between us.

Our inverted relationship was so irrational, sometimes I could float the most outrageous notions and be tolerated, whereas at other times she would shriek at me for the most innocuous verbal lapse on my part. This was before the term 'sexist' was common. To her credit, she was showing a burgeoning interest in depth psychology which I respected, even if I dared to scoff at her addiction to the 'I Ching' and her love of astrology and even end of pier fortune tellers. I had been reading some mystical literature; I was a huge fan of Robert Graves and his 'White Goddess'. I loved medieval English music too, part of my romantic Anglo-Catholicism. I suddenly had a vague memory of an Old English poem.

"Glenda," I said suddenly. "Do you know a poem called 'The Baillie hath taken the bell away'?"

I hummed the refrain I'd heard on an erudite Radio-3 programme. Usually, my singing, or even an attempt at reciting poetry, would see her fly into a rage but I sensed we had found one of those precious moments of physical and spiritual convergence. Was it a perverse kind of love? A kind of a state of grace? I had begun to wonder if there was something slightly wrong with me.

I put my arms around her but from behind; it felt not as confrontational but I wasn't expecting to be rebuffed now anyway, such was my deep assurance of our strange bond and she leant her body back into mine. I kissed her rather drab hair, tied into a plait something that drove me wild in Scandinavian type blondes like her. She rocked back on her heels and it was OK.

"The Lily, the Rose, the rose I lay-the Baillie beareth the bell away," I crooned softly to her and was gratified to feel her relax trustingly in my arms.

"Don't be cross but do you know what I think it's about?" I asked.

"Go on," she replied, not in a hostile way.

"Well, I think - and Graves says it somewhere - that it's about a young girl coming to the menarche and her fear about that - her first period, don't you know, the knowledge that she was coming to womanhood?"

I stiffened, anticipating a tantrum but she hugged me a little closer.

"Mmm," she said. "Interesting."

"I've got a good memory," I said. "I'll try to remember it in a bit. Music is such a great mnemonic; our medieval ancestors were no mugs."

Then I told her that she smelled beautiful and for the first time in this situation, I meant it. Like many menstruating women or those suffering from PMT, there seemed an extra layer of skin, minuscule as it was, or maybe just a discernible layer of nerves flayed from her. Her suffering was palpable to me and I felt the deepest empathy with it and madly, insanely privileged. In my current sense of transgressive liberty, I told her exactly this and how I found it deeply attractive but in a totally inchoate way and again, half-expecting shrieking contumely and damnation but she sighed and returned my embrace with the tenderest caress of her hands.

Rather theatrically, I thought, she sighed again.

"David, you know what we have in common?"

"No," I said.

"Pain."

I was slightly disappointed by the bathos of this, so I slowly and gently detached myself from her and retreated into the sitting room.

"I think that tea's brewed now!" I said, laughing.

She brought a tray into the room. I told her to sit down and I poured, knowing it would be Earl Grey and I wouldn't have to be bothered with milk and sugar. A companionable silence followed and I didn't feel as I usually did with Glenda, that I had to perform or amuse.

We just seemed to gel together. It was like a scene in a very good play. Stan had enlightened me about this when explaining the finer points of Beckett and Pinter. So, I just sipped my tea and savoured the moment.

"Remember the time you showed me a bit of Greek dancing?" I said.

"Yes," she replied. "It was here wasn't it?"

"Aye, lass," I said, feeling it appropriate to drop into a West Yorkshire brogue.

"Aye, lad, 'appen," she returned.

"You better now, our lass?"

"Aye, lad 'am reet!"

"Well, I'd best be goin' then, Mrs, 'Olroyd," I joked. "Weer's me 'at and coat?"

Glenda's eyes, usually a dull grey, shone.

"Don't go, Dave," she said.

I didn't. I slept the night there, holding her in my arms, she suffering, while I stroked and gently fondled her plaited, bruised and golden hair. During the night, I gently sang snatches of the medieval carol and after sleeping for a bit, I woke to her gently snoring. I stroked her hair again and buried my nose in it. A bit rank, I thought but I felt a stiffening in my loins and profound compassion for her, and her sex well up from somewhere. Suddenly remembering and sensing her stirring, I gave her a special hug and nibbled her earlobe playfully. She squeezed my arms in return.

"Listen, Glenda, I remember it. The Maidens came when I was in my mother's bower; something, something,

The Baillie beareth the bell away

The lily, the lily, the rose I lay,

The baillie beareth the bell away."

I forgot a lot but some were archetypal images and I knew she was into Jung.

"The silver white, the gold so red

The rose they fell in fold,

and through the glass window shines the sun

And why should I die so young?"

She turned her head and planted a soft and lingering kiss on my mouth. Foul as her taste was, there was something sacredly intimate about it. She was my Goose-Girl again, my Lawrence Woman, my Goddess, my Muse.

We talked occasionally through the night, nothing much but our words seemed to drop down into deep wells of significance, reverberating echoes of voiceless meaning, of affirmation. Church bells throughout the universe, the Birds of Paradise.

The next morning, I gently kissed her forehead and left. As it was early, I wandered uptown to James Street, making my apologies for an unused bed to my temporary Landlady and went on to eat a hearty breakfast. Something had been consummated, the ground had shifted beneath our feet and even if I never saw her again, I thought, we had connected. My heart singing, I took the earliest train back to Victoria and then back to West Yorkshire. A page had most definitely been turned.

'Something understood.

The Land of Spices.'

George Herbert's great poem resonated in my soul the whole of the journey back up north.

Chapter 45

I was beginning to like being back up here a little more. Every Friday evening, Eliot Ness came for his rent. I noticed a good thing about northerners, that they were more inclined, like Irishmen and Scots, to put you at your ease. My landlord and I would share a joke and a glass of malt and he would sign my rent book, pocket his cash and leave with a cheery 'See you next week, Dave!'

However, the job was beginning to get me down and although I liked the lads, I felt almost heart-broken for them. On my third week, Jack called me into his office, seeing I wasn't happy. I warned him I might not be staying long and told him I still had things to sort out down south, loose ends and stuff. He knew and shared my political despair and kindly suggested that I joined the Communist Party of Britain (CPB), a break-away and less revisionist party than the Communist Party of Great Britain (CPGB). He mentioned a name, an ex-RAF bomber pilot in Otley, of all places just over the border in Tory North Yorkshire. Jack had hopes for a Labour government, which I shared but my despair and cynicism was such that I expected little.

I knew Stan was courting an Irish girl, or London Irish at least and he was supply teaching in the great city. Tony C, coolly building his career as a college lecturer, remained in Brighton and as I considered these two blokes my best mates, I hoped to keep in touch. Tony had some of my books and art materials, so it was a good excuse to go and see him and to hit the London and Brighton trains, my 'Lotus Land'. I seemed to be recovering from Glenda and had little desire to see her again, though I wished her well. I still cherished my home-made Stalin icon and kept it, caressing it even sometimes, in my right breast pocket.

I have mentioned that the meteorological atmosphere was heavier up north but something else was becoming apparent, a certain 'swinishness' in the air. Norman Mailer had recently referred to that in the States; I read it in the Encounter magazine, a Trotskyite periodical that I occasionally indulged in. Maybe it was the emergence of what looked like a serial killer on the loose but I began to despair at what felt like a gratuitous nastiness in the air.

The word games Stan and I used to play, brought forth in me a renewed passion for poetry, particularly in the ballad form and my romanticism encouraged a passion for the Border ballads, I was half Scots after all. Just before leaving Brighton, I had enjoyed researching them and anything that moved me - all of them usually - I either memorised or scribbled down in my notebook. They seemed to go straight to my guts, expressing a primordial grief almost beyond words and with a superb and stoic economy, making Shakespeare and modern poets look effusive. Yet in all of these I detected and half-heard a woman's voice, a bit like my Scots Mum but more resembling any nameless old crone in our dark and cruel past. They seemed the poetry of the people. The old girls at the back of the cave? Could they point to that 'aboriginal disaster', which the great Cardinal Newman wrote so expressively about? Stanzas came to my mind from 'The Black Douglas.' Anon:

'Out of the lady's grave grew a bonny, red rose,

And out of the Knight's a brier..

And they twa met, and they twa plat

And fain they would be near;

And a the world might ken right weel,

They were true lovers dear.'

However, then came the bad thing, the gratuitous insult:

'But by and rade the Black Douglas,

And aye, but he was rough!

For he pull'd up the bonny brier

And flang't in St. Mary's Loch.'

An elderly Dutch lady, from 300 years before had known that too.

Chapter 46

One weekday lunchtime, I went to The Carlisle pub, just to forget myself amongst the crowd of Asian bus drivers, whores and racing punters. It was one of the first pubs to have a big TV screen and there was a constant racing commentary going, news flashes announced just a little of what I knew was the real horror happening in Chile and the current Heath Government disgusted me with its uncritical support of the US in the UN.

I went to the payphone outside the Saloon Bar and Snug, rang into work and told Jack I couldn't carry on. He was sympathetic but sounded disappointed and I agreed to call in for my wages and any holiday pay due on the next day.

I had befriended a few Hungarians in the St Paul's Road pub and one I particularly liked was little Joe. He had an open and friendly, innocent face, as I imagined Billy Budd looking. He told me about the Steel Works on the other side of Bradford where he worked. I relished something physical and I was feeling very much a 'worker', both spiritually and politically. Joe brought the odd Jamaican friend into the pub, big, powerful and guileless blokes like himself. I liked the idea; I was lost anyway but I thought Joe Stalin would have approved. I decided to see Hungarian Joe in the pub the following evening and look for accommodation, nearer the major bus routes but still in Manningham, which I had grown to like.

I found a large, damp-smelling room above a baker's at the bottom of Oak Lane, the hub of Manningham actually, with the bus stops just outside. It was shared accommodation and I liked the baker, a cheery soul and the tenant, Mike, I vaguely recognised from an older generation in the Jazz club in town. Still sporting an Acker Bilk type beard, swarthy, dark and beer-bellied, I disliked him but thought it a convenient stop-gap. There was a huge kitchen and a main entrance up the ubiquitous, clanging, iron staircase out the back. Some wag I noticed had painted in now peeling white emulsion, the letters 'V-3' on the Gothic like ventilation hood over the bakehouse. I wondered if some late '50s, early '60s Bradford Art College Student had done this; David Oxtoby, or his trendy inferior, David Hockney.

Mike gave me the run-down, all highly masculine and in a 'hail-fellow-well-met' fashion said I was welcome. He made it very obvious who was the boss, one of those Alpha male types I thought I had left behind in the playground and the Rugby Club years ago. He was the exact type of the 'Black Douglas' and I bear the scar over my left eye today as a witness to that.

He liked to make a day of his weekend drinking and as we 'messed' together, such was the arrangement that we had a ritual of doing the weekly shopping in Bradford town centre. I introduced him to Malc in the meat market who was merrily chaffing with his old lady customers and other jolly butchers across the aisles. I saw his face darken as I introduced him to Mike. Of course, Malc being a jazz drummer, he would have known Mike from years ago at the Jazz Club, Bradford's only pretensions in the early '60s to being 'hip'. Mike had been the compere and I could just imagine him, the overbearing, beer-bellied Yorkshire sod.

It had been an ordeal shopping with him, bargains and 'good value' being the main topic and I think in the course of our conversation he was beginning to suss out that he might have a 'Fletcher Christian' on board. Clutching my arm fiercely at one point, while we were both enjoying a pint in the Market Tavern, he threatened that any hint of 'dope' in the flat and he would throw me down the stairs.

I was expected to join him back in Manningham later in the evening at the Park Hotel. I dreaded it but I seemed now to be his 'creature' and anyway he was buying the drinks, so I thought I would humour him while I looked for another place and I was too knackered after a day at the Foundry to look around in my spare time. That night across the bar I noticed Elliot Ness who gave me a hearty wink. I regretted then leaving his flat as I had become fond of the old bugger. The Black Douglas Redux! I detested Mike now, an overbearing and vulgar brute, pompous and condescending with it. Christ, he could drink though and closing time found us down in the old Edwardian villas, that harboured the drinking clubs of the Baltic states, groaning then under Soviet occupation, that I was to come to know much later, bedsit land and haunt of a mass killer.

I sobered up slightly in the Lithuanian Club, a haven for out of hours drinkers, coppers posing as human beings and as usual, there he was again, Elliot Ness! Up until fairly recently, most English blokes avoided the place.

Lithuanians, Latvians and Estonians were mostly ex-SS and violently anti-Russian and Polish, their homelands known as 'Captive Nations' in the Cold War rhetoric of the time. When the old Wehrmacht marching songs started up, chairs and fists would start flying as ex-British Forces blokes got stuck in.

It was calmer these days and Mike relished the dour atmosphere, tapping his feet to 'Erika' the marching song of the Waffen SS. I was introduced to tall and hard-faced men who bowed stiffly and shook my hand as Mike intoned warnings in my ear as to what not to say, knowing my political leanings.

It was stirring in a sinister way, 'Devil's Music' as I joined in the chorus and even the foot stamping.

"Und das heist Erika!"

It sent shivers down my spine, even though my skull cinema evoked goose-stepping and bawling Germans soldiers.

I looked forward to meeting little Joe and his Jamaican pals the following evening though. We were to be introduced in a Lumb Lane pub, frequented by black guys and then go on to the Spotted House, on the Keighley Road, which was a great venue for music, even since the youth of my overbearing new landlord. We often reminisced about the old Bradford Jazz Club, something we had in common. It was full of big, beery and heavily-bearded Yorkshiremen who I didn't particularly like.

I seldom went into The Queens or The Percy, which was short for The Perseverance and also popular with the Jamaican boys. I only popped in when I went to the launderette next door, the couple of times I needed to in my few weeks back from the 'Sarth'. It was rough, really rough. The joke was that the punters mooched around the joint with daggers in their teeth and that was just the women!

"Ya' fuckin' black bastard!" screeched one of the working girls who used this pub as a base, just as I opened the main bar door.

I managed to catch sight of Joe with some crew.

"Dave!" he cried cheerily as I headed for the bar.

I stepped past the throng clamouring around the loud lady and met my company, a bonny brunette, a real Irish colleen and a couple of black men, Jamaicans by the look of them. One of them resembled a huge and handsome Adonis, with a face of almost beatific innocence.

"Yes, man! You'll be Dave! Me, Curtis, man!" he said, gripping my hand firmly.

Then Miller, a crazy but benevolent-looking man whom I'd seen around and was working some girls around the Lane. I doubted Miller was the object of the aforesaid lady's ire, he seemed the genteelest of his profession and would prove a great workmate.

"Yeah, man," he said, shaking my hand.

He had some sort of attention deficit disorder and immediately moved sideways to an ancient upright piano, to make a splendid if cacophonous riff and a couple of scales, while chatting up a group of his girls and appearing to be asking what the hassle was about. He re-joined our company with a huge grin on his face.

"Ras clart!" he exclaimed, putting his arm around me and leaning into our company.

"Miller, ya cunt!" said the Irish girl, with Joe's arm warmly and protectively around her.

I guessed she was no St Bernadette but the love in her eyes, as she gazed up at the ginger-haired and radiantly innocent-looking Joe, was a joy. Curtis was just a beaming and magnificent rock of happiness holding us all together. I imagined Billy Budd again and his comrades of the 'Foretop' just like this onboard HMS Indomitable in 1796!

We bonded in that first round then with Miller staying behind to attend to his business, we went on to the Spotted House, posher and with some good jazz. It was also easier to hear each other speak and Joe and Curtis filled me in on the job. I was to meet them tomorrow morning outside the works at Low Moor, one of the oldest steel mills in England. Joe and Curtis still had some of that deference of our class to learning and seemed glad that I was to be their workmate.

"You'll learn a lot from us, Dave, about real life," said Joe. "What men's work is like!"

Pat pretended to bridle at this.

"You blokes-ha-big lumps o' shite ye are," she said. "Ya don't know REAL work!"

All was good fun though and I left early as I needed to be fit the next day. These were tough blokes; innocent and kindly but hard as nails and I would have my work cut out trying to keep up with them.

Little Joe, my 'Billy Budd', looked like any pressed English sailor back in those days and Jamaicans and freed American slaves were ubiquitous in Nelson's wooden dreadnoughts. I was also not yet too hooked on the booze to be unable to stop drinking, so having 'Dropped Anchor' I smugly headed back up the road to dark Michael's grim castle.

I arrived at Osborne Steel the next morning at a reasonable hour, in case I was taken on for the afternoon/evening shift. The foreman, a Mr Ackroyd would be around and I was told to just ask for him.

"What you want to see that daft ole bugger for?" asked the security man.

A massive, corrugated-iron, open-ended shed loomed up past warehoused billets of steel, supported on what looked like 18th-century brickwork. I got glimpses of Herculean-looking men, rowing at some rolling device under an overhead gantry. I introduced myself to a couple of blokes who were sitting on their heels, drenched in sweat. One of them, a black man, took a swig from a bottle of Lucozade.

"Ah, the new lad," said the other, a white man who volunteered to take me to find the 'gaffer'.

We found him in one of the two changing and restrooms. I quickly sussed that it was just by coincidence that the larger one happened to be the base of the black guys; Curtis had warned me about that. There was to and fro between the men and no overt racism at all. I stepped into a genial chaos, Jamaican and Yorkshire voices in banter with Mr Ackroyd.

"Get thi' face weshed," said one obviously from South Yorkshire.

This was followed by ribald cheers then I detected Curtis's broad grin in the gloom of the hut.

"Ras, Captain!" he said, slapping his muscular thigh.

"'Nah, lad," said George. "So you're t'new lad - must be fecking mad!"

He deputised Miller who was on a quick break, to take me to "t'stores" and get me fixed up with safety boots and gloves, visor and protective helmet.

Any road, I was on the team and I got to stack. Mervin, a criminal-looking Jamaican whom I had seen around Bradford, showed me how to stack the completely rolled billets, black, hot and tough to work with. We both resembled medieval devils, equipped with long-handled tongs which Mervin showed me how to 'fettle' at the back of the furnace, where Miller, the comic pimp and musician from the previous night, presided. His task was to put the 'pigs' of steel through the furnace and by judging the right gaps, give us our well-deserved breaks.

The main engine of the apparatus were four massive rollers, half-submerged under cast iron plating through which the 'pig' was gradually stretched and squeezed into the long billets which Mervin and I stacked on old railway lines. With a Captain or foreman to sway the gantry and two big black men, stripped to the waist, to nudge the 'pig' through ever-narrowing rolling pulleys it looked a highly dangerous but antique and aesthetically pleasing sight.

There was a rhythm to it also and though it might be racist or condescending to say so, the beauty of it seemed to suit these heroic, almost chthonic figures. A sea-shanty seemed called for and I thought to myself, yes, Shaller Brown, originally a Jamaican one.

I think that sight, the gently rolling figures, the chiaroscuro, white/black/white, the fires from the furnace, the dark shadows, Burnt Umbers and Indigos over the gantry, the sweat reflecting indirect and sporadic Yorkshire sunlight and the red heat from the steel ingots was simply beautiful and reignited my joy in pictorial art, though this was more a ballet, manly and elemental.

The Jamaican guys had got to calling me Catweazle, after a kids' TV character of the time, maybe because I sported a beard then, either that or my fart-arsed way of presenting myself. I noticed some of the men would send themselves up, making me the representation of 'Da Man'! Big Roy, one of the most intelligent men I ever worked with, had a habit of rolling his eyes like the 'simple nigger' portrayed by Stepin Fetchit, the first black actor to have a successful film career, in ancient US films I used to see as a kid at the local Saturday morning matinees in our flea pit of a cinema. They knew I was a softie grammar school white boy who meant well and they were remarkably tolerant of that.

Later that day, when Curtis gave me a lift back to Manningham, I rhapsodised about the job, even though my wrists burnt where my grip with the tongs had slipped or where a flying cinder had winged me.

"It's de felicity, man!" he said.

I was amused by the use of a word which had died out in England but I saw what he meant. These lovely Jamaican blokes had got the job sussed. Ever after, until I had to leave, I looked forward to work and Friday payday with the British Queen, a Tetley's pub, right next to the works doing a roaring trade, with huge, thirsty men quaffing pints, a sight out of Viking Saga!

It went on for a few weeks and then the Black Douglas, the bad thing, happened. It wasn't about the job. I'd done a double shift and even though I was pretty fit by that time, I was exhausted and retired to my grim bed after a couple of joints down in the dismal community lounge. Mike meanwhile was in the pub. I had just turned out the light and was descending into blissful, dreamy sleep when I felt the bed covers yanked off me. I was dragged across the room by a drunken, darkly violent Mike. I remember the first blow but must have been a bit concussed, as I don't remember any more, only staggering to my feet and beyond fear, not able to see for the blood streaming down my face. I screamed at him and he stood still, swaying drunkenly, muttering something about him smelling 'dope'. It was when I brushed the blood away with my pyjama sleeve that I noticed the signet ring. I spat blood in his face from a now swollen mouth and continued shrieking imprecations until the other flatmate, a timid and boring journalist from the local rag made a plaintive query as to what was going on. Mike slouched off and after I glared at the hack, so did he.

"But by and rade the Black Douglas

And aye, but he was rough!

For he pull'd up the bonny briar

And flang't in St Mary's Loch."

Cromwellian!

The next day, Curtis and Joe moved my stuff into Joe's house which he shared with his uncle and a seedy-looking Hungarian cousin, a bigger Joe. By the look on Mike's face as we clanged up the iron stairs, I would guess my moral victory was assured. He was white with fear.

I had a little room next to Little Joe and it was like being back home with my brother as a kid. In his charming way, he would knock on the thin partition wall in our attic when he and Tina were about to make love and I would dive coyly beneath my sheets. Sometimes he would just knock gently and say:

"Goodnight, Dave. God Bless, sleep well, my friend!"

They were good times but I felt that I had stared into the jaws of hell elsewhere.

Thrawn is the word I'm looking for, an adjective of Scottish origin, meaning perverse and ill-tempered. I just knew I had to get down to Brighton again, or London, so I still hadn't settled. One Saturday after payday, I took a seat on the 10.36 train departing Leeds Station. After that, everything's a blank.

I woke up in hospital on the way back north from London so I must have been hitchhiking. Apparently, a couple of days earlier I had been found unconscious at the side of the slipway from the Stevenage exit of the A1, by a passing lorry driver. He must have been a real knight of the road, as I was wearing my RAF greatcoat and would have been near invisible, as it was dusk when he stopped and rang the emergency services.

My few weeks of fairly healthy living and hard work helped me make a quick recovery, although the Doc at Stevenage was concerned about probable mental issues. I had been given a lumbar puncture and a stiffish dose of barbs had been found in my bloodstream. Slowly and embarrassingly, I began to realise that I had spent all my money and scored some downers, my way of 'eating' my alcohol and possibly a way I had of finding temporary oblivion.

I still don't know to this day what I had been doing. Did I stand outside Glenda's flat as I did before, smoking cigarette after cigarette? Did I stand under the arches of the West Pier, one of my most evocatively interesting places, tripping out of my mind?

Chapter 47

I'd put in the hours at the steelworks, so when I called in for my cards, I was pleased to find I had a bit of a wedge of cash.

"See ya, man- Catweasel!" shouted Curtis.

I said goodbye to the rest of the boys and almost miraculously, instead of heading straight for the British Queen for a couple of pints, I decided to walk back down the Wakefield Road into Bradford then maybe reward myself with a drink in town and say hello to my mates in the Meat Market. I still flattered myself with the thought that I had the booze under control.

As I walked down the hill, I was amazed, it being a fine day, how superb the view was across the industrial defile of Bradford and to the Moors beyond. Something stirred in me and I started to wonder if it might not be a bad idea to get away from the red-light district of Manningham. A reconnaissance might be in order and I didn't trust that the relative truce between Dad and I would continue long.

I had a pint or two in the Manville and Jacob's Well, near the Exchange Station where so long ago I had fantasised about joining Julie Christie on the London train. I noted in the Well how it had become quite a haven for radical young people, working-class mainly, unlike the bourgeois Trots with whom I had fraternised in Brighton. The Manville made me think about Glenda again and in a fit of common sense, I gulped down the dregs of my pint and left her ghost there, forever, I hoped.

Heading back down into town, I enjoyed looking at the hard-bitten and stoical faces of my now fellow Yorkshire folk and the seductively beautiful Punjabi girls. I liked the way my Asian neighbours had blossomed from the emaciated and tubercular old men of my youth into the strapping young lads and lasses I saw now, despite a revival in the hard right. I felt full of optimism for the future, knowing in my bones that I only needed to sort myself out.

Malc and Pete were joshing and joking with Russian Annie, a well-loved, though tragic Bradford character. A huge and muscular Russian peasant woman, she pretended to frighten kids when I was young and getting older herself now, tended not to brandish her ubiquitous staff but lean on it, whistling her party-piece bird calls at the various butchers' stalls. What scant hair she had - rumour was the Nazis experimented on her ovaries - was covered in a knitted woollen cap and the whole of the front of her man's suit jacket was decorated with British Army Badges. Today she had a posy projecting from her close-fitting headwear, a present from the kindly lady everybody loved in the Flower Stall. The Butchers, rough and hearty as they were, never saw poor Annie short and Pete and Malc had a meat parcel or a pound note ready for her.

I felt a pain in my left buttock and suddenly Mother Russia was beaming down at me.

"You Good Boy! You friend of Malc, you friend of mine!"

She proffered her massive hand, I gave her a tribute and she was off for another conquest, great staff aloft, whistling and raising waves of ribald cheers ringing down the aisles of Rawson Market.

"Dave, old friend!" said Malc, laughing heartily. "What can I do for you?"

Pete Taplin winked over to me from his stall opposite and hoisted a huge side of beef into the freezer behind him.

Anna always left a hush in her wake so Malc had time for a chat. He invited me to dine that night and when I told him of my plan, he enthused that it was a great one. He had one or two places in mind, a caravan and a couple of cottages.

Malc had long ago joined the flight from the city and now lived in semi-rural Cottingley, a fine old village and well-appointed housing estate near Bingley. Sorted, I went on to Bingley to look for a job at the little Labour Exchange there. That's how simple it was then and I was able to report back at 'Dotheboys' by teatime, possible accommodation sorted and a job. Malc had offered me a bed for a couple of nights. And so began my pastoral interlude.

My job was at Jonas Woodend's Springs in Harden, a village not far from Bingley on the Haworth Road. It's now been gentrified and turned into upmarket flats. Then it was an old family firm, typical Bronte Country and probably originally a cotton or woollen mill. It had good union representation and the job itself of grinding the footings of industrial-sized springs in a vertical and automatic grinder needed little effort or intelligence, only some attention. So long as I kept my eye on the swishing and trundling device, I could have a joke with a colleague or roll a cigarette. I was now smoking Golden Virginia and I fought the monotony by recalling lines of poetry, painting imaginary pictures and recollecting some of Stan's and my wilder nights in the Bristol.

When I eventually moved into my old but decently-equipped caravan over the fields, I felt that I was living in a rural, early 19th-century idyll. I could have been the intense and idealistic Paul Morel out of 'Sons and Lovers' hurrying over the fields and down the lanes of North Nottinghamshire to meet his Miriam. It was a twenty-minute walk over a field and down a walled packhorse track, of the sort which abounded in these parts, to Goit Stock, the tight and hidden valley where my new home was situated. There was even, up in the woods and on the high road back to Bingley, an 18th-century folly, St David's Castle which had something of the fairytale and Arthurian mystery that I was connecting with, in the northern landscape.

The site manager, George, turned out to be an amiable fascist, who quite took to me. He offered me odd jobs around the site, painting old caravans and helping to refurbish the more dilapidated ones which I loved doing. Though he was rude to Winston, one of my old Jamaican comrades who came to see me with his white wife, he soon backed down when I told him off. He was partly mad, like a lot of country people I was to find. Many people of a more conservative disposition seemed to be paranoid about the new Labour government and full of venom for the famed Arthur Scargill, now in his pomp.

Apart from the beginning of the 'Ripper' murders, things seemed quite good in the north. There was little shortage of work, Vietnam was nearly over and some sort of detente appeared to be working with the Soviet Union. OK, I felt a bit lost as an artist and when I had time to think, it occurred to me that my exile in the south and metropolis had failed. I consoled myself with the thought that at least I had tried and was now in the process of starting a new adventure.

I still had my political idealism but little bitterness. Indeed, when the boss's son brought the wages around personally on a Friday, I shook hands with him.

"Ah, you must be David!" said the gentlemanly and obviously public-school educated young man.

"Yes, Mr John!" I replied with neither insolence nor grudge, adopting the customary language when addressing the squire or young master.

I joked to myself and Reg, the shop steward, that come the revolution we would let young Master Woodhead keep his job, his Jag and his big house up by the moor. Master John graciously laughed and in his deferential courtesy and charm, I thought I saw something of the look of the doomed young Subalterns of the Somme and Ypres battles of only 60 years ago.

I seemed to be breaking out in a rash of common sense. I bought some strong working shoes and a pair of well-fitting hiking boots with my first wage and slowly started to build up a collection of art materials. I bought Ordnance Survey maps of the area, determined to explore every inch of the lush and bracing countryside around.

When the first rains of autumn came, I rejoiced to hear it pattering on my caravan roof just over my head and when I couldn't see out of my windows for the scything and puddling rain, I felt that I was in a yacht at sea, or even becalmed in harbour. I was still reading my Hopkins' poetry and building a library of slender and portable volumes paid for out of any spare change on my fortnightly shopping trips to Keighley, Leeds or Bradford.

Memorising lines of poetry helped to lighten the monotony of machine work and keep my mind and soul alive. Even the metronomic beat of the vertical grinder - *swish, grind and swish* - beat the time of my mental recitations: "Oh, is it not passing grand," - *swish, grind* – "To be a King," – *swish, grind* – "And to ride in triumph" – *swish* – "To Persepolis!" Followed by a Teutonic stamp of the feet and a final, Wehrmacht-style click of the heels!

They were good days and my soul seemed to settle.

I liked to drink in Bingley only a short bus ride away or a delightful 40 minutes' walk down the tight and winding Harden Valley, so beautiful and pastoral that if it wasn't for a lusher and slightly harsher light, I could be walking through the lovely mystical landscapes of Samuel Palmer and William Blake in Sussex and Kent, down on the sunny south coast. I could even imagine myself as a young Billy Caspar with his hawk, Kes, on his walk through the woods, near t'pit head in South Yorkshire, missing his dad and feeling alienated, but full of love for his only mate, his pet kestrel.

I drank in the Ferrands Arms, named after the old aristocratic family who used to own the land around here, some of it was park-like and incredibly reminiscent of a Jane Austen landscape. I felt at home with the Bingley Training College students but strangely alienated too. I was yet to learn that you can't step back into the same river twice. Somehow, I was losing my student-like patina of innocence and for all my socialism, I still felt that I couldn't get on with the local yokels, preferring the whores, deviants and dykes of the Manningham red-light district.

I walked the length and breadth of the glorious heather heathland, ancient green roads and packhorse roads around Bingley and Goit Stock, named after a delightful little waterfall. I discovered Templar remains, follies and stone circles and this was only on the edge of the Dales. One Sunday before winter really set in, I enjoyed a mammoth hike up the old Coach Road of the Ferrands by their great Estate called St Ives, situated on its own plateau above the Aire and Harden valley. I walked on unpeopled tracks and old quarry workings and even a stretch of ancient Romano-British road over to Haworth where I visited the Parsonage, continuing to Top Withens, rumoured to be the inspiration for Emily Bronte's great and barbaric novel. In the gathering dusk on the way back, exhausted but exhilarated I could almost imagine 'Soldier Emily' stalking the heather and crags behind me. Her ghost was said to haunt the moor tops all around.

Calling into a pub near the top of the steep main street, I chaffed gently with a couple of old blokes in the taproom who sat contentedly with their dogs and enjoyed a companionable game of Dominos. I noticed how people up north seemed to age more gracefully and it was good to see dogs welcome in bars, not just for the county set, as in the Home Counties. To the clacking of doms, we carried on an amiable if desultory conversation. Cannily, the old boys had sussed out my plans and where I'd come from.

"Tha' likes thi' ale, lad, tha' knaws," said one.

I heartily concurred, saying frothy beer took a bit of time to get used to after the flat stuff down south.

"If tha' can fuck and fry bacon, lad-tha's welcome i' 'Aworth!" said another.

With the rejoinder, that I didn't know about the first bit but I could certainly fry bacon, I drained my glass and with a cheery wave was on my way.

Home, at last, I thought to myself as I braced myself for the long but uplifting walk back to Bingley, up through Crossroads, then sheer exultation, as I breasted Long Leigh, then Harden Moor where the views encompassed to the north, the Dales, Lothersdale and upper Worth Valley, to the east the brooding and majestic massif of Ilkley Moor and south, the high fields above Bradford and a far distant Leeds. To my back lay the moors over Lancashire and Halifax way and such poetic names: Mount Tabor; Ogden Moor; the Forest of Trawden; Queensbury and Scarlet Heights. Scudding purple shadows glided up the fell sides like the hand of God. The sense of freedom and glory was palpable!

This was my first experience of living in the countryside and though hardly roughing it or camping, the caravan made me feel closer to nature. I could almost sense the pull of a full moon, particularly if it hung over the west, framed by the surrounding moorland and spruce forest and for the first time I began to sense in my bones the joy of nature. I got Thoreau's 'Walden.' out of the library and felt privileged by sheer chance, to become an aficionado of the new British nature writers: Ronald Blythe; Roger Deakin and Richard Maybe and the Scots-American, John Muir.

I was sophisticated enough intellectually to know that I wasn't seeing nature unmediated. I was embracing what I thought was the moon, of course, but reflected in a puddle, through happy memories of contemplating the end-of-chapter vignettes in Enid Blyton books, half-remembered catches of ballad and minstrelsy. Already though, I was rediscovering for myself a life of the mind, a not unexamined life, the best definition to me today for that dread word, intellectual. For all some of my new Bingley College lecturer friends' academism, it was always a thrill to see them in the student pubs and to exchange our thoughts and perceptions about things.

I still worked in 't'mill, although boring, it was a good place, civilized, and I often had a chat with the convener and lady chargehand, who being Bradfordians tended to scoff a little at the conservatism and deferential attitudes of the Aire Valley locals. Peasants' they called them.

In Harden village itself, there was a very well-run launderette and I did my usual routine the first few washes, filling a washer rapidly and rushing to the pub next door. I ceased this after being accosted by Melvyn, the very camp proprietor, who after offering a cig, liked a chat. I had enough experience of gay guys down south to know that he wasn't chatting me up. He was just a bit lonely, intrigued by me and was bored. It turned out that he knew Mum who had worked in a confectioner's shop next to his tobacconist in Girlington, the next inner-city parish to Manningham, though not quite as bohemian.

He adored my Mum and told me that he owned some property in Eldwick, the posh suburb up Otley Road from the Careys and with a garden sloping down to the lovely Shipley Glen, a famous beauty spot for most Bradfordians. He offered me the chalet next door to him, furnished and no strings attached, for a very reasonable rent. I leapt at the chance to deepen my experience of fresh air and the bucolic life!

So, passed two of the finest summers of my youth, 1975 and 1976. I still socialised a bit, stopped smoking for 6 months and Malc, an enthusiastic cross-country runner, encouraged me to train with him. Malc and Pete on their days off in summer would take me up the Dales to the Folk Concert in Hubberholme on one weekend of camping, in lovely upper Wharfedale. One special day, on his Wednesday off, Malc pulled up at the Chalet in his Land-rover to take me for a run, up Pen-Y-Ghent. I wasn't fit enough to keep up with him all the time and lay beside a crystalline mountain stream gasping with pain and joy until he rejoined me and we both wolfed a huge bag of his mutton sandwiches with horseradish dressing. We drank about eight pints in a farmers' pub in Horton-in-Ribblesdale and I believed I would never feel so physically vibrant and well again.

I had another spiritual experience, on seeing the purple-grey shadow of a cloud as it crept up the fell-side of far Whernside. The shadow of a deity's hand, the fitful sun highlighting the mountain limestone crags and screes seemed to reveal the very bones of the earth itself. I think the landscape painter in me was born then.

Chapter 48

There is a beautiful scene in "Dr Zhivago", one among many of my favourite films of my teens and Glenda and I saw it together. The Poet Yuri, in a brief reprieve from such tragic times in the Russian Civil War, is seen returning to meet up with Lara (Julie Christie) in winter, at their old dacha. To the music of balalaikas and the heartrending 'Lara's theme', Yuri (Omar Sharif) marches over to the desk, now covered with snow from a leak in the roof and sweeping it with a gloved hand, reveals the woodwork of his old writing desk, beautiful mahogany with a gloriously antique patina. It seemed also to suggest magically, the joy of the artist's, or poet's work, the promise of the pristine canvas, the sensuous potential in the naked page; the eye's 'Latin.'

That's how I felt that first Christmas morning in my chalet. I had only moved in the week before and I felt just like Yuri must have done as I looked out on a winter wonderland, my long and sloping garden leading down to a drystone wall with great elms and oaks obscuring the ravine of Shipley Glen; and beyond, snow-clad bracken and heather leading up to Baildon Moor and slightly to the left, the huge and brooding hulk of Ilkley Moor and exquisite Wharfedale beyond; a winter wonderland, sleighbells and Lara's tune.

There were times when I felt a bit lonely and often it was such a joy to get a letter, either from Stan who had returned to Merseyside with his lovely Irish wife, Adrienne or sometimes Tony, still living in Brighton, that before I opened them, I went through the ritual of a makeshift bath, a change of clothes and at last a cup of coffee and a roll-up before I opened and read them. Stan, a railway Guard now, always included a comical cartoon and some hilarious story about the railways of Lancashire and the Wirral Peninsular.

I had a succession of jobs; labouring I liked still, as I had no responsibilities and I was content at this time to just 'be' and build up my strength. If asked, I would say that I didn't know where I was going 'But I ain't lost!' Somewhere back down my timeline I had crossed that invisible class barrier, in this, the most snobbish country in the world. I was no longer a student but working-class, even worse, a drifter and unclassifiable.

I enjoyed my 'Walden Pond' period though, however false it was in some ways. The nearest bus and railway termini being either in Saltaire or in Bingley, both of them nearly 800 feet below me so that when I came back with my shopping and other supplies on a Payday, through the woodland and then up old bridleways or ancient sheep trails, I felt that I was coming home to some Shangri-la in the clouds. These were good times; yes, the occasional pang of loneliness, of youth passing me by, anomie and even alienation but all so thrillingly fashionable! But it was also a time of physical wellbeing and even some spiritual insights. I had started taking the liberal Roman Catholic weekly, the 'Tablet' and I read it intensely. I think I have already said that I had a copy of Simone Weil's collective and edited works at my bedside.

I remember one gorgeous July Saturday, opening a library copy of Jane Austen's 'Sense and Sensibility' and not picking up a cigarette until I had finished the book and my stomach craving food, I stood up, staggering almost, muscles cramped, my soul rinsed and my mind alive and on fire. Throwing my roll-up away, I felt hooked by something else and didn't pick up another cig till going to university in late 1976.

I suppose I was a happy Pagan at this time, suffering no illnesses and enjoying a fairly athletic body. One late spring evening I got caught out as night fell, on the smaller, Baildon Moor, a part of the great Ilkley Moor massive. I panicked somewhat not realising how little light pollution there was in Yorkshire and I felt the most profound joy as I gradually got my bearings; and then a gloriously silver moon rose just as I avoided stumbling into a pond, a huge glaucous moon reflected therein. The owls hooted from a nearby thicket of hawthorn and my heart sang. I imagined a Goddess, androgynously Bowie-like but brunette, very much a woman and a liberated one. I also imagined her smiling upon me.

I read Wordsworth's 'Prelude' voraciously and made a mental note of taking it with me to my dream desert island.

They were great times in retrospect but at the time I now realise, I felt a nagging anomie, a searing sense of my irrelevance.

One day, I felt it was time to leave the realm of the Hawthorn Goddess behind; I was getting restless again and worried about intellectual and political isolation. Feeling the need for some discipline and connection, I decided on going to university as a mature student. It might mean my getting some sort of a grant but at that time, if I was accepted, fees were low and often waived and I could still sign on and study as well as taking on part-time work. I also was intrigued not only to learn about current left-wing ideology, particularly feminism and to be honest, I wanted to meet more feminists.

One afternoon in that idyllic summer of '76, Graham and Kate Carey, my Lecturer friends, invited me to some Summer School public lectures. I enjoyed going to hear and later to shake hands with Arthur Scargill and to see and hear the beautiful and intellectually-challenging Juliet Mitchell give a Lacan-based critique of 'Wuthering Heights'. I didn't understand a word of it but I swooned to her blonde radiance and voice, imagining Jane Austen's Eleanor Dashwood sounding just like her. American summer school students, gushing and drooling, mobbed her afterwards, while I muttered platitudes to dear old Arthur, then almost untouchable and even now my God and my 'once and future King.'

I went for an interview in the hideously brutalist University building in Bradford, up past the art college of my halcyon early youth, a hostile and militaristic commissionaire and introduced myself to Ken Smith, as instructed by one of Graham's uni colleagues in the 'Interdisciplinary Human Studies' a charming northerner about my age; bearded, unassuming and friendly.

Chapter 49

I liked the university staff on our course, all were about my age, politically sound and mainly Oxford men and a couple of women. There were also a few mature students about my age and our sister course, 'Peace Studies', seemed mainly made up of older students, cosmopolitan also, continental and British militants and some mystics, ageing Christians and exiles from the idealistic 'Commune' movement of a few years before.

It was exciting to be introduced to our personal tutors and it felt almost as I had imagined my old man's Bomber Command comrades doing 'chumming up' for aircrew in those dark but exhilarating days of their youth. My Tutor was Ian Vine, an unassuming and hirsute Psychology Lecturer.

Two of the most attractive of the new students were G, an animated, highly intelligent, yet strangely philistine and extremely sexy ex-Canterbury student and her room-mate in Halls, A, tall and dreamy but with the gentlest of eyes and endearingly big ears, with Brighton written all over her:

"Oh, I bummed around for a bit before coming here," she said to me.

Both were to prove highly PC and very feminist, nauseatingly so, as I came to find.

A woman nearer my age, Sue, an intriguingly sexy and highly independent woman, a soul sister almost, I became close to, both intellectually and spiritually. I would say she was the one person I most regret losing touch with and the best reason for my decision to go to uni. Jim, a strange lad nearer my age seemed a nice fellow, not so much an academic but a bit of a mystic and an autodidact. He struggled academically but I liked him very much. He had the benevolently fanatic and spiritual look, like Dominic back in London, of a Saint Aidan or Columba.

Most of the youngsters were pleasant but more conventional than the art students I had known and a bit tame. A startling brunette from Southampton, Elsa, surprisingly seemed to take to me and I hit it off with a mischievous, anarchic Jewish Girl, Ruth who became a drinking companion and friend for a while. For the rest, it was the socialists who I got on with, Angie and Ginny at first, many of them much more serious and committed than I had imagined, even more so than I.

Drifting between the two student bodies, the Peaceniks and our more staid but younger set, I set eyes for the first time on Steph whom I usually assumed to exist in a permanent haze of dope, drifting mystically above the floor in a maroon and velvet, sequined gown, with I imagined wistfully, little bells and shards of glinting mirror; the Queen of Elfland. But we weren't to be introduced until later.

Things were ok at home for a couple of weeks and the old man tried to show interest in some of my set books. I was finding increasingly though, his oppression of my mother beyond tolerance. Every day I was seeing vibrant and intelligent young women, aflame with the search for knowledge and a better society and though I might find one or two irritatingly ambitious for justice and radical change in society, I found my mother's acquiescence even more obscene and egged her on to resist him which only made things worse for her. I had the strongest feeling that she, even more than my father, wished me out of the house.

Contrary to my leftish beliefs, I was finding the semi-rural boorishness of the white working-class around Bingley, ugly and narrow, brutal, mean-spirited and Cromwellian. I had romanticised at first the genial poachers and 'outlaws' in the Bar at The Fisherman's, with their dog companions and gun talk, without realising how close I had been to the company of a sadistic and soon to be notorious serial killer, the 'Ripper'.

Poor Jim worried me. Like me, an older student, intense and eccentric and also like me something of an idealist and seeker. He rented a caravan up towards Haworth and not far from a couple of my favourite Bronteland pubs. He felt less relaxed about academia than I and was beginning to have a hard time with the other students. There was something strange but rather pure about him. Students were beginning to bore me now and I felt disgusted by the conformity underlying their superficial social deviance. They found Jim a bit queer and I suspect they looked on me as an old rogue and degenerate. But I liked him. He didn't have a bad bone in his body but he seemed a strange lad and looking at him on the few occasions that I saw him those days, he appeared fraught, a bit of a crank; and with his strong but kindly fanatical features, he reminded me of photos I had seen of the young Lawrence of Arabia.

Jim had been taken up by Gail and Alison as well as the motherly and spiritual Sue. Then they dropped him, ruthlessly I thought, after which Jim received some support from a very sweet and innocent looking Christian amongst our year, in a group that I grew to like but who had been eclipsed initially by my far more assertive feminist friends.

Feeling worried and low one day, having to find a place to live, I caught Jim walking down the road outside the Manville and suggested a drink. Sat in a corner with a tonic water, he poured out his heart. A Gloucestershire lad, from a small village, he had come up north to 'find his soul'. Not as hard-bitten as I was, he had spent time in the lovely Whitby on our county's northeast coast, then further inland, to West Yorkshire in isolated communities. He was disappointed by the simple life and like me, hoped for intellectual and spiritual companionship at University. Maybe, like me, he just needed a girl but his spiritual yearning was real and he claimed, vociferously in Seminars, that he had direct contact with a Higher Power and not a Christian one.

I often had a drink with my tutor Ian Vine; apparently, Jim's written work proved poor and the staff, my friends and contemporaries surmised that he felt alienated and had made a massive mistake in coming to university as a mature student. I felt almost the same myself at that time. The second-wave feminists now disturbed me and I was growing to heartily dislike them.

Drinking up, I promised to go and visit him. The large caravan he rented from a University Physics Professor, as it happens was close to where I had rented. He gave me his phone number; we shook hands and Jim headed for the Haworth/Colne bus.

I eventually found a room in Frizinghall, thanks to a charming Christian couple in the second year. The house was full of engineers and physics students, not my favourite people but it stood just a couple of houses up from one rented by a charismatic Feminist Lecturer on 'Peace Studies' along with other Quakers and activists. It wasn't too far from Mum's fish shop or Manningham and though I didn't like the area, dank and dreary and below the main Bingley road and near the railway line, it had reasonable access to Shipley and the Aire Valley beyond.

I took it and moved into a depressingly masculine atmosphere with the gloomy subaqueous light I had never quite got used to in Bradford.

However, I managed to settle down and enjoy my studies, still earning a few bob in the Uni bar and just the once going up Emm Lane by the great and bosky Manningham Park to see Mum at the chippy. She seemed glad to see me but I knew she felt happier after I left.

Settled, or at least so I thought, I gave Jim a call and agreed to drop by him on Saturday, my day off from the Uni bar and lectures. Enjoying the late Autumn air, I walked from Keighley Bus Station then up through Hainsworth, on the old packhorse trail I had discovered the months before. Striding down Long Lea towards Crossroads and Haworth beyond, I drank in the sweeping views over to Mount Tabor, Ogden Moor above Halifax and the green bliss of fields sweeping below to my left and all the way to the hills above Bradford. The last of the migrating curlews burbled and scolded me as I approached Long Lea Farm and Jim's Caravan.

I don't remember much but I enjoyed his company while detecting a certain defensive arrogance about him. Gail, to her credit, had visited him in her little Austin A30, which resembled her I always thought! And while I made appraising and somewhat sexist remarks about her intellect and physical attributes, Jim proved surprisingly dismissive of her. I got a bit tired of him, realising that he found me gross and a disappointment. Though no atheist or committed believer at the time, I found his 'hippie' mysticism tiresome and made the mistake of telling him so. However, we discovered some affinity talking about Whitby, a town I adored; even then he was dismissive of the locals there.

After a polite interval, I said goodbye and called in at the 'Guide' pub not far back up the hill, an old packhorse inn with splendid views over Bronteland and Lothersdale to the north, where I gratefully necked a couple of pints. I caught the bus back to Bradford and thence to my dreary new lodgings in Frizinghall.

About ten days' later, in December and approaching end-of-term, I bumped into a distraught Jim as I descended the mezzanine to IHS and Peace Studies. Jim was raving having just fled a lecture. I grabbed him and calmed him down, which I felt he wanted me to do, sat with him in our cosy foyer and asked what the trouble was. He said the Feminist/rationalist contingent had just ripped him to pieces in the lecture. He was humiliated and raging.

"Look," I said. "It's my birthday tomorrow. I'll come over and see you!"

Threatening all sorts of silly things, he raced off and I climbed the short staircase to our department, where I met flustered and embarrassed looking youngsters, most of them girls, emerging from one of our lecture theatres. They were not much wiser than me and I said I'd visit him the next day. There was to be an end of term party on Friday and the girls, mainly the Christian and mystic party said graciously that they would look forward to seeing me there. They felt that poor Jim had really 'lost it' but even so, they thought the feminist 'wolf-pack' who demanded a rational explanation for his loudly protested spiritual convictions had been unfair. They were worried for me and feared I was in for an unpleasant experience.

I caught the bus to Bingley, it being a cold but fair winter's day, my thirty-second year and took the steep walk I loved so much from Bingley and up to the 'Guide' pub, where, knowing Jim's abstemious tendency, I replenished my energies with a couple of pints. Having done so and joyously, I bought a couple of take-outs. It was MY birthday after all.

When I entered the farm gates, having jogged down Long Lea for a happy and anticipatory twenty minutes, I sensed a deeper chill in the air. It was getting on now into the afternoon and I could dimly see Jim's outline, obscured by either a trick of the light or some murk or other. As I got closer, I saw that it was a cascade of blood and when I got right up to the caravan, guessed it was almost certainly arterial blood. Jim's fanatical face, in profile and showing the grinning rictus of death, stared sightlessly out over the fields to Mount Tabor, Halifax and the Lancashire moors beyond.

I managed to alert Jim's landlord. His wife was distraught, though she did manage to assure me that he was not liked and the children hadn't taken to him. I suffered, while we waited for the Police. Needless to say, I didn't like poor Jim's Landlord or wife especially either. The Police came and I was interviewed; the Station Sergeant at Keighley Cop Shop seemed sympathetic whilst the interviewing DI, a shifty and cynical southerner wasn't and made it clear that he despised me and Jim.

They did not offer me a lift home and I returned to my chill and unwelcoming lodgings. My University Staff had been informed and I rang Ian, my tutor to tell him I was ok. I was asked to go into University first thing in the morning. As expected, Roger, Ian, John and Ken were all great, Roger Fellowes in particular which surprised me as he was the closest to the 'Oxford' stereotype of ex-public-school alumni. He gave me an address and insisted that I contact him over the Christmas period and even gave me the date of a party he was throwing for academic staff the following week. I was asked to keep my counsel; apparently, there were other circumstances but by all means to get to the Department Party that night. I did so and many students, in shock just sat around staring into space. I got drunk and managed to sleep. Still shaken, the next evening having drunk steadily all day in the miserable pubs around Frizinghall, I went to see my kind neighbours from Peace Studies a few doors down. Sarah Parego, the bossy and dungaree-ed Feminist lecturer I'd seen striding around our two departments was an absolute brick. Two Jewish girls gave me a big hug and Pete's girlfriend, a gorgeous Dutch Christian girl, threw herself through the kitchen door and into the Windsor chair by the cooker, crying that there'd been a stabbing just after the party. The name Tricia Moore came up; I knew her, a petite and kindly Northern Irish redhead.

Darkness fell and the next I heard about Tricia she was in hospital having been stabbed by a woman but would pull through. Thinking that was enough and the year had seen the Devil arise from his lair, a Lancashire lass and Quaker Peace protester, burst in saying there had been a murder in the flats down Oak Villas, Manningham. Knowing the area and almost sure my mate Sue had a flat down there, even that Eliot Ness was her landlord, I scrounged the cash for a taxi and shot down to the bottom of Oak Villas where a Police Incident structure nearly blocked the rear entrance, which I knew led down to a communal hallway and stairs. A friendly and concerned WPC lifted a flap of the tent and I ran down the stairs to Sue's place in a second. I found her flat door wide open and the whole joint stripped of her hangings; only some well-used cat and dog litter remained in her hallway. Sue, a Devon lass and a country girl with a tough-looking giant of a west country boyfriend had had enough.

The following day we learned that what was now becoming officially known as a 'Ripper' murder had occurred. Some poor prostitute, apparently. It wasn't until the press photos hit the shops after this terrible weekend that I recognised the smiling young brunette, Irish-looking Pat, Hungarian Joe's girlfriend on that happy night out in Lumb Lane and The Carlisle a couple of years ago.

I had to go to the Inquest for Jim's death at the Aire Valley Hospital, in pleasant countryside opening up to Skipton and the Dales. It was snowing and as I had to squelch through a couple of inches of the stuff, my threadbare desert boots leaked prodigiously and I could hardly concentrate on what the Coroner said. Roger, as Head of Department, sat next to me, his big rugger player's body rigid and shell-shocked in his elegant Burberry. I heard nothing because of my discomfort and was nervous about my feet beginning to smell. I didn't want to hear the details anyway and afterwards, as I turned to leave, a wiry old man in obviously what was his only suit took my arm.

"It's Mr Greenwood here, I'm sorry for," he said.

I was near to tears, choking them back as I introduced Mr Eames to Roger.

"He wor' a good lad, zurr!" said Mr Eames, poor old Jim's Dad.

Roger, bless him, looked crestfallen and soul-stricken.

"Eee would do anything for you, would Jim. He wor a nice lad, he wor!"

The poor man looked frantic and Roger, for all his manly Guards Officer appearance, seemed to be fighting back the sobs. I had often thought Roger a bit distant but today I loved him; his honesty and sincerity were so transparent. I held on to Mr Eames' elbow and gripped his hand as firmly as I good. Eventually, in a spontaneous gesture, Mr Eames gently released my hand and extended both his to Roger who enclosed them in his great fists and for some time the two good men communed in silence. Spluttering that I had to go, I rushed out of the room, skidded and slid across the car park to a fence and a short-cut that I knew over the fields to Steeton and thence the railway to Bradford.

The funeral was a bit better, high on the moors in Lothersdale over Oakworth and I noticed only one IHS student there as well as Roger and I. Thus, in misery, ended 1976.

Chapter 50

Because I felt duty-bound to hold my tongue until my fellow students came back for the Spring term of '77, I had every license, or so I kidded myself, to keep tanked up. I could hardly concentrate on my books anyway and now on the edge of the red-light district, couldn't walk straight out of my back door and into the bracing fresh air and windswept vistas of moorland and majestic cloud-stacked, dramatic skies. I even suspected that many students, who had still been schoolkids a short while ago, might be prevented from coming back to this mean City. For mean it seemed, even though I had heard that the poor Irish student had recovered well from her wounds, Patricia A was dead, very dead, her body eviscerated and long gone.

I was mainly alone in the flat. T, from whom we sublet, was away at home and most of the other rooms being student occupied were locked, so I felt pretty desolate. I was also beginning to slip into a kind of slough, alcohol becoming my crutch during the day, although I hoped to wean off it after the necessary grieving process was over and then return to maybe keeping a bottle of Scotch strictly for medicinal and emergency purposes. Social drinking was the way forward, I lied to myself, but being sociable, even though I was lonely was the last thing I wanted.

I was becoming even more disillusioned with the working class, preferring the far more cosmopolitan and sexually deviant purlieus of the inner-city. I would have an occasional pint in a local pub, the Turf, or the Bradford Arms or Brittania on the bottom road at Shipley, a short cut to Leeds but one mainly used by heavy goods and service vehicles. The occasional serial killer, too, of course as it turned out later. They were places of unfathomable gloom. No-one talked to me, apart from a concerned Scots couple on Christmas Eve, from a Hotel nearby who had noticed the vomit down my trousers and my woeful look.

Brian, my fellow tenant, a pleasant-looking and hard-working plumber, I found asleep sometimes in our sad communal 'living' room. A gentle and woebegone soul, like Jim he hadn't a bad bone in his body, but I could see he was cruelly exploited by his brother and boss, a pig-eyed, walrus-moustached dullard and several flint-hearted floozies who Brian dragged back from t'Con club in the next street. Conservative Clubs in West Yorkshire are not exclusively political and I occasionally drank in the Frizinghall one but the almost infinite dreariness of it suffocated me.

Brian would say how he hated Pakis and though I knew he didn't mean a word of it, this saddened me. Even the darts and card-playing white working-class youths in the taprooms in this white enclave seemed not only Roundheads but dour and heartless savages. I was beginning to hate the North but also my country, humanity even, intensely. Slowly, it seemed the shutters were falling over my hopes.

Gradually, flatmates started drifting back.

"Ah, hello, old boy. Had a good Christmas?" said my landlord, T.

Ex-public school, a minor one in the Midlands probably and totally insincere, he had dead eyes and a flabby mask of a face, the ubiquitous, scrubby dark beard popular at that time, shifty eyes and a pronounced nervous tick, in the form of a sudden shake of his head to the right. In any other man, poor Jim or gentle and simple Brian, for instance, I would find it endearing.

The Black Douglas Redux! I thought to myself. A few more drifted in, a pleasant but surprisingly teetotal Aussie and a nondescript engineering student, who had the disconcerting habit of leaving his pot-holing wetsuit in the bath after Dales-ward adventures. He could drink though and was slightly mad, like most cavers and I could usually get a bit more than the usual grunts of conversation out of him.

One day I looked out over the backs of North View Road, the gutters dripping from above and rain drizzling over the blue-grey and indigo slabs of the midden tops, a forlorn washing line swaying in a grudging breeze, a dispiriting and festering rank of overflowing dustbins below and my heart sank and I thought that I was at the fag-end of the universe. A long and grim year stretched ahead, probably two years, maybe nearer three, if I was to finish my course. It all seemed impossible. Futile.

Thankfully, my uni mates also started drifting back. Though there was never to be anything else between us, Sue and I developed a firm friendship. Formidably intelligent, she was a fairly recent divorcee and always had a boyfriend in tow. Though she liked me, in all honestly, I think she found me a bit wet. Then, one morning in a sociology lecture, she shot me a glance of deep concern. It was a great gift and I think that from that time my spirits began to revive. Sue, of course, was wise and profound, even inscrutable and rather forbidding. I think I was in love with her. Her looks weren't conventionally pretty and with her long Stuart tresses she looked like the Duke of Monmouth or the ill-fated James the Second; definitely a Cavalier. I was rapidly becoming to dislike Roundheads, both left and right-wing. She also encouraged my burgeoning interest in feminism and as we both loved novels, we enjoyed some great discussions. She hated Kingsley Amis with a passion, I less so but I saw what she meant.

We often went to the University Film Club and discovered we both had a passion for Italian movies and I thought she liked my company. She had a ruthless streak, just my type! She was also quite scathing to me about other students, surprisingly even about the 'sisterhood'. I was just beginning to get a bit cross about some of them, the 'Roundhead' tendency in particular. Sue had strong spiritual leanings but little interest in Christianity. Like me, a Francophile, she loved Sartre and Camus and I loved Simone Weil. I also enjoyed my Stendhal and, of course, the magical Alain Fournier.

Though Trevor was nowhere near as brutal as my flatmate a few years before in another dismal dive above the Baker's Shop, I never overcame my distaste for him. We were on civil terms and usually bandied banalities, as he liked to like to sit in the Common room watching TV while, strangely enough, experimenting with atomic models. There was little he didn't know about Spectroscopy, electronic chemistry. He was Tory candidate for the University Ward. I laughed at him as a scion of a dying breed, because I drank occasionally with Tory students and they found his politics almost fascist.

Brian, bless him, got me a job in the 'Ring-of-Bells' another white English enclave but not aggressively so, as on the top road and near posher Saltaire and Nab Wood, most of the locals were white. I was quite a good barman and got many tips. Came the day though, that I couldn't stand 'Middle England' any-more and at the time of the Queen's Jubilee later that summer, couldn't stand the bawling of the National Anthem. Unlatching the door to the bar, I walked out of the place, only to come back, humiliatingly, for my wages.

Summer followed what had felt like a very long winter and one of the spirit too. Elsa was using her room only as a stop-over during term time and for her few lectures, and anyway she had a long-term relationship with her steady, a man of incredible virtue, a Post Gradual medical researcher. Marjoribanks, in the Oakleigh Pub I had recently discovered, who fancied Elsa often expressed his incredulity at this in his cynical way.

I had been painting and drawing more seriously and when I had a visit from Sue, a lisping hippy and art student type, I was able to show her some rough pastel sketches, as well as natter and gossip about our course. She liked what I was doing but kept quizzing me for symbolism, where it was honestly unintentional. She was very ideologically driven and possibly focused on this because she was an ex-art therapist.

I got myself a new job as a barman at the Fisherman's Inn, by the canal at Gilstead, a rural backwater near Bingley and on the Eldwick road. I had reverted to something of the Pastoral. I got on well with the Landlord, Hartley, a Leeds man and city slicker, from an older generation than me. He'd been a bit of a card in his youth and rhapsodised about 'Ole Blue Eyes, Dean Martin and the rest of the 'Rat Pack'. He was a bon viveur and loved to hold court in the corner of the Saloon Bar with his business cronies, Tories all and fawning racists, after closing time, while I played his willing 'Figaro'. I was pretty good at fielding the repartee and Hartley's barbs and though it was hardly the Brighton or Uni scene, I was able to hold my own. I thoroughly enjoyed working for him and I used to walk there from Shipley and back along the canal tow-path, a bucolic contrast.

I also had a part-time evening job in a Plastics factory at Stocksbridge near Keighley, to which I usually took the bus from Shipley, a short distance from Frizinghall. I was feeling a bit better, even in this year of Ripper murders and assaults. One pleasant late summer's evening while I was at the Keighley bus stop, two sharp-looking and tough young men approached me, one discreetly produced his warrant card.

"Regional Crime Squad," he said and politely asked me to accompany them to the Shipley 'Nick', a short distance away.

I assumed that my Sunderland connection and having been known around the Manningham area, as well as being about the correct age, made me a 'Ripper' suspect. Brian had already been pulled in and it was true that his handsome and neatly bearded face bore a resemblance to one of the earlier photofits that had been published everywhere in West Yorkshire throughout the past year.

In fact, though the subject did crop up, it was over a completely different murder that they wished to interview me. Flashing a photo of a harmless-looking middle-aged housewife they said that the lady had been murdered on the canal tow-path at a point I regularly passed on the way to the 'Fisherman's'. Hartley had been able to give a good character reference of me and it was unlikely given the time scale that it was me. However, they wanted to eliminate me from the inquiry and now seemed satisfied with this. After showing me some photos of possible suspects, they told me it was highly likely that the killer was lurking in the bushes in Hurst Wood when I passed, heading for Dowley Gap and just beyond that, the Fisherman's. I noticed that they looked at my feet and when I asked about my Sunderland connection, as an alumnus of Sunderland Art College, they clammed up. One of them vigorously shook his head, the other repeated no, no, no, no! rapidly under his breath.

I was trying to close my ears now to the increasingly horrible news and when I got to Lacrinoid Plastics, the Boss hauled me into the office. The Police had very considerately phoned in my excuses, apologising profusely. He seemed genuinely pleased and surprised to see me.

On wage night, I thought me it might be a good idea to check out the 'Oakleigh' Hotel back in Manningham. I was getting heartily sick of Frizinghall and was even put off by the Pastoral idyll. Now I had got used to serving the 'Dowley Gappers', I found them ignorant and narrow, not the wholesome country folk and outlaws I had romanticised. I thought the Oakleigh Hotel might be a nice place to take Elsa if Pete Marjoribanks could keep his filthy mitts off her. I loved Marjoribanks, pronounced Marshbanks, an 'Oik-Detector' spelling, beloved by my class-conscious fellow countrymen and his sardonic humour. I think it was I who got him to go on our course instead of wasting his time pimping and supping in Manningham. He was now in the year below me, generally considered by the wee feminists to be a sink of sexism and chauvinism. Pete M was seen as the resident 'Naughty Boy', a Cavalier, of course!

The Oakleigh proved everything I had hoped for, a touch of Brighton and even the old London 'Cafe Royal', that back in the day, Dick and I had romanticised about. The French windows opened on to a dark garden outside that late summer's evening and long, damask curtains billowed fitfully, gently and gracefully into the high and exquisitely corniced room. In the corner, sat an elegant old gent in a dinner suit, playing Chopin and Debussy on a grand piano.

"Dave!" said Marjoribanks, raising his glass to me.

"No, later," I mimed, raising an index finger to my lips and shaking my head, giving him the thumbs-up sign and a mighty grin.

It would spoil the moment's perfection! I thought to myself.

Marjoribanks gently bowed his head. Something nameless and priceless had been understood. The Cavaliers were back!

Indeed, they were back. A half-asleep Brian told me when I walked back into Cromwellian Frizinghall, that someone called Stan had been round and left his card! Sound the trumpets and beat the kettle drums!

So, the summer of my spirit had come eventually and I began to feel a bit better.

The only pleasant occasion apart from snuggling up with Elsa at times was a day trip to the Dales on the day Elvis died, with Michaela, a Physics Post-Grad and new flat-mate. She was ok if a bit hard but I knew her type and knew not to let myself to get too involved. We had a bit of fun and as she had her own car, a Hillman Imp, we were able to get up to the Dales. She was a good walker and one of the few good things about that dismal year was our trip up to Buckden Pike, the day Elvis died and as we were both young and VERY fit, we went on to climb Whernside and visit an aunt of mine near Grassington, one of the wealthy members of our family. Hospitable and no fan of Greenwoodian Patriarchy, she was able to encourage me in my estrangement from the parents. Her first husband, who I was supposed to take after, John, was my uncle and dad's much younger brother. Barbara, a still stunningly beautiful brunette, of Russian Jewish origin, told me how she used to stand up to old Walter and hinted that she despised my mother for her meekness. On parting, she said I reminded her of John, a keen and courageous rock climber and craftsman. He had died suddenly in the early years of their marriage. He had not had my opportunities, born at an earlier time. I was chuffed because I liked him, as he was the nearest thing to a kindred spirit and elder brother in my strange and reactionary family.

It had been a great day and honestly, that's the best I can say about 1977. I'd made my old room presentable, the lovely Elsa moved in and I got a few more visits from uni friends. When Brian and I were alone together in the sitting room, usually both of us either pissed or knackered from work, we would hear her door opening and Michaela would emerge for a bit of teasing. She was a shocker and Brian and I, brothers almost now, would writhe embarrassingly, tumid and erect as she cavorted or twirled around that room which was dismal no more! I continued in my fear and wonder at women.

I stuck with my bar and factory job not far into the autumn term of my second year at university. Though the workload wasn't difficult, I valued my free time on the hills and my sketch pad so I found my study harder than my younger friends though I was gratified at my reasonable grades. I loved the Seminar system and shone at it.

I worried though, that I was becoming a snob as I couldn't stand the plebbish friends which the other students in our house brought home. I liked the people in the Taproom at the Fisherman's and even Hartley agreed, though he socialised with the small-time accountants and spivs in the Saloon Bar.

"Basically, Dave, you've got to understand most people in pubs are cunts," he said, waving over to the now-deserted corner of the Saloon Bar, long after closing time. "This lot, for example, are all shagging each other's wives and husbands and half of them should be in jail. That lot," pointing to the Tap Room, might look rough and many have been in jail, are the salt of the earth!"

Hartley was a Tory but a Cavalier at heart.

The year dragged on with more murders and assaults by the maniacal Ripper but I was too sickened to think about it much. Drink, as usual, helped. A pall seemed to hang over West Yorkshire and the only cheerful people appeared to be the sort of white and thuggish predator class I had seen too much of and lived amongst this past year.

I spent some time with Elsa, on her occasional visits up from Southampton. She loved me to read to her from Jane Austen, saying she found it soothing and that I had a nice reading voice. I occasionally hugged her and we had the odd chaste cuddle. When in funds, I took her to the

Oakleigh and such was the camaraderie amongst our generation of students, she would sometimes treat me to a drink too. Marjoribanks liked my voice, too. He said it was one of a confidence-trickster. He often invited Elsa and me back to his flat to read his pornographic, though delightfully witty stories.

By this time, I was sharing a flat with Ian. After Stan, he was to be the most charismatic and powerful influence of my youth. Curiously, I had met him through Stan and I delayed the meeting because it seemed so contrived a plot, so providential, seeing Stan like that even though we had kept in touch by letter our correspondence had fallen off once I'd started university. I used to relish getting his letters, when I was isolated in my countryside retreat in Eldwick, often going through an elaborate ritual, having no shower or bathroom, with the aid of a couple of plastic bowls, my kitchen sink and water heater, I made a total scrub down and after brewing a pot of tea, and with eager anticipation opened a letter usually relating Stan's adventures as a railway Guard for the then nationalised British Railways and his patch throughout Lancashire and North Western England. Sometimes, with his characteristic generosity, there was a £5 note or a bit of 'blow' the current slang for marijuana. In fact, at this period, one of hiatus after leaving University, I was feeling under something of a cloud. I felt lost and though my academic work had been good, I was beginning to feel that I had made a mistake. I didn't like academics, or at least this younger generation of students. I don't think they liked me either and though I was fitfully beginning to paint again, I felt lost and out of tune with what I could see in the art world, at least from what I could glean from the 'Guardian' and 'Observer.'

I had a job in a Greetings Cards Factory near Heaton, a more salubrious area up the hill from Bedsitter Land and almost in open country. It was my Saturday afternoon off and I was slowly mooching down the hill and into the mainly Muslim area of Girlington, and with Manningham just down the road and a nice new flat, I was looking forward to a scrub and some shopping in Bradford.

"Hey, Stetson! You who…" something about ships and Mylae.

"Who the fuck?" I thought, half-recognising the quote from T.S Eliot's 'Waste Land' and then the Scouse accent. "That skull in my garden…!"

Then I saw Stan across the road and suddenly remembered: Oh, my God his card, that Brian had passed on to me weeks before. He looked hardly changed and I think he saw me first because I saw his still athletic figure give a little jig, heard my name shouted and his broad smile and shaking, blond locks. We rushed into each other's arms and hugged.

I laughed to myself, thinking that indeed that skull "had sprouted", death being so much in the air.

"I thought you didn't want to know, young David!"

I relished hearing again the Merseyside twang.

'If only you knew!' I wanted to reply but stopped myself as it seemed a bit effete.

After very little consultation, the consensus was that a libation must be taken and we repaired to the nearest hostelry, the Upper Globe on Whetley Hill.

His lovely wife Adrienne was pregnant and she had work over here, so he had packed up his job on the railways in Merseyside, married Adrienne in London and come up here. She was London-Irish and I took to her immediately. I was invited to supper and went there often, even babysitting for them. Just a short while later I was to meet Ian, the other great male friend in my life. Things were about to get better!

Chapter 51

I shared a house in East Bowling with two charming young Indian men, one an art student and an eccentric individual on the younger, nicer end of the Manningham bohemian scene. His brother, Terlok, was the most perfect gentleman, like many south Asians I was ever to meet. I remember the only Pakistani punk too, with the most resplendent Mohican and lavishly studded jacket. Though not as much on my sardonic wavelength as Stan, or Wes and I, I was meeting a younger art college set, still Peter Pan! Scots Mary, a friendly, Glaswegian punk and art student, Tim Nuttall, younger son of Jeff Nuttall of 'Bomb Culture' fame and Bradford Art College lecturer, guileless and amiable kids. They were more easily and naturally bohemian, and being creatives, far more congenial. I was flattered, that these young people saw me as a friend. I felt that somehow the wand of youth still lingered over my ageing head. I preferred this crew to my university contemporaries and it was good to be in a multiracial household too; a vibrant and sassy Anglo-Jamaican girl, Charlene, shared the house with us. They were a talented and a kindly bunch and we took it in turns to cook a community meal every payday, or in my case as I was out of work temporarily, every dole day. I never tasted such delicious curries and for the first time ate Jamaican fried bananas and sweet potato, stockfish and peppery West Indian cuisine.

It wasn't the same as Manningham and I didn't like that side of Bradford but I was more on my own and I wanted to take stock and somehow resurrect myself, for I felt I had been drifting dangerously. The Thatcher government was setting a brutal tone; I feared for my academic future and was uncertain of my near redundant talent as an artist.

One dole day I went to Bradford town centre and the college precinct, so near to the Manville Arms where I had celebrated my first glorious day at Art College, an aeon away. I had almost forgotten Glenda by this time, though we had exchanged the occasional letter; hers, even after all our vicissitudes, in a scarlet and scented envelope. She wished me well and seemed to be settling into teaching as a Supply Teacher in London, an unenviable job and I admired her for it. She was a brave lass.

I bought a fistful of pastels and another sketchbook and called at the

Central Library for some art books on the way back to East Bowling. I didn't like the local pubs, lumpen Cromwellian, so drink was less of a temptation but sometimes when the craving and lonely yearning for Manningham engulfed me, I bought a bottle of cider or a couple of cans of Special from the nearest Off License on Wakefield Road.

Curiously, on one such dreary trudge back down dismal East Bowling, kicking through sludge and sleet, the winter was turning out to be a bleakly depressing and chilling one, I recollected seeing a film as a kid: 'No Love for Johnny' one of those post-war British films that had pretensions to a kind of continental socialist realism. Self-indulgently, I wondered if that applied to me. Alienated from my family I didn't know what the immediate future would bring. I felt lost and with no luck, quite alienated. That 'Anomie' again. I had no inclination to finish university because I loved my tutors, all about my age, Oxford-educated but as left-wing as me. I loved the academic gaiety and tolerance, something cavalier again, though I felt spurned by the feminists and a younger generation of fellow undergraduates, who, unlike art students were much more conventionally minded, and probably looked on me as a living anachronism. Love seemed far away. I was as bereft and lonely as at any time in London. An exile in reverse. A 'double exile'. I saw myself at such times and melodramatically, as my father's ghost. I fantasised myself into some sort of sense of reality, self-harming almost, drinking deep and playing silly games with razor blades, testing my courage, crossing busy roads, even standing teeteringly close to the platform edges on my forays to Leeds or Skipton.

A fantasy Spitfire pilot, I almost fell out of bed with my nightmares at such times.

"Watch your tail, Johnny. Break! Break!"

But then I heard a voice:

"Dave! Dave!"

It was Wes, my hermaphrodite Cicerone, shaking my shoulders, as I festered and sweated in my tousled bed.

"Come on, girl. We're going back to 'Electric City!"

And we marched back to Manningham. Drinks were on him.

I got Germaine Greer's latest book 'The Obstacle Race' about the difficulties besetting women artists and a noble attempt to rescue some of them from oblivion. I liked it and one or two paintings captivated me, particularly those of the Italian High Renaissance and more recent artists. Gwen John enthralled me and in the story of her tragic love life and her Edwardian self-portraits, I saw something of what I loved about Sarah and Steph. I had just one female friend, apart from Elsa left from my course at university whom I respected, Sue Cole. We were like siblings and I found her very encouraging, an ardent feminist and stimulating intellectually. I immediately set about a pencil and charcoal portrait of her and as another present, a small head and shoulders portrait by one of La Greer's finds, a Madonna by one Sebastiana Della Piombo. I treated it like an icon, playing down the colour and emphasising its sculptural and monochrome qualities. The eyes were sculptural then, with no pupils. My 'Muse', my 'Goddess'?

Why I did this I don't know, and I had a strangely involuntary and guided feeling while very tentatively painting it. 'Limning' would have been a more appropriate word as it had the feel of one of the Elizabethan English miniaturists, or Limner, Nicholas Hillyard. No longer taking for granted my art college studies of years before, I was beginning to find something transcendental and almost mystical in making marks in a sketchbook. In my anomie I felt like some aboriginal, or Cro-Magnon, deep in his limestone Dordogne cave, a burnt piece of bone in my hand and lit fleetingly by an animal fat lamp, I exulted and trembled at the flickering shadows on my inner cave wall, my 'skull' cinema.

It almost seemed as if, in the right frame of mind, I could penetrate and then enliven an imaginary spiritual membrane just floating above the surface of the cave walls; red oxides and indigos, a wound, an outline quivering with a haunting presence, a passionately summoned ghost. However, icon-like it hung on my wall until I could give it to Sue. Was Sebastiana my Goddess, my Muse? I rather thought that she was. Or, did Rembrandt's old Dutch lady still linger? I felt the numinous shadow of the Goddess and sensed trembling wings over me. Sue didn't laugh at me and being an ex-art-therapist, she sympathised enthusiastically when I showed it to her. Looking back now, I think Sue was one of the most deeply spiritual and intellectual beings that I had ever met. She took the pastel painting back to her new house in Hebden Bridge, another friend dis-enamoured of Bradford.

I painted another, this time from an illustrated Folio collection of El

Greco. Sue paid me something for this so it was my first sale. Again, it was another religious one, of a young Cardinal, intense and icon-like, El Greco being from a Greek Orthodox background. Retrospect tells me that at that stage, I was making tentative and even desperate forays back into a more orthodox religious faith.

I started a habit of packing some pastels, sketchbook and a flask of tea in my rucksack and heading for the moors. It kept me off the booze, limited my smoking and cleansed my spirit. Before long, though I only had a vestige of my youthful bloom, I was in pretty good shape and growing a beard, becoming quite the outdoor man, if not an Adonis-like Stan, or an athlete like Ian.

Part Six:

LOVE STORY

Chapter 52

A big man, with a Paratrooper's body, his legs extended from a bear-like torso and hulking swimmer's shoulders. Incongruously he seemed to waft, wraith-like into my sight, or so it seemed at our first meeting at Stan's house in Girlington. This was just up the hill from Manningham, a mainly working-class area, like my childhood Manningham with its serried rows of terrace houses and a largely well-mixed Pakistani and working-class English population. It was in Stan's attic, his den and while Adrienne was knitting clothes for her expected baby and watching tv downstairs, we boys had been granted permission to watch the soccer, a great Merseyside Derby, Liverpool versus Everton. Ian seemed drawn into himself and hunkered up against the low sloping roof of the attic, like some great roosting raptor. Stan told me later that Ian was unusually quiet, as he was recovering from a bad acid 'trip' in the 'Pool and intent on moving over here.

We were both, Ian and I suffering from hangovers of a kind, and I was pleased with my new flat but worried if I could afford to rent two rooms. So, we were both desultorily watching the soccer, while Stan, a fanatic Liverpool fan gave a lively running commentary. Bill Shankly, the famous Scots Liverpool manager at that time, of course, Stan's 'God'.

There must have been some subliminal psychic 'groping' between Ian and me, as he seemed to shift on his perch under the eaves, or perhaps Stan had given us wine, knowing well his hospitality, because I remember the big man becoming the butt of my half-inebriated jibes and his beard splitting shyly into a smile that seemed to break up his face in an unselfconscious and unspoiled, uncool way, like that of a toddler. I thought of him as a shy man for a short time.

He became my new flatmate as we both had come to a mutual and instant decision, our bonding being so sudden and spontaneous. Much banter followed.

"Come on you two comedians!" said Stan, at last ushering us out into the indigo Bradford night. Ian was to have Virginia's old room and presumably her none too virginal bed, for the flat was furnished, cheerfully and elegantly too. I quietly rejoiced to myself that night as I had a flatmate and what looked like a fascinating new friend.

The rooms had been formerly occupied by two female students on my year at university, pleasant and ardently feminist but socialist too. Angie, whose room I had taken over, the more mature of the two was a 'salt-of-the-earth' socialist feminist, a lovely woman and almost a muscular Christian in her compassion and voluntary work with young lads and single women parents; a committed and brave anti-fascist too and on the few anti-NF demos I had been on she had always been present, a real trooper of a person and a northerner like me. Her flatmate, Virginia, whose room Ian was about to occupy was very 'Home Counties' but fashionably leftist and vocally feminist, as well as somewhat disapproving of me. I often used to visit them and because I borrowed books and the occasional bit of cash off of them, I believe I came to be distrusted as a 'user'.

Angie was more sympathetic, to my financial desperation and my social isolation and I was pleased to know that apart from her course books and the obligatory 'feminist' approved reading of the time, such as Marilyn French's appalling tome: 'The Women's Room' and 'Emmanuelle', she had books by Flann O'Brien and Jane Austen, favourites of mine that we could enthuse about over a cup of Earl Grey tea, and maybe a spliff.

I liked to think that this literary vibe might linger in Angie's room. Anyway, it was larger and with a dip of the mansard roof towards the elegant dormer window facing more or less south, the room was full of light on a clear morning and I felt I could settle in for a long stay. It still stands in my memory after my room in Eaton Place, Brighton, another south-facing and light-filled room, as one of the happiest and most formative spaces of my youth.

Sometimes during this quiescent period when I was settling in, as did the weather, into a very atmospheric and evocative Autumn, I must have started to forget Glenda and begin, in my not so young fogey-ish' way a similarly Autumn period of my life. I almost relished what had become my permanent bachelorhood but also some hopes of a gentlemanly decline. I thought that I understood my limitations by now, had loved and lost but now was wiser. I played with the notion of taking up pipe-smoking and Chinese Cliff in the ground floor flat had promised me his cat, Peter, when he left the house, which he did within a month.

Halcyon days over, it was time I started growing up. Somehow, I would finish my course, with a good degree and get a job teaching. Sometimes, I could hear Ian, or both him and Joyce, his girlfriend, on a weekend visit from Liverpool, clattering about our galley/kitchen at the head of our landing outside my normally slightly ajar door. Sometimes, dear old Mrs Hill, our genial 'concierge' who rented the whole floor below us, and had been there since she was widowed a century before, white-haired and with beaming features, she would appear near the top of our stairs, offering us some tit-bit, or even a 'nightcap', a very welcome glass of sherry or a malt. Sometimes she would have the beautiful and neutered Peter, snowy white with a dashing black eye and ear patch, in her arms as she retrieved him from his post outside my door. He had already 'adopted' me, it seemed!

In my almost 'spinsterish' way, my heart would thrill at a tap at my door, as I 'dog-eared' the tome I was studying and stepped up to answer, at that time a still diffident Ian, or an almost effusively kind Joyce, offering me a glass of wine, or an invitation to share their meal. A trainee Solicitor but with absolutely no side and a friendly Merseyside accent, she respected me, which seemed to promise that she had had a good report from Ian. I felt that I had entered civil society at last.

One evening, in mid-October, I was savouring that sweet feeling of regret and nostalgia, typical of the season and even parody of what I was becoming, half-listening to Vaughn-Williams on Radio 3, the latest Rowan Williams, the Arian Heresy? at hand, when Ian called to me through my half-open door.

"Dave! I'm playing at the 'King's Arms'," a pub in the more salubrious Heaton just a mile up the road. "Do you want to come and give me some support? Pints are on me?"

I agreed with alacrity. It was Thursday and payday the next day, so perhaps I could return the favour. By this time, I had discovered that Ian, like me, loved a drink or two and I had noticed with some horror, his guitar. But at the promise of free drinks, I donned my anorak and we both set off at a brisk pace on the pleasant evening walk up the hill to semi-rural Heaton.

On the way, with the Victorian public park to our right but an invisible presence now in the dark, blue moonless night of early evening, gently pierced by the light from the occasional elegant Edwardian street lamp, we both chatted concernedly as we walked, about the latest murder; some poor prostitute in Huddersfield way, it was reported. I nodded with approval as Ian too expressed his disgust at the attitude of the Police. Local feminists were incensed and rightly so, we both agreed, that they had warned that an 'innocent' young woman might be the 'Ripper's' next target!

And what a star Ian proved to be! Gone for good was my first impression. He held a smug and cosy folk-club audience in thrall. I was consumed with admiration for my new friend and flat-mate.

On the way home, the reservoir at Wilmer Road reflected a full moon in its chill waters, it shone now, as it must have rained while we were in the pub, in a freshly-rinsed and a deep indigo-coloured sky. With carry-outs of Carlsberg Special cracked open, alternately imbibing and exclaiming at the stars above and like art students of old, freshers again, we shared our passion for music, for the paintings of Georges Rouault and Van Gogh. Picasso was cruel, clever but no colourist, we agreed. We bawled out our respective contempt; in Ian's case for the Merseyside Folk Scene and mine, the sanctimony and snootiness of the academic left on my course.

"It's almost unpaintable!" I cried, comparing the sights of my Brighton experience to the ambient Victorian Gothic here in Bradford, the steely light now glistening off Scots Baronial turrets and steeples of long-dead, wool Barons. Indeed, as we passed the birthplace of J.B Priestley near the park and I was clamouring for his rehabilitation, we agreed that only a writer could express the spirit of Bradford, its mixture of Teutonic excess, lumpen brutality and meanness of spirit. The ghosts of Emily and Charlotte Bronte stalked the moors up and back of the now rising silver moon above us as did those of the wretched victims of a serial killer, the weather now changing dramatically, the dismal and still dripping streets below in an enveloping fog and drizzle.

It must have been the Sunday evening of the following weekend, we were now bonding well and funds being low, we 'dropped anchor' for a sober Sabbath evening. It was to be an intense act of communion between us. Often spending an hour together and sometimes even sharing a meal, we were swapping our reminiscences that particular evening of our 'golden days' at Art College.

Ian had stuck around West Yorkshire longer than I, having done his teaching practice at Bretton Hall, near Wakefield, not far from his home in Liversedge and in the mining district near Ossett. It was a crazily innovative

College and he had been a student at Liverpool, much further away of course, but still in the north of England. All that seemed to explain much about what was to be revealed in his outrageous character. He talked passionately about Stan Barstow, the writer of strong and moving working-class northern life, a fine and manly figure who I had felt honoured to meet and chat to in an Arts Forum while at university, a year before. Stan, as a part-time Lecturer at Bretton Hall, had encouraged Ian a lot. Though not really a writer, Ian had an original way with words and wrote much of his own music, some of which I and the Folk Club audience had enjoyed so much a few nights before.

He talked about his dad, a WW2 veteran and like my dad, a bit of a hero, in fact, an ex-Paratrooper and survivor of the desperate battle of Arnhem in 1944. If it hadn't been for our generation's better opportunities, Ian was destined to be a soldier or a policeman, as surprisingly he failed his 11+ and this the most intelligent man, along with Stan Engel, my other best mate that I was ever to meet. Those for whom Art College had indeed been a liberation.

He rhapsodised about the escapades he got up to; an 'Outward Bound' course he went on in art teacher training at Bretton Hall, abseiling down huge rock faces, pot-holing, paragliding and wind-surfing, much of which he could have done in the armed forces but not without the usual military bullshit and brutalisation. Even ex-Etonians would have envied him and I often marvelled at the privilege the both of us had enjoyed, 3 years on a full maintenance Grant; no College fees to burden us for the rest of our lives and as Ian went on to say:

"How' ya gonna keep 'em down on the farm after they've seen Paree?"

Ian fully realised his lucky escape, unlike mine, which was more personal, grasped now his opportunities with both hands. By comparison, I seemed to have an old-fashioned and gentlemanly diffidence. Ian saw through this and it was often to be a source of friction between us. Ian's forwardness to me seemed rather pushy and yet to him, my diffidence seemed phoney and snobbish. So, for him and his family, he was an only child, going to Art College was an advance in the world and yet to my father, my trajectory after getting a place at university, and good ones too, Oxford and Durham, was a step downwards.

Perversely, I had been proud of my decision to sacrifice better academic and social status to satisfy my ambition to be an artist. However, I had liked the progressive liberal attitudes and personalities of my Art College interviewing board, so I guess I was showing some integrity. On that, Ian and I could heartily agree. I said once to him around this time that my attempt to get a university Humanities Degree was an attempt to redress my apparent sacrifice. He gave me an 'old-fashioned look'; an almost cynical half-smile and a twinkle 'I know YOU!' in his eyes.

Glenda still loomed at the back of my mind but I didn't want to mention that. I had the feeling that he would have slight patience with my agony and like Stan, have given her short shrift. The evening was still not too advanced and both of us clenched ourselves to avoid looking at the clock, 10.30 Sunday Pub closing time would see us safe from temptation. We went on to the issue of 'class' and the state of England. Neither of us missed tv and I think it was plain that we enjoyed each other's company.

Sunderland, where I spent 3 years as a student was just an alcoholic blank to me now so I went on to try and evoke my memories of Brighton and at what I saw as that pivotal time, the beginning of the '70s and the end of Mr Wilson's first Labour government.

With delight, I noticed that Ian had nipped into his room and having raided his secret 'stash' he had emerged to pass me a freshly opened can of Carlsberg Special. Bliss!

"Picture this, Ian!"

"Go on," said Ian, avuncular and expectant, his pipe now going nicely, eyes twinkling.

"I'd had a late-night, partying and was having a lie-in, the late morning high summer sun streaming into my chambers. I had recently finished my Brighton Art College teaching course and was signing on, as one could at leisure in those more civilised times until I could find a temporary job, while maybe applying for a teaching post in the Brighton and Hove area, later in the Hols. I liked it there and even my student accommodation, sharing a house with other art students at the top of the hill at Montpelier Crescent, was really nice. Outside my bed-chamber window, I could look out over sedate allotments to a glimpse of the Sussex Downs and a cheerful Cerulean Blue sky, with almost cartoon-like and fresh-looking fluffy clouds.

"A knock suddenly came at my door; 'Hilloo, David, it's me-Bridget-the lady downstairs let me in. Are you decent?' 'Never, Biddy, you should know that!' I retorted. A chortle from her, the sound of politely shuffling feet and a manly guffaw and she pops her head around the door jamb, a gorgeous vision of Edwardian London; Bloomsbury, and the 'Arts and Crafts' movement, South Kensington and all things nice. Her hair braided with vivid green and scarlet ribbons, a long and Iberian-Irish, pale-skinned beauty, with amber and green-tinted eyes which blazed in the light, as she wafted to my bedside; a very 'Knightsbridge' accent: 'Fulham actually, darling,' she had corrected me at our first meeting at an arty party in Sussex Square. Such was England, or as I saw it then, and at its' best."

'Go on!' Ian nodded, unvoiced and with an accompanying wink, giving a ruminative pull at his pipe and I knew then, that I 'had' him. We were like two 'yarning' sons of Empire out of a Conrad novel, I laughed to myself.

"Anyway!" and trying to sound 'bloke-ish', the Carlsberg was getting to me now and had become well-established as my 'take-out' tipple. "This geezer with my bird at the time follows her inside and: 'Mind if I take a pew, old boy?' plonks himself on a chair by the window, very Gwen John sort of a tableau. And I see a rather splendid-looking chap, smartly but casually dressed but not intimidatingly so. A Guards Officer to a 'T'" I mused. "Scots or Irish, I was thinking; rugged, and yet refined good looks, breeding, of course! Moustached and kindly eyes, the sort of face you were beginning to see less of in England, he was in his late twenties or even early thirties; Biddy liked them mature. He had a brotherly manner and seemed sincerely anxious to put me at my ease, regimental blazer, Grenadiers, I noticed from his badge and regimental tie, madder and indigo flashing, discrete grey flannels and gleaming Oxford dress shoes and a singing cream-white, pure cotton shirt.

"Well-liked by his brother officers and loved by his men, I surmised.

Mumbling an apology, I threw a sweater over my bare shoulders, I had apologised for my decadent behaviour. 'We-e-e-e-ll, old boy,' he drawled. 'One could hardly expect to be in ONE'S best Dinner Jacket!' Said Guy, as he introduced himself because Bridget was in the kitchen or bathroom adjoining my chamber. He truly looked like one half of a lovely couple and in my mind, I conceded defeat. I was outclassed. I liked him a lot."

Ian took a deep pull from his can and drew pensively on his pipe.

Eyes twinkling.

"Nice one, Greenish," he said. "Pray continue?"

"Bridget was a delightful gel,' Fulham-Irish, poor girl's Chelsea, darling! A latch-key girl, she had told me in the Fifties, so genteel poor and slightly bohemian; liberal-leaning and having met the type in the 'Young Communist League' on Aldermaston Marches, I both knew and trusted her set. Daddy was a successful sculptor up in London and a distinguished Army Veteran of the war, with an 'interesting ', wound, having stepped on a German 'Teller' mine in the Italian Campaign. 'The old 'Silly!' said Bridget. And Mummy, step-mother was a highly regarded opera librettist and translator. Bridget," I continued. "Once confessed to me, almost in tears how her actual mother, who died of cancer and had been a professional nurse, had been one of those brave and compassionate young women who escorted and danced with savagely burned and blighted RAF fighter pilots in the early war years. One of her charges had been Richard Hilary, author of that Battle of Britain classic: 'The Last Enemy' whom she found quite conceited, though grievously disfigured and even arrogant.

"Bridget of the cascading raven hair, knee-length and curling slightly at the ends, how I had loved to comb it, while she, naked, her face obscured, apart from her Japanese Doll lips, purred softly and yet lasciviously! She had hugged a black and loosely-crocheted shawl to herself, something rather exquisite bought in Notting Hill or the King's Road, as she emerged from the bathroom. A pale lemon light had streamed then into my room.

"Bridget now beamed down at me and then at Guy, almost proprietorial, inclusively as if I was the equal of Guy, that august 'Colonel Brandon' figure.

And then I said: 'I'll make myself decent. Do excuse me, you two?' Hurriedly, I had scrabbled under my tousled bedclothes for some underwear. 'Then, I'll make us a pot of tea, boys!' she cried. Then before I rose from my bed, half-smothering me with her patchouli-scented hair, she whispered: 'You funny old thing, David!' Then she gently pecked my nose.

"While in the bathroom, I could hear through the frosted glass, her contented humming and singing and my heart sang."

I feared Ian was going to say something crude but he showed great empathy, nodding his head and pulling gently at his pipe.

"Nice one, Greenish."

We went on into the small hours, lovingly bonding with each other, chatting about our student pasts and respective family histories, the state of England, which was worrying, we both agreed! The Folk Music scene, irritating, both of us mourning and loving Sandy Denny, my loneliness at university and generally setting the world to rights, while wincing at what looked like the dread prospect of a Thatcher government.

It felt exhilarating after the 'Cromwellian' darkness I had experienced the previous few years. Though not as high octane as my earlier halcyon Brighton days, I felt that a new chapter in my life had just opened. It was liberating and I felt reborn.

We had become brothers.

We agreed to call it a draw for the night and promised some class analysis the following Monday night and more vignettes of the South Country and perhaps our hopes of a different England to come.

The following night Ian told me about some of his art college experiences and the darker ones as a schoolboy in the Secondary Modern he attended. A firm socialist like myself, he had no romantic delusions about miners and the working class as I still had. He hated the barbarism and brutality of his schoolmates and interestingly, found schoolboy yarns about our social betters liberating; Billy Bunter and William Brown and for over an hour we both rhapsodised about Orwell's great essay on public school stories, a kind of a 'false-conscious' escape for that generation broken by the horror of the trenches, a so-called eternal summer of Edwardian England. My jibes about 'class collaboration' and escapism seemed rather crass and insensitive. But Wodehouse we both agreed was a master, a magician of 'Happiness' and superb English prose.

For my part, I evoked my strange experience with the Russian Princess in Brighton, the 'Saffron Lady' and went on to say how I saw it as some kind of Epiphany, a sign of God's grace breaking into my narrow world. Ian went into his room to ransack his mysterious stash and re-emerged with a couple more tubes of Carlsberg, so we continued reminiscing and yarning. Then it got boisterous.

"Gussie Fink-Nottle!" I threw at him from Wodehouse's Jeeves.

"Pongo Twistleton!' he countered.

"Stiffy Byng!"

"Tuppy Glossop!' shouted Ian and collapsing onto my bed, we exploded in Homeric laughter.

We almost but didn't quite embrace; male bonding at that time still had its limits.

"For God's sake, Ian! It's just after midnight!"

This came from the top of the stairs outside my door, punctuating the previous scene in my memory, followed by Mrs Hill's foot landing on a creaking floorboard.

"Come on, boys," she said. "Dave's got work in the morning!"

Snatching up my dressing gown, a Colombo-style, ancient Burberry, I rushed out of my door and halfway down the stairs to calm the old lady down, as I knew that she was fond of me, if a little disappointed now. It was quite an easy job because she was a wonderful old girl and I genuinely loved her. She was always offering us a bit of food, or, even better a nightcap of whiskey or brandy. She was a comfortably devout monarchist and High Anglican of the Old School. No fan of the emerging Thatcher, she often waylaid me after I had run a little errand for her - and get yourself something, Dave! – about: "That monster, Thatcher. Ooh, what I could DO to her!"

While I held Mrs Hill's hand and tried to calm her, which I feared was a fat chance with Ian in full flow. He, graciously I thought, passed me on the stairs and took my place to break the ice with the old girl. His charm worked as I heard the occasional chuckle from her and even a burst of laughter. Then:

"Eeeh, ya young bugger!!" from the genteel Mrs Hill.

When I jumped out of bed again and headed downstairs for a bathroom visit, I marvelled at the tableau of Ian still holding the plump Mrs Hill's hand as she smiled benignly, so Hanoverian-looking with her silver-white halo of hair and her cream satin gown. Ian had made another conquest.

My job was undemanding and thankfully after an interlude, Ian dropped by my room to drain his can, pick up his smoking materials and declared it a draw. Relieved, I took up my Austen novel and struggled to get to know Miss Eleanor Dashwood, the gentlemanly Colonel Brandon, and the delightful Marianne Dashwood. I eventually put out the light, sighed happily and fell on my pillow.

So, my infatuation with Ian continued, my Grande Meaulnes, and though I could sometimes shrink into myself in trepidation, such was my weakness, often his footfall on the stairs, or his rattling about our joint kitchenette and sometimes - be still my heart! - his tap on my door, set my pulse racing in anticipation of joy to come, or sometimes a sense of dread and outrage as he collapsed onto my bed in the early hours, drunk from a visit to Manchester or the 'Pool.

And such it was, one Thursday night, just before payday at work and as I was grimacing for want of a nightcap, he crashed through my door and like a huge and amiable Old English Sheepdog, landed on my bed. Annoyed and yet thrilled at the same time, I gratefully accepted a tube of Foster's Australian Lager which had suddenly become fashionable that year. Then: 'Here, have a toke on this! Some 'blow' or in Ian's peculiar terminology, some 'Bob-Nonsense.'

He staggered to my armchair and proceeded to regale me about his appearance as a guest at the Manchester Free Trades Hall and having a drink with Maddie Prior in the dressing room there. He had shared a whole crate of brown ale and Maddie's beloved cider with her, hence his present state. He went on, a bit boring like most drunks and anyway I was still half asleep and disorientated but he was interesting.

He moaned again about the folk scene although he loved Maddie. Some guys dressed in the working-class fashion of the fantasised history of the PC folk brigade had been knitting in the pub, while strongly objecting to the smoky atmosphere of another pub nearby. We went on to share our disgust at the Roundhead tendency amongst contemporary youth.

"You know, Dave," he said, suddenly. "I met some of your university chums in the Oak a few days ago and why, by the way, are so many of your mates such twats and desperate men?"

What he said next devastated me and destroyed my sleep for the night. I was known as a bit of a racist and a sexist. I wasn't too worried about the latter as I was growing tired of the new feminists but I felt incensed at the implication of the former. These young prigs had been comrades in the recent struggles with the NF and other growing fascist groups.

We bitched for a while and thought of a few choice nicknames for what looked like my enemies: Juggernaut, for the girl with the gentle eyes but huge sticky-out ears and Bo-Peep for her nubile, baby-faced sidekick, G who always wore long Kate Greenaway dresses. We coined imaginary names for the more Roundhead feminists: Glenda Thrang, the Hampstead Thinker; Beatrice Hardcastle, the Barnsley Sybil and fantasised about an imaginary yurt in Thornton, up on the edge of the moors, occupied by Feminist artists; all 'shit and twigs' as Ian apostrophised their 'Wimmin's Art' which was fashionable at the time. Ian was not well-loved by the more severe feminists either.

Feeling a bit nasty and sour, I eventually went to sleep and knew that I would get drunk the following evening. I felt that I didn't fit into the academic life, much as I loved my tutors, all a similar age to me, highly intelligent, progressive, and kind.

Ian had started to encourage me to paint and he even enthused about some of my recent sketches. On the few sober evenings we shared, we enjoyed drawing each other.

That's it! I thought. I'll skip a year. I needed to save for my uni fees so I needed quite a bit of money and I knew, apart from Elsa, who was spoken for, that I had no friends at university. Nobody ever mentioned poor Jim either which puzzled me, coming from a bunch of young people who professed highly PC and humanistic views.

Chapter 53

Late Winter/Spring. 1979

I resigned myself to the idea of not returning to university and was growing increasingly restless and bored with my humdrum job. I still smarted at the opinion of me expressed by my ex-comrades at university and was in a rut. My life began to revolve more and more around alcohol, though the rut was enlivened by Ian's stimulating company. I sensed an increasingly swinish mood in the air and felt hardly surprised when Thatcher had become PM earlier that year. The pettiness and barely concealed racism of my workmates at the Greetings Cards factory, not to mention the plethora of blue Conservative Party posters in a working-class community like mine that had benefited so much from Labour governments, disgusted me.

You could sign on for unemployment then quite easily. Jobs were plentiful and in fact for near drop-outs like me, successively being in work and signing on was a revolving door and an accepted way of life. I needed to cast around for something else, although I was not sure what that would entail. I toyed with the idea of working in what was then West Germany. I had mates on the building sites, the money was good and I could make enough to resume my uni course or maybe even start on a sole trading career as a professional artist, or at least earn enough to give me time to build up a big portfolio. Plus, there were still opportunities to lecture part-time at an Art College.

I thought that Ian was away in Lancashire, in Liverpool or Ellesmere Port. Sadly, he and Joyce had split up months before. The 'Port' as Ian called Ellesmere, sounded as full of loonies as Manningham. He used to have me in stitches at some of the tales he told me about the characters there. But marriages, overdoses and prison sentences, even early drug and alcohol deaths seemed to have taken their toll amongst Bohemia over there and despite the Ripper murders, West Yorkshire seemed to hold more promise Ian loved Manningham, his so-called Electric City.

That evening I craved alcohol, not just company, as I had never done before. I felt that I could 'neck' a whole gallon of the good, foaming ale.

Such was my thirst, a Viking Mead-Horn's full!

Ian was good with people and had started to take me out of myself. We were almost becoming a double act. I filled the role of the straight man or fall guy in our public drinking performances. I was always the best one to hit on a likely 'mark'.

"Go on, Greenish!" he hissed to me once. "One o'clock, the bloke in the 3-piece by the piano. He likes you and he's loaded. I was drinking with him t'other lunch-time!"

Shamelessly, I went over to discuss my financial position and a uniquely inviting remedy for it, requiring but a small investment.

But this particular evening, I felt lonely and desperate. It seemed cruel that it was such a balmy, early summer's evening. I didn't like foraging for drinks on my own; I needed Ian's charisma to break the ice, to set the narrative. In despair, I plunged my hands down the backs of the couple of upholstered chairs I had in my room.

Oh, plunge your hands in the basin

-plunge them up to your wrists!

Nothing. I frantically scanned my bookshelf, remembering that my bible might be a good bet. Opens at the Psalms, I remembered! And It suddenly came to mind that on the rare occasions when I was in funds, usually in the middle of a binge, I would secrete a couple of notes there, a good sign of being a burgeoning alcoholic, against future drought. And then, Oh joy!

In came Ian and laughed uproariously as I found a fiver among the Psalms of David.

"No point in looking in my place, old Boot," he said, using my current nickname. "It's well-scoured!"

"Tee-hee, though. We've got the entrance fee so let's go!"

Which we did, at a fairish lick.

Sometimes, usually on my payday, we liked to affect a Red Army style march, as Stan and I had done in a former epoch in Brighton. Arms swinging transversely across our chests, imaginary Kalashnikovs, barrels pointing up and to the right, a semi- goose step, heads tilted upwards and to our left, right hand slapping the breaches of our machine pistols, balalaikas and stirring Russian Tenors, from massed Red Cavalry, a soundtrack in our skull cinemas. Stalin's soldiers, marching up the few steps into the 'Oak' Lounge Bar, singing:

"Slava! Slava Rossya! Slava Stalin!"

Chapter 54

The new year of 1980, in the highly unusual weather conditions following the St Helens' volcanic eruption, I was walking over to Electric City. I was still living with the two Indian boys on the other side of town and showing Ian my work, viewing his stunning self-portrait too, Rembrandt-like in its depth and pathos. He had suffered a lot the previous year and I felt I had neglected our friendship. I began to see more of Steph, too and her strange but noble boyfriend, Paul. Sometimes Ian and I and the pregnant Sarah would go for a quiet drink in the countryside together in her Morris Minor estate and then call into a curry house back in Manningham. These were nearly the last days when they were still cosmopolitan and full of cheer. We liked to imagine something of pre-war Paris in the air.

The Ripper had either died or was lying low. Still, those chilling tapes though, left in public places:

"I'm Jack-oh, my dear, George…!"

I was heading to see Mrs Hill and Ian one evening, in this late and strange Spring, having got my old job back. I was just outside my old place when I had to step aside between the late snowdrifts, for my Goddess. The woman had a loping, graceful stride, not dykish. She looked stylish in her long boots and sported a chic cloche, the hat fashionable among Feminists at the time, on her short, brunette hair. I caught a swift and short-sighted glance of recognition in her beautiful eyes, a Bowie, androgynous look. She stepped aside for me simultaneously, submissively. One of the Bradford Festival crew, I thought, no lesbian her.

I imagined she was an actress or a musician. Then suddenly it hit me; the Hawthorn Goddess! I had played darts with her years ago, on my first night back north by myself. I had been so awe-struck by her, only one of my arrows hit the board and I had been far too overwhelmed by her to chat.

And so the year went on, all of us wondering when the rain would stop after midsummer; indigo nights when it did, hot and steaming and we never tired of listening to Meatloaf, the leitmotif of that weird year. Even Steph came out of her shell, as we all danced; Sara, Ian, Paul and I, clumsily together like summer ghosts out on the lawn at Oak Villas, well into the scented indigo twilight.

Dear old Miss Busby, like Mrs Hill, the landlady and concierge, last of a small Manningham gentry, smiling gently and vaguely down at us from the faded elegance of her lonely bed-chamber under the Victorian eaves, an ageing Lady of Shallot.

The first time I saw Miriam, at the Oakleigh with her minx-like brunette friend, Polish and sexy Julie, Ian nudged me into action.

"'Get in!"

We both hauled the rustic tables together out on the back lawn and made our introductions. The vibes felt good and Ian kept nudging me vigorously underneath the beer-laden table, while Sarah beamed at me with a knowing smile. It was decided that Sarah, not drinking due to her condition, should drive us up to the Sugar Cane night club while it was still quiet and on we went.

Another day in that crazy year, I spotted Steph, alone in the corner of the Oakleigh lounge, nursing a pint and twisting her long cascading hair, contemplatively around her delicate fingers. Her myopic gaze met mine but she didn't acknowledge me. I didn't feel offended, as I found her self-absorption totally appropriate. I experienced that freezing of time when seeing the face of a Goddess. She looked like some medieval illumination from a Book Of Hours, a cloistered nun and so deliciously feminine.

"Dave," she said, in her girlish voice suddenly, looking up at me. "I've just written a Testimonial for you!" then collapsed into sexy giggles. "You have an admirer!"

I told her I hoped it was a good one. Collapsing in on herself like some Pre-Raphaelite Maiden, she hugged herself into her long gown and shook her delicious tresses.

And so the year drifted on, wondering when the rain would stop after midsummer; indigo nights when it did, hot and steaming and we never tired of listening to Meatloaf.

On a hot summer night, the torrid indigo night of the Deep South of the US, and 'What's it gonna be, boy?'

I remember first hearing that classic Meatloaf record in Germany the summer before, where I worked with some other British lads. It became the anthem of that strange and exalting year.

"Like a bat out H-E-E-E-L-L-L-LLL!!!

'I will love ya for the rest of ma Life!"

I remember the Sugar Cane and then going on to the more hip Palm Cove and then my first morning with Miriam.

Chapter 55

Miriam

I woke up that first morning, shirt drenched with sweat, in a strange bedroom flooded with a silver-gold September light. It was an attic room, a typical Manningham garret that I recognised and with a feminine neatness about it, a cool refinement, that I remembered admiring in Gwen John's great painting of her Paris apartment. The Velux window in the mansard roof shed a more distilled northern light than in Gwen John's Paris, but there was a similar cane chair in a corner which was desecrated by my cast-off jeans, socks and underwear.

The woman, petite but all of a piece, breezed in with a hint of garden freshness. She came to my bedside. She came so still and I sensed as I had the previous night, her compactness, her muscularity and her excellence.

"Well, good morning, David, what a night!" she said, drawing her dressing table chair up to the bedside and sitting down.

"Indeed, E-E-Erica," I spluttered.

"Miriam," she replied, looking faintly amused. "I think I am going to clean you!"

As she leaned towards me, her handsome and finely-chiselled features became clearer to my myopic gaze.

"That beard HAS to go!"

I couldn't help but stare in silence at her porcelain complexion, at her refined and calming gaze, her Baltic grey eyes freighted with intelligence and kindness. A high buttoned and light Prussian green/grey blouse was fastened discretely with what looked like an Edwardian dull gold brooch, obviously some family heirloom.

"You said last night, David, that you wanted to be my friend?"

My throat throbbed and I felt an almost delicious choking sensation. I was speechless. I moved my hand slowly towards hers which was now resting near my lower left arm, so still. With an elegant and rather surprising gesture, she withdrew from somewhere beneath her, an inhaler, which she drew on, swiftly yet deeply and holding her breath for a moment, prolonged our silent communion. I still don't know why I was so profoundly moved by her gesture but it had a sacramental look, one hinting of infinite grace and my soul suddenly ached for her.

"I would rather like that, Miriam, to be friends," I managed to say, huskily.

"And I would too, David. You made that quite clear last night."

With a toss of her blond and bobbed hair, she moved to stand up, half-turning towards me as she did so. I could still not take my eyes off her, nor did I wish to break the silent communion between us. Mesmerised, as I now obviously was, she stretched towards me, radiating some of her physical and spiritual fragrance and leaning over me, blinding me momentarily with an elegantly drooping wing of hair, she kissed me, oh so gently, and tenderly. Then briskly and with a little wiggle of her joyous bottom, she clapped her hands authoritatively and with her shapely, sculpted back now to me, looked at me over her shoulder.

"Righto, my David; coffee for us and stay right there!"

Now in the golden dawn of my second day in Paradise with Botticelli Girl as Ian had described her. I had woken up again in her bed to a glorious late summer's morning in this crazy year of 1980.

"Hello, you!" she said. "So how was it for you, boy?"

This was to be her name for me for a short and blissful time. I laughed, half-remembering how pissed I had been the night before last, in the Sugar Cane but how I had summoned up the courage to ask her for a dance and her graciously accepting. Her friends and some of my former uni acquaintances, Gail and Alison and even the rest of the highly PC and Cromwellian crew, had collaborated in forming a cordon sanitaire around us, as we found a corner to chat and bond in. Bob Marley provided the theme music; Ali, the charming Sudanese disk jockey and a mate of mine winked at me through the fug and flashing coloured lights on that fantastic night, indigo and vermilion, satin blacks and ambient Afro-Caribbean joy.

A while later, washed and breakfasted, we set forth to show ourselves, on what looked like our wedding breakfast. She dressed in a smart, casual style, suiting her clean-cut and slightly masculine features. Petite, yet muscular, an early mark Spitfire, I thought to myself. She wore short heels along with her denim jeans and a smart, tailored jacket. I don't think I was ever to see her in a dress. Her vigorous and firm yet nicely curved body seemed to mould itself to mine as with a little wiggle and a grin, she made a space between our singing limbs and offered her left hand, tugging urgently at my sleeve.

"Paw," she said.

How I loved this ritual command, as we set forth towards Manningham Lane. Dutifully I hugged her hand with mine, marvelling at the strength of hers, despite her sheer womanliness; a delicious coolness issued from her, my body resonating to this, her blithe and crystal spirit.

"So, Botticelli Girl," said Ian later. "Ya fucked her yet?"

I mumbled something about her being more of a Donatello girl, as her androgynous good looks reminded me so much of that fine sculptor's 'David'. If anything, Steph and Sarah were more Botticelli.

The previous evening in the Oak, Pete Marjoribanks had intimated loudly to Ian and company, both Steph and Sarah being present, how Greenwood was cunt-struck at the moment. I learnt this later from a laughing Steph.

"Well, I… er…" I spluttered, wiping my mouth as I passed over my can of Carlsberg Special, my calling card, my libation to the Jovian Ian.

"Tell Uncle Ian, go on," he said.

"Well, for starters, I see her as more of a Monteverdi girl now, much more spiritual."

Ian guffawed at this.

I mumbled a string of shamefaced excuses; erectile dysfunction, temporary of course, too much ethyl alcohol in my system, first sex for about 4 years and so on.

"Tha'll be reet-get some ale down thee, lad," he said, laughing at his Yorkshireman's panacea.

This exchange took place in Sarah's flat while her baby, Jo-Jo, gurgled away in her cot. Mrs Hill was still in hospital and seemed to be recovering from her cancer. Both of us had been to see her at the Royal Infirmary and at first, we felt concerned at not being able to find her in that sad ward. Finally, we saw a shock of platinum white hair, just another old, crumpled body among other old ladies, warehoused against the walls.

There had been some recovery on our last visit.

"You know, Dave," said Ian. "I think she's coming out of this. She seems set to little old lady mode forever and we'll be seeing her back at the old place before long!"

His optimism was not ill-founded, having lost his mum to the ravages of cancer, earlier in this momentous year. And indeed, the old girl did get better. I was able to take Miriam proudly to meet her.

Miriam was only too pleased to share her life and accommodation, so I returned to Electric City in the year of the St Helens' volcano. We had had hot summer nights in April, hence my gift to Steph and I remember us; Sarah, pregnant with Jo Jo in early summer, then later in that magical year Ian, myself and Steph and Paul her boyfriend, all sunbathing and cavorting about on the elegant lawn of the house on Manningham Lane. Just about all of my Manningham friends seemed to have lived there at one time. I remember pacing the back streets around dismal Bowling and heading for Manningham sometimes engulfed in sub-tropical rainstorms and throughout that summer when I wasn't working on my night jobs, the crackling and flashing of lightning storms.

The latest Police ID posters about the Yorkshire Ripper had started to peel now and in the pubs and clubs, though the fear had not gone, people felt that the Police had lost their way. The latest news was that Scotland Yard had been called in on the case. Even big Ian and I still chilled at that perpetual refrain, the dispiriting sound of that Wear-side voice: "I'm Jack, Oh my dear, George-have you lost your way!"

I snapped out of my musings, not having slept much lately when Paul came in to relieve me of babysitting duties. He was an intense and sometimes difficult man, with a kind of lean inscrutability.

With no little enthusiasm, Miriam having gone down south to see her parents for a couple of days, we ventured forth to the Oak at Light Infantry pace and to the sound of Eric Coates' RAF March Past, with a swift foxtrot, marking time as we waited for the lights to change on Keighley Road. Merlin engines from the 1940s roared throatily in our ears as we continued and after a sharp right turn, arms a-swinging and bags of swank assaulted the few stairs and with gun-buttons set to 'FIRE', we roared through the Saloon Bar doors.

"God Save all here!" shouted Ian, to an empty lounge.

A late summer light streamed through the French windows, beyond which I could just about see the elfin and gracious figure of Steph, with the Lady Sarah, her equally gracious sister. No-one behind the bar, so we cut our throttles and undercarriages down, myself wallowing in Ian's slipstream, we shimmied and chicaned over to join them. The two ladies, well Regency gentlewomen, had brought the gracious ambience of Home Counties England with them, something Cavalier and the gentle late Summer light enveloped us in raw sienna with maybe a touch of yellow ochre and a tint of Naples Yellow to cool it, the painter in me saw. The huge sycamores and oaks, tending slightly to the sere and yellow as the lawn certainly did, loomed nobly over us, as we gently conversed until I sloped off to the bar.

For some reason, in this strangely exultant yet elegiac mood, my thoughts went back to Brighton and a certain poem, which had moved me so much and inspired me to think anew of the promise and the hope of art.

I heard the refined voice of the poet, Officer Class:

'The branches

Hold in the gardens their silent, eloquent gestures,

Which in our case we have not got.'

I could almost smell the close sexual bond between Ian and Sarah, something more adult and fecund than the one developing between Miriam and me. Their baby girl must be at home being babysat, a future job for Miriam and me, I hoped.

"Hi Dave," said Steph giving out her inimitable little girl giggle, with just a touch of West Country brogue and a shy grin as she shook her long, dishevelled tresses.

Sometimes, most endearingly, she would gaze myopically up into the clear air. Looking for 'sky babies' I thought, for some strange reason. Both sisters always wore long dresses which suited them; gowns, I thought to myself would be even more suitable. Were Eleanor and Marianne Dashwood like these two? What did they smell like? Wood smoke and witch hazel with a tang of female sweat? Visually, I thought deep maroon and sequinned highlights for Steph, shimmering iridescent when she moved. Russet Madder, glimpses of Officers of the Foot-Guards attending their muslin and calico-clad ladies, even the indigo and old gold of naval officers, Nelson's Young Seahawks. I thought, ah, Sandy Denny and Fairport Convention as I called to mind suddenly a lithe and be-gowned girl at the Hyde Park concert so many years ago, with a tambourine and turning backwards somersaults, wafting ethereally across the stage, twirling, diaphanous, an incandescent and medieval dream; a Benedictine manuscript come to life. Sarah, more athletic and 20th century with the same refined but slightly more sober face, bespectacled and focussed, concerned and yet thrillingly kind.

"So, where's Miriam?" asked Sarah.

She had an endearingly lopsided grin and her voice sounded a more contralto register than her sister's Pixie fluting, with a slight catch in it, like a brave and precocious adolescent boy. Ian, as ever with the Lady Sarah, somewhat subdued, smiled shyly, as when I first met him. When I told them Miriam was down in Plymouth, Steph let out a girlish, flirtatious giggle.

"I gave Miriam a testimonial about you, Dave, a good one!"

She giggled uncontrollably as I basked in the love and golden vibes of these beautiful people. She held out an LP to me.

"I've been dancing to it all night, with Paul, Dave!" she said.

It was the Meatloaf album that I had bought on impulse for her when I had been in town the day before with Marian.

We finished our drinks, Sarah and Ian tasked with relieving their babysitter and driving to Wakefield, in Sarah's slightly battered Morris Minor estate, to see Ian's widower Dad and show him their baby, Jo-Jo. Steph was to return to her very feminine little attic garret in Oak Avenue, the most genteel cul-de-sac in the once elegant and fashionable Manningham and myself back to Miriam's flat up St Paul's road, where I had been tasked to clean up, as her dad was bringing her back and introductions were likely. A further suggestion she had made was that I should drop anchor on the booze. At this stage, I could easily comply. Parting with the ladies and a subdued Ian, felt like a portal to a new life, something distinguished and unforeseen. The grace of the Goddess seemed to be shining on me and Ian, now a very proud father.

As I walked back to Miriam's place, I looked forward to the domestic tasks ahead and called in at the SPAR shop on the way for a couple of cans of Carlsberg to ease the workload. I cut up to Oak Lane, gazing wistfully up at the small dormer window of my old abode. Such times, I thought. It would never be the same but I looked forward to what seemed the end of my bachelorhood with no regrets. The Life of Riley was over; a sober and loving married life beckoned.

Chapter 56

Ops-Heilbron-December 1944

Dad, from his folding seat right of pilot and skipper, gritting his teeth and clenching his stomach muscles, looked up and to his left at Skipper Bert, who in turn, very briefly glanced then looked back and up at the face of Peter, the Navigator just visible in the astrodome and taking a quick star-shot with his sextant. If he had looked around and down, he would have discerned in the dull yellow light, Lobbie Lobsinger, the bomb aimer's Mae West and his prone figure in the nose of the Lanc.

"Right," said Bert over the intercom. "Dutch Coast ahead; no chat, fingers out and keep your eyes open for fighters."

"Roger, that, Skip!" from all the crew; from Gungha, in the rear turret, sphincter tightening, as were his gauntleted fingers over the triggers of four Browning machine guns.

"Roger, Skip," from Ron, in the mid-upper, already foot-pedalling his 2 Brownings in a near-full circle, midway down and atop the fuselage, scanning the indigo sky above and around his lone perch.

"Roger, Skip," Jock, the Sparks and Peter now ensconced behind his green curtain and at his compasses and slide rule.

"Roger, Skip," said Dad, fumbling with the fuel mixes at his lone panel but standing up now and prepared for fire control in the event of a fighter attack, maybe even taking over from Bert in case he was chopped or more likely, helping him heave at the controls in an emergency.

"Roger, Skip!" crackled Lobby over the intercom, in his Canadian accent.

They were headed south and east for south Germany, south even of Nuremberg which Dad and Gungha remembered so vividly, that dreadful February night only 11 months before and what seemed a lifetime ago. Dad and even more so, Gungha. He had his face cut up a bit by shattered perspex as a Jerry night fighter had made a swift pass at the rear of the Lanc. Dad had to drag a profusely but superficially bleeding Gungha back up the fuselage. It was a miracle that the Ju-88 had been scared off by Ron's' hammering twin Brownings in the mid-upper turret. They must have remembered the funeral pyre of burning Lancs and Halifaxes strewn across half of northern Germany on that fateful last leg back to the Dutch Coast. They must also have remembered the 'Abbeville Boys', yellow-nosed Messcherschmidt 109's and Focke-Wulf-190's, even more infamous among the daytime US aircrews of the 8th Airforce Fortresses and B-24's who had been decimated by gallant Luftwaffe fighters, on one of the many Schweinfurt 'Daylights' only a year before.

Lancaster 'JO-E' droned on, well west of the Ruhr with its almost impenetrable flak batteries and night fighter bases but perilously near the Saar basin and upper Rhineland.

"Corkscrew Por!" screamed Gungha's voice over the intercom, from the tail end Charlie position, his 4 Brownings clattering with Ron joining in from the upper mid turret. Dad must have shrunk in on himself, grasping for Bert's armoured seat as the huge Lanc started a plunge down and to port, his flying boots kicking at the throttles and his arms around Bert's ready to lend some heft to the gyrations of this emergency move, 4 Merlins suddenly roaring as negative 'G' threw Dad and Bert together, dust, pencils and even maps flying past them as now the mighty Lanc climbed and corkscrewed over the loop, cannon shells, and machine-gun fire raking them from the Jerry fighter, muffled screams over the intercom, panicked and heavy breathing, the Banshee scream of unleashed Rolls Royce power.

Miraculously, there was no burning and the Ju-88 seemed to have vanished into the velvet but menacing indigo night around them.

Bert did an intercom check and on not hearing Gungha, released Dad to stumble back down the cramped fuselage, over the terrifying obstacle of the main spar, under Ron's swinging stirupped feet, as he still traversed his guns. Then tentatively, Dad must have groped through the narrowing and yawing fuselage to the hell of the rear turret that he fearfully anticipated; no fire but Gungha lay slumped over his guns, then he moved and his oppo's face looked up, even with his oxygen mask obscuring his lower face, he seemed to be smiling and gave the 'thumbs up' and as Dad leaned, over the howl of the slipstream and the roaring of the Merlin engines and with Dad's arm about him, Gungha was able to partially remove his oxygen mask.

"Guns jammed, mate!" he said. "Harry mate, maybe I got the bugger?"

Fighting back and over the main spar, that last refuge for many a doomed crew spinning to their deaths, Dad was able to reassure Bert and watch the fun ahead as JO-E, the vanguard of the Main Force saw the first Target Indicators and incendiaries from the Pathfinders ahead, inverted and iridescent Christmas trees and searchlights groping the sky frantically, insanely, from the doomed little town below.

"Christmas coming up for somebody!" cracked Gungha and over the intercom sounded stifled but nervous guffaws.

"Shut it!" said Bert. "Bomb run coming up."

Bomb run, no hitch, not even stroked by a probing searchlight, no fighters it seemed but flak all over the shop.

"Bombs gone!" shouted Lobby and the Lanc seemed to leap as it released its burden.

"Steady as we go! Hands off cocks!" said Bert.

They had to keep their course until the cameras had taken photo-flash pictures of the target below; a gut-wrenchingly nervous moment.

"'OK, boys, home! Good prang!" said Bert and a collective sigh of relief came from the lads as Bert heaved the Lanc up and away from the burning Heilbron below.

Being at the spearhead of Main Force, JO-E had a head start and a better chance of avoiding the probable carnage to come behind them as throttles, opened wide by Dad, they headed north for home.

I was born shortly before take-off and only the rest of the crew knew. After a good landing back in Lincolnshire, the lads formed a guard-of-honour for Dad as they emerged, exhausted and exhilarated, onto the tarmac. Backs slapped all around and from that time, Little Heilbron was my name amongst the crew.

Bavarian Heilbron fried beneath an unforgiving and indigo sky, smouldered for weeks and that terrible night is commemorated every December 4th since 1944, in Southern Germany.

Chapter 57

It was nice meeting her Dad. We went to the Oak and then a curry, which he loved.

"Call me Huw, old boy. Dave, sorry!"

He was medium-sized and getting a bit porky, an ex-Rowing Blue from Emmanuel College, Cambridge and looked it. He had kind eyes and an Auden- look about him, exuding gentility and liberality, a very kind and loving father and a graduate, like Miriam's mum who was an ex-Girton Scholar in literature Tripos both immediately pre-war and after wartime service. A rather old-fashioned and liberal-minded Englishman of the best sort.

The next few months, years even were great. I think the old man was shrewd enough to be disappointed that I was on the bones of my arse and not quite the social catch he might have hoped for, for his beloved daughter and that I was fond of a drink or two. However, at that time I was fairly presentable when scrubbed up and could counterfeit the air of an educated man, even a gentleman.

I was determined to get a job as soon as possible. Huw agreed that the Thatcher government was intent on repression and I felt that I should make a better contribution to our income, dire as the general economic situation looked for Britain.

We settled down to what looked like a long relationship. I got her an engagement ring, a cheap brass one from Bradford Market. I wince with shame at this. We moved to a bigger flat; I got a temporary job labouring in a sheet metal factory in Bowling and we survived the darkening times ahead. We had found each other and I resolved to put halcyon days behind me. We even fantasised about our first baby; our new flat further down St Pauls Road had a backroom big enough and Thatcher hadn't yet got her grasping hands on the Housing Associations. On evenings together, we seldom hit the club or pub scene now, we fantasised about our coming family. Rosa (Luxemburg) for a girl, Ziggy for a boy after Siegfried and because we both loved Bowie.

We survived the assassination of John Lennon, a kindred spirit of my youth and I met her Mum, Shelagh for the first time, at Christmas near Plymouth. She was a deep and serene gentlewoman, shy and kindly. She had a comfortable and genteel house, and her brother, Ralph was a delight, charming, very funny and handsome. I couldn't believe that I could deserve such domestic bliss; my new family.

Back in Bradford, our quiet life continued. Miriam finished her post-graduate degree and I accompanied her on the odd trip to London, as she was a left-wing bookseller and needed to see her publishers down there. We were so preoccupied with each other that we had hardly noticed the murder of student Jaqui Hill in Headingley, the student area of nearby Leeds. The horror had returned and we both lay awake telling each other second-hand reports of possible sightings of the ripper. He loomed as some kind of a giant, a spring-heeled Jack, the stuff of Grimm's Fairy Tales.

One evening, we thought we heard voices raised outside on the street and as I rushed to the curtains, Miriam switched on the TV for the News.

"They've got him!" she cried.

One Peter James Sutcliffe of Heaton, not far from where Ian and I had bonded so strongly one indigo night years ago. A Bingley boy and Christ, if he didn't frequent the same pubs I used to haunt many years before when I rented a cottage up on the moor near there.

The wave of relief around Manningham was palpable. All of our crowd headed for the pubs in Electric City. The horror that had blighted so many lives was over.

That night, Miriam and I snuggled together in our new bedroom with the large window looking out on parking spaces and vacant lots at the back. She pummelled her feet on the backs of my legs, an endearing habit of hers and grasped my enveloping arms to her tummy.

A 'Gunners' Moon' shone down on us innocents from an indigo sky.

"Paw," said Miriam a few days' later, as we stepped through the front gate and into St Paul's Road, her left hand extended and as a couple or an item in today's parlance, we headed down to the Oak.

It felt almost as if she was showing me off. Me! Very strangely for I was, as by now should be glaringly evident, never hesitant over the prospect of imminent pints, I felt reluctant to curtail the delicious sensation that I felt burgeoning between us. I wanted flowers, sweet birds singing, corny stuff like that, her in my arms and us blending. So, we cut left at the Bradford and Keighley Road and instead of heading across it for Oak villas and the Oakleigh Hotel, we cut left through the great Victorian cast iron and ornamental gates and through to the most romantic Manningham Park. At that time there was a blind persons' garden between the mock Baroque Cartwright Memorial Hall and the Lake. There was also a bench where we could hold and savour each other as well as the most delicious ambient smells.

So, we had our walk through paradise Garden and to prolong our bonding, went into the great Gallery, holding hands, welded together.

And then we went down to the pub.

Marjoribanks was there and Ian and the Lady Sarah, Stephanie and Paul, Ellie, Pansy – "Yo-Bicycle-Face!" - Scotty, sundry others and then Terry and June behind the bar. I felt like I was King Arthur and Miriam was my Queen Guinevere and around me here at my Court at Camelot, were met the greatest Knights and Ladies of all Christendom. I remember an uncharacteristic beam of delight from the cynical Pete Marjoribanks, across the groaning table.

Later, we took a turn around a still summery garden, though with an Autumn breeze getting up and Miriam shivering slightly. I hugged her and we went back through the French doors. I had found my Miss Dashwood at last, the older and slightly sterner one, the true Roman, my Lady Eleanor.

We were both working; Miriam in the office of the Bradford Council Depot and I was working for an employment agency, my usual default occupation when not in regular employment. This being a Saturday we went into town and I had forgotten how thrilling it was to go shopping with a loved one. She liked her food and as I promised to make a fish pie, a speciality of mine, we went to the old Fish Market with its white tiles, crushed ice and seaside smells. Then we headed off to the covered market at John Street, to the Slavia stores. Miriam liked a good Polish rye bread and a weekly delicacy, such as herring in horseradish sauce, stuffed olives, delights I would never have thought of and then, with bags full and no 'paw' command this time, we went for the bus the short way home to

Manningham. Then changed our minds and went for a quick drink in town, before late afternoon closing time.

I was walking on air. Suddenly I realised it was the first time I had thought of Glenda in nearly 10 years. It was nearly 20 years since both of us, rumpled and dishevelled, myself desolate in spirit, I had walked her to Chester Street bus station, for her journey back over Scarlet Heights and Ovenden Moor to Halifax, when I was so puzzled and lost as to what our relationship was about.

At home, Miriam and I ate, drank some Chablis and went to bed. We stayed there some time, only going out over that enchanted weekend for walks together in the park and up through Heaton and Northcliffe woods, merging our bodies and spirits and blending into each other, the light of love in our eyes and birdsong drenching us from the late September sky.

That Sunday night, in between lovemaking, Miriam having taught me most of what I knew, we talked to each other about our past, our families, our joys and disasters, our hopes and fears and the next morning, I just had to sit at the bedside and watch her put on her makeup.

"Here," she said, pointing to the bedside.

I marvelled at her artistry, her gentle poise and the minimal craft she applied. I marvelled too at every stitch of clothes she put on, spare and classical and even the engineering that had gone into the manufacture of her pristine court shoes, with two-inch heels and strapless, which seemed designed solely for her; her cheap but tasteful tights and panties, her short - but not too short - skirt and black leather Suzi Quatro jacket, the rage at the time, giving meaning to the Jacobean poets' trope: A nakedness with its clothes on.'

She had made me sandwiches because I had a long day ahead, working in a soft drinks' factory in Honley on the other side of Huddersfield, with two bus changes. I didn't expect to be together with her until late evening. It was the happiest day's work I've ever had, before or since.

The days settled down and the following weekend when Miriam had gone into town shopping; both of us feeling we needed a little space, Ian rang. It was psilocybin time! Ian knew a field just between Heaton and Northcliffe woods, where Miriam and I had done our bit of courting only the previous week. On the way, Ian and I bought a bottle of cider and a couple of cans of Special Brew to refresh us in our hunt. I had mixed feelings about psychotropics but for a time we goofed about, sometimes at grass root level, talking to the strange little fungi, with their witches' hats and evil colouring, like Plague marks. We rolled about like puppies and surfaced to view what looked like thousands of nodding Gandalfs in a Hobbit landscape, sometimes a disenchanted old West Riding waste and then the booze came in handy.

We got back to my place and bachelor no more, I was determined to clean myself up. Ian in a similar spirit did the same and though we had brought a bottle of Chablis for Miriam, I brewed a strong coffee or two for us both, while we waited for her. We also had a carrier bag packed with magic mushrooms. Miriam had told me she was no stranger to drugs, though we both rarely indulged these days. Ian was up for everything, as I think I have already illustrated!

She was very gracious and welcoming to Ian and we eventually sat down to a hearty meal. Miriam loved her food, something I liked in a woman. We had Polish sausage and salami with some quickly-cooked oven chips with mayonnaise and Slavia Store's best Coleslaw and stuffed olives.

We popped a few mushrooms after this and Miriam, by the light in her eyes, seemed to like it. This surprised me as I was beginning to find her a very strong and rational woman, despising the Hippy ethos and sceptical generally.

"Dave," said Ian, nudging me. "Why don't you just let go and go for a stroll in Wonderland with Miriam?" and tactfully for him, made to leave.

I was beginning to feel itchy and uneasy with the side effects of the drug; my peripheral vision was beginning to lose form and wave, the tiny room coming alive but in a creepy way. Yet Miriam looked at me yearningly, holding out her hand, her hand so firm yet gentle. I was frightened and demurred. I now wonder what might have happened if we had walked through our fantasy Magic Garden?

We came down gently and washed up in the kitchen together, chatting generally, gradually becoming sober and wondered where to go that night, the Bavaria or the Oakleigh again? Suddenly, we heard a knock at the door. Ellie stood there with two bottles of Newkie Broon - Newcastle Brown - held aloft.

"Thought I'd leave yees' two to settle down before I came to the House Warming!" she said, with her tomboy, naughty boy looks,

We welcomed her in. I truly had arrived; Ellie, Queen of the Gays, or so I thought at the time. I marvelled at the gossip and craic the two women enjoyed and laughed with them. Ellie had a distinctly Cumbrian accent, a working-class lass too, ex-RAF van driver and with several convictions for driving and taking away, she was even more of a tearaway than Ian and I. By turns comic and serious, the conversation turned to the Ripper. Ellie and the girls knew some of the prostitutes down the 'Lane' and St Paul's Road being nearly the heartland of the trade, had kept an eye out for potential dodgy punters and younger men like me. Even as a Lesbian, she had given a good report about me to Miriam, thinking that I was a nice lad but who drank a lot.

"And he doesn't drive," said Miriam.

Ellie knew poor Yvonne Pearson and one or two others. We were sad for a bit and then we recollected our fantasies as to what made this maniac like he was; a bedtime preoccupation for Miriam and I almost every night, as for many others at that time. And, such is the banality of evil, he turned out to be a little petit-bourgeois shit from Heaton, my stamping ground. And in government, we had Margaret Thatcher.

Chapter 58

Neither of us, of course, was so 'uncool' as to want to watch the Royal Wedding on TV. In those darkening times, it was a bright spot, the nasty little Falklands war being now behind us but still, at least up here, in the cold grip of Thatcher's recession, it was seen as something to celebrate. I scoffed at it, as did Miriam, saying she had lots of academic work to catch up on and as I'd been taking my artwork seriously and resumed my solitary walks, Miriam not being much of a rambler, I resolved on a sketching trip up at my beloved Shipley Glen. This was a popular and exquisitely beautiful valley just a few miles from us and near the edge of Ilkley Moor. I took our portable radio with me though and I am sure that Miriam watched the wedding, probably ironically and in a 'post-modern' way!

I took my tartan shortbread biscuit tin, an ancient Christmas gift from Mum, containing the few pastels, pencils and sticks of charcoal that I'd accumulated and even used during a session in winter at the Art College for unemployed people. I had done three of my only completed pastel paintings that I thought worthwhile since leaving college so many years before. And today, despite my divided concentration - I enjoyed the service on the radio - I painted my first decent landscape.

I walked farther than Shipley Glen and up to the summit and watershed of Ilkley Moor, so full of renewed energy and the joy of love did I feel. I noticed for the first time how the North Country held more of what I wanted as a landscape artist. Looking over into the Wharfe Valley and across to Blubberhouses Moor, pretty as I acknowledged Sussex to have been, I was overcome by a kind of spiritual grandeur, something old too. I was still, like my father something of a late Victorian and rejoicing in the bronzed and burnt golds of old bracken and the crags amongst the burned patches of heather, the sudden clockwork 'whiiirrr!!' of a startled red grouse at my feet, I felt really at home.

Looking north, I could see the Craven limestone uplands and I could just discern the bone-grey choir of Bolton Abbey in the far distance. I knew this scene well, of course, and had rejoiced in it on my early return from the south and from when in the mid-seventies I lived in my chalet on the glen.

But this time my soul exalted and especially on this special day to see the cloud shadows in the slight early summer breeze chasing up the fell sides of Beamsley Beacon, over Addingham in the distance and straight across and above Ilkley on Middleton moor. They seemed like the Holy Spirit caressing the moor-side, something that was never to pall and to me was a moving symbol of God's grace in the North Country.

I enthused about this to Miriam later, but though a Devon girl, I was a little disappointed that she just returned an amused grin. Just a slight cloud seemed to have appeared in our bliss.

I chose a stack of rocks overhanging the post-glacial gorge that formed the glen, funnily enough directly opposite the chalet where I had enjoyed what seemed my semi-retirement 7 or 8 years ago. It was a lovely early summer's day and feeling fulfilled and pleased with myself, on the long hike back to Manningham, I hummed to myself Parry's great hymn of praise from that splendid occasion: 'I was glad…'

I can still see her happy face as I stumbled through the door, sweaty and my face streaked with charcoal and I rushed to crush her in my arms after I had hurled my easel and rucksack into our little hallway.

"Bathroom, Dave and wash your face first!"

And I did and my heart sang and afterwards, we rushed into each other's arms and mutually agreed that we had time for a bit of love-making before she had to turn the roast.

Our honeymoon over, we decided to find more serious work. I got sick of travelling so far and for such monotonous work and low Agency wages and Miriam, who came up north originally to study for a PhD needed to find work that enabled her to finish it. She was a bright lass, I knew that and I was pleased to find that she was an MA and an excellent scholar as well as political activist, a feminist and a Trotskyist. She had struggled at Grunwicks in the anti-union battles of the dying Labour Government of the late '70s and she had a job as an agent for left-wing bookshops. It paid little. However, we were able to go down on a quick day trip to London, meeting some publishers and dining in Clerkenwell and near the Guardian offices in what was still a working-class part of Islington.

Chapter 59

Sadly, for Miriam but as a sign of the times, left-wing book clubs were on the wane, even Fourth Idea in Bradford was struggling. My last agency job was in a Dickensian Pop factory in Fartown, Huddersfield, hard by the Viaduct where poor Helen Rs' body had been found. During a short break at the works, I casually remarked on this to one of my Huddersfield comrades. "Ah, that slag!' was the rejoinder. My cynicism deepened about England, even though my personal happiness had never been better.

I had dropped anchor on the booze and Miriam and I stayed in a lot more, to work out a plan. She resolved on getting a teaching job in Further Education; both her parents were ex-Cambridge, her mother had been a public-school teacher and her Dad something administrative in local and county government in Devon, but related to higher education and the Arts in particular. Miriam was 'posh' and I have to admit, that I liked that. I also liked the sound of her parents, liberal, upper-middle-class, something interesting in the war and with colonial administrative backgrounds, of the less exploitative sort. Ralph, her not so academic, social worker brother seemed a gem. He and Miriam were very close and I found it touching. I seemed to have found a home at last though neither sets of our parents were to meet.

Miriam started a short course, interestingly enough near Huddersfield, for Lecturers in Further Education and her bus journeys soon replicated mine. I got a job, and a very dirty one in the old engineering side of Bradford, near where I had lived with Des and the two lovely Indian boys. An ancient family steel plate works, manufacturing industrial ventilators and ducting wanted heavy labourers to help them move the factory further up to the Leeds Road. It must have been the only industry growing in England at that time, for the feeling was that though Thatcher was rapidly losing any popularity, here was a government willing to stick the boot in. There was a new ruthlessness and swinishness in the air. I noticed it when part of my job turned out to be going to the shop for bacon sandwiches for the lads. There was little of the bantering jocularity I would have seen only a year before, only a sullen stoicism and snydy-ness. I liked to bring my transistor radio and left it tuned to Radio 3 with its shortwave aerial extended. On returning from one sandwich foray in the rain and after a long wait, I found my aerial had been sawn in half with a hacksaw. Sniggers all round. The Black Douglas redux?

I needed a bath every day as one job I had, with another lad, was sweeping a hundred years of carbon dust from the rafters in the new building, an old forge and steelworks. I was jeered at by my fellow workmates. My moral and political re-education had begun.

A high point before that Xmas was that we were offered a flat change. We were to leave the present flat and Rob, my Hawthorn Goddess, was to take ours and then we were to move down the same side of the road to another Housing Association flat, but a larger one, vacated by a rather pleasant lesbian artist called Bert.

I loved our new place, not so high up and with a huge bay window in the sitting room looking out towards the still rather fine, late Victorian terraces, with their mansard upper roofs, almost Parisian in their elegance; a tidy little bedroom and an extra one large enough to be a guest room/study, AND I hoped, my future studio as sporadically, and despite my peregrinations and craziness of the previous twelve months, I had got down to a bit of serious work; drawings and crayons so far but I was getting into a working habit and had taken up doing my own framing.

Bert had left us a huge faux-antique desk, Heals, possibly, but which cried out for study. When our move was accomplished, I had to go over to the desk, admiring the view; the late summer afternoon had painted the gritstone of the terrace opposite a golden yellow ochre and with indigo and burnt umber shadows, the view sang to my soul. I swept an arm over the desk top, marvelling at its antique patina, its madder and Indian red hues and the mahogany and dark oak of the drawers and carcass. I was Yuri Zhivago near Smolensk and deep in the Russian landscape of Pasternak's masterpiece. Lara/Miriam was brewing a pot of tea in our light-filled kitchen to my right; Peter, my cat was acquainting himself with his new litter tray in the corner by the cooker and I fancied I heard balalaika music.

The next day we went to see Bert's show at the Cartwright Hall. It was bloody awful. Ian who was with us agreed and so did Miriam! Like "Jules et Jim" we three best buddies headed for the Oakleigh for a libation to the Goddess of course. She had done it again!

Chapter 60

Eventually, Christmas came and seemingly a class betrayal, for I was travelling deep into Tory territory and something of the England of Enid Blyton's smug and snug little fantasy of the '50s. But they were books that I devoured as a boy, along with 'Narnia' land, with passion. How could I reconcile that with my leftism, my Stalinism, even? I don't know and I still don't; maybe with my Anglican background and my constant interest in god-bothering?

Anyway, I loved it; getting up occasionally to check Peter, poor thing, our cat, in his basket in the Guard's van; yes, they still had them then. The run across a wintry central and southwest England that I had never seen and the enchanting and most civilized Exeter Station, everywhere that Dickens' Christmas bustle and superficial kindliness. We had to wait for our connection to Plymouth where her Dad was to pick us up to take us to the Brooks family home in Plympton. All new territory for me, the pre-war, teak-veneered waiting room and the rather deferential 'Mummerset' and 'clotted cream accents of the railway staff on the tannoy - as was the very Knightsbridge lady, fussing with Peter. "Oh, what an ADORABLE pussycat!" and gushing at me, whereas in London I would have been totally invisible to her.

It was still light enough to spot a cormorant drying its outspread wings as we seemed to steam through the sea at Dawlish and at Plymouth, we emerged to meet:

"Call me, Huw, old boy, please do!" Miriam's Dad, kindly still, and still rumpled-looking, like my dad, his pipe a constant fixture to an ageing but once handsome face.

We had met briefly before, of course, when he had made a flying visit to her old flat. Broad-shouldered, though gone to seed and an ex-Cambridge rowing Blue, Emmanuel College, he had the kindly vagueness of W.H. Auden, very English and like Miriam, the best of the breed. Class fraternisation had its charms. For a while.

We drew up at a Regency Villa, sub-Palladian and one that Jane Austen would have approved of. Mommacat, as Marian called her, shy, and retired was as I expected, with kind eyes and almost Chinese submissiveness. I detected her daughter's steel though, beneath all that. A Girtonian bleat:

"Te-a-a-a, first-my dears?" After shaking hands, or holding hers, gentle and a little frail.

The facilities having been pointed out, I raced up a gently curved and elegant staircase, with a splendid central window covering three floors, my hand caressing the while the splendid Georgian mahogany handrail. Drinks were served in a snug parlour, where exquisite Christmassy smells emerged from the Aga in the kitchen. We toasted each other:

"Call me Sheila, Dave!' from Momma, as we eagerly awaited Ralph, or the Ferret, his family nickname. He had to drive across the southern heft of England from Colchester and far longer than we had done from the north. From the excitement I detected in Sheila's eyes, I guessed he was her favourite. He proved to be charming and amusing, a kind and handsome young man, a 'Doll' as Miriam admitted, a real Cavalier!

Chapter 61

Thanks to Miriam and the good offices of Maggie Chilvers, our friend and later to be my colleague teaching adult literacy and even later, my boss, I got an interview in the old Alexandra Hotel Annexe building. This was below the main college, on lower Great Horton Road, the 'Rive Gauche' of Bradford, just opposite the rear of the Alhambra Theatre and below the Manville Arms, Daley's Art Materials, where I was to spend thousands! and the art College and Poly.

I remembered having a drink with Glenda in the old Chaplin Bar in '65, while I was at Sunderland and she was up from Kingston-on-Thames. It was on the ground floor of the 'Alex'. Chaplin, like many other great old Music Hall acts, performed at the Alhambra. I remembered seeing Christmas Pantomimes, 'Brigadoon' and Priestley's 'An Inspector Calls' performed by the Bradford Catholic Players. Bradford people loved choral music and I also remember going to see Dad in the Bradford City Police Choir many times, and once even in the splendid Red Army Ensemble. Though the Civic Theatre over the other side of town was the avant-garde centre of theatre and film - as a Sixth Form aesthete I used to adore watching French and Italian films, smoking half a pack of Gauloise at the time - this side of Bradford always had more glamour for me.

Huw Evans, my prospective Boss and I could see, a bit of a ladies' man with secret Bohemian tendencies, seemed to take to me and offered me a maximum of 12 hours teaching General Studies and literacy to vocational students.

As Thatcher's axe hadn't yet swung over further education,12 hours at an average of £12 an hour seemed pretty good and with Miriam already on full-time hours and myself anticipating the same in a year, 1983 looked like being a pivotal year for us. Miriam and I even started looking wistfully at potential homes. Property, of course, was all the rage, though we only wanted a home to call our own, maybe with a bit of garden, Miriam being a country girl and maybe at some time soon, we would need a safe place for a toddler or two, to play in. It would get us away from Manningham as well and temptation for me, or so I thought, and already the atmosphere, though it improved slightly after Sutcliffe's arrest, had deteriorated again. The area was becoming not so much genteel and run down as sordidly criminal, with even more wretched 'working girls' on the street.

My first class, a morning session with a tea break, was an Auto Vocational one and as I had been warned by Steve and Miriam that the lads were ok, day-release Trainee Mechanics, their staff were difficult, some of them bastards who hated us 'leftie' General Studies lecturers. Such was the social and intellectual climate of the time. I faced the lads that morning in the brutalist '60s, Jacobs Well Annexe, with trepidation.

The main task of General Studies seemed Social Science-based and a mainstay was teaching the writing of reports and doing surveys. This was all familiar ground for Miriam and Steve and most of the rest of my colleagues but apart from teaching basic adult literacy, which I was quite good at, my major skills were in open-ended teaching, discussion about current affairs and some basic life skills. The latter was great only after building up a rapport with students, which over time, I think I succeeded in. Even the art skills I had, had to be fitted to teaching non-art students like hairdressers. I was good at this too but it took time and all I had to go with was a rigid-looking syllabus; trade union rights, wages councils, health and safety at work, ALL of which was under threat by the ideological battle commencing in Britain at that time. Throw in the hostility of some of the vocational staff, not all by any means and the task was looking almost impossible.

In that ghastly setting, I felt that I was at the cutting edge of the propaganda offensive being waged by the Murdoch Empire, the Investment Bankers and this fairly new and ruthlessly reactionary Tory government. I felt that I was in enemy territory and that years of the Ripper menace had softened me and my colleagues up for this. I was scared and soft and wet and felt abandoned by my much stronger and capable Miriam. Pathetic as it may sound, Miriam, Steve and Maggie were not there to hold my hand.

I don't think I was able to teach them anything that morning but I learned something from the lads and later had some of my fears about the political side of the situation confirmed, indeed emphasised.

Getting the register filled in gave me a bit of time to appraise the class. Despite my recently-acquired cynicism about young men in general, I thought they weren't a bad-looking bunch of lads. I had a very basic questionnaire worked out with the aid of Miriam, just to give a bit of structure to the void I was feeling. Also, to give me some time. Moving around the room, I mentally grouped the lads: Stevie, one of nature's gentlemen and a born leader. In the short time we'd met I'd had a few words; I was good with accents and surnames and I think he liked and respected me. Then there were a couple of jokers, Wiggins and Broadbent, with a couple of hangers-on, camp-follower types, two lads not very bright I noticed but pleasant, one slightly bohemian lad who could be an ally and a couple of Asians, who I knew could be incredibly loyal if you treated them with respect. A black lad who looked ok.

I sat down and started to roll a cig and almost panicked. Though not overly religious at that time, my mind a blank, I sort of prayed or leaned into whatever help was out there. The door opposite banged open, obviously, a private office and tall and sleek, a sneer already forming on an already petulant mouth, stood the Head of Department of Auto-2: The Black Douglas.

I should have said: "Can I help you?" but, I was back in that dismal room in the flat above the Bakers in Oak Lane, 1974.

Standing up, I merely said: "I have a class right now. Name's Greenwood, I'm the new General Studies Lecturer." I did not hold out my hand.

Snapping closed his briefcase and not replying, he snarled voicelessly and headed out of the main door. A thin-lipped and cruel fascist, if ever I had seen one.

"Our gaffer 'ates you lot," said one of the jokers.

"Does he indeed?" I said as I retreated to my seat. "Just a few more minutes, lads, while you finish the questionnaire and then we can carry on; nothing too heavy, just a case of getting to know each other!"

As I sat down, I noticed that my ciggie, Golden Virginia, had been rolled and there, by its side were four different makes of tailor-made: Craven A; Senior Service, B&H and Embassy Filter-tipped.

"Got 'owt in that joint, Sir?' said Wiggins.

"Dave!" I corrected him.

"Tha's reet, Dave!" said Broadbent, winking and I knew it was going to be all right.

"Maggie's alreet, an 'a!' said the gross and 'orrible Wiggins.

Maggie Chilvers, how to describe Maggie? She was to become Miriam's and my Boss in General Studies, or at least our line-manager when we were seconded to try to teach youngsters, who now found themselves underemployed with Thatcherism in full swing. They were just shoved off into vocational training, cheap or even slave labour for the local chambers of Commerce up and down our blighted land.

I had heard of Maggie and probably rubbed shoulders with her the previous year, now well into two years of my relationship with Miriam and going strong. Although Miriam was ahead of me, she was an MA after all and was only at Bradford University originally to study for her Doctorate or PhD. She had already qualified as a teacher of Further Education the previous year while I, very fortunately and only three months into our time together, got a post as an adult Literacy Field Worker and teacher, just down the road from us, in a rather splendidly housed adult education centre.

Against the reactionary tide of the time, I had done well, though it was Miriam who had pushed me into getting part-time hours at Bradford College and who knew, a foothold on the ladder of an academic career?

Maggie had seemed to like me and though I was back at university in that 'Annus Mirabilis' for my final year and with a grant to finish my degree, I was lucky also in that our new boss, a charming and suave Welshman, Huw Evans, took a liking to Maverick and Arty types like me, Maggie and a few others and our stars seemed to be rising.

I had heard a lot of 'Maggie this' and 'Maggie that' and all of it good, around Bolton Royd Education Centre where I had been based. I remember now her booming laugh, friendliness, her warmth, and her vitality. I had glimpses of a tomboy figure, a bit like the up-and-coming TV personality and entertaining Lesbian Artist, Maggie Hambling, who she reminded me of, though neither of these dynamically charismatic women was remotely like 'La Thatcher'.

She came to represent to me, like most tomboys, pure and liberated womanhood, socialism with a tincture of feminism. Her 'womanliness' was so evident, that unlike most of her kind, not even Miriam, she could wear a Harris Tweed jacket and jeans with ease while OOZING femininity. She was bloody marvellous and symbolised those happiest of times.

She epitomised to me what Keith Waterhouse wanted to express in his superb novel 'Billy Liar' in that part which Julie Christie played so well, the beginning of that amazing film and near the beginning of my novel. Maggie could have been Julie in that opening shot where she's swinging her tote bag, carefreely, just arrived in Bradford and back from London! She was the 'new woman' of my time, the girl who had been to London, the nice girl from next door who strove for freedom, like Glenda too, in her way?

But much as I loved Julie, the young lady from Bexley-on-Sea, Maggie to me epitomised that new free spirit of the early female versions of the Texes and Kens, working-class lads who had been to India, to Morocco and were starting to grow their hair long; the Oxbridge lads from all the rat-holes in Britain, who were discovering Marx and Raymond Williams, Brecht and Beckett, and were coming back home to build a cultural Jerusalem.

She was; 'Maggie's back in town!'

'Yeah, Maggie! Help us out here?'

'I'm working with Maggie Chilvers, with the problem kids, ya know?'

'Lucky you!'

Yo, Maggie, a female Figaro!

It was Maggie and to a lesser extent, the Sues and Sarahs, even my Miriam who wept with rage at the sight of the wretched WICS, Work Introduction kids, girls in just a cotton slip and boys, in winter too, wearing just plimsolls and only a shirt. I can hear Maggie now, storming into Huw's office or shaming the venal vocational staff.

"This is a FUCKING outrage!"

Maggie did not mince her words.

Miriam and I worked together with Maggie on a couple of interesting projects, helping non-art students with basic design skills and literacy. They were great times of class struggle and Maggie, more than just being an academic, was a great socialist, an enabler and trouble-shooter and a real leader. And yet she was still an Earth-Mother, carrying multi-tasking to the extreme. Youngsters, whom she loved and easily related to, clamoured around her, a tigress and her kits.

Chapter 62

I think it was that day, exultant almost, that I'd passed that first hurdle, though worse was to come with the Auto staff. I took my break with the students in future or went out onto Great Horton Road and the little college car park to have a smoke. The braying pigs of Auto lecturers disgusted me, as Maggie C so accurately described them: 'failed foremen.' You could understand why the British motor industry was on its back!

I needed to expend some surplus energy, so I decided to walk back to Manningham, thinking sorrowful thoughts as I strode up Lumb Lane remembering the poor 'Ripper' victims over the last years. Crossing Carlisle Road and on to St Mary's Road, past Blenheim Road and its faded elegance, I rejoiced too in the change of season. A bright spell between late March showers blessed the area with an Olympian radiance, freighted, for me, with nostalgia. Spring in London, Westbourne Park Road and Notting Hill, Bayswater Road and the 20-minute walk to Chiswick and Turnham Green and my first London home.

I thought too, with a catch in my throat, of the short walk down Eaton Place in Brighton after a night's gruelling shift at the Royal Sussex, the morning sun lighting one side of Lewes Crescent and the elegant terrace opposite my flat. Stan, departed now but where I once lifted my eyes to see darling Molly, poor wretched Molly from the 'Bristol', standing at her Juliet balcony, waving ecstatically and mouthing kisses to me; poor 'Death Kiss Kate'.

As I swung into St Pauls Road, marvelling at the truncated turrets of the villas at the road's end, pale indigo and slate blue roof tiles, charcoal and indigo ashlar and that golden ochre washed stone, I saw her. Miriam must have just seen me as she emerged from the Bradford Road and just started the short walk from her bus stop to our flat and my heart stopped, then raced and my tears sprang to my eyes as I saw her afresh again in all her beauty. I hadn't noticed how she wore her tailored jeans with her high heels and how ravishingly sexy it looked and coming closer, I saw the light in her eyes and we rushed into each other's arms as if we hadn't last seen each other this morning but an aeon ago, at Troy or Carthage, with the beached ships.

We decided to get married later that year. I began to enjoy the job more and had some wonderful teaching sessions with Maggie and on the whole, I loved the students: brickies, electricians who were possibly the brightest and hairdressers. I enjoyed a trip down to Manningtree to stay with the old folks and one day, on taking her brother Ralph's dog for a walk, I realised that we were in Constable country. We saw a fair bit of East Anglia that year and enjoyed the bracing sea coast and big skies that summer, even doing some dinghy sailing with Miriam's scattered East Anglian family. We even had a fortnight in the Basque country of south-west France and northern Spain. I marvelled even more at this 'Queen amongst women' who I had found, at her expertise in French and her fluent Spanish.

In late June, I discovered that I had got a good degree, Miriam having gone down to the Department to check my results, I was so nervous. Mum and her constant lady companion, Dorothy treated us to a meal in the countryside after my graduation ceremony and I even got the chance to shake the frail hand of my ex-P.M and now current Vice-Chancellor, Harold Wilson.

I was managing to get some painting done, even building a small collection and we both looked forward to the short autumn term, our wedding a simple Registry Office one in Bradford in December and a reception at the Park Hotel, our current pub below the 'Oak'. The only cloud over the wedding was that my father declined our invitation, though there was a cheque for £50 from him. My brother, Jean, his wife and his growing family; he now had a daughter, Amanda came and with a lavish gift of wines and spirits.

For our honeymoon, Huw and Sheila drove us down to Manningtree, to where they had recently retired and we spent a warm and loving Christmas down there.

1984 found us looking forward in hope to the new year and we found ourselves back in a gloomy, Cromwellian Bradford browsing through Holiday Mags of Greece and Property papers. We thought it best not to try for a baby until either of us had some job permanency.

Miriam must have got her permanency of teaching tenure, which was a great relief to us both as the government did seem to be preparing to attack us in Higher Education. Though I was glad for Miriam and Steve, now our 'best man' who had more hours, full time even, I seemed to be losing hours if anything. Though I don't think I had a bad reputation yet, I knew that I had a problem and I used to discuss it with Miriam.

Departmental and College politics became a constant talking point and the easy camaraderie of the Department seemed under threat. Splendid as Miriam and Steve were, I was astonished by the level of gossip they got down to; a Trotskyite trait perhaps? They both knew each other at Essex and Steve was an experienced activist having been a Shop Steward at Asda. I was getting a bit conscious of the fact that in their eyes, I was seen as intellectually inferior.

There was a small contingent of Gulf State students as well as Iraqis, whom I liked and even some Iranians but there was glaring evidence that some of our staff were lapping up contracts with Gulf States students. We expected this sort of thing from Vocational staff and Maggie and I had noticed with the complex study in work schemes which she and Huw had devised, how mercenary and exploitative the attitude of the Chamber of Commerce was and other businesses who sponsored the courses. The stench of corruption in public life was obvious. There was a sickening sense of bad faith and treachery, a new ruthlessness about senior staff and a lowering of morale amongst our colleagues.

Huw left us as Head of Department and we had two more in succession, while I was there. Richard, a born-again Christian, whom I disliked intensely and John Dixon, whom I liked but distrusted.

Stu and sometimes his girlfriend were often visitors, living just across the road and though I was never jealous, I did feel so unworldly in their company. Never sure whether I liked Steve completely, I was increasingly in awe of Miriam's toughness and political worldliness in comparison to myself and the nice West Country, middle-class girl her parents knew.

I was getting some painting done though and when not doing that, I enjoyed building the occasional Airfix kit. Miriam looked upon it with amused tolerance, as did Stu but whereas Stu really liked my pastels, in fact buying a couple of portraits I did of him plus a view of his apartment block across from us, I had an increasingly uneasy feeling that Miriam didn't take my art seriously. Her parents did though and while we were away in Spain the previous summer, they went to the Private View of the Pastel Society show in London. I subsequently realised that they were being polite.

The year moved on, a darker one now. The Miners' strike worried us and we tried to help a little but it all seemed hopeless. I was beginning to do stupid things like losing my keys and having to call Miriam at college for her to come and unlock the flat because we were too high up for me to risk an exit through our window. I was beginning to waylay Miriam at college, for small change, ostensibly for cig money but really because I was dying for a drink. I was suffering my first howling hangovers and at least once, Miriam had to call an ambulance. My back ached so much some mornings, to her amusement it seemed. She knew how hard some of my labouring jobs had been and understood but slowly, ever so slowly I think, that I was becoming a bit of a social embarrassment, a bit uncool.

I started to buy strong peppermints to disguise the stale alcohol on my breath. I would have the urge to buy a can of Carlsberg from the 'Offy' or a miniature of whiskey or vodka and drink it on a park bench by the park lake and I once came back to see her in tears. I knew then that I had a problem, as did Miriam and I resolved to drop anchor on the alcohol. I told her so and she responded by nodding and blowing her nose. She was not given to moods or little tears. I volunteered to make a coffee and then we watched Newsnight, both of us saddened and beyond anger as the Miners' strike looked like it was going down to inevitable defeat.

"Oh, bloody hell, Dave, let's have a stiff one," she said.

Digging into her purse and giving me a tenner, she told me to get a bottle of plonk from the Offie, a Chablis and a bottle of Cider for me. Later we both wept for the miners, for England, for socialism and what looked like a darkening time for us.

My burgeoning alcoholism was forgotten for a while. We made love gently and sadly that night and we both forgot about my problem for a bit, However, things generally had got VERY serious.

Part Seven:

HEARTACHE

Chapter 63

It seemed like everybody was cultivating his garden. Stu's talk was all about money and guns. A dry alcoholic, he had taken heroic steps in replacing one obsession with another, his 'shooting club'. He hated anything smacking of spirituality and a strong-minded person, he had stuck to that. He despised AA, which I mentioned when the subject of alcoholism came up. I at least was open about the issue and Miriam was content about that and didn't seem to mind my having the odd lapse. Also, she liked most of my friends down the pub; though, ironically, I was getting bored with them and preferred a drink on my own, or with her at home, or even better in the park, on some bench, or even in town in some bar, the more unwelcoming, the better. I should have recognised the signs; the spiritual malaise accompanying a physical addiction.

Becoming slowly resigned to the death of many of our political dreams, Miriam and I decided to buy a house, not just as a base for our future family but as an investment. Her dad had offered to pay a deposit and my brother who I kept in contact with now my marital position was clearer, had offered to guarantee a Barclays Bank loan. He was a bit of a conformist and now as a Company Treasurer, he did a lot of business with that Bank. It was Miriam's as well.

So, we swallowed our political hopes, or put them in abeyance for the duration and went around Estate Agents in our spare time. It was something that I could do as I had more time and I only had the slightest moral qualm, that I was a non-contributor to our finances. Miriam seemed to think that, on the whole, I was doing my best, but I was beginning to sense a howling wind at my back.

So, early Summer and almost as an afterthought, with Didier's help who was a French drinking pal from the 'Oak' and the loan of a car from my brother, we drove up to the more salubrious Daisy Hill, on the 'tops', the watershed looking into the Aire Valley but fairly built up, if still a bit rustic. The Bradford Royal Infirmary was handy for any future little events, tiny feet perhaps? And as I joked at the time, Lynfield Mount Psychiatric Hospital also.

It was a charming and sturdily built late Georgian/early Victorian cottage with a small back garden accessible from 1960s-constructed French doors and looking south over some wasteland, some other gardens and a small builder's yard at the back of a similar row of even posher 18th century stone cottages. Though longer views were obscured by this, and Alms Houses owned by the Psychiatric hospital at our rear and on the main road from Bradford over to Haworth, and the Aire valley below it, we were at the top of the hill and there were pleasant walks down to two elegant and now disused Victorian reservoirs. There was another village beyond, Allerton, and then Cottingley and fresh open countryside over the hill country and moors to Lancashire. Our bedroom blazed with light on a summer's morning and our sitting room was nicely proportioned and cosy. We should have been ecstatically happy.

Her Dad had bought Miriam a second-hand Ford Escort so now we had transport. We still had our little black cat, Magic and the old folks had made a home for my Peter down in Essex, who was getting a little old but now had a huge East Anglian garden to play in. We looked forward to the new year but I was increasingly uneasy. I was losing myself.

Miriam had stopped taking the pill, knowing that our situation was hardly likely to improve financially and that I was so keen to be a father and still fairly fit, I was prepared to take on a labouring job or even factory work to support a wife and child. Miriam's biological clock was ticking. One exciting night, Miriam swore that I had hit the spot; false alarm alas, as her period came again only a day or two later than scheduled. Miriam insisted she was fine, gynaecologically but I suspected that maybe I was 'firing blanks. We even looked tentatively into the possibility of adoption and I sometimes whimsically referred to our spare back room as 'the nursery'.

I fantasised about our little baby gurgling up from her cot at the sight of a gull framed in the Velux window above her, with a background of the freshest Cerulean blue sky, baby blue. And again, I saw myself as a lone house Dad in the garden of the 'Oak', with Rosa tucked under my chin, as I buried my nose in her little blonde curls, inhaling her delicious baby girl smell.

It was the beginning of a period when I began to have terrible nightmares, obscene even. I can't think that my alcohol consumption had increased much, or whether it was just my increasing sense of inchoate guilt, that the eldest son should hate his father so much.

My aunt Mary, the Sergeant's elder sister, died, a Tory Imperialist like him but deep down, kind-hearted and despite her snobbery, uninterested in money. I know that she was fond of Miriam, probably because she saw her as 'Top-Drawer socially but I was fond of her and even her husband, Uncle Tom, similarly Tory but kind-hearted and sadly for both, childless. I always felt that despite their Daily Mail opinions they meant well, deep down and Uncle Tom was a wounded survivor of the terrible battle of Kohima/Imphal in Burma, where Commonwealth troops at last fought so well and indeed trounced the Japanese, clearing them forever from the Indian frontier and eventually most of Burma and Malaya.

Even knowing that the Sergeant would be there and we hadn't communicated since 1976, passing each other silently on the streets of Bradford, Uncle Tom urged me to come to her funeral and knowing he loved me like a son, I complied. To her great credit, so did Miriam. I resolved to dress as smartly as I could, knowing Uncle Tom and the deceased Auntie Mary would appreciate my effort.

It must have been tough for Miriam because out of the corner of my eye I saw her approach him and later she told me that he had rebuffed her. In his grandiose and overbearing ex-cop manner he dominated the reception. My contempt for the beast became boundless and clenching my fist and looking out for a weapon, I awaited my moment. Uncle Tom, who had worshipped Auntie, despite his grief, grasped my wrist, saying under his breath:

"Don't, lad, Miriam can hold her own!"

By a strange transference, I saw Uncle Tom, a small man as a giant and my real father as an insignificant midget.

"Son," said Uncle Tom. "You two have already won. He's shown himself up for the windbag and bully he is!"

He tipped me a wink, something I always remembered from being a boy, the wink and the surreptitious palming of a ten-bob note, latterly even a 'fiver' to my hand.

Eventually, Swine-belly, Pig-Face, the Sergeant and pig of the finest swill, my Dad, approached with an unctuous and alderman-like introduction and an outstretched hand.

"Now, who's this smart young fella?" he said.

Looking over to Miriam who was charming a group of Uncle Tom's remaining family, I looked back, stared into my Father's dead eyes and keeping my hand to myself, about-turned and walked away from the company.

Mum was in the kitchen washing up. Somehow, I felt that I didn't want to speak to her; there was a hint of betrayal about her, not just sheer cowardice and after a turn around the small garden, I went back inside where, Miriam was in conclave with Uncle Tom. With a gentle cough, I was able to squeeze my uncle's hand, compassionately and with synchronicity, I thought really wifely, so did Miriam. Hugging us both to him he said:

"Mary loved you both."

He seemed near to sobbing, at which we left and a cousin, Brenda, up from Sussex gave us a lift back to our little home. I rejoiced in Miriam and my heart glowed with pride for her. She had conquered all. I don't think I had loved her as much as that day. On such are true and strong marriages built. Yet it wasn't until much later that Miriam told me that Father had deliberately snubbed her.

I felt something truly irrevocable had happened but something I can only now begin to accept, that the hatred between me and my Father was something aboriginal, fathomless and beyond redemption. Either he, or I had been a 'wrong 'un' from the start.

The nightmares got worse. I had to find a reason for such evil. I woke up drenched with sweat again that night; an airman, parachute-less, fell backwards into the flames of a burning Reich; my back arched and burned at the lashings of the maniac's whip; my mother's voice somewhere in the night: "They'll take the boys. Harry, don't, don't!" and her barely stifled sobs; the memory of her telling me that my brother had also started wetting the bed, as had I some years before I left that Prussian Lunatic Asylum that was Dotheboys Hall.

I was coming to realise that there was something uniquely evil about my father, even that archaic term, so question-begging seemed redundant. I was old enough to have worked with by now and even drank with ex-RAF bomber command personnel and most, though only willing to talk after a few beers, said that it had been horrendous but that was the case with all war. What about the experience of tank crews, having to face the almost dead certainty of being roasted alive, along with their crewmates in their crap American Sherman tanks? Tommy Cookers, German tank crew called them; having to brush aside the putrid and rotting remains of former comrades as they leapt from one burning tank and into what seemed like a deserted but safe one; of having to disembowel another young, enemy soldier with a bayonet or hand grenade, to endure hour after hour of superbly accurate German shelling, or to walk into a hail of machine-gun fire without turning and running away as any sane man would do; to see best friends turned to a pulp before your eyes? It just didn't compute.

When did the Pig become such a monster? Was it when Lobby the bomb aimer took Dad aside after an op, Heilbron or Duisburg, perhaps and retching against the side of a Nissen hut, told him about the 'Sunday Roast' smell coming up from thousands of feet below, as another target burned. "A Good Prang' as Dad had described the Dresden raid in his logbook, for February 1945.

Did he lose his soul when the Flight Sergeant in charge of the maintenance Lancaster JO-E pointed out swatches of blonde and burned hair in the intakes below the huge propellors, maybe the minced remains of some German aircrew, some Lothar or Eric felled by other Lancs in the hectic and crowded bomber stream just a few hours before?

Maybe he was just a bastard and he filled the bill for what Butch Harris, AOC of Bomber Command wanted from his boys, stolid, unimaginative courage and blind and unquestioning obedience to orders and rank. A Loyal Soldier as tough and indomitable as an SS Infantryman?

Father had served his masters well.

The Lancs, Bomber Command's 'shining sword' even grounded had heft and power about them, a Shakespearean epic feel to them; their grim majesty even symbolised the dread chivalry of an older England. They stirred my soul, as did the feminine and almost vicious grace of the Spitfire in the battles that had raged over the shattered skies of Kent and Sussex only a few years before. Was father his eldest son's grey ghost? The RAF obsessed me.

I choked with guilt and shame. I shuddered as I imagined the stew, the bouillabaisse of writhing and dying German children below those coldly indifferent skies, on those indigo nights only forty-odd years before.

Chapter 64

Sometimes, my hours finishing by lunch, I would take the bus home back up to the heights, at Daisy Hill and buy a bottle or a couple of cans on the way home. Somehow, the house seemed bereft without her. If I was not active, afternoons were always a bit depressing for me. Black Dog time I rather pretentiously called it, that 'anomie' that I had first encountered in my heady days of freedom and my fumblings with Glenda and often Miriam would come home to find me in bed, half drunk.

I had embraced a great emptiness. Was I indeed a 'wrong 'un'? What had happened to that noble young man? Why was I so unhappy yet with a wife such a pearl of great price and my dream woman?

I awoke once in the early hours to a baby crying and myself in a cold sweat. This period seemed something out of time. Had I had, or was I, enduring a nervous breakdown? It must have been boring for Miriam. I would screw myself into a corner of my seat, even Magic our little black Persian, stared disdainfully down at me from the back of our sofa. I would analyse endlessly why my father was as he was or why I needed to drink, sat here by the best wife and comrade in the world, both of us with some hours of an interesting job, still fairly young and in good health. Sometimes I lay awake and stared at her gently breathing body, her exquisitely noble profile and leaned into a body that seemed to fit me like a glove and my heart sang, but the next moment, I sobbed within, knowing that I was not good enough. I was rotten, I was a 'bad 'un', and I knew that she had married beneath herself.

"I despise you!" Miriam said, as in the morning and at my bedside, I scrabbled in my jeans and hers, for coin. I was desperate for a drink and for the first time, begged her for one. I was surprised, looking at her noble and yet stricken face, when she conceded.

"Oh, go on then, back pocket of my jeans!" she said.

I felt a momentary, masochistic and even sexual rush at my humiliation and dashing into my clothes, I staggered down the stairs and out of the house to our nearby Asian-run Off-Licence.

"Ah, early, Mr Dave!" said Imran, who by now was well aware of my burgeoning alcoholism.

I bought enough to take the edge off, two cans of Carlsberg Special and a bottle of Old English as a 'Parachute', my recipe for getting me through a couple of hours and time to think about where my next source of booze would be. It was black medicine. I had now long gone past the stage of alcohol being a prop for celebration, rather it was now a crutch to get me through the day. I had read enough around the subject to realise that I had got to the stage where I could neither live with it nor live without it. It was a kind of a Hell, both for myself and Miriam. I was now physically and mentally sterile.

I don't know how I got through that particular day; I must have done and it was to be the first of many 'Rock-Bottoms.'

Miriam rang Al-Anon, AA's sister organisation for the spouses and families of alcoholics because she told me later that she had been advised just to let me get on with it: Detach with love, I was later to hear it called in AA. Thinking absurdly enough that this was my let-out, I stiffened a bit but at the same time, just gave up pretending that I was struggling with my demons; it seemed cool just to accept that I was a drunk and what the hell, why didn't I like some of the blokes in the pub? Give a roguish laugh and just get on with it. Why worry? The country was going to the dogs under Maggie and it was obvious that our class had suffered a historic defeat during the crushed Miner's Strike of the year before.

I didn't think, or rather the superficial part of myself didn't think of Miriam's growing disrespect for me, her unhappiness and her shame at being married to a loser, a drunk and what I rapidly was becoming, a bore. The ground, no longer imperceptibly was shifting beneath me.

I was still welcome down in Manningtree, though Huw, an outspoken man at times, observed that I was a dour-looking chap these days. I thought that I heard the dread tread of The Black Douglas at night. I began to feel disillusioned with my teaching. I was given classes out of Maggie's purview and hours all over the place and now decreasing. I had taken to having a miniature vodka in my pocket and taking a surreptitious nip before an awkward class as 'Builders-101' started. One morning in the vile Jacob's Well annexe, a member of the Hairdressing Vocational staff, noticed my miniature Smirnoff bottle by my already opened register. I was called in to see my bosses, John Dixon, who expressed concern and Richard White, who gave me a sanctimonious sermon but a polite warning and nothing else. But my card had been marked.

It was inevitable, of course. My hours at College petered out early in '86 and a part of me was glad. I wasn't sacked and I went along to a few Department Parties and Steve was able to confirm that I was not the only member of staff with problems; 'issues' didn't exist then.

Being on my own back at the house, I could discipline myself sometimes and be hard at work on a painting come 'Black Douglas' time, or out walking on the moors, or in the nearby woods. For a time, I was a model house-husband and I expected any day to have hit the spot and welcome home a rejoicing Miriam who would tell me that I would be a father by Christmas. I tidied up our small room and we got a Velux window installed. A little baby girl, my preference, would look straight up sometimes to Cerulean blue skies or racing white clouds. For the time being, our larger back room which faced onto the main road was a good spare bedroom for visits by the old folks and sometimes Ralph. He now had a lovely girlfriend who brought a little girl, Emma to the relationship. On a visit by them, I noticed how Ralph loved babies genuinely, as did his sister and he took joy in changing 'Boon' as he called her.

Ralph had a deliciously idiosyncratic sense of humour. And we got on well. Despite his public-school education, he had no 'side' whatsoever and not a snobbish bone in his body. I knew that he was a terrific social worker at a time when Murdoch and Thatcher were demonising with full force, anything socially committed or kind.

Stu still came up to see us and was full of his apparent conversion to the Insurance business and revealed himself as ruthlessly ambitious. I remember one time, me in my dungarees towards the end and fresh from my last job as a chargehand, Miriam looking back from a smart and enthusiastic Steve to me with the faintest twitch of disdain over her aristocratic features.

That was later, so maybe I had been out in the garden building a pond, nature having disappointed any likelihood of my being a father, the safety of any future toddlers was academic.

The bad news had come earlier in '86. I still had a few hours at College left to teach and I remember joking with Marjoribanks and kindly Scottie in the 'Oak' about the possibility of my taking fertility treatment. Miriam and I had booked an appointment at the Infirmary down the road. She booked in for an appointment the next day, to get an almost immediate result, she was fertile. I was given a couple of plastic containers to ejaculate into and told to phase my activity over a few specified days, returning the brimming vessels the following week.

Anticipating no big problem, we both reckoned my binges over the few months previously would be of no account now and I had been pretty abstemious on the booze front, or home drinking at least. Huw and Sheela had been pleased to see me drinking water at Christmas.

I could hear Miriam laughing outside the bedroom door as I struggled with my aim, even suggesting she might come and give me a hand. Job done and after writhing around the bedroom floor for half an hour, I was able to seal the containers and deliver them to the hospital that afternoon.

Miriam was on the town that night with Maggie and some of the girls in the department; some sort of a hen party and they popped by at the Oakleigh in Manningham for a bit of slumming. Marjoribanks was there and pissed himself laughing when a mellow Miriam reported on my polyphiloprogenitive adventures. Calling in for a weekly pint, which was my new regime, from job hunting in town, Pete Marjoribanks regaled our table with images of 'Greenish' wanking into Guinness bottles and rolling around the bedroom floor with a Dominatrix-suited Miriam!

The following week, the blow fell. Miriam called into the Fertility Clinic with me. Expecting good news, I grinned roguishly, man-to-man at the youngish doctor, who told me with tears in his eyes that my sperm count was almost non-existent and completely sterile.

I had another terrible night, a baby crying again. I must have had the mother of all binges because my memory began to fail me. I think we had a Spring visit to France; Burgundy and back via Auxerre and Chablis. I remember having my photo taken with Miriam and toasting the camera. I vaguely remember Sens, its cathedral and that of Auxerre, and I am almost sure the Beauce, country which I had loved in my imagination since being so moved by Fournier's "Le Grande Meaulne" or more honestly the French film based on it that I saw in Notting Hill in the early '70s. Miriam and Steph I thought had something of the quality of Yvonne de Gallais and I dreamed too, like poor Alain of someday finding 'The Lost Domain' which she haunted. I thought too of how Ian, in the great days, reminded me of the eponymous hero, the dashing-and working-class, Meaulnes. I thought too of all the brave Frenchmen whose lives were destroyed in that terrible Great War and the one that Fournier was killed in. I marvelled and took some pride in the fact that Grandad Greenwood had been at that battle, which saved Paris and France; the Marne.

I made quite a lot of it to the old folks AND Miriam, as in my increasing sense of insecurity, of lostness, I was picking up more strongly the feeling that I was not quite good enough for their daughter, not quite 'the thing'; not officer material. I could almost overhear and thought that I had heard, Huw say to Miriam's Uncle Peter back in Norfolk that Christmas something like:

"Dave, good type, bags of guts, and initiative-but hostilities only material,

eh, what?"

My class chippiness was coming to the fore again. Huw and I were no longer friends and I was beginning to resent him.

I always loved France but I was dying a little spiritually. To paraphrase Coleridge: 'Dejection: an Ode' I could see but not feel how beautiful France was. My vision was narrowing down. Shelagh asked me politely, while we were waiting for service in a Routier just south of Calais, why I never carried a sketchbook anymore?

I felt it with a stab of pain, this burgeoning resentment, when A, one of my oldest friends from uni, and Miriam in the women's movement there, came to visit us at Daisy Hill. She brought her little boy. I was in my dungarees and tried to be amusing, showing him my pond, now nearly built, but I detected a sneer on A's face.

"Don't go near that pond."

I used to really like her but now a flash of anger consumed me. I put her on my mental hate list. As Dad's crew must have painted an extra bomb symbol on the nose of their Lanc after another 'Prang'.

So, I was discovering my malicious side. I raged deep down with resentments. But on clear and indigo nights, I found myself, Miriam gently snoring in our bed behind me, staring out with pride on the moon's reflection on my brimming pond, musing what it would have been like for our children, our 'sky-babies'.

Chapter 65

I woke up in Lynfield Mount Psychiatric hospital about the time of the Chernobyl disaster but it shows my state of mind that the import of this catastrophe hardly touched me. I was lost in self-obsession. Later, I got a job on the strength of being an ex-Psychiatric patient on another MSC scheme, of much less status now, based just around the corner and in the Infirmary grounds. I was to be one of four chargehands in command of a ragtag of other 'loonies' but worse than us, lost souls and misfits. Our boss was an ex-Police Inspector with what appeared to be a social conscience. He had an assistant, Jack, a salt of the earth type who had been in business as Head Gardner at several Stately Homes but now in semi-retirement.

We were to spend a lot of time in the hut, that horrible summer but though I knew there were two murderers and failed suicides amongst us, I found them a nice bunch. Some were heavily sedated, some of them beyond help and needing tactful and sympathetic supervision. These were heart-breaking cases and sometimes, it being nearby, I would bring the odd one home for lunch or a tea break. Some were to break down on the job and we charge hands were tasked with calming, even hugging them until Jack or Trevor, our boss arrived.

I developed the habit which was noticed, of sloping off to the nearest 'offie' for a miniature vodka and as we worked in hospital grounds all over the Bradford area, I got a chance to sample the local pubs, usually increasingly forlorn places. This was the time of increasing gentrification into wine bars and Irish-themed pubs beyond my purse. England seemed to be dying, or at least the one I used to love was.

I think Miriam grew tired of my tales of woe, and the sight of me in my dungarees. The parting jibe of the side-parting had been:

"Oh, I never knew what a chargehand was until now, how quaint."

Ralph and Bridget came up to see us with their new baby, Tom, and the house heaving, I sat in my corner with a half-drunk bottle of cider. Miriam, Bridget and Ralph gushed over Tom and little Emma, 'Boon', looking up at me and piping;

"You're rubbish!"

Miriam went back down south with her brother and family and I stayed to work out my contract which would end soon. A few days later, I got my first and last letter from Miriam telling me when to expect her home and ending with the romantic postscript; "I don't want a shit-tip when I get back."

I tidied up the place and after I'd helped her unpack the car, which she had loaded up with wine, a hamper of fresh food and veg from the old folks' garden, we relaxed over a glass of wine while watching the News. Miriam was an enthusiastic TV fan. At the end, she switched it off and turning to me said:

"Dave, I want a divorce."

Summer still lingered in that dreadful year. Miriam came to see me in my garret back in Manningham. There was still a pretence at civility, even intimacy, as she gave me a packet of money from an insurance policy I'd surrendered, the premiums paid by her or Mum. There was an academic folder containing a few forms and photos. I'd insisted on one of her. And there were wedding photos as well, an item of her clothing, a discarded 2-inch heeled shoe. I knew I would want something to cling to, a comforter. She knew how obsessive I was.

There was a bit of a nip in the air and her black ushanka framed her happy face. I could see that she now knew that she was free. My flat was so high up that the light in the room that sunny early autumn day was dappled in green-gold, blazing through the upper branches of the huge sycamores outside. I knew about Jorge by then and in fact, he and I had had a drink in that same room only days before and embraced each other like brothers, after a libation of Special Brew. I had looked sincerely into his handsome Iberian eyes, saying:

"Look after her, Jorge. You have a pearl of great price there!"

Even then, I knew what a failure I was, a phoney also, but nearly choking, I offered my hand to shake and then led him down the stairs. In my insanity at that time, or my confusion and emotional turmoil, I still harboured an illusion of Miriam and I getting back together again. It had seemed like a bad dream or nightmare and suddenly I would wake up in a sweat, as in a magical morning over seven years ago and dream that I was looking at that same dear face.

I looked at the golden vision before me; her ears always got cold first and I wanted to clasp her sweet head, ushanka and golden hair. I reached out my hand tenderly to her face. She flinched. I then said:

"It's over, isn't it, Miriam?"

"Yes," she said, calmly and undramatically, but not coldly, but with the temperate rationality of those kind but Baltic grey eyes.

I went out and got drunk.

I think she gave me about £70; more than enough to get drunk and before I set out to do just that, I had enough sense to buy a stock of food and a couple of books. I forget what I was reading at the time, though slowly I seemed to be accepting the reality of my situation. Miriam, bless her, had bought me a radio, knowing how much I loved my music and Marjoribanks, in a brotherly aside, later in the 'Oak' advised me to have voices on in the background, like Radio 4, and not just my favourite music on Radio 3. He had been through the same thing and revealed his less flippant side.

"And avoid some of that human dross at late afternoon doors, Greenish."

As they were at that time, that desperate last hour before afternoon closing on a lonely weekday. Scotty just nodded assent, his kindly face shining with empathy.

I must have known it was the end, that her life was beginning afresh and that mine might as well have been over. Stinking, self-indulgent and self-pitying thinking as I knew to call it later in AA, but at that time I felt like a falling airman without a parachute.

Taking the bus into Bradford was a rare indulgence for me and in my soul, I floundered and flailed for some footing, some last shred of dignity, some faith in the old Dave and failed. And so came the utter fucking misery, the utter selfishness and in the early hours, waking up in a cold sweat and with such loneliness as I had never known before.

I had seen her again over some business, she had ungraciously handed me some old photos and papers she had found while cleaning up any evidence of me. Already, to my childish chagrin, she had filled in the pond that I had built in the yard of our marital home. She was pregnant after all and smiled proprietorially at her tummy and before leaving my flat, she let me tap it. Then she beamed triumphantly and on leaving, waggled her arse provocatively, cutely, almost as she left me.

That night the dream came again: Robert Southwell's great 'Burning Babe' and I knew in my seared soul what it meant.

It wasn't all depressing. There was the usual elderly lady downstairs, in my new flat, the proprietary spirit of the house, someone I could pretend to help and condescend to. Ann was even older than dear old Mrs Hill, whom I still saw around.

With little old Ann, a southerner by her accent, something of the better part of my mixed feelings for the South Country re-emerged. One morning, she appeared on the landing below my attic, being helped by a Mrs Smith, another neighbour, one half of a just recently retired couple and probably reflecting the economic crisis of the time, having just come down in the world. Genteel working class, she and Mr Smith had a bed-sitting room next to that of Ann.

"Oooh! You must be David!" cried Ann, a slash of crimson lipstick in the strangest shaped and powdered face, rubbery in expression, simian-like, balding and hennaed hair under a dashingly lopsided and coquettish hat over a rumpled chiffon headscarf and still holding on with both hands, sporting light beige calfskin gloves, to bulky and kindly Mrs Smith.

"Well, this will be my new young man!"

Chuckling cheekily and touching her head to my chin, which would turn out to be her favourite gesture. Then fussily reaching for her long-handled bag and turning to her door, she turned to me, another profile and a slightly raised and joyous ancient face, a friendlier Marguerite de Greet.

"We shall be friends, David!' She exclaimed.

I was smitten and after offering to help her take her things inside, she shook my hands. She was Dame Edith Evans, Grace in Brighton, the Saffron Lady, dear Old Mrs Hill; Miss Ramsgate,1913 and a new and dear friend, altogether. An angel, in fact, a goddess more like.

Ann loved for me to take her to the shops. I had to be patient but it was worth it. On our first particular day, she wore her rakishly-tilted hat and a feather boa which wouldn't have looked out of place in Brighton of the 1920s, and linking arms, we made stately progress, cavaliers on a spree, up Oak Villas and along Manningham Lane, past the various greengrocers and off-licences, not yet boarded up or turned into estate agents, waving cheekily at passing motorists and:

"Oooh, look, Captain Birdseye!" to one of the regulars at the Oak, a bearded and rather fine looking older fellow, who coincidentally was Magnus's Dad and fancied himself a bit of a ladies' man, always with a young lass in tow.

At one stage she insisted on a taxi and we drove in style to Bradford City Centre, and went to Spinks Bar, still clinging onto some sense of gentility. Then we had tea and cakes in Rackhams, at one time the favourite of well-upholstered Bradford woolmen's wives. All the time she regaled me with her experiences as an ambulance driver in London and Brighton during the war. There were huge anachronisms: why had she married a Surrey Tory MP and what brought her up to Bradford? She seemed so typical of the dotty old ladies I'd seen in Hove and Brighton, as well as in Bloomsbury cafes and pubs in London. Yet, I detected no interest in the arts or literature. For weeks on end, she liked to be on her own with her cats then there would be rapping on my door to her landing, or a note, lavender-scented for me to join her for drinks or to go out on an errand. She loved her Dunhill cigarettes and her TV and on such occasions which she referred to as our little parties, she would give me a couple of £20 notes and invite my mates, Magnus or Blackburn Dave and she would get rather fresh, waving her Dunhill about, fixed in her long cigarette holder and reminiscing about some adventure in pre-war Hastings or Eastbourne.

Chapter 66

Timed Out. 'Gungha' Dean, Dad's Rear-Gunner

I forget precisely when I met up with Dad's Aussie rear-gunner and oppo, Gungha Dean but it must have been after Dads' death in 1985, as Gungha would never have knowingly agreed to meet up with his old comrade's estranged son.

Anyway, I'd heard from Mum that he was due in the UK for a squadron reunion, so presumably, some of the crew were still alive or he cherished his WW2 links with the 'Mob': RAF Bomber Command. The last time there had been a reunion, in the 1970s, many Aussies and Kiwis, Rhodesians and the odd Caribbean went on to Germany on an invitation from former Luftwaffe night fighter organizations. Strangely, Brits and Canadians were reluctant to do so and Polish and Czech ex-Bomber Command types... well, what would one expect? Partly I reckon, Aussies were up for anything and had come all this way and I reckon for Brits, memories were a bit harsher and Canadians had had some bitter memories. There had been bad blood between German and Canadian troops and wounds were still raw. Canadian aircrews had suffered disproportionate losses too.

I remember the old man, not long before we fell out, never to speak to each other again, joking that the Aussie/Luftwaffe Reunion might be really interesting; either a terrific time or the biggest punch-up since the disastrous Nurenburg raid of February 1944.

I was hoping that we'd meet up in the opulent environment of the RAF Club in the Mayfair end of Piccadilly but I remembered that Gungha was an NCO like most air gunners and being an Aussie anyway if he was like the ones I drank with in my London days, would not have given a fuck!

I think he and Mum had a bit of a soft spot for each other. She lent me the money to go down to London to meet up with him. I was with Andrea and sober a couple of years and as things were a little strained between us, and I was between jobs and a bit lost again, I thought it would give both of us a break from each other. Gungha and I exchanged short and civil letters. I booked a Travelodge room with breakfast and we agreed to meet up somewhere conspicuous and well known. I suggested Westminster Bridge by Big Ben and opposite to where the old Lyons Corner House was which I remember from my lonely days, nursing a long-gone cold cup of tea and a stale buttered scone. Gungha would have remembered it too, as a famous rendezvous for wartime Commonwealth and American airmen.

On the coach down, I had plenty of time to muse about how our meeting would go. I think I have already said that I loved Aussies and from what I had heard, Gungha was typical of the breed. I anticipated a good few beers, some reminiscences of the Mob, news of the rest of the crew and maybe some sympathy from him when I poured out my heart about Dad.

The Corner House had long gone of course, so I paced up and down Westminster Bridge Road by the statue of Boudicca, that I knew he would remember and I occasionally took an appraising look up at Big Ben as I strolled up and down. I still felt, even then, a certain patriotic pride in the setting.

I didn't have to wait long, melodramatically throwing my Burberry over my shoulder, adjusting my tie as I gazed wistfully once more up at the great clock tower, Trevor Howard in 'Brief Encounter' style, looking down and self-consciously stubbing out my cig, I heard a cry:

"Dave!"

There he was, built like a scrum-half, short and compact, cheeky Aussie, and ageless grin, a tough little fucker, I'll be bound, I thought. Raising my hand to stay his efforts and looking both ways, I loped across Westminster Bridge Road.

"Gungha," as he had given me written permission to address him. "How did you know?"

"You're just as your Ma described, mate and a bit like your Dad!"

Strangely, I thrilled to that and suggested we repaired for a drink, one of my faves from former times being the 'Shakespeare' at Victoria, a brisk 30 minutes' walk away, opposite the Rifle Brigade memorial and the equestrian WW1 statue of the French Field Marshall Foch. He seemed fit enough for it. We marched in step, briskly, airmen together and I fantasised that I was with my Dad. The first surprise was he didn't drink! I suggested a bit of a walk, maybe Westminster Abbey or, the weather being fair, a stroll along the embankment, past the Air Ministry and then back up via Charing Cross to Trafalgar Square and we could get a cuppa on the way. We did so and I asked him about his family, two daughters, apples of Dad's eye and a loving wife, Marian, still alive.

He chivvied me about my long hair and skinniness and he went on to tell me, when pressed, about the rest of the crew. We went over to the riverside balustrade near Cleopatra's Needle, knowing he would glow with nostalgia at this, another famous trysting spot and fecund too with memories for me, half-starved and trudging the streets so long ago.

Suddenly he looked weary and suggested we sit down on one of the elegant benches facing across to the majestic County Hall, recently abolished by Thatcher I earnestly pointed out. Breathing a heavy sigh, which was emotive for an Aussie, he told me swiftly that Peter, the Navigator and who together with Dad had formed an unholy trinity, had passed away in Bahrein to where almost straight after the war he had emigrated and prospered as an engineer. Bert, the Skipper, after continuing in service and flying 'V' bombers had died only recently. He'd lost touch with Ron, the mid-upper gunner years ago, and Jock, the 'Sparks' but 'Lobby' Lobsinger had died many years ago in Canada. He sighed again. He had taken to drink and intermittently religion and died in a clinic in Ontario, ten years ago. Of German extraction and being a bomb aimer, we concurred it was hardly surprising. Gungha agreed but seemed inclined to be more judgemental.

"We had a job to do, mate."

Foolishly, taking this as a hint to speculate about the bombing campaign, I voiced my own opinion. He looked uneasy, so I shifted ground to some of the good times they had in those dark days.

"Mate, I was bloody scared, shit-scared most of the time!"

He remembered Grandad and Manningham, pints in the Beamsley' up on leave in Bradford and the posher 'Kings' Arms' in Heaton, sing-songs around the old piano chez Greenwood in the home at Victor street, reminiscing about days in India and Mesopotamia in the first war with old Walter, my Grandad. Then he exulted about Mum, her beauty and gentleness, her Scottish accent and the more than mild crush that he had on her.

He regaled me with his memories of Dad vamping at the old upright in grandad's house on Victor Terrace, Manningham; Dad and Gungha bawling out 'Roll out the barrel…!'Mabel, Mum's oppo in the WAAFs on leave also, and with her arm around David Bayliss, Dad's best man and Stirling bomber co-pilot in a different squadron, later to be blown up with his crew over Magdeburg. This must have been late '43 or early '44 and Dad and David must have recently started on 'ops' and losses still high, and on this their first leave and Mum and Dad only just met, they must have felt the desperate need to let off steam. I could imagine Mabel singing Gracie Field's 'Wish me luck when you wave me Goodbye' Mum's favourite and Gungha was telling me how, pissed by then, he had started a 'conga' which, neighbours, squaddies and matelots on leave joined in and which wound out the back door, nearly into Oak Lane and back as far as Leamington Street, only stopping when their young knees ached and it was time for Black Out.

We got up and wound our way up Charing Cross Road. I wanted to linger at the bookstalls but I sensed a change in the atmosphere between us. I must have let slip something about the Police Force, a sour remark about my Dad, or something and on turning down St Martin's Lane and towards the Square, I could just discern Nelson's cocked hat up high, he gripped my elbow savagely and spun me around.

"Look, sonny, your Father and I were mates; we would have died for each other. Same goes for the rest of the crew. Grow up, kid, look after your mother."

I suddenly lost it.

"Fuck you and all. I've worked in Germany, replacing the homes you bastards destroyed!"

I must have blurted out what a pig Dad had been too.

"I'm a vet as well you know. I always loved him as a kid, he was my hero! I always wanted to join the 'Mob' but my game foot would have stopped me." I didn't add though, my very left-wing views!

So saying, he smiled.

"That's Harry, Heilbron, that's my 'Oppo'!" and he took my hand.

I was too angry to cry but I discovered a cold rage I had never known before, a steely determination. The crystal spirit.

"Don't fucking call me Heilbron!" I shouted suddenly, my heart racing. "You staying at the RAF Club, tonight, Gungha?"

"Yes, Heilbron- Dave, sorry- and the next and after that, I'm flying to Germany to meet up with some ex-Luftwaffe Night Fighter boys with some other mates. You wanna come?"

Here he laughed and, inspired, I suddenly shouted:

"But I want to stay at the RAF club. tonight!"

"You're on, mate, you bastard!" he said, digging me in the ribs, then hugging himself to me. "Luckily, I've got a spare RAAF tie!"

It was a very posh, typical St James club, one of the most prestigious in London, after the Cavalry Club, and Atheneum. I didn't like it and I don't think Gungha did either. It didn't take a clairvoyant to know what he was thinking, as we sat down to a silver service meal that evening, ex-RAF Catering Corps waiters, fussing around us, chillingly polite, and 'top brass' and fragrant wives much in evidence at adjacent tables. I sensed Gungha was seeing the ghosts of former comrades, so I kept quiet.

We ate in sullen and smouldering silence, the honking and fluting voices of our 'betters' clamouring the air in the now crowded restaurant, like fulmars and guillemots in some sea-girt cave. I didn't need to be a psychic to read Gungha's thought; flashbacks to some dismal Nissen hut in war-time Lincolnshire, the heart-wrenching and stomach-churning anticipation of that night's Ops.

He stood up suddenly. I had already lost my appetite and pushed my plate away. Gungha, crumbling his napkin and raising it, then hurled it down with a 'Shitehawks' gave me the wink and we both marched out of the room, me steadying Gungha as in his fury he stumbled into gilded chairs on the way out.

We had both achieved something; something understood, a kind of closure. When we shook hands on parting the following morning, both of us had agreed on fore-going breakfast, I knew that he was anticipating a much friendlier reception in West Germany from his former enemies.

"Old Jerry will see ya right, mate!" I told him. I sympathised. My alienation from England was increasing.

"Goodbye, Heilbron! You scruffy airman!" he said and winking mischievously, he grasped my hand firmly. "Look after yourself, son."

He turned on his heels and dodging the Piccadilly traffic nimbly, disappeared into the crowd.

I saluted, about-turned smartly and 'left-right, left-right' arms swinging in an airman-like manner, I marched briskly across Hyde Park Corner and down Gloucester Terrace, past the huge Royal Artillery and Waterloo Memorials and then by Knightsbridge corner to Victoria and the coach home to Bradford.

On the coach, I discovered that I was still wearing his RAAF tie.

Part Eight:

THE MAKING OF NINA

Chapter 67

Fitzrovia. 1990

I had been sober for over a year. Nancy, a delightful American lady I had met in AA, and I had split up but in a gentle and friendly way. I felt that I had got over Miriam and that the most important thing now in my life was my sobriety. My artwork was improving and I was becoming more professional. I loved AA and though I was unsure about my faith at the time, I seemed to have lots of friends and though near penniless, felt that I had hope for the future. I had something of my old serenity but rarely felt thrawn and my old restlessness and anger came back. I hit on some kind of a solution. Though I was fairly conventional sexually, I had become aware of a feminine side to me and a submissive, even masochistic streak. I was selling more than the occasional painting and on the verge of success, and now having few expensive habits, apart from smoking, felt occasionally financially flush.

I felt in need of an adventure, something new. I feared that I was getting stale and soft, old maybe? My reading had been verging to the dark side and though the internet was yet to be all-pervasive, I haunted some of the seedier shops around Leeds Station and Manningham Lane as I had done in Brighton and Soho years before. Nostalgia for London also made me thrill at perusing some of the sleazier pulp magazines. I didn't think that I was a dirty old man, still in my 40's but with inchoate sexual urges, I decided on a new adventure. London and the bright lights, if even for a brief period, still appealed to me. Maybe better luck this time? A Dark Goddess beckoned.

Mistress Spiteful, the Dark Side, I had previously called her, both on the train from Bingley on my first Motorola mobile! and then again in Centenary Square, Leeds where I had to sit on a bench in a state of trembling anticipation-my first personal contact with a Dominatrix! As the dialling tone purred, I had felt that same transgressive thrill as on donning sheer stockings, a spiritual as well as physical slithering, a fall, both sheer and elevating. Then the answering voice, educated and very Home Counties, pleasant matter-of-fact introductions and her instructions as to our rendezvous in Bloomsbury the following week. Being a fan of the eponymous literary group and frequenter of the darkly melancholy pubs around the area, the student pubs and cafes and pubs redolent of war-time Bohemia, I thrilled at the adventure ahead; eros, melancholy and that vivid sense of the present slipping away, that I loved so much about that part of London.

Ah, Fitzrovia, I exclaimed to myself as I emerged, as instructed, from Warren Street station. I soon located her street and the basement stairs to her flat and having been texted by her to wait 5 minutes - the excitement! - I paced up and down Warren Street, marvelling that here Gwen and Augustus John shared a bedsit in the pre-Great War days and I studied the gaps and brash new frontages in the elegant early Victorian villas, where here and there a V-1 or V-2 rocket bomb had shattered such civility in late 1944 and early 1945. Splashing my chest with cologne; Mistress Rachel had been insistent on the strictest hygiene, I, at last, opened the wrought iron gate and descended stone stairs to a small patio and frosted glass, 60's-style door.

Heart beating, I rang the bell, wondering, as I waited what vision would reveal itself. A red and black blur through the dimpled glass and the door swung open on a demonic fairy tale embodied, a proffered slim hand, a mane of tossed back and copper-red hair and then a sophisticated, yet surprisingly husky voice:

"Ah, but you must be Davina. DO come in!"

She ushered me down a corridor in a typical North Central London 'Pied-a-terre' flat, which in my London days would have been either tenanted by medical students at the nearby London University Medical School or better-class prostitutes.

Pointing to a corner dressing table and a seat, she asked me to strip while she graciously took my proffered tribute of £150 in notes. I was thrilled straight away by the ambience, a dark chamber was just discernible, spots of scarlet and black, a glimpse of a throne and enticingly, whips and tawses hung from racks upon the wall. I delightedly saw a bathroom with lots of fresh-looking towels. Re-emerging, Mistress Rebecca smiled reassuringly and offered the bathroom to me to 'freshen up'. There was underwear; black lace panties and bra and hold-ups for me to don after which I was to be summoned to the dungeon for an interview.

Having done so, she took a notebook from a black, enamelled drawer and pencil poised, asked me questions; whether I liked bondage, forced feminization or whipping. Helpfully and almost kindly, she pointed to a rack and even suggested 'electrics'. After a very civil 'to and fro,' she told me to drop my panties - I thrilled at the word - and put red velvet trimmed cuffs on my wrists. Then: "Oooh, I nearly forgot, Davina!" a chastity device which she spent some minutes, hilariously, struggling with. Taunting me with the key, she said, grinning menacingly:

"I might even lose the key, my Davina if you are naughty."

Specifying a default position, kneeling with arms behind my back, she then calmly read from her notes.

"Well, I think you're a mild submissive and with all the accompanying traits, but more than anything, a transvestite, with, as I suspect, and I'm playing the Doctor here, late-onset gender dysmorphia. I think I am going to collar you and maybe after a few more sessions, I will make you a slave. I have many." She mouthed the word lasciviously and I somehow felt that she was the real thing.

She pointed to a rack of collars, black leather, pink, and spiked like those of a mastiff and even with little bells or flashing lights. Each had a pendant medallion with an engraved name; Fifi, Pansy, and the like. My heart beat and I thrilled as she pointed to the throne room where she sat herself, ordering me to get into position. She introduced me first to a series of floggers and canes; I was to shuffle on my knees to the various wall-lined racks, grasp the commanded implement in my teeth and after shuffling back, proffer it to my Mistress high on her throne, a dream of scarlet and black and of cascading red-gold hair.

"You will kiss my boots first, slave!" she commanded deliciously and she then ordered me to stay licking them, while - oh so thrillingly! - she flexed a tawse or cane over my exposed back and buttocks and after first, in a delightful ritual asking me to kiss the business end of said implement, to resume slobbering over her now bootless feet, sheer fishnet while she began to slowly and accurately lash my back and buttocks. She had already given me the 'safe signal' a raised right hand and as I was not much of a masochist it was not long before this experiment ceased.

"Goooood!" she exclaimed, in something of an almost matronly tone, at once thrillingly strict and frighteningly kind! "I thought so-slut!" And she dragged out that word lasciviously; "Submissive little bitch, that's you!"

A long mirror graced the far side of the dungeon.

"'On your feet, slut!" A hint of a cheeky grin from her 'brave boy' face, kitten teeth and a throaty chuckle. "Girlie-time now... Davina!"

I couldn't see too clearly but this enhanced the dream-like ambience and still with my arms akimbo, I was told to get nearer the mirror where Mistress R slipped a couple of breast forms experimentally in my bra,

"Not to make the mistake you girls ALWAYS make, my Davina, small is better!"

It felt good and I involuntarily shimmied and she playfully slapped my bum cheeks which still glowed from my light spanking.

"'Now for a wig!"

A first for me and even from what I could myopically see, I was amazed, liberated!

"Well, Hello, Tina!"

My feminine side was born; I was euphoric and after a few experiments with nipple clamps - hurt! - and her whipping my plastic en-sheathed penis with a sable flogger, both of us spluttering with laughter, she gave me a brief make-up session and painted my nails, the while chuntering to each other like girlfriends. In an almost poetic moment, she let me brush and comb her ravishing hair.

Afterwards, and after a brief shower, we shook hands and I found myself promising to see her again, her now devoted slave! And I no longer had to undergo the humiliation of being flogged. Somehow, I had gotten the half-baked notion in my undisciplined study of psychology that maybe I suffered from the Stockholm Syndrome, that identification with my tormentor. I had yet to get rid of my obsession with the wartime RAF but what was wrong with that? I was proud somewhere in there that Mum too had 'served' and at least Dad's comrades were decent men and saw Bomber Command as a way of fighting the Nazis.

I'd gotten hold of the notion of my humiliation feelings being best served by being treated as a woman and who knows, Piggy Boy had often warned that he would turn me into a woman and had often slyly, and even in a good mood referred to me as 'she', and anyway it was better than being an 'it'!

Madame Annunziata, my next Mistress, over the next few years, was to say that she would TOTALLY destroy David and that I would become her TOTALLY obedient and shivering and submissive slave. In my state as a lapsed Anglo-Catholic and failed lover and husband, some dank cellar in my being thrilled to this. My totalising catholic metaphysic rejoiced, even in my fallen way, of my sacred symbol of St Pancras, just back up the Euston Road, being desecrated; a gigantic House of Torture, scarlets and blacks, Piranesi-like impossible perspectives disappearing into canyons of delight, of bondage, torture and delicious pain. The old but magnificent railway hotel had not yet been completely refurbished and like the ruined abbeys of my native North Yorkshire, but on a Gargantuan scale, seemed vastly more spiritual and mysterious in that state; bare, ruined choirs and echoing vaults, a yearning for transcendence made physical, over-weaning, and Cyclopean.

Madame A posted me regularly instructions and a pocket catechism I had to sign in my blood and that she after receiving it, posted back countersigned with her menstrual blood. She sent me sentences, passionate declarations of servitude, to write out long-hand and return to her; sometimes a hundred at a time. She set me little but humiliating tasks; I was to go and purchase a bra for her but ask the shop assistant if I could try it on. I had to post photographic evidence of this, just before the introduction of the new digital technology and the development of smart mobile phones.

Gradually, the pain of Miriam's loss waned and an almost narcotic obsession with Madame A took its place. I thrilled now to the sound of the post hitting the linoleum of my ground floor, Manningham flat and sometimes she wasn't mercenary. As well as being something of a literateur she was a serious Sadist and rejoiced in my burgeoning bondage. Once or twice, there was a return railway ticket, sometimes, made of very expensive silk, French knickers that she commanded me to wear AND to provide photographic evidence for. I had also to write a paper on how exactly I felt.

I was her property and bizarrely this kind of love suited me. She held out the promise much later in my training of being permanently tattooed, even being branded and 'collared'. I loved the smells associated with her; synthetic, plastic and rubberised-away from the too vulnerable and all too human ones; of unclean flesh, discharges and rank breath, the bathroom smells of matrimony, that Marital Sty, the foetid stench of domesticity... of... luuuurrrrvvvv!

Alienation was looking like a good thing.

It was amazing that I did not drink again but part of me felt that I must concede this humiliation, that it was not about alcoholism but that something inside myself, or who knows, a transcendent power; 'La Belle Dame sans Merci' or 'Hawthorne Goddess' was working her magic on me and I did feel a kind of narcissistic sickness, the 'sedge withering by the lake.' I felt helpless and in thrall to 'evil' women.

One day - One Day! - Mistress S took me by the collar and hissed that she wanted to castrate me, in a ritual. Was I the 'Fisher King' the impotent knight languishing at some mysterious illness, sterility, a vast void of meaningless? Anomie.

"Hang me, Domina! Hang me, I beg of you!" I had cried once, after a deliciously heavy session. I was swinging around, feet barely touching the ground, block and tackled by a silver chain to a transverse beam across the corner of the dungeon where I seem to have entered subspace, an almost mystical feeling, one of sheer and blissful transcendence. I felt like a St John of the A-frame, our favourite bondage device, engineered such as, that she could spin it to any point of the compass, sometimes leaning down to spit and snarl in my ear, tightening her grip on my thick leather collar, taping sparklers to my body and setting me spinning, whipping me savagely about my nipples and my crotch.

Sometimes in a parody of domestic bliss, after a session on her electrically-powered rack, she would order me to shower, then drench me with her perfume. I was always ordered to wear the same as her, a strangely uncharacteristic and mumsy 'Noah' and she would make me up, cuff my arms behind me and ordering me to kneel, my head resting on her thighs, she would read poetry to me and she would stroke my wig and mutter softly:

"Nice girl, Davina, nice girl," and then: "'Oh, is that the time?" And she would shoo me again into the bathroom, with an: "OK, slut, end of session. Your new instructions are by your coat."

And I would feel ten feet tall as I almost floated back up Warren Street and foregoing the tube, would walk along the Euston Road, past the massive and eviscerated St Pancras, my mind's 'House of Torture' and to King's Cross Railway Station' and home, my buttocks singing deliciously as I occasionally had to shift throbbing cheeks, or take a relieving walk up and down the coach.

I preened myself and when I could, bought better clothes for Davina, though under my Owner's strictest instructions. Luckily, I was making a lot of picture sales and enjoying being single and now teetotal and hardly smoking, had more cash to spare. I was enjoying my madness.

I think I have said already that Madame could be generous and on my trips to London, she would love to take me down Jermyn Street, sometimes stopping me in the streets of Knightsbridge or Chelsea to shriek at me and sometimes, deliciously and in full view of a sun-bathing Green Park, slap my face, once, twice, and after an exhilarating pause, three times, or until I came in my trousers when she would make a show of cleaning me, waving about her head to demonstrate to passing nannies and wealthy matriarchs, her box of Kleenex. One time in Fortnum's, she leaned over the china tea-service, her breasts palpitating, obviously aroused and hissed through the scarlet gash of her lips that she would make me wear a tampon to coincide with her periods. I swooned with a new-found ecstasy and back at her chambers, writhed in joy as she lashed my whole body as I hung in her chains and then she would gag me and sodomise me till I collapsed in a perfumed heap, heart hammering and my soul singing. I adored her

I kept in touch with her and with her encouragement, became a subscriber to quite up-market and even intellectually respectable BDSM magazines over the years of my recovery from alcohol addiction.

But I digress, though I am a bit confused about the time sequence, I had yet to get really clean and despite my inchoate religious and spiritual leanings, that I had massive emotional issues. Time didn't heal my yearning for Miriam, my loathing and obsession with Glenda and my deep bitterness at my father's sadism.

I was to become sane enough, at least thanks to AA and my persistence, to realise that, paradoxically I was not quite 'all there' but maybe I could be forgiven my apparent self-obsession, when mostly I despised myself and felt under an intolerable burden if I was to realise anything of my hope as a youngster, of becoming an honourable man.

I liked the idea of being crushed.

My art, my 'aesthetic' was such as to be original enough to look after itself. I would begin to discover over the next 10 years how difficult a market it was but I achieved some sort of success and though most of the time being near destitute, I was occasionally, being single, able to afford the odd 'adventure'-usually a 2-day trip down to London to see a couple of exhibitions but mainly to follow my emerging dark side.

Chapter 68

My recovery, with several lapses, began after my first miserable and drink-sodden Christmas apart from Miriam. Though I wasn't to get really sober until over 2 years later and even then, after a short term in an addiction and psychiatric unit, AA laid the foundations and a superb support network for my recovery from alcoholism.

I could never get over the heartbreak of my Divorce, the madness, the walk on the wild side and the feeling of enveloping evil at that terrible time but I was to learn how to cope with that, despite occasional plunges into despair and to be honest, self-pity and hurt pride.

I suppose I was growing up. Or growing down?

I had other demons though, which, even if they didn't take me back to the bottle, could easily destroy me. I had grown to understand that though I had been deeply wounded when young, that life could be a sad affair and it was mainly a question of learning how to cope with that. For the time being though I knew that my main issue was my alcohol addiction and that I had to deal with it. In the process, I was to find help and friendship and a new way of looking at the world. I had always been a believer but thanks to AA, I was able to learn to trust God a little and even find joy.

"My name's DAVE. I'm an alcoholic! There, I've said it!" I muttered to myself.

"Hiya, Dave!" echoed male and female voices from around the tables.

Around it went; to my left:

"My name's Yvonne," from a brassy but stunning blonde in her late 30's.

And so on around the tables, adorned with the naff-looking AA sign and copies of the 'Big Book' of 'Alcoholics Anonymous' our bible. Saucers used as ashtrays abounded around the table edges. This was still the 80s and amongst alkies, it was almost compulsory to smoke.

Rolling a ciggie, Golden Virginia, I sat back and a warm feeling beginning to glow between my ribs.

"I'm home," I said to myself.

I forgot who the Speaker or Share was that night but at the end of the meeting and after holding hands with the people to the left and right of us, we chanted the Serenity Prayer in unison: God grant us the courage etc and we contributed to the collection plate passed around Then we scraped back our chairs and thronged towards the coffee and tea area, chatting and laughing. I really did feel on the team.

"Hi Dave, I'm John."

"I'm John, too!" from a rugged and tough-looking bloke in his mid-forties, extending a calloused hand with some fingers missing. "You can call me Scaffolder John. Nice to see thi' lad!"

"Gavin," said the Chair for the night, a cultivated and slightly familiar, aesthetic gentleman in his fifties. He had London written all over him, with his BBC Arts programme voice but a comradely twinkle in his eye.

"Scots Mary, hen," said an elderly, grizzled, motherly lady with a Glasgow accent and a grip like a Clydeside riveter.

"Fred," a big, beaming, kindly man whom I suddenly remembered from Grammar School over a quarter of a century ago. He was a nice lad then, I remember. He was in the year higher than me and always to be seen on a drop-handlebar bike, his school cap placed perilously at the extreme flank of a Brylcreamed Elvis quiff. He seemed a nice lad even now, with his bear-like grip, barrel chest, twinkling eyes and a ready grin.

I stood at the table with a big pot of sweet tea in my fist; I was still slightly hungover from the night before and feeling edgy. A Jethro Tull look-alike came and shook hands with me.

"Hiya, man! They call me Mick-Man. Don't know why!" he laughed.

Then from a Bradford-Irish lad, with red hair and an open Irish face: "Mick. Tyre Mick!"

Still feeling a bit shy of females, I steered away from the handful of them, chatting together around the literature section, which displayed pamphlets and books by Bill W and Dr Bob, the American founders of this motley group. I felt like a man's man again; it was great to bond and be one of the lads, without resort to the pub.

Fred gave me the wink from over by the coffee table and nodded towards a quiet space. Taking the hint, I went to join him. Scaffolder John loped over to us with some pamphlets.

"Na lad, our Dave, take these and 'ave a look when tha' gets 'ome!" he said.

Fred beamed a look of sheer benevolence.

"We're supposed to be anonymous but don't I know you, Dave? It wasn't in a pub, I know that; so, I'm not breaking your anonymity."

"Thornton Grammar School, about 1962?" I replied.

"Right," he said and we were off, cracking on about hated and loved schoolmasters and old school pals.

I wanted to stay all night but eventually, we were shooed out into Market Street. A blizzard coming on, Fred offered me a lift back to my attic in Manningham. I had a list of meetings, many of which were within walking distance from my place and on parting, Fred told me to take my time choosing a Sponsor, that I should just listen and try and keep an open mind.

"Eee, I'm reet glad to see ya, David, lad! You'll get better here lad! Keep coming!"

Wondering if I looked ill and why I should want to get better, I headed for a cocoa and bed. For the first time since being little, before I shut my eyes, I uttered a silent prayer to a God I didn't believe in and had my first night's sleep after three months of sheer mental anguish.

Chapter 69

So, 1988 came around and I had my dear friend, Old Anne, downstairs to share a drink with when I 'slipped' and even Magnus and his girlfriend, Alice, a tormented soul and double addicted but who had first got me to an AA meeting. It was when I was with Miriam and had first got frightened by my possible alcohol addiction. I had been full of false pride and went along with Alice to the Quaker Meeting House in the old professional and residential part of Bradford, around the University. Shearbridge was the nearest thing Bradford had to a cathedral close, like those of more ancient cities such as York and Ripon.

"Ah, it sounds just like an early Trotsky-ite meeting!" said Miriam when I came home enthusing about the spirit of comradeship at AA.

This had been at my reconnaissance meeting a couple of years before our break-up and when I was determined to at least demonstrate that I was trying to do something about my addiction.

Much later, after Miriam and I separated, I was to be a regular. Magnus, Alice and I made for an unlikely trio and I think some people, in AA, in particular, regarded us as an unhealthy menage a trois. Many people thought we were bad for each other. Even Miriam, only months before our parting, believed we were dragging each other down. But when I had my 'slips' during the following 18 months, there was always a bed made up for me by the kindly couple.

Alice had had a tragic history of alienation from a prosperous but cold family and Magnus, though of warm-hearted, Halifax working-class stock, had suffered childhood illness and alienation at school. He had been so poor as a little boy that he tore cigarette machines off the street walls to sell the contents, there being no money in the house. Sometimes, in his cups, he told me tearfully about his stay in clinics in the remote Calderdale Valley, where wretched children, severely facially deformed and some hydrocephalic were fellow patients but how he learned to play with them and love them.

Miriam had warned me that Magnus was a leech, though where she got that knowledge from amazed me as this was around the time of our break-up, with both of us home-based wine drinkers. He was hardly of her social circle but neither, as I would prove, was I.

Magnus had his dark side. I knew his brooding good looks hinted at underlying violence. I also knew that he had been a soldier in Northern Ireland. He was no fascist though and often surprised me with his liberal attitudes and political radicalism, unlike a lot of ex-squaddies. He had mixed feelings about the IRA, being like me, a Catholic fellow traveller. I knew he had punched Ian and as at this time, I was alienated from Ian, I saw it as a point in his favour. Ian could be an obstreperous bastard and I had had him by the beard a few times.

So, we might have been a motley crew; sometimes Alice and Magnus had to be parted when they had their rages. Both people had a howling wind behind them, however, and the more I was beginning to know them, I could see how small my problems were compared with theirs; and, yes, also, I was beginning to love them.

Came the day, all three of us, and now I remember even poor Wes who had had a bit of a 'fling' with Alice was in our company, were walking across the huge common, on the Keighley Road side of the great Manningham Park, towards Cartwright Hall, near where I had walked through Paradise Garden seven years before when I noticed far away a heavily pregnant Miriam, Jorge, Ian, the traitorous bastard and one or two colleagues, one my ex-best man at our weddings.

Magnus and Alice knew that something was up and pulled me back. A sweet little girl of that company whom I babysat for a year, impulsively ran towards me, followed by shouts and screams from Miriam's party as if I was a paedophile. I stood rigid with rage, looking from their party and back to my mates, my rag-tag army of misfits and then back to them and saw my class enemy. The tragic irony of the whole scene was that Jorge and I, Catholics, antifascists both, liked each other, even though my star was in the descendant and his rising swiftly. A noble part of me rejoiced that Miriam and Jorge had found each other, for deep in my heart I knew that it was true love.

I looked back again at my degenerate comrades and knew who my real friends were. My anger and humiliation did not end there.

Puzzled in recollection now as to what my team were up to, heading up through the park towards Heaton; none of my companions were likely ramblers or museum visitors, I rather think it was a question of killing time before a meeting so we might have been doing a bit of 'cold turkey' together.

Time can drag in bedsitter-land if you're fighting both addiction and loneliness. So, we were showing comradeship to each other, weaklings and losers as we were. I remember now, Magnus and I were the self-elected cooks and after our walk, we could reckon on killing a couple of hours cooking and quaffing huge draughts of hot, sweet tea. Wes and Alice's addictions were worse than Magnus's and mine. There was a telly and maybe some music after supper. Magnus was a superb disc-jockey and knowledgeable about African and West Indian music.

A walk together across Bradford to the Friends Meeting House in Shearbridge and we reckoned that we would be safe from the perils of that night.

For me, it was not to be. We walked up through Heaton, the village beyond the park gates and up the hill, where Ian and I had bonded on that evening so long before and to the edge of the countryside. There was happy talk as we passed through Heaton village and to the allotments and a splendid view over the Aire Valley beyond, of our renting an allotment together; of our getting well together and growing fresh food. Maybe it could be our Dacha and I could take to smoking a pipe. And so, we stood there, looking over Heaton and Northcliffe Woods beyond and then across the vast Aire gap to Ilkley Moor beyond. It seemed a promise of a clean and new life to come, the wide sweep of the great Ilkley Moor, dappled with early Spring cloud shadow and just a hint beyond of the great limestone country of Buckden Pike and mighty Ingleborough, guardian of Wensleydale and Ribblesdale to the north-west.

It came to me suddenly, despite those fraught times, a way ahead for my art; a drawn line around a shape, or form, the 'naming of parts, that great mystery of perception; that it was the probity of art, the eye's Latin'?

'Ye Heelans' an' ye islans', Ah, weer ha' ye been?

'Ye hae slain the Earl o'Murray'

'An lain him on the green.'

Happier now and looking forward to a pot of tea, we passed back through the north park gates, I for a short detour into the Cartwright Hall Memorial Gallery to take a look at an exhibition jut recently opened, probably by some Feminist or Lesbian Collective up on Ovenden or Haworth Moor.

The Side-parting, in her ubiquitous Doc Martens and big Afro hair was there with her little boy and Rusty Rose, one of the street theatre 'Pantouflards' of the counter-culture of the time and another arch enemy also. I spoke some endearment or other to the little boy: "Hya Tiger,' or some such harmless endearment. I was resentful of Rose as an old mate of mine, Ross had offered a room in one of his properties, up on the moors near my old school. It would have been ideal as I knew the place well, Lady Sarah and Ian having stayed near there years before. Rose refused to share. I remember, when Miriam drove me down to the Oak to meet Ross about the time of the break-up, and not feeling my best, the outrage and fury I felt, even Ross looking embarrassed as he said:

"Look, Dave, sorry, mate but he's my tenant. I have to stand by him."

"He's got a name, you, know!" sneered the Sapphist.

I had always thought it a cruel nickname not only because I had known her from Uni, even liking her gentle melancholy and kindness, but today I saw the sneering face and bourgeois mien and hated her like fury I felt debased, insulted and deeply hurt. I wasn't big enough to handle Rose but at least he had the grace to turn his back on me. With a sneer of derision of course.

I knew then with crystal clarity which side I was on in the now raging class war.

My hatred was incandescent, trenchant and adamantine.

I could kill.

And I would do so.

And with relish

I needed a drink, a big one and rushing past Alice and crew, I told them. They had the grace to look at me with horror but Magnus came over and put his hand on my shoulder.

"Dave, I'll look in later. I know how you feel," he said.

Indeed, he did because he had often told me how as a soldier on parade he had to hold his head up and not dare to look into his CO's eyes, probably some snotty little shit from some minor public school. Like Rose.

Like Huw.

Like the Juggernaut.

In my mind, I chalked up two pluses for Comrade Stalin and two more bomb symbols on the nose of my beloved Lanc. I learned then, also, of the point of gulags. I knew now what hatred was and loved it.

It was liberating.

Epic.

'For he was a braw Gallant

and he rade at the ring

they hae slain the Earl of Murray

an' he might hae been a King.'

That night, I had the worst nightmares I ever had in my alcoholic career. I was to drink again but never like that night: Vodka, Whiskey and Tequila and never with such terrible physical mental torture.

I dreamed I had charged at Miriam and her company, some sort of a firearm or battle-axe in my hand; Magnus, redcoat, tricorn hat and musket at my side. I gave Juggernaut a magazine full of 9mm, KGB style, blowing his head off and somehow, Magnus was bayoneting Rose and was already leaning over his bleeding body, boot on his sternum and twisting the rifle by the butt, Miriam screaming the while and Juggernaut crapping herself as I emptied the rapidly reloaded magazine of my Makarov into her smug and sneering face. Then I was kicking the shite out of her twitching and jerking body. Jorge had gone and anyway, I'd no beef with him. Like in the Border Ballad, I'm kicking Miriam's severed head against the wall of my flat and Ian is twitching on the end of Magnus's bayonet. I'm standing at the sink in my garret with Miriam's dripping head and trying to cleanse the foaming blood from what was left of her neck.

A baby cried.

I woke up drenched in sweat and screaming, Miriam's name with it echoing around my room and a concerned Magnus looming over me with little old Anne - how did she get there? Saying:

"I'll make a pot of tea."

Magnus turned around and told her where the kitchen was, then leaned in:

"Dave, you want a Doctor?"

"No, I'll be OK!"

And I was and I slept well that night, almost miraculously with no more nightmares. The next night we all went to a meeting. I don't remember much except Fred looking over towards me and once more, making to shoot me with an imaginary carbine, saying;

"Recovery Bullet."

"Keep on coming, it gets better," said Scaffolder John ruefully, whilst shaking my hand. "It really does, brother!"

It did. A bit later.

Chapter 70

The Grammar of Addiction

I dried out and found myself a couple of horrible temporary jobs in quick succession; I was becoming almost unemployable. I got dry a few weeks at a time, even did some serious painting and managed a couple of exhausting hikes up to my beloved moors. I still slipped and woke up in East Bowling on Alice's settee, hauled myself back up the slope, drank in company but never on my own anymore, though that just meant drinking in a 'cider school' somewhere around the squalid backs of Oak Lane with down-and-outs and other low-life and went to Saint Stephen's church with Magnus and Anne in East Bowling.

Sometimes I went to Mass with 'Tyre Mick' who, as he always insisted, was a Bradford Catholic. I loved the Cavalier ambience at St Anne's in West Bowling, so near to the old Irish quartier of Bradford and the old HQ of the Independent Labour Party, sadly mired now in Trotskyist deviance. It was all reminiscent of my days around the East End of London, that mixture of the ghosts of Russian Jewish refugees, Italian Socialists and wretchedly poor Irish Fenians. I was beginning to see it was Ok to need people. Need, not use.

One morning, just after leaving a group of cider drinkers on Lumb Lane, I heard a squeal of breaks behind me and again 'Tyre Mick's' gravelly voice and his open Irish face looking down from his truck cab window:

"Get in, ya cunt!"

A helpful hand and I was up on the seat next to him.

"Step one, Dave! Meeting tonight in Dewsbury; you're coming home with me, fry-up then meeting, bath and change of clothes if ya want," digging me in my ribs. "Morning Mass at St Anne's! Ya cunt!"

Dewsbury were hard-liners and took no shit; it was boot camp for drunkards, 12-Step AA Fundamentalism and I'd bet on Scaffolder John being in the chair. Cromwellian but more 'Levellers' and 'Diggers' and so unlike the snotty Presbyterian faux-radicalism of Bradford and Leeds.

I must have shared my recent experiences, finding myself in low company and hating myself for being snobbish. Pigeon Ken, a kindly bloke from Bury opined that:

"Dave, we alkies get to the stage where we are the guys our parents warned us about."

I got it, the new twist in the grammar of degradation, from 'he' to 'it' and then to 'them'.

The general ethos of the 1980s was getting more conservative politically, if not culturally which was confusing. People at meetings were anxious to reach out to ethnic and religious minorities and I was proud, in a small way, to contact Muslims about AA. Gay and Lesbian people had been welcomed in AA for some years despite Thatcher's reactionary government and an increasingly rabid and scurrilously right-wing press. There seemed a genuine drift towards Christian revivalism but very latent in AA, mainly because of its American origins.

The nearest I came to a row with Fred and that must have been a little later when more or less sober and Fred chauffeured me around the galleries in the Dales. A countryside we both loved, Fred was extolling the virtues of TV's Hannah Hauxwell, an old spinster farmer who lived in heroic isolation up in remote Teesdale. She was known and revered for her wise and traditional values. I strongly insisted to Fred, as we motored through idyllic Wensleydale, that she was a reactionary old shitbag. That was unwise as books on her were on almost everybody's coffee table that year; it was like insulting the Queen Mother or Mother Theresa. Fred took it well though; he was that sort of a man.

Then Yvonne, the bottle blonde, brassily and forthrightly came out with one of the things that was to stick in my mind and what Fred would later call; 'knower-knowledge.'

"Dave," she said. "They shouldn't have been drinking with 'them'."

I got a bit better, then better still and Fred invited me for breakfast in Thornton the following weekend. It was my favourite meal and since I was feeling physically well, I accepted. He was my sponsor now, so I looked forward to the weekend with enthusiasm.

"Sit yerself down, Dave, lad and don't let Ella hassle ya, but she will!"

said Fred with a hearty laugh.

Ella, a barrel-chested Bull Terrier bitch, looked up at him adoringly while she wagged a curly stub of a tail, transferring her look of undying devotion to me and snuggling down between my legs as I slumped into one of Fred's chunky, comfy chairs.

A man after my own heart in so many ways, given Fred's obvious practical construction skills, the floor of his old cottage was littered with G-clamps, saws, drills, and hammers. The place was undergoing a massive restoration. We shouted through to each other, Fred in the kitchen, peeling potatoes and preparing onions for what looked like a gargantuan breakfast, favourite meal for both of us as it happened but for Fred, his and Ella's Saturday morning treat.

Petting Ella's noble head resting between my knees, her adoring eyes looking up at me, I half-shouted to Fred through the door of his kitchen. He stood at the stove, cooking spatula raised aloft and waving it like an orchestra conductor, to emphasise a point. Ella, with her tongue lolling, shifted her bulk up to my lap and moved her noble head to focus her eyes adoringly on him.

"Dave, it's the steps; do the steps!" he shouted back.

"B-but, but," I demurred. "Aren't they a bit crude? And the book and all the literature a bit naff? I mean so much of the stuff we lay out at a meeting, even the AA logo looks like a mid-50's Rotarian Meeting in Nebraska or Indiana. Ugh, so un-cool!"

"Dave, lad, if someone's thrown you a lifebelt, you don't moan about the colour of it."

"Oh," I said and my Catechism continued until, Fred, tea-towel over his shoulder brought through to our little coffee-table two laden and steaming plates: a King's Breakfast. Nudging an ecstatic Ella out of the way, he dumped the two plates down, along with eating irons, giving a joyous Ella a big kiss the while.

"Right, Dave, breakfast for champions, tuck in!" said noble Fred, and Ella, looking over at me with joy, and then likewise at Fred, almost seemed to applaud.

"So, you see how it is?" said Fred, as he wiped the delicious gravy with a chunk of bread from a now empty plate.

I did the same, though I slightly cheated as I had discovered a willing ally in Ella, who despite her Master's command, had wriggled her heft under our little table and nuzzled my hand to liberate some of my burdened platter. I marvelled at her Killer Whale jaws and shining ivory teeth, as she delicately, almost demurely took my proffered food.

I had known and liked Fred from school days. In the form above me, he was hardly likely to have remembered a sprog like me but it was a token of his quality that as well as the bullies of his year, I remembered the rare examples of kind and friendly boys like him. He was everything that a clever but happy and outgoing working-class Yorkshire lad of that time was. With his school cap perched precariously atop a well-Brylcreamed Elvis quiff, house-tie askew and pushing his drop-handled BSA bike between classes, his bursting satchel hanging on his scrum-half shoulder, he was everything that I envied, with his happy-go-lucky nature and his comradely mien. A clever lad as well, he was on the science and Maths side of our grammar school cultural divide and had some august and talented contemporaries. We chaffed and reminisced about some of the characters we had known, hated schoolmasters, like 'Slug' who had been the bane of both of our lives, then more lubriciously, because ours was a mixed-gender Grammar school, some of the beauties, fine, strapping farm and village lasses, our school standing near the edge of Bronte Land, hill farms and Thornton village.

While we both lustily reminisced about the succession of gorgeous Art mistresses and snotty French teachers, Fred waxed lyrical about how he had always been a Thornton village lad and indeed he rang true as I know that his ex-wife-who briefly disturbed us to drop off some of his washing, had been his first and only love. The more Fred went on, the less neurotic and unlikely alcoholic he seemed. He was the only son of two salt-of-the-earth village parents who had doted on him. Though a well-qualified, high-end technology salesman and German-speaker who had served as an apprentice there and been around the world several times, he was the type who always returned home, a one-woman man and he was proud that he lived just around the corner from the folks he had known all his life.

Totally unlike my alienated, neurotic self, I could easily imagine him as the pub 'good bloke' standing at the bar of the taproom, chaffing good-naturedly with the bar-maid while before sinking his first pint, he finished the Guardian crossword. A man, our Fred, who though just back from Iron Curtain Poland, wasn't above taking his seat with the old boys in the Tap Room at their 'Doms', their dominos. Such was and still is Fred, my other 'Grande Meaulnes.'

"Coffee, Dave?" said Fred and he threw himself onto his settee, making a place for himself among the hammer drills and chisels, screwdrivers and manly stuff; honest, chunky and straight, very much like Fred!

"Now then, lad, where were we? Oh," with a massively ironic grin, "the Steps!"

So continued my education in the mysteries of alcoholic addiction but with a message of hope, resounding and clear!

Chapter 71

I was getting to the stage Fred was to warn me about, that a bellyful of AA and alcohol was REALLY toxic. I had endured my longest stretch of sobriety since being a youngster, about 2 months I think, when I found myself peering up through the bushes across the road from my former marital home and in the half-light from the landing stairs shining into the back bedroom, I had half expected to see a little 'Rosa' or 'Ziggy'. It was an early autumn evening, always an evocative time for me and totally impulsively and irrationally, I found myself smoking cig after cig and revelling in my emotional pain. I even heard her little baby cry and then her calming voice, with the same endearing words she used for me: "Boo-Boo!"

In a torment of self-imposed and near exquisite pain, I at last ground my cig out, baffled and almost half-mad with grief. I headed in total misery back down the hill to my flat in Manningham and miraculously, I did not pick up a drink.

I was to learn later that though not drinking, I was still suffering from alcoholism. It was 'stinking thinking.' I had begun to accept that I had an alcoholic mind!

Good Morning, midnight! I awoke in the early hours after my crazy vigil. I knew enough now about addiction that abstention though necessary is not a sufficient cause of recovery. But, hell! I thought to myself in the early hours, life can be bloody sad. Self-pity, I know but life seemed bad. Though some hard-liners in AA and in some of the literature around the subject that I'd consulted, thought that recovery from addiction was worth losing friends and lovers, family and even children for.

I didn't accept that but what I had learned in AA and through bitter experience, was that in the end, I drank because I drank. I bridled when I first heard that, as it seemed boringly simplistic; I was looking for a key, a trigger, what AA called 'stinking thinking' or as I was later to call it, 'Magical thinking.' However, I had already been given that trigger a few years before when accompanied by a dutiful and very concerned Miriam, my University Doctor had retorted to the saga of my abuse at the hands of my father, that there lay the key and that turned into an excuse for further drinking. I now had a passport for continued addiction, sealed with the imprimatur of the British Medical Association! No, this wouldn't do, I realised and knew in my bones and it was to be one of the foundation stones of my recovery from alcohol addiction, one of many, among them being the 12 Steps of AA. Gradually, my defences were breaking down.

I was heart-broken, truly so and this was no maudlin drink-fed emotional binge. It was reality. "Too bad, Johnny, the Hun's got you in his sights!" I ruefully thought. I suffered for an hour, enough to hear a few floors below, our rude and aggressive milkman, a Thatcherite obviously, throwing his crates around. We lower dregs of Bohemia not to be respected as really human. Then the crash of gears and screeching tyres and revs as his vile little van hurtled back up Mount Villas to respectable Heaton. My anger was returning and I rejoiced in it.

"Fuck it! I'll remember this!" And I did and I write this in a kind of clinical, frigidly determined spirit of revenge. This was real; I could build on this. I had found firm ground. Wretched and full of rage as I felt, I had touched base and I think that my foundation, though not pretty, was sure and that with good friends and an open but bleeding heart, I would survive and rebuild a life.

"Break port, Johnny, break!"

"Roger, Blue Leader," and suddenly my spirits soared. I had a 'wingman' in good old Fred and laughing to myself, I imagined Ella, his dog, in Biggles' style goggles too.

I eventually got up, having gone on to sleep for four solid and dreamless hours, a pattern for those early months of recovery. I remember sneaking past little Anne's door, not feeling sociable that morning and for some reason, I headed up the hill to the Library hard by the Carlisle Pub where I had caroused with Jo and the Jamaican boys, in what seemed like a lifetime ago. I despaired a little - in a non-racist sort of way! - when I noticed the pubs near St Paul's Church where I had met Ellie and my first Manningham friends on becoming an exile from the South, were now Asian Shops or even Muslim Centres and that the Carlisle pub, sordid but lively as it had been, was almost a derelict shell of a building. The Library was still open though and I enthused to myself when I saw the many young Pakistani girls in there, that future novelists were here fertilising their minds. Who knows, a future Emily Bronte or Jane Austen writing a book entitled Lumb Lane or

Manningham Heights?

I opted though for the latest Patrick O'Brien, author of 'Master and Commander' a passion that I shared with Ginger Dave, alias Square Man. I think I would have got out a Jane Austen as well, as she helped clear my mind, not in a therapeutic way but almost like a kind of mental hygiene or house cleaning. I would most probably have chosen something on addiction and spirituality, also, as I was an enthusiastic as well as living expert on the subject.

Feeling refreshed and not a little excited at the prospect of a good few hours reading before the night's AA meeting, I swung and almost swaggered, a bit later out of the library and into an increasingly shabby and dour-looking Carlisle road and down towards my garret in the depths below Manningham Lane.

As I came to Bertram Road and nearer to my old haunts, my swagger ceased and on turning left, towards Oak Lane and very quickly, St Paul's Road, my heart stopped almost as an early summer just a few years before came to mind. I was looking down towards number 19, or maybe even worse and to my left, number 51 and high up to the garret where I first woke up to her voice and then I looked to where I was going, heart hammering and tears starting in my eyes and I saw the ghost of Miriam, MY Miriam, as she approached the door from Manningham Lane bus stop and she saw me and her face lit up with joy, and the tears were now cascading down my cheeks.

No luck for 'Johnny-Head-In-Air'.

I think I got to a meeting that night. I don't see how, in my state of mind, I could have avoided one.

I think I have already said that I was no AA purist; I wanted to be with people and AA seemed a good idea. Some months before, if I had wanted a drink, I would have done so. I had no defences, unlike now, where I knew deep down within and with what dear old Fred had called 'Knower' knowledge, that I could not afford even ONE more drink; from being a mere slogan it was now written and with pain upon my body that: 'one drink was too much and 20 not enough' for a practising alcoholic. I knew also, in my bones, that I was an alcoholic, not just maybe, or someone with some vaguely defined addiction issue but that I was an ex-drunk or, in one of

Square Man's pithy and downright turns of phrase, a slurp-merchant, a piss-head and a drunk. It was a solid, if demeaning truth, and I was beginning to value truth, to THIRST for it, even if that is not quite the nicest choice of words. In a way, it was a part of my alcoholic personality, something I had begun to take on board, which was all about some object-less, metaphysical need, a void. A lack.

Chapter 72

I had a strange dream. Whether I had been fantasising about Glenda and my not-so-halcyon days in Brighton so long ago, or my reading of my favourite medieval poets I kept to deter the night watch horrors, surfaced but I had what was to be the first of several mystical experiences around this time.

"Lullay, Lullay, the bailey hath taken the bell away!"

I knew I was getting better but I was suffering, although AA support and some of my increasingly more spiritual studies may have exacerbated this turmoil. As an artist though, I had faith in the creative process and clenching my mental teeth, I grinned to myself and suffered patiently. Waiting on God, I suppose?

Something happened.

It was the Corpus Christi Carol and had overtones of that exquisitely evocative and mysterious 'Lily and the Rose' song that I remembered singing to Glenda in Brighton so many years ago. It might have been on 'Choral Evensong' a favourite programme of mine on BBC Radio-3. I was still such a not-so-young fogie and yet it was not till much later that I heard the late and great Jeff Buckley's version. It had the Carol and Ballad form that I felt most moved by, of all the arts and I think I was now beginning feel and see the beauty of art as I had never before in my life. Slowly, sanity was returning.

It went something like:

'He bear me up, he bear me down, the Faucon (falcon) hath borne its mak (mate) away.

Lullay, Lulullay, lullah

The faucon hath bore my mak away

He bore him into an orchard brown

and in that orchard stood a hall, Hang/ed with the Purple and the Gold,

Lullay..

And so on and something-something-and in that hall there was a bed and on this bed there lay a knight who bled both day and night

and at his feet there knelt a maid

she was weeping both day and night

Lullay Lullay the Faucon hath taken my mate away,

and out the door there stood a stone with 'CORPUS CHRISTI carved thereon.

Lullay, lullay and etc…

I shivered with awe and I felt something shifting and stirring deep within me, something understood but impossible to analyse. Something of the old woodland, the stone circles and the timeless megalith and the soft and shifting light of these, my islands and the whisperings and snatches of ancient voices I half-heard on my moorland walks; a Hawthorn Goddess and Emily Bronte, her ghost striding manfully beside me, the curlews burbling and scolding about us, the piping skylarks above our exulting heads.

Though I was to take another drink at that time, I had found my higher power. I had by no means become perfect but my healing was near completion. I indulged occasionally in what I learned later in AA to call 'Magical Thinking', a kind of wishful thinking or sober day-dreaming, common to alcoholics and people suffering from grief. I also seemed to have discovered a streak of misogyny which shows how little recovered I was from my divorce from Miriam. I tended to veer away from the women in AA and Fred had to take me aside gently to warn me about this unpleasant trait.

In one of my jolly exchanges with Square Man on his regular nightly visits to my flat, I remember rejoicing at his quoting Kipling's splendidly dark Barrack-Room Ballads: 'Miss Kitty O'Grady and the Colonel's Lady are sisters under the skin.'

Though I was gradually learning to be honest with myself, I still slipped back into 'stinking thinking' that somehow things would turn out all right, that it had all been a big misunderstanding; I had suffered bad luck and been grossly misunderstood. Most people didn't realise it but I was really a Prince, robbed of his inheritance, or my parents were killed in a car crash when I was a baby and I, the rightful King of Scotland, had been brought up by Yorkshire peasants.

That sort of thing; or, come back from making my fortune in the Indies, as a sun-tanned but distinguished-looking Heathcliff, I turn up, elegantly attired and in my Bentley at my former marital home, asking my chauffeur to keep the engine running while I step tentatively through an opened and child-begrimed door and picking my way with my ash-plant through scattered toys, I greet a stressed and bedraggled Miriam; I lay a £5 note on the telephone table in the hall and turning on my well-shod heel announce: "Miriam, you really have let yourself go. Here, take this and buy yourself some new clothes!"

They weren't such bad times, though on this particularly bad day, I probably sat and brooded or maybe Ginger, Square Man, came back for a companionable cup of tea or coffee. "A brew, a mighty brew!" he would always enthuse and I would enjoy half an hour or so of what I called his 'abrasive bloke-ishness,' his reminiscences, funny in the pub but funnier now! his refreshingly politically-incorrect remarks and thrusting manly shafts of honesty from the hip and four-square!

One example and a graphic and typically Square Man remark about 'Denial' which is very much a part of the '12 Step' ethos, both of us being roll-your-own smokers at the time, he would lift up a packet of Rizla ciggie papers, yes, with a torn-off sector! and read out the Government Health Warning: "Smoking can be dangerous for your Health. HM Government. But you're alright, Ginger, you're the exception!"

"Substitute Dave or Greenish," he continued, in full fling. "Or any alcoholic fucker," both forthrightly and squarely. "And THAT is a profound truth, my friend! Thank you very much, me darling. I'll take me coat now and thanks for the brew!"

His departure would leave a sense of emptiness but I was sufficiently disciplined to enjoy a little serenity, despite that particular day and before bed, I had recovered the hope I had felt at my first AA meeting. I had a little ritual, mostly AA inspired; the Serenity Prayer or some kind of thanks to an unknown higher power for getting me through the day without a drink and then, cocoa in hand, I retired to bed with tobacco at my bedside, my hot drink and a good book: a jolly Jack Aubrey Saga, I probably got from the

Library that day, a sea yarn from the time of Nelson's Navy and I would read and smoke for a time, putting out the light, shutting my eyes and as on this occasion, crying myself to sleep over my loss of Miriam.

I think that was the last time that I cried over her.

Chapter 73

Blackburn Dave, Square Man, had centred me somewhat in his abrasive bloke-ishness, No tender plant or male feminist he. His Dad too had been a para and had fought after Arnhem but he was a loving and happy family man I found, on a trip over to Blackburn with him, Fred and Magnus. So, heroes' sons all. Magnus's Dad had been a naval frogman. We were even more bonded, a happy bunch of misogynists, as American Nancy laughingly accused us of being.

One day, Nancy, at the coffee table, approached me after an AA meeting; it had been my share, I remember and though sober now over a year, I had shared my hatred of my father. Nancy suggested I pray for the strength to forgive him. I later marvelled at the wisdom of this and tried to 'Walk in his shoes.' I had no trouble being a hero-worshipper but I dug out a couple of the Sergeant's wartime diaries. Behind the stilted slang of his time; 'Ginger Mitchell chopped over Hanover last night. More bacon and eggs for us.' 'Hanover last night. Good prang, though lots of flak and fighters. Gungha saw flames over H all the way back to the Rhine. Fuck them, if they can't take a joke. (From Gungha.) We all roared with laughter back in the Mess after de-briefing! Extra bacon in the mess. 3 crews chopped and apparently 11 Halibags (Handley Page Halifax's) from 4 Group. 99 bods in all chopped. Bad show.'

Dawn came, usually and the morning coffee seemed good and another day in recovery beckoned.

Next day, I felt a bit better about the Sergeant. I could even see in his increasingly shaky writing, in fading copying ink, that he was disturbed. I even made a formal prayer at my bedside that night, childishly uncool as it seemed. I went on to read more of his diaries and got a couple of books out of the library. I saw deeper into the horror: the OTHER Holocaust.

He had played his part in historic and world-changing events. A tiny, VERY tiny Tory inside me glowed with respect for him but with the sudden realisation that I was now easily old enough to be his father, I felt something like love for him.

That night, I got down on my knees again by my bed to pray to my Higher Power, for strength to forgive him. The following morning, I felt a strange but pleasant lightness. I was my father's ghost now. Something, however inchoate, was understood.

It was as corny as that but like a good love story, or 'AA' 'share', true and honest. The law of Love I am sure was taking root in my life. Real Love. I thought fondly of Mikhail, ushanka at a rakish angle, Kalashnikov held aloft, as with one hand gripping the turret of the T-34 he was riding on, he raised a fist in a 'Stalin' salute, as his tank, with it's characteristic 'Headlong' Red Army look, ducked and weaved through the ruins of Moabit and towards the centre of a burning Berlin. Of old Bill, like the 'Third Policeman' genteelly pedalling his vintage bicycle along the front at Hove, dear Polish and consumptive Chester, a dishcloth over his shoulder, aproned and coughing compulsively, writing another aphorism for me on the back of an old menu back in the Brighton Hotel. I adored, in recollection, these lovely men.

Meanwhile, providentially, as my lost love of Miriam - why that clinical word: obsession? - got even more intense and I knew now that alcohol was no solution, I received a letter from Madame Assumpta. I remember the thrill when opening the rather posh envelope and I noticed the heading: The Corrective Institute. I remember in a moment of my walk on the wild-side, posting a letter to her on a Contacts' site in a transvestite magazine. Something about her short piece of prose, in her advertisement, fascinated me, something highly literate and out of the ordinary.

My recovery seemed to be keeping pace with the innovations in the new digital technology, as I think I have already said. The latter script was done by somebody with access to desk-top publishing, though stupidly I should have known that this had been around for some time. Rushing to the bathroom for a quick scrub - she had trained me well - I, at last, sat down and read her charming letter. After the usual civilities, she said that she and another couple of Dommes had started a BDSM-zine, available in most 'SLEAZY' outlets - her words - and commanded me to buy a copy and subscribe.

I knew of the recently-opened Sex Supermarket in Manningham Lane; a place I sneered at in my PC way when I passed it and even remember making approving noises when Miriam had told me that a couple of the gay girls, Ellie one of them I could imagine, probably had smashed its windows. I was still too snobbish and prudish to go there but knew of similar places in Leeds and Manchester. I loved the ambience of these places, so similar to that small area in Brighton near the Pavilion where I had contacted the local fascists, years before. I loved Conrad's 'Secret Agent' and of course Graham Greene's evocation of the underworld of Brighton, the sleazy dark side, the feeling of being a subversive and the outsider that I knew I basically was, and even though I had never had the need of the services of 'Ladies of the Night' I had always a fascination for such places.

I imagined the next visit to Manchester and I had business there, as I now exhibited in a typical walk-down Gallery in Portland Street. I also, and more conveniently for me, knew of a similar store down Briggate, the Soho and Charing Cross Road of Leeds. I saw it as an aesthetic adventure, exploring the 'underground' of literature and in this early digital era, I had an antiquarian passion for searching out minor graphic works, even if they bordered on pornography and especially criminality.

It was in an alley, just before the massive IRA bombing in '92, that I discovered the gay American 'Tom of Finland' erotic comic books and a whole plethora of US West Coast porn, the most thrilling being BDSM literature, Gay and Lesbian fanzines, 'Tom of Finland', some of which had vividly written and illustrated, though bizarre stories.

I discovered a very slick early British Transvestite magazine and on the back pages discovered a full-page advert for 'Transliving', a shop near Manchester with mail order for trannies exclusively. There were even stacked shelves of classic Fetish Magazines and hard-backed copies of classics like 'The Story of 'O', which were to be my bedside reading for the next few years.

Then one day, I had enough cash for a reconnaissance in the Leeds shop in Lower Briggate and appropriately, underneath the arched and run-down part of the city, pure Graham Greene land, or the haunt of Lilli Marlene. Imagining seedy-looking old men in gaberdine raincoats, I was surprised to meet bright-eyed and extremely sexy lady assistants and a bright and trendy clientele; my first 'Metrosexuals.' At last, maybe, I thought to myself, I had found a new way of being sexual but without the emotional pain and physical tackiness of 'Vanilla' sex. I had discovered a way of dealing with my unrequited passion for Miriam. My love. My wife.

At last, I discovered in a little A5 magazine, what I was looking for. After all the adverts from various semi-nude ladies from Stockport to Hunslet, there was a little questionnaire under the heading; Are you a submissive? And GLORY, a heading at the top of the page in the same typeface as Madame A's letter: The Corrective Institute and with a Devon address, my beloved Miriam's home county and not a place one usually associated with metropolitan sex.

I immediately purchased a copy and a couple of 'BDSM' mags and a pair of fur-lined handcuffs. You never know! I thought to myself. The nubile blonde counter girl wrapped my purchases up in a shiny black paper and gave me a dazzling smile. I felt quite 'hip'. Rushing for the Bradford train, I could hardly contain my excitement and on sitting down in my compartment, signed a cheque for the Institute and in Bradford immediately bought some envelopes and posted my application for slave-training and feminisation.

'I wake and feel the fell of dark, not day.'

Chapter 74

I think I had been sober for over a year; I was still living in my flat in Manningham and had found much stability and happiness in my life. I had even enjoyed a brief but happy relationship with an American fellow AA member, Nancy, a University Professor and as left-wing as myself, and like Miriam, a feminist also. She was similar in many ways but I think quite rightly, she found my self-centredness annoying. Despite my best resolutions, maybe because I was an artist, I was always thinking of my next painting, always yearning for the far horizon. I had read later that it was an alcoholic trait, the 'Yonderly look' as we say in Yorkshire. Maybe, I was to think, years later and with horror, my narcissism. AA doctrine insisted on a constant self-appraisal - Step-Four, or an ongoing moral inventory as a way of coping with a sober life and living a spiritual one, with or without religion.

Nancy and I had many trips out into the north countryside as she had a car and I enjoyed being her guide. I had been able, thanks to Fred and his red Volvo, to get out to galleries to show my work and already had a solo show in Leyburn where I continued to be invited and had renewed my friendship with Pete Taplin from Bradford Market. He had moved up to Wensleydale and started a country house style hotel and a friendly one. I was invited to stay there for free as long as I left Peter a painting and found my way up there. Thus, I became something of a Dales' artist and found a second home in Wensleydale.

I had great days throughout the Nineties, staying in the Stonehouse Hotel near Hawes, in comfort and meeting lovely people, sketching around upper Swaledale and Wensleydale and coming back to a lovely meal with no temptation to drink and pleasant company in very pleasant surroundings. At the other end of the Dale, at the Chandler Gallery, I was always to receive a warm welcome from the curators, the latter herself a superb artist and my best critic. I was not only painting but I was learning the skills of making my own frames, so my chambers were a hive of activity and a creative mess. However, this time I could hardly move for canvases and easels, not empty bottles and the miasma of despair that accompanied it; an almost physical sensation.

Then one morning, up early as was now my habit, I headed out of my back door to the corner shop for my milk and the Guardian when I bumped into Vinnie, a casual acquaintance and former drinking crony.

"Hi, Dave," he said. "Have you heard the news?"

Thatcher's fallen down a hole, I thought to myself, but no.

"Ian's dead."

"What! I only saw him the other day, on his bike. Looked as fit as a fiddle and he winked at me as I waved to him."

"Apparently, he had been drinking back at his flat with some crew. There had been an altercation; Ian could be 'difficult' and he'd collapsed - an embolism apparently. I knew the bloke, Liam, a mate of mine and he was cut up about it. As I'd had Ian by the beard I few times I felt no animosity."

I don't remember much after that. I didn't pick up a drink but I vaguely remember going back to my flat, drawing the curtains, throwing myself onto my bed and sobbing voicelessly into my pillow.

"Baldur is dead! Le GRAND Meaulnes!"

Square Man, Magnus and I went to his funeral over in East Bowling. His little girl, Jo-Jo Sky, whom Miriam and I had babysat for in those halcyon days of 1980, placed a little bouquet on his coffin and a distraught but stoical Lady Sarah played a tape of Ian singing "Salty Boys" his party piece that I heard that Autumn night at the King's Arms in Heaton years ago.

Though I was sad, my sobriety continued and I was overjoyed when Ginger told me, Ian and I having become a bit estranged recently, that he had always rated my painting better than his and wished us both well in our recovery. The big fella used to joke that he was thinking of joining us in this AA lark as he was running out of drinking companions!

I eventually moved to Bingley so I was nearer to more open country and as Dave and Magnus had moved out of Manningham, I felt the place, now I didn't drink any more, was too full of ghosts and memories of my happiest time with Miriam.

Many happy weeks followed and sometimes I was able to log on in the new Internet cafes to the Corrective Institute site. Amusingly, I had no idea at first and in Bradford had to ask the bearded and serious-looking Muslim proprietor for some help. Scrolling through several lurid-looking links, he grinned and said to me:

"I see you are sexually somewhat adventurous, sir?"

I was sure the address was a fake but I enjoyed the theatre of it and I had met the charming Madame Assumpta in London in Mistress Rachael's dungeon, or at least one of her sisters. I was never able to tell, such was the mystery that she wove about her person. Maybe it was Annunziata or Theresa? I was hooked and decided to bask in the illusion and enjoy what I knew of the reality of this strange way of 'loving'.

From my Contacts mags and until such times as I could visit the Institute or get a reply from Madame A, after sending her a cheque for £25, I passionately posted off to various housewives around Yorkshire and Lancashire. In one magazine I came across a course advertising 'Female Domination'-tongue in cheek, I know and designed for sad men like me but I rang a given number and heard a pre-recorded message; a feisty, young West Country girl by her accent and I could just hear her suppressing a chuckle before the message ended.

I took down the address of the 'New Age of Female Domination,' somewhere in the East End of London, surprise-surprise! I loved it; working-class girls taking the piss out of mainly American radical feminism and I could indulge my fantasy of getting even with Juggernaut and the not-so-fragrant feminazis of my university years AND have a bit of fun. I was surprised at how educational Princess Sabrina, the Matriarch in charge of the New Age, turned out to be and how sexy.

Eventually, I received a string of beautifully-crafted letters from the Institute of Correction, mainly with a covering letter from Madame Assumpta and more from Mistress Rosemary, her colleague, who as a Fetish Dominatrix had taken upon herself my feminisation. However, there was only a cartoon of her, the image of Madame A when she was younger. Even if I had not met the real Madame, I would, from her style of writing put her on the top end of my social class and generation, as you will soon see!

I was given the task of buying a pair of plain white panties from British Home Stories for my first piece of homework and I well remember the fear attendant on my doing so and the subtle smile of the store assistant when I stammered that they were for my wife who had been suddenly rushed into hospital.

If Mistress Rosemary had been pleased with one of my assignments, I would be sent a gift. Once, to my slight horror, a black and scarlet Basque and for Christmas a shining black patent leather collar with stainless steel studs.

I often received short missives from a slave, Tarty Tina or Fifi, house slaves who ran the Institute when their owners were away in France on wine-tasting tours. Like all Dommes I was to meet, they were 'Cavaliers' and hedonists. One of the things I loved about my new passion was that in largely Cromwellian Yorkshire and Lincolnshire, I had hit on something that I had learned to treasure about the more cavalier, or liberal South of England.

By now I was set up in a studio in Bingley and could receive mail either there or through the PO Box of the main Post Office of my new town. I remember the thrill when I first got a reply from the New Age of Female Domination. For my £35 fee, I was given a whole raft of information: photocopies of literature from US bondage and Fetish sites where my perversion was taken with a Teutonic solemnity. It was all tremendously exciting and of course, hopelessly wicked and decadent. And much better than making Airfix WW2 aircraft kits.

But for a time, my yearning for Miriam ceased, as did my nightmares about my dad and past humiliations seemed as nothing. This was real and like my art, only a little lie, to embody a greater and deeper truth. I really was now a secret agent and devout servant of the demi-monde!

I was still painting and NOT drinking and had even stopped smoking. On my own, I felt I could indulge my obsessive behaviour and I had no desire for another woman, only Miriam. Glenda lurked in the deeps of my soul though.

'Dive, Faustus,

Dive thy thoughts

Deep.'

I had learned a lot from Princess Sabrina and enjoyed my daily worship of her image and the mantras I recited daily to Female Domination. I laughed to myself thinking what my uni enemies would think. I who was being embraced and schooled in the Arts of Womanhood and by real beauties, women of wit and dazzling grace and fashion.

Sometimes on my trips down to London, I would visit Mistresses recommended by Princess Sabrina or Mistress Spiteful. Mistress Rebecca, a sylph-like redhead, would beat me into 'Sub Space' an area beyond pain and mere sexual release, more akin to the ecstatic visions of Medieval Christian mystics.

'Batter my heart,

Thrice Blessed Trinity!'

On one long and rather expensive weekend, I was part of a group of three of Mistress Spiteful's chosen body slaves who, in various stages of bondage were put through our paces by our owner and two other Dommes, one of them I am sure, the elusive Madame A, on a garishly flood-lit stage, the 'Skin-Two Rubber Ball'. I remember we slaves in the gents comparing proudly the great welts and scars that our glorious Owners had written on our flesh and the cigarette burns punctuating our torsos. The whip-crack of some boy being flogged by screaming Dominatrices was music to us bitches!

Such were my joys then but at least I wasn't crying myself to sleep with Miriam's name on my lips, or the sound of the footfall of my father overhead as a boy, as he prepared his descent to rage and flog me on the mildest pretext. I was dealing with my demons, I thought, in my own way. And sometimes I hallucinated, outside of my bed-chamber window, the voiceless spectre of a 'Burning Babe' and perversely, the catholic recusant in me was comforted.

Chapter 75

At last, after a pause of a couple of years, I had the money to go down more regularly to London, often in connection with my art practice too and to visit Mistress Rachael again. She was worried that I was getting a bit frail for regular flogging and suggested after a long interview that I emphasise my feminine side. I had told her about 'Tina' and we agreed on a quick course on my feminisation, with maybe a view to taking it even further. She was a serious sadist and feminist, passionate about castration but as I had become a friend as well as one of her cherished slaves, she wished to feminise me as much until, seeing how I felt, seeking professional medical advice. She had a string of prostitutes, formerly male as part of her property but knowing my basic heterosexuality was willing to grant my freedom at such time as the NHS took over. I did have delicious fantasies about being one of her 'working girls' though! She had been very pleased with my progress with the New Age of Female Domination and knew some of the girls there. BDSM was not all a big scam and I was to be impressed by the honesty of my Dommes.

Life for a man about to enter his 60's was getting rather exciting. I seemed to have worn well and presented even better 'en femme'. I was highly inspired in my art by my new secret life as a kind of secret agent, though curiously the subject matter was very 'vanilla'; only a very discerning eye would detect the frenetic emotional and spiritual state behind my painting.

I was advised- commanded rather, to save enough money for regular trips to London for feminisation training and possibly a professional makeover. Rebecca insisted that despite my age, I could make a convincingly beautiful woman and already I was being moulded by her, and she was sure, to my other Domme's satisfaction. I was wildly excited that I had found an absorbing and elegantly sexy solution to my demons.

In a short ritual, Mistress Spiteful renamed me 'Davina' and told me to inform my other Mistresses, recommending a Dressing Agency called Fourth Space in Windsor. After a mild spanking, she commanded me to kneel and kiss her boots and with a ritual slap on each cheek of my face, plus a short list of reading materials, sent me on my way. Like quite a few 'Dommes' she was quite intellectual and literary and recommended to me the extremely radical trans and BDSM author, American, Pat Califia.

A bit later, I posted off to the 'Corrective Institute' details of my new plan, and a request for permission to proceed. By return of post almost I received a delighted reply and the delicious present of some black, silk and lace panties. I was requested to post polaroid photos of me wearing them.

Though I worried a bit about my perversion, I had it deeply entrenched in my 'Knower' that I was an alcoholic and knew I was now embarked for the rest of my life as a sober and recovering alcoholic. I also had deeply impressed in my 'Knower', that I was not recovered and that just one drink and I would be back to the horror I had been delivered from! I still had my Demons, of course, though my life had turned around. I had discovered that limits defined and celebrated life. The Soul's 'Latin'?

Chapter 76

Mailly-Le-Camp. 1944. Part 1 of 2

It must have been a good few months, maybe nearly a year into sobriety. Fred was driving his great Volvo Hatchback and we were heading towards Hemsley on the old Scarborough Road, one of the nicest runs in England. I had four framed pastels in the back to show to a gallery recommended by Charles and Daphne Chandler from Leyburn, Wensleydale, where I had had my first Solo show as a professional artist months before. With Ella, Fred's beloved bull-terrier bitch with me in the passenger seat, I was full of hope on this early Spring day and so was Fred, my AA Sponsor and friend. These were great days, getting out to galleries all over Yorkshire, seeing some lovely countryside and sharing enthusiastically 12 Steps' lore and recovery with Fred; my hopes for the future and his as we enjoyed the varied and magnificent countryside of our county.

Not far from the bottom of Sutton Bank and very near the more manicured beauty of the Howardian Hills and North York Moors, coming up to Skipton-on-Swale, I suddenly noticed just over the gate of what looked like a beet-field an unmistakable, lichen-covered and squat WW2 Nissen hut. I had been reading desultorily recently about old WW2 Bomber Command airfields and in particular those of '4' Group, Bomber Command. There had been many Canadian and even Free French Squadrons this far north and I had also read about so-called 'Chop' Squadrons, those with a reputation for enduring even more losses than most in those terrible times.

Fred heard me exclaim, stopped with a squeal of brakes and found a passing place on our side in which to park. I told him all about this and being a good and sympathetic friend, after a reassuring pat to Ella, we crossed the road and without permission, clambered over the ramshackle gate. We could still see tarmac and concrete and I was overcome with a kind of melancholy which couldn't have been nostalgia as I was only a baby by the end of the war. Strolling further into the field and looking out for the former Control tower, I saw a farmer standing beside his tractor and raised a shout and an arm and the farmer, a friendly one, returned my greeting and called me over. On the way, I imagined what it would have been like just over 48 years ago, very much like any other Bomber aerodrome, I knew of probably? I shook hands with the farmer and introduced Fred.

"We get a lot of enquiries, lad, particularly these days, for some reason," he said. "Mainly Canadians and some French."

I knew about the Canadians and also that the Free French flew aged and battered old Halifax bombers, 'Halibags', to Lancaster crews. There had been some bad feeling recently in Canada at the allegedly higher losses of Canadian aircrews, that they had been fobbed off with 'Duff Kites' in RAF parlance. Whether true or not, I knew that even before that, mainly British aircrews around here had to make do with flying coffins like the 'Armstrong Whitworth Whitley' and Handley Page Hampden bombers, even the ubiquitous and reliable Wellington, well up until 1943.

I had heard sinister rumours of 'Chop' Squadrons, like RAF Melbourne and to the south, Linton-On-Ouse, home of RCAF Moose Squadron, where losses were so dramatic as to close a station down temporarily and eve of aircrews refusing to fly.

Crossing the A19 outside Thirsk, we passed a famous pub with Canadian airmen at the time: The Busby Stoop. I was able to persuade Fred to nip in for a glass of tonic water and see the wartime Squadron Photos on the wall, as well as the famous Windsor Chair where it was rumoured any airmen who sat in it got the 'chop' later.

The farmer didn't say much more, nothing about ghosts or sudden aircraft engine noises in the night but he said that the big field was not much use yet for tillage, there still being a lot of tarmac and concrete about but hard man as he was and looked! he never felt comfortable there and was aware of an oppressive sense of melancholy.

I suddenly remembered The Alouette Squadron and asked the farmer.

"Tha's reet, lad, I remember French lads? T'lasses round 'ere aren't likely tae forget!"

We said our goodbyes and headed for Hemsley, up Sutton Bank and a coffee and toilet break in what, over the next few years was to be a favourite spot on the way to the East Coast, Whitby or Scarborough, the romantic and exquisitely beautiful abbeys near here of Rievaulx, Byland and Guisborough, or a regular visit to the friendly and hospitable gallery curator,

Nicholas Coombes, of the Look Gallery, a lover of dogs and a great fan of Ella!

It had been a lovely Spring morning and I thought of the French and Canadian lads so far away from home nearly 50 years ago and some of them with their bones resting here. I noticed that the countryside was not unlike Normandy with its rich farmland and honey-coloured stone. The medieval churches and the great abbey ruins had a French feel about them and were probably designed by Frenchmen. Being mainly Cistercian orders, many of the early monks were probably Frenchmen too. Though I hadn't yet got into an unselfconscious way of praying at that time, I muttered a voiceless prayer for the French and Canadian dead.

After Fred, Ella and I had our break at the top of Sutton bank, we drove through a beautifully-farmed landscape of corn and well-tended woodland, with distant views of sweeping moorland. The sun was bright and with the window down, although still smoking, I savoured the fresh spring air outside, Ella occasionally and good-naturedly licking my forearm resting on the passenger window sill.

'The early bees are assaulting and fumbling the flowers'

They call it easing the Spring.'

I couldn't help bringing to mind Henry Reed's great WW2 anti-war poem and continued to myself or maybe aloud to Fred - we sometimes liked to sing!

'They call it easing the Spring; it is perfectly easy,

if you have strength in your thumb; like the bolt'

And the breach, and the cocking-piece, and the point of balance,

Which in our case we have not got; And the almond blossom

Silent in all of the gardens and the bees going backwards and forwards,

For today we have 'Naming of Parts.'

Chapter 77

RAF Waddington, Lincolnshire. 1944

Briefing done and it looked like a 'Milk-Run' to France. Gungha went back to his billet to snatch a couple of hours kip in this, the most stressful period on normal Ops. This was when the Lancs were being 'bombed-up', flight-tested by a skeleton crew, guns rearmed and cleaned, gun magazines reloaded. A few 'bods' might be kicking a football desultorily, bowling overarm at an aircrew batsman yielding a tennis racquet, or with the few Americans and Canadians playing throw and catch with a baseball glove and spare cricket ball.

Lying back, his peaked officer's cap, unusual rank for an air gunner, over his eyes, Gungha lit up a Players. He had been avoiding eye contact with the sprog crews just come on the base that day from their OTU. It was only a week before that 'Mitch' Mitchell and his crew had gone missing near Texel on what had seemed at the time like a routine mine-laying exercise off the Dutch coast,' market-gardening' as it was known. He had not come back and neither did a Sprog crew whose skipper's name he had forgotten.

It wasn't unkindness that experienced aircrews kept their distance from fledgeling crews but the heartbreak of getting to know new men and losing them almost immediately; the statistics were harsh. The first 5 'ops' were always the most dangerous. Up until halfway through a Tour, about 25 ops, the chances of a new crew surviving those first ones were negligible.

So, Gungha was not very friendly when one of the new intakes approached him, saying as he held out a hand tentatively - seated officers were not expected to salute or expect the same courtesy among aircrews) – saying:

"Ridler, Sir. Pilot-Officer Alan Ridler, and over there," pointing to a baby-faced but animated looking teenager, "Geoff Jackson, my Navigator. Have you any tips? I understand this evening's show is routine and only worth half a normal OP?"

"S'right, mate, just keep your eyes peeled and tuck in close to the main force."

"Anything else, Flight?"

"Nah, just fuck off, Ridler, won't you?"

So saying, Gungha picked up a nearby Daily Mirror, ostentatiously snapping it open at the back page and the 'Jane' comic strip.'

"Hey, Ridler," he continued. "Ya see this Sheila? Once she gets her full kit off, we know we've landed in France. Ever seen a pussy?"

Ridler, a tall and sensitive-faced youth, large-eared and slightly myopic, blushed and stammered: "Not quite, Flight."

He went back to a concerned-looking Jackson, another nice, baby-faced boy, who commiserated with a shocked Ridler.

Poor buggers thought Gungha and throwing the Mirror to one side, put his whole cap over his head after dousing his cig and slept.

Come the time for take-off, the crew of JO-X were dropped on the apron by their mount. Looking up to thank the WAAF driver, ever the lady's man, Dad and the rest doing the usual ritual, pissing on the tail wheel then lighting up, fingers shaking, for a final cig, Gungha saw a new face, a new 'Popsie'.

Strewth, I like her. This is the one! Gungha thought.

"What's your name, LAC?" (Leading Aircraft Woman)

"Thanks for not calling me Sheila, it's Marian!" she said in a firm and slightly manly voice, with a lopsided, cheeky grin.

"Thanks for the ride, Marian!"

She returned a just discernible grin in the gloaming of this Spring evening. She had cropped but waved golden-blond hair and from where Gungha stood, what looked like a petite and compact figure. She had a kind of a shine about her, a radiance, an intelligence, an excellence. Something understood.

"Well, Marian, places to go, little French children to kill, you know how it goes. Name's 'Gungha by the way-to my mates. Gungha Dean-get it? May I see you again, Marian?"

A faintly discernible grin, a crunch of clutch and gears, then:

"Just come back, Gungha!" a wrench of the steering and she was off.

The Merlins were coughing and propellers starting to windmill, as heart racing, Gungha rushed to the rear door and with a helping hand from Ron the mid-upper, yet to climb into his turret, he heaved his Sidcot-suited bulk into the rear fuselage. All around the apron and runway throaty roars and bellows of Merlin engines assaulted the evening air and it was still a pale indigo twilight when JO-X hauled its bomb-laden heft into the Lincolnshire Sky.

Molly had already saluted the Lanc, somewhat apart from the rest of the send-off committee: brass hats, a few off-duty desk-wallahs and Popsies. She did her little ritual march back to her billet thinking she might come back later, to see the boys returning. Looked like a 'milk-run' tonight and most of the girls knew D-Day couldn't be far away.

Back at her tiny dressing table in the WAAF officer's billet, she wistfully thought of the young Ridler, such a charming boy. They had climbed the Spire of Lincoln cathedral together and kissed after he pointed out the main aerodromes of Bomber Country spread out below and as far as The Wash. They had kissed tenderly and over a beastly Woolton pie and brackish coffee in a Gainsborough cafe, Ridler had proposed, and on being accepted, gave her a temporary brass ring. They spent an unshriven night making clumsy but passionate love in a Sleaford Hotel.

"Ah, well!" said Molly to herself. "Poor boy, let's see what dawn brings."

By dawn, all of the Lancs had returned except Ridler's. Molly, ashen-faced and in the cold light of an early summer's dawn, about-turned and did her 'death-Kiss Kate' routine, marching back to her billet and a new day.

Chapter 78

It was as corny as that but like a good love story, or AA share, true and honest. I had shared with an almost gut-wrenching pain, my rock-bottom, the dark hours of my descent, marital breakdown and uprising with the likes of the old-timer, Pigeon Ken and black Terry, a streetwise and witty, Anglo-West African kid. Just to be held by Ken's honest workman's hand was a spiritual experience and Terry commiserated with me saying:

"You learn from hitting the bottom, Dave, not from the mountain tops, they make you arrogant."

But my life was unmanageable, blessedly so. I don't know what happened; maybe I picked up a resentment at an AA meeting. I really had a problem with women by this time, as I imagined a radical feminist front trying to capture Bradford AA; memories of slights or otherwise I'd witnessed around Electric City, what had been my Camelot just a few years ago. Maybe it was a frosty glare from the Juggernaut or other former mutual friends of Miriam's and mine. Frail as I could feel, not being so strong in sobriety, I could easily be hurt. I felt exceptionally sensitive to my reduction in status, now being just an early middle-aged single and poor man back in Manningham. This was at a time of triumphalist Thatcherism and I sensed an increasing harshness in the social climate. My alienation from contemporary Britain was profound.

I was desperate for a drink but knew that I couldn't. I walked up the Hill, my Calvary I thought mawkishly and right past Miriam's home and through the gates of Lynfield Mount Psychiatric Hospital. I knew in my 'Knower' that my drinking days were done. I spent some weeks there, mainly in the recovery centre, once I had overcome some heavy sedation.

At last, I was back in Manningham, painting as I had never done before, eating well, going for long hikes over the moors and AA meetings, as many as I could manage.

I sensed changes in the air and not good ones; returning students from universities drooling over money and designer clothes, a certain shiftiness among former friends, a closing of ranks, a hint of treachery, a sense of evil?

The occasional curled lip and blank look from former drinking associates, the flashing of car keys at the bar, ostentatious and somehow obscene. I've got mine! It cried; the increasing thudding of devil's hoof-beats, the dark riders thundering across a darkened Bradford nightscape.

I had my first exhibition ever at the age of 46! It was at the little Bradford Gallery and I enjoyed some local success, with my first review, a positive one in our local paper, the 'Telegraph & Argus.' Then Mary Sara, art critic of the Yorkshire Post, a conservative but well-respected newspaper came and praised my work highly, giving me contacts in the art world and introducing me to a superb framer, whom I am with to this day.

Another contact who proved a real friend and supporter was Little Barry, a lovely man, very conservative as well as gay and Curator of 'Hunter & Greasely's Art Gallery. In those heady days of early recovery, he would often call at my place for a late-night coffee, always enthusiastic and encouraging about my work.

Even Miriam deigned to come to my Preview and though no enthusiast for my painting, conceded that my work looked professional. A part of me, the superficial, social part, pretended to be cool to her but in my heart, I felt an agony of loneliness and regret. I could sense she only came to see me out of an almost totally faded sense of obligation, like a Duchess on a visit. Now a young Mum, she still looked lithe and athletic and I sensed in her a woman satisfied sexually a strong and happily fulfilled animal. My pain was near exquisite.

However, that night, after helping Barry and his partner, Mike, close up, with my best Burberry and my fairly smart Burton suit, I walked singly back up to Manningham with only a slight sense of anti-climax and a feeling that the art world was at last about to embrace me, that a page had been turned. Tony Sharpe, my landlord hero and artist of so many years ago had come and even bought a painting!

Though I was never to drink again, my body yearned for some kind of release. I needed to forget Miriam for a while and if I couldn't, I almost wanted to BE her in some way. I wanted some humiliation too; my father's ghost still loomed; Cromwell or the Black Douglas!

By the time I got back to my empty flat, I knew what I had to do, go down to London. After researching the BDSM Press in the sleazier quarter of Leeds, always a 'Walk on the Wild Side' I needed to get down to London. I had sold 6 pictures, enough to settle any pressing debts and pay for a couple of hours with a Pro-Domme and maybe, if she was still around, Madame A!

I had been pleased to meet Miriam again and though I knew that she didn't rate my painting highly, I felt that it had been a dignified last meeting and that I had earned some self-respect. Too excited to sleep, I changed into my painting clothes, even donning an ancient Rembrandt-style smock and set up my easel. I put on my new CD of Rachmaninov's Vigil in the Russian Orthodox mode, set up a fresh piece of pumice board on my easel and thinking of painting a portrait of Miriam in an exorcising ritual, started on a portrait of her as a kind of a tribute, a valediction. A full moon was shining over Manningham, a typical Indigo night. I was just around the back of the road where, in the glorious days, we had lived and loved together.

I had decided in the end to paint a portrait of Glenda. She still haunted me; I still raged, even more in my new-found sobriety. But I found myself, head bowed, numb and catatonic, before my easel. No hate.

In the great Rachmaninov's Night Vigil service, I sensed the echoing vaults, the million partings on long-ruined platforms of St Pancras and King's Cross railway stations, the aching farewells, the gentle whisperings in the background of the great Orthodox Mass, the receding night lights and the hushed and reverent female voices, the long echoing corridors of the hospitals of my youth, the poor, shabby and broken men in the Hammersmith Spike and semi-ruined St Pancras, the Bellman waking us for our shifts, the melancholy white, enamelled London brick, sepia and indigo transepts and aisles, Gothic turrets and high, pointed gables. The fitful stars shining on a thousand streets. The aching heart. Church bells through the universe. Something understood. The Land of Spices.

I sometimes hear the dread footfall of the 'Sergeant' on the stairs but less often now. I think fondly of his comrades in Bomber Command and the boys of the Luftwaffe night fighter squadrons.

No hate.

I bless Miriam and Glenda for inviting me into their lives.

I sense a shining; maybe I will find a use for my iridescent pastels after all. A burning babe?

I sense a hush and a presence. An old Dutch lady and so much older, a Russian, 'Our Lady' of Vladimir?

I pick up a big wash brush, garden spray and a fistful of pastels; let me see, as I gaze through my tears at her photo; Naples yellow, raw sienna, light purple grey and palest lemon yellow, a stick of indigo, burnt umber and green grey for her superb and heroic bone structure.

I hear a voice: "What yer like, Zac?" A Halifax accent from so long ago.

And I dimly see her hand fixing a stray lock of blonde hair into her 'Mary Jane', beneath her dark, cobalt blue beret. I begin, with the tenderest of caressive strokes and I am being kissed by her as I have never been kissed since then, her blonde hair cascading over me, recumbent on my camp bed in my monastic room so, so long ago; hair that smelled like crushed vanilla, her body that I yearn to swim in.

Some firmer strokes now, my fingers gently massaging the lustrous pigments, as I summon up the magic of remembrance made physical, the supple young female flesh over bone, those elegantly buttressed cheeks, the dome and turrets of her skull, the balcony of her brows, the jellied perfection of her calm, deep and fathomless eyes.

Silence in the studio as the great Vigil closes.

"Silence in the Life Room!"

Part Nine:

THE TEMPERING
OF THE STEEL

Chapter 79

I knew in my 'Knower', as Fred called it, that I would never drink alcohol again. One day, not long afterwards, I received a reply from the Institute and in Madame Assumpta's typing. It was to be the most charming and non-Cromwellian letter I have EVER received, exquisitely crafted also; I can only quote in full:

'The Corrective Institute.'

PO Box..Exeter, Devon.

Ah, dear Nina,

Thank you so much for your tribute and your beautifully-written fantasy.

There followed a string of commands, sartorial mainly about the correct sort of lingerie I was commanded to purchase, with advice on bra-sizing, make-up etc. Then she continued in a chatty way about some of her recent experiences, just like a sister or intimate girlfriend. It was sheer bliss and I loved her prose style as well as her waspish but sexy humour.

She continued:

You say you worry about being fucked by males at nightclubs but this would not happen to you unless you wished it to. There is a code of behaviour in these places, where 'no' really does mean 'no' and you would be quite free to go as slowly as you wished. Frankly, I believe that a club like this is one of the safest places there is to explore one's desires, so I hope you won't dismiss it out of hand. Perhaps we could go together at one point.

Now, I know that you mislaid my last letter during your move to your new address but there were a couple of questions you failed to answer. We wanted to know if you ever go out dressed and if you would be interested in going to a sauna or sex club on a TV or Bi night? I ask this because it was Tina's birthday shortly before Mistress Rosemary and I left for France a few weeks ago and we gave her and Fifi 24 hours off to a place called Chameleons just outside Birmingham. They had a simply marvellous time and Tina ended the night lying in a leather sling, still (just about) wearing her pink party dress, whilst men and women crowded around her and, in one case, actually fucking her! How would you feel about something like that happening to you, Nina?

Are you still in touch with your first wife? I love the nickname Mizzie Messerschmidt, by the way, how did that come about? It does sound as if she was quite understanding and helpful, and that for a time you really loved each other.

But, as for your various Mistresses, well, some would call you a bit of a slut, Nina, the way you spread yourself about, but I am not a possessive woman, and am just glad that you are exploring your submissive femininity so thoroughly. A lot of subs think it it's impossible to be warm-hearted AND dominant, but to my mind, it's the ONLY way to be.

I must rush, as I have news of my sister, Annunziata in France. Apparently, she is rather ill with the drink so we are temporarily closing the Institute down here in Devon.

However, Fifi is care-taking the Hall while we are in France. Do keep posting, my dear Nina. I have great hopes for you, dear girl!

In the meantime, much love.

Assumpta XX

I was intent on exploring my dark side; obsessive, as I was in so many other things which is an alcoholic trait, I learned. Sometimes, as I think I have already said, I had enough of a successful exhibition to spend a few days in London, usually in a 4-Star hotel in Bloomsbury, or as I prefer to call it, Fitzrovia. Russell and Bedford Squares were my favourites, being only twenty minutes down Southampton Row to Charing Cross Road and then straight into Theatreland, St Martin's Lane and the West End. How well I remembered those hungry and desperate days so long ago when I roamed those streets.

On one of my trips, I walked straight past an elegant, if slightly dishevelled Dirk Bogarde and I even fancy he raised a quizzical and characteristic right eyebrow at me and made a barely discernible 'moue' with his lips. I was sad to see that he lacked the pencil moustache of Von Aschenbach.

I think I have already described well the excitement and passion of my burgeoning sexual deviance. Going to exhibitions and stocking up with art materials from the Dickensian 'Cornelissen's Colourmen' on Great Russell Street was always a good excuse, as was the nearby British Museum. October to Christmas was my favourite period and I have already rhapsodised about the Elgarian ambience of those noble squares: Russell, Bedford, and

Tavistock, not to mention the Mayfair area and Shepherd's Market. Truly, I fancied that I DID once hear a nightingale sing in Berkeley Square.

I had worked out a little scenario with Mistress Rachael, not only a Dominatrix but as she described herself, an Initiatrix.

Oh, the Black Douglass-but he was rough!

On my most recent visit, in November last year, I had asked her to wear a blonde, bobbed wig over her usual immaculate 'Betty Page' bobbed red hair. We had worked out a routine and I had written a script. It went like this - and yes, maybe I heard a cock crow 3 times that night!

Fitzrovia. The Dungeon. I've lashed out on paying tribute to two Dommes; a cane chair stood in a corner near me and I am strapped, bound and gagged to an A-frame. I have just been kicked around and screamed at: "Take that, bitch-boy-and that!" by Mistress Betty in 'Glenda' mode before being strapped to the frame.

Follows:

"Well, Good Morning, David, what a night!"

Miriam (A hooded Madame A?) reaches over and snatches the ball-gag from my mouth.

"Indeed, Erika," I splutter.

"Miriam!" Mistress Elena retorts.

Leaning over she says; "I think I am going to clean you! You said last night, David, that you wanted to be my friend?"

Me: "I would rather like that, Miriam, to be friends?"

Mistress Elena: "And I, too, David, actually. You made that quite clear last night!"

Mistress tosses her blond wig bob and turns around slowly towards me and oh, so softly, she spits in my mouth."

Mistress then turns her back to me again, slowly raises herself and picking up her crop from the nightstand at my left, wiggles her bottom, holding her crop with a hand at each end, looks around and down at me, haughtily but frighteningly, then kindly, says: "Righto, my David, coffee for us," grinning. "And stay right there!"

And the beatings began.

"And here a great Prince, in prison lies."

Chapter 80

I became 'Nina' legally, and started on serious transition with the NHS and by that time, much help online.

The NHS has been kind to me. I started on a short course to treat what my excellent GP, Kate Eldred, diagnosed as 'Depression' induced by 'Gender Dysmorphia'. She was also to refer me to the Gender Clinic in Leeds, as I was beginning to be serious about my transition.

I felt I had finally taken my revenge on my father and Cromwellian Yorkshire though, curiously my military obsession never finally left me, despite my becoming ever more left-wing and pacifist with age. Father had wanted me to be a girl, or rather threatened to turn me into such and the Roundhead type of Yorkshiremen that I hated, used that as their greatest insult, to be like a big, silly girl.

Deep down in me, a burgeoning female voice cried: "If that's what yer want, Duckie, so be it!"

One night, about the time of our split, I had a strange dream which I couldn't understand at the time. I had been walking either in Northcliffe or Heaton woods, a favourite childhood truant spot; a short evening walk from my home in Manningham. Miriam and I had had our 'Paradise Garden Walk' there some years before.

Anyway, a WW2 German soldier seemed to detach himself from a hawthorn hedge where sometimes I had startled a fox. Holding out his right hand and tipping his Nibelung-style helmet slightly to reveal handsome blue eyes amongst the sweat and stubble of a front line 'Landser', he gripped mine saying:

"Wie gehts, JUNGE?"

I shivered and as he readjusted the sling of his Mauser rifle on his shoulder, he continued:

"Mailly-Le-Campe, I am 21st Panzers-Infantry section. I am the enemy your father killed, meine liebe freund."

"So am I!" I replied.

He clasped my hand firmly with his other hand.

"I am with your father… but we must sleep now."

He walked towards some cottages below and down a deep ravine that I knew was there and before he disappeared, he turned and saluted, adjusting the strap on his Stalhelm and with just a grin on a somewhat noble face, he sang softly and sweetly in a Tenor/Baritone voice, a few lines of 'Erika' about the heather blooming on the heath - I knew that much German - then nothing, just the birds resuming their singing. I suddenly remembered a late summer when Miriam and I had first met and our walk through paradise garden. It was precisely down there, that she had knelt on her haunches and pulled me down to kiss her, saying, country girl that she was: "Look, David, here's wood sorrel!" And I remembered the smell of wild garlic and the certainty of love found and returned and forever.

I received another charming letter from Madame A but the new technology didn't suit her or maybe she had retired. Sadly, and almost tragically, I lost it as I moved to my new flat in Crossflatts. I wished I had read her letter closer the first time because I realised that I had encountered someone remarkable, even more so than Robin, Stan or Ian, but that had been the story of my life. I got a few garbled emails from 'Tarty Tina', her TV maid but heard nothing more for a bit. I continued to post letters to her though and Fifi emailed me instructions.

Very little money was asked of me and I was beginning to think the 'Institute' in Devon was for real. Fifi hinted that Madame had been upset by the state of her sister and was somewhat depressed and withdrawn.

Princess Sabrina retired to Spain with some select slaves but I still kept up an online link with Mistress Rachael, even meeting with her for coffee at Claridge's or Fortnum's, the Cafe Royale being no more, alas; sometimes the V&A or Courtauld's down by the Embankment, my favourite.

Whenever I am in London, I love to stay in Bloomsbury and I get a terrific pang when I walk along Euston Road from King's Cross and turn into Warren Street, then Fitzroy Square and deeper into Bloomsbury. That place, St Pancras Station, now nearly restored to its former opulence and the memory of the Hammersmith 'Spike' are my cathedrals, both to exquisite pain and ecstasy.

Eventually, I found a lovely little evangelical church that accepted me as Nina. Then, one morning last year, I decided I could not go ahead with my transition and I returned to being David.

Part Ten:

LARA'S SONG

Chapter 81

Well, my dears, here we go! Where shall I start? Now that I've laid Dave and Zac to rest for a bit, I need to explain myself. I know I've been hovering over these last chapters like some Jungian Anima spectre, a figment perhaps of David's frenzied, and fallen soul?

I know that I had a walk-on role in one of his rather irritating Time-Out pieces, or even when poor David, bless his confused soul, played on the Dark Side but I can assure you that Madame Assumpta is, or was, poor girl, for real. We used to meet in the old Cafe Royal in Piccadilly before it went TOOO down-market, then latterly in Fortnum's until they had that ridiculous lockout of their staff. You can call Madame A and me many things but SCABS we are not. So, towards the end - she passed on a couple of years ago, bless her - we used to meet just outside the West End, in Bloomsbury; David loved that part of town, you know. Fitzrovia, he liked to call the area, dear boy, in that mawkish forties' way that he had, how he rhapsodised about Russell and Bedford Squares, autumn leaves and the lights going on in the late afternoon and of nightingales singing in Berkeley Square. "But That's MAYFAIR, darling!" I would have to correct him.

I don't think he's been back on the sauce but maybe he's been taking a look at Calvino, having pretensions way beyond his plot-making capacity and fallen into some kind of a time-loop. He made a good stab at Evelyn Waugh though, dears, you notice it? Poor old Dave was becoming more and more like that snivelling Papist bore, Guy Crouchback until Nina came along. Maybe he has been listening too much to his snotty ex; I know he got caught at warp-speed in a protracted and rancorous Facebook argument with her. Apparently, I'm a result of his channelling a desperate desire to make his fantasies about me, his obsession, concrete.

Nina is for real, I assure you, darlings; only Dave and I share the same space. I've got my corset just about right now, or my changing body is leaning into it. M might call it fetishistic but to me, it's real-and enormously liberating. How can restrictive clothing have that effect and I feel no sexual arousal? I worry about the word 'spiritual'. It seems dishonest and twee to me but I feel something inchoate, turned on and in touch with myself;

wonderfully so, HAPPY, maybe?

People ask when I was born. I know I'm a bit of a minx, unlike David who let's say can be a bit dour at times, a bit intense? I think Dave was moderately kinky, though fairly typical of his age and sexual tendency, and mum's bottom drawer was such a healthy and corrective balance to that of an Alpha male father, with its uber-butch contents: spanners, WW2 medals, Flight Engineer's notes, black leather police gloves, fuse-wire, RAF logbook, wartime 'snaps', pipe cleaners and handcuffs; stuff that reeked of authority, false masculinity, the prison house and the barrack square.

Zac had loved Mum's drawers, even the way her dressing table was so beautifully carpentered, a parting present from the Duchess of Kent when she had joined the WAAFs. How seductively even it slid open, to reveal to his enraptured gaze, glazed pink lingerie, her black and sheer nylons, for best only and from her brother in the States, mysterious gynaecological-looking engines, cotton panties, bras and bliss, one of those new Playtex girdles he'd seen on commercial TV that had the boys in his class talking in subdued and reverend tones.

A kind of a radiance shone from the open drawer and a corresponding glow lit up his own soul. It was a bit like when he donned a freshly-laundered surplice and helped serve the Eucharist at Holy Communion, that iridescent sheen from freshly-laundered linen, that deliciously fresh ozone smell, that sacred light glistening on the upraised chalice, the proffered Host, the ruby red wine, 'The Blood of Christ'(sotto voce), the same thrill as when he tenderly inserted his hand into the deep beige tops of her nylons and stroked the silken texture of them and caressed his still beardless cheeks with them. Ecstasy!!

Mother's gentle Scottish voice, her Snow White looks and lithe and girlish body. As she covered Zac's eyes and ears with her soft hands that smelled like summer rain so long ago: "What are the wild waves saying, little one?" Was it by the big, cold and dirty-grey river at Rosyth or Grangemouth, perhaps, by the grey and chill bulk of the great warships, when for the first time, they were alone together, Mum and he, up in Fife with her family, Dad at home and at work, little baby brother with Grandma Greenwood back down in gloomy post-war Bradford. They'd been to the pictures the night before Zac remembered, in Cowdenbeath, with some of Mum's lovely and warm-hearted mining family. Zac had loved some of their archaic sayings:

'Goodwif' and 'Mistress Kirsty'. Mum's Aunt Marie from the Western Isles, her deep and gentle Erse courtesy and her curiously Mediterranean long dress of almost black plaid, with an off-white shawl always thrown delicately and elegantly across her bird-like bones.

Such feminine grace and gentle courtesy, when he first learned to know 'a kindness of women.' Yet the rough kindness of their men also, tough and wiry miners, all recently ex-servicemen and Zac remembered the 'kriegies', lines of handsome foreign-sounding men, ex-German and Italian POWs with no homes left back in the Reich just over the water; our men shaking hands with them, giving them small packs of pipe tobacco and sharing family photos, regimental cap badges. One Teutonic God must have lifted Zac up in his strong arms with an 'Ach, JUNGE!' And Zac remembered a cold North Sea and setting sun glistening on the blonde stubble of a former warrior's cheek; perhaps an iridescent gleam in a half discernible tear, as he was put down and with a hearty handshake, a Siegfried said his goodbyes.

Was it Scotland Well, or that Queen of Scots' forlorn palace at Falkland, or Forres where they skipped together? Mum and he down a long avenue of majestic elms, sad, yet grand in the big park near the great, posh houses? 'We will walk down the avenue, though we haven't got a dime!' Mum would sing and get Zac to follow in step and skipping by turns through puddles to the beat. 'We're a coupla swells-we live in the best hotels!' from Judy Garland's great song from the 'Pictures' the night before where they had both delighted in the new and exotic colours of Hollywood, of joy and glamour and escape!

Her legs smelt like Spring rain also and exuded a blissful coolness. Zac thought her the most beautiful creature in the world and he adored and worshipped her as she sang softly, songs of the old country while she undressed at the simple night table, then leapt over to join him in a freezing Fifeshire bed, as she wrapped her arms around him, kissing his ear with a 'Coorie down, ma wee son!' Then she turned off the bedside light and Zac fell into bliss.

Chapter 82

I think Nina became something more concrete around the time David and Andrea, his last partner, parted or rather Andrea had decided she'd had enough of his self-obsession/downright selfishness, his obvious lack of success in the art world and his obsession with religion.

Hi, it's Dave again! For a short time, I thought I was on the verge of success and I had some wonderful times with Andrea driving, motoring around the north and southern Scotland, taking my work and sometimes some of hers, as a good if less committed artist, to galleries and with the group exhibitions we were in.

Out of the blue some years ago, coming back from a short break in Venice with Andrea's Art Group, I received a call from Glenda on my first mobile. To my astonishment, there was not a trace of the old Halifax accent but it was her voice alright, strong and authoritative. I couldn't describe it at the time but now I imagine that it was how Emily Bronte might have spoken. She was wondering if I was David, or Zac Greenwood, the former student she had met so many years before? In an idle moment, she must have stumbled on or Googled my name. I was on an Ilkley Gallery website and I found out later that she had phoned the curator, Geoff, a friendly man with whom I enjoyed much success in the late '90s.

We reconnected, even saw each other. She was still down in Sussex and a few times, especially at Xmas, we all three met for a meal. Andrea and Glenda seemed to get on well, two strong Yorkshire lasses and I discovered later they were email friends. I still found her attractive, though with a strange undertone of mystical awe and horror and I retained my distrust, fascination and admiration of her.

About the time Andrea and I split up and I was making lone experiments in cross-dressing and generally the dark side, Glenda met me on one of her trips up north. It was the usual mixture of pain on my behalf and that inchoate yearning I had always felt for her. But the evening with her, though tense, ended almost amicably. I think she realised that I had no hopes of an affair with her and was aware of my total ineligibility at that time too. We came to a moment where despite her dislike of 'Trans' issues,

Glenda gave me some sisterly advice on the ear studs I was wearing. Saying as much, that I saw her as a soul sister, her eyes lit up, affirming that she kind of liked that and then a bit sadly, we parted at the railway station. But on the long, cold journey back to Bingley, my heart was warmed by the fact that something - I did not know what - was understood.

So, while I struggled to get my act back together, with Andrea generously helping me to get a nice flat, we occasionally emailed or phoned each other. Then something happened during an email conversation; harsh words were said, all of my anger and frustration boiled over into a tirade of grief and hurt pride. About a month later, on the way back from shopping in town, my mobile buzzed. It was a Detective Sergeant from the Sussex Constabulary. After asking me to confirm that I was indeed Mr David Greenwood, he cautioned me that he had been charged to inform me that a Ms Sugden had seen her Solicitor, who had, in turn, contacted them and to warn me never to contact her again, in any shape or form-blah-blah. After I had expressed astonishment, he calmly asked me 'man-to-man' what it was all about? Then reassured me that he was sorry but he was only doing his job.

My rage and fury inspired me to start on this memoir. The 'Black Douglas' had struck again, but was he her, or me?

The only good thing that I can say about that terrible time is that I didn't pick up a drink-oh, and…

And that's where I came in, Nina! Poor old Dave, a total fail- but I'm anticipating!

Well, how Dave didn't just ram her teeth down her throat beats me! What an overbearing, arrogant bitch. You could see Dave was on the bones of his arse and not at his best. She picked up one of his books he'd bought for the train: the poetry of Swinburne, recommended by Mistress Rachael down in Fitzrovia and a collection of the Border Ballads picked up in Piece Hall Yard nearby, disdainfully saying that at least he was reading proper books. Picking fault with everything he said, jumping down his throat with a 'That's sexist!' Or laughing at his ear studs. He was nurturing me but had not yet realised I was for real! Lol!

I could sense Dave tensing for a rapid departure; what a way to spend a Saturday night in freezing Halifax? Personally, darlings, I would have

HOOFED her down fifteen flights of cast iron stairs!

I was with him on his way home on the train and of course, I couldn't hold his hand but I hugged him metaphorically and I think he seemed happy. I worked on him subliminally as he went to his sad and blameless bed in his new apartment. I resolved to work on him overnight and come out the following morning. Time for Nina to take control. Sound the trumpets!

Chapter 83

It would have been a year after Andrea and I had split and I was settling nicely into my new apartment. The first thing I did, I remember was to luxuriate in my new bath and shave my legs. It was a new-build and quite smart. Now I was on my own I felt I could really develop my feminine side, Tina or Davina, I seem to remember me calling myself. I had also started seriously studying the Trans magazines I'd bought in the sex shops in Leeds and Bradford. I know I must have got over my sleazy masturbatory fantasies because I was beginning to find some more intellectually stimulating stuff among the mild porn I'd bought.

I discovered the existence of the Beaumont Society, a straightlaced support group for very straight and middle-class transvestites. I read some interesting features about the history of my condition, discovering the Chevalier D'Eon, that fascinating French aristocrat who lived and fought 24/7 as a woman. However, what interested more was the existence of men who wanted to be women, who identified with them and felt ill at ease in a man's body. I wondered where I stood on that spectrum, having no desire to have sex with a man but a confused desire, a passion at times to smother my body in female garments, drench myself in perfume and just BE.

A part of me still liked the seedy and what I thought of as a socially subversive aspect of the BDSM spectrum. I used to love the camp and rebellious humour of gay and 'pretty boys' in the various bars and hotels I worked at in London and Brighton. Not only did I sympathise with their anti-establishment leanings but I felt strangely exhilarated in their company. Such social life as I had now, much as I loved the serenity of the moors, canal and woods nearby, seemed dull and reactionary. I had also felt strangely exhilarated in the company of gays in a way that even a loving marriage couldn't compare with. I think I was always deep down one of the boys who loved the greasepaint and the motley.

At the Fourth Space Dressing Agency, Nina discovered!

So, the great day came, when single again, thoroughly shaved all over, I found myself on the train to London and then Windsor. I booked a hotel overnight in 'The Smoke', Bloomsbury and then took the Slough train and changed for Windsor.

In Endsleigh Street, part of University College, I had already talked to Jo, the female part of the couple. Her husband Tim, a photographer was a transvestite also and that promised to help me feel at ease. From what I had seen of their website, they seemed a highly hip and professional young couple.

Windsor, I knew was very posh which was reflected in their prices but self-indulgent as it seemed, I was in the mood for something radical, something sophisticated and exciting!

I was asked to call Tim on my mobile when I arrived at Windsor and arrange a meeting place where he would pick me up and drive me to their studio/home. On the journey there, I was immediately struck by the social differences between King's Cross Railway Station and Paddington, only a short hop away on the tube. The former still had a desolate and melancholy feel about it, even more so following the terrible underground fire of not so many years ago and I hugged myself mentally as I walked smartly through the throngs of people through that seemingly endless pedestrian tunnel to my connection to Paddington.

Paddington immediately appeared a more sedate and ethnically homogeneous area, with a hint of the suave and luxurious Kensington a couple of miles to the south. The station itself confirmed that, with its prosperous stalls and the elegant cantilevered roof of Brunel's masterpiece. Ghosts of the old Great Western Railway were evident to my still nerdy and boyish mind. This, of course, would have been where Holmes and Dr Watson (Don't forget your Service revolver my dear fellow!) would have embarked, in fiction at least, for their adventure in the far West Country with the Baskerville family.

The crowds inside the station were more relaxed, more middle-England and I couldn't help but feel that chip on my shoulder itching as we rode out of the station and headed west. Though the chatter among my fellow passengers was mainly on mobiles, those in conversation seemed to do so with old friends, had interesting jobs in town or were taking time off for some casual and genteel shopping in the West End. After changing trains at the less salubrious Slough, I was treated to memories of my Surbiton days, the lush suburbs and wooded Surrey of the middle Thames Valley, Eton College glimpsed briefly beyond the hymned and famous playing fields and soon the great battlements of Windsor Castle.

Only the constant and low-flying Boeing Jumbo jets, coming into land at nearby Heathrow brought me back into the early 21st century as the train gently came to a halt in an exquisitely-preserved, boutique-lined station concourse, one of two. After calling Tim, I was told to meet him in the car park at the other, a short walk away, down Peascod Lane - how twee-sounding - where after the briefest but heart-throbbing wait, I was to meet him. A toot and a friendly wave from a huge Range Rover: "Climb in Davina!" which was my girlie name at the time, a manly shake of the hand and Tim drove us as far as the old village and just past the Castle main entrance.

I arrived at the 'Fourth Space' where once inside the elegantly restored, late medieval cottage, I was introduced to a slim and stunningly well-groomed Jo-Jo.

"Tim will get you ready, as soon as you've washed or would you like a shower, Davina?" she said. "And then we'll begin on your make-up. We like to take our time and would you like a coffee?"

They seemed a delightful couple and Tim filled me in on some biographical details, how he was an ex-Royal Marine and fitness fanatic and whose transvestism had only been discovered a year into their marriage and how it was a miracle, really, as on finding one of his bras in a trouser pocket, she suspected he was 'playing away from home' but that it was ok when she found the truth because as a trained beautician, she was delighted and it was a stimulus to their business.

I was to realise how successful, or at least how professional they were when, coffees in hand, Tim showed me around while Jo-Jo prepared her boudoir and make-up kit. The walk-in wardrobe was just that, as big as my own bedroom back in my new apartment near Bingley and well-stocked with rows of glistening fabrics. There was an Imelda Marcos fantasy of shoes, row upon row of gleaming patent black leather and lethal-looking bayonet heels.

"Just let me tuck you in a bit, old girl!" said Tim, the bloke-ish banter and the knowledge that he was ex-military, making me feel less embarrassed as he tied me into a corset. "Not too tight, I hope, Davina?"

Then he chose, with an expert eye some clothes from a rack nearby and ushered me back onto the landing near the boudoir, saying with a knowing wink:

"Put this bra on. I think you'll know how!"

He went over to an antique chest of drawers and withdrew a pair of black hold-ups and black lacy panties.

"Oh, and put these shapers on, gives your bum a bit of a curve?"

He winked again, then after I had put on my bra, he deftly inserted a pair of breast forms and showed me how to press my male breasts which were quite well pronounced by now, into a presentable cleavage. He topped it all with an exquisitely hugging Brazilian body-shaper and helped me to step into some 4- inch, shining black patent leather court shoes. Finally, he held one of my arms courteously and ushered me into the boudoir, saying:

"I've sorted out an ensemble for you: three probably for the afternoon when we can have a long photoshoot."

"Davina!" cried Jo as I was steered gently over to the dressing table, which blazed with lights around a huge mirror. "This is how we professionals do it, Davina!"

While Tim took a seat in the corner, Jo began her work, first throwing over me a white protective gown, while complimenting me on my new figure. Then she bound what was left of my hair in a tight headband after stretching the skin of my forehead and cheekbones with powerful tape. She vigorously applied 'Derma-blend to cover my beard and then began her magic, while regaling me with her experience as a professional beautician in the theatre and TV. Tim joined in occasionally. One plan was for Tim and me to go dressed up to the West End, probably to Soho or Chelsea and have a bit of fun 'out and proud'. Happily for me, he said that he didn't feel on top form. As I had to get back to my London hotel that day and we had what was looking to be a great photoshoot ahead of us, we agreed to give it a miss.

What followed was one of the most sensuously self-indulgent afternoons of my life. The conversation was vibrant and interesting. Jo was a bright and vivacious lady and the anecdotes flew thick and fast and not just gossip; we talked about films we all loved, even hitting on politics. Tim, like a few soldiers I had met, proved surprisingly liberal in his political views, saying that though he loved the comradeship of the Corps, he would be happy never to fire a weapon again or don a uniform. He had married the girl of his dreams in Jo-jo and they enjoyed the most wonderful of partnerships, where on the occasional weekend Tim would become Tamara and they both would go 'up west' and do the clubs.

The time came when she permitted me to open my eyes after doing, like an artist, some meticulous work on them. Choosing some false eyelashes while I recoiled at the almost obscene-looking, wig-less image before me in the mirror, she asked me to close my eyes again while she placed my new lashes on my eyelids.

How to describe my feelings? A sinking and slithery sensation, as if I was degenerating fast and sliding into a primordial stew of vice and depravity; quicksand sucking me under as I sank further into degeneracy and the ultimate in debauch and yet the thrill of what seemed like walking through vanilla custard and ice cream, of being in a new skin, a second one, an unfamiliar but longed-for wholeness, just like a butterfly emerging after a long gestation from its chrysalis.

"And NOW, my Davina!" Jo's exclamation woke me from my reverie. "Your crowning Glory!"

She gently lowered the wig over my head, asked me to give her one hand at a time while she applied false nails and I gloried at my transformation in the mirror. She then sprayed me briefly with the most delicious fragrance from what looked like an ancient obsidian flask.

"Well, hello Nina!" said Tim as he came around my chair and helped me to my feet.

He put me into a short, clerical grey skirt, the most elegant blouse and waistcoat with a fine-knitted black cardigan - very Knightsbridge - over my shoulders. While Jo smiled lovingly up at me and started to clean up her things, he scrabbled around in a huge bronze chest for some jewellery.

Tim was to show his stuff as a photographer now and helping me up and down the rickety stairs of the old cottage, he snapped hundreds of exposures on his expensive-looking camera and the rest of the day passed with two more ensembles and photo-shoots, with Tim giving me glimpses from his camera memory of my new persona. I was astonished, enthralled and enchanted. I knew I had to pursue this woman, this alter-ego and thus

Nina was born.

Chapter 84

I had been on my own now for over a year but I still felt a small pang of loneliness and the wrench of the past, a little sadness too, as I opened my apartment door after the short walk from the small suburban sub-station after my connection from Leeds and York. I had taken some paintings, unframed to my York Gallery and loving the old city, I had made a day of it, even attending Evensong in the majestic Minster there. I was pleased to see some mail in my box and hurried up to my rooms where I brewed a coffee, kicked off my shoes, booted up my laptop and threw myself into my armchair.

I opened the letter first, noting excitedly its Exeter and Devon postmark. When I saw the letterhead: 'The Feminising Institute, Devon' I knew it was from Madame A. A glance showed three pages of elegantly typed script and knowing I was in for a treat, I set it aside for later and went over to my laptop to open my emails. I was still selling quite well and I eagerly anticipated requests from galleries for more work or even notice of recent sales. I had also posted the CD of my 'Fourth Space' makeover, and photo session to the Institute 10 days before, so I was excited as to what her reaction would be.

First, two short emails: one from Fifi:

'Oh, Nina, just to tell you that Madame has put me in the dungeon thingy for 10 days on bread and water and I'm now out. Just to tell you that I am ordered to write that Madame's sister, Annunziata, in France has got bad with the booze and her and Mistress Rosemary (My Fetish Mistress) *have gone over there to sort her out. Me and Tarty Tina are left looking after the Institute and as I'm not going back in that fucking hole of a dungeon again, we're on our best behaviour and doing the joint up. Luv, Fifi xx'*

The second, from Tarty Tina, confirmed Madame Assumpta's French jaunt but the great news that they'd received my CD and were delighted with it. With some excitement, I leapt back to my armchair and my coffee and Madame Assumpta's amazingly beautiful letter.

The Institute for Feminine Domination. Devon.

Friday 4th December 2009.

Dear Nina,

First of all, dear girl, thank you for your patience. For various reasons, our trip to France had to be extended and we have only just returned. This, combined with Fifi's failure to forward urgent mail to me, for which she has been severely punished! has meant a long delay in replying to correspondence and whilst other so-called submissives have BOMBARDED us with whining letters, you, Nina, have kept a very feminine and dignified silence. For this reason, I have placed your letter at the very top of the pile.

I understand that Fifi has been keeping you informed about our various troubles here and please do NOT beg for mercy on her behalf, I can assure you she deserves everything she gets, and more but it is nonetheless very nice indeed to be writing to you at last. Thank you once again for your patience and I do hope that communication between us in future will be less intermittent. Annunziata seems to have found some sort of stability at the moment and our sister, Theresa, a senior Politician, as I think you know? is still with her, so I am hopeful that I will not have to rush over to France anytime soon.

Well, what can I say? My dear, the CD you sent is EXTRAORDINARY! You look quite beautiful, and VERY feminine, in fact, I have had to remonstrate sternly with Tarty Tina, who was caught doing rather more than having a LOOK at your photographs.

Please do not worry about this. I know you are thoroughly heterosexual and I do promise that if ever you come to visit us here, which I sincerely hope you WILL, I will not let him/her put his sordid hands on you in any way, shape or form. We may have to lock her in the dungeon, but if that's what it takes, then make no mistake, that is what we shall do. You are very much our favourite here and we will not see you come to any harm. He would dearly love to shag you senseless but as I explained to him, that will be MY prerogative, not his.'

This delicious banter continued and then she got more literary, something which increased my excitement and she wasn't the first Dominatrix I had communicated with who had literary skills. Was 'she' really a man, I wondered? I had only seen her masked. A writer and one of her slaves? Somehow, I don't think so but she was nearer my own age I guessed. She also seemed a kindred spirit, like a sister, from whom I had been separated at birth?

'Your letter to us was wonderful!' she continued after a hilarious passage about her recent experiences 'dogging' at some squalid night club in Birmingham.

'We always look forward to them and I chuckled out loud over the likening of your first ear piercer to a harpooner from Moby Dick! However, later I got to thinking that you were really onto something there. It's a famously allegorical book, one of my favourites in fact but when I started to think about the central relationship in the novel, it struck me that if I were Ishmael, then you would be my Queequeg: Ishmael undertakes the journey through affection for the ocean -sexual exploration? - and you are a prince who has renounced everything, marriage, conventionality? to explore the same thing. There is a real intimacy there too, which I think is also true of our relationship. Incidentally, it is an unusual pleasure to be able to bandy literary references about in this way, most of our slaves here are rathe… LIMITED, in this regard.'

Nina: Well, me dears, you can imagine how poor old Dave was feeling then? Or not? There was much more of this and David continued breathlessly to the end. These were the last words he read from her:

'Do write again soon, Nina. You are indeed a contrary gal and I find you both intriguing and enormous fun.

In the meantime, much love, Assumpta XX'

Need I rehearse for you, darlings, the agonies and ecstasies that poor David went through in the following weeks? Frantic searches online; the Feminist Institute website closed, emails to Fifi and Tarty Tina, Google searches, sex shop visits in seedy quartiers of Leeds, Liverpool and Manchester? Poor thing, I know that we girls are not always radiantly fragrant but I enveloped him in mine and became determined to capture him, body and soul.

Nina: Poor Dave never met Miriam again, or Madame A either. I shall look after the silly old thing. That's me for now, lovelies.

Chapter 85

April 2019

But I saw her again at the station. Miriam, my wife.

I had been to a new Gallery just opened. In Ilkley once more and now about fifteen years on, I was single again and beginning to sell my paintings well. I had been to sign a few documents, print copyright and banking details and was dressed fairly smartly, my RAF tie worn proudly around my neck. I had even polished my brogues and sensing a bit of a nip in the air, I wore an elegant maroon silk scarf. I had grown to love silk next to my skin. County-style strides complemented the image, bought in Jermyn Street on a recent visit to London and a genuine, expensive Barbour jacket, newly-bought in Harrogate, on a trip to see my gallery there. I was freshly shaved and enjoyed a lingering eau-de-cologne fragrance. I even affected a tweed-style Trilby hat.

She was coming towards me on the concourse of Shipley Railway Station. I was waiting, seated, for the Skipton train, my connection to Keighley, where I now live very happily. She came near me and my heart, surprisingly, fell still. Instinctively, I rose, touching my hat brim with my former respect. Our eyes met but hers glanced away, a look of contempt swiftly shadowing her expertly made-up features. She walked on by and I slumped back down on the cold metal seat.

"Fuck her!" I thought, as I watched her retreating, her arrogant arse.

On the Skipton train, I picked up a copy of Murdoch's Metro, while leaving my Morning Star conspicuously on the vacant seat opposite. Spread the word, comrade! The Metro's headlines joyfully proclaimed the RAF bombings in Yemen. I needed to go to the toilet, I was getting that old! Once inside, I spontaneously tore my tie from my throat and flushed it down the toilet.

When I got back to my apartment, I booted up my laptop to see a whole page of the news of Julian Assange's abduction from the Ecuadorian Embassy. I knew it well. It was in Fitzrovia where I had first met Mistress

Spiteful and where I was to find a strange kind of love.

I knew then, that my England was finished. Russia. Holy Russia. Or my mother's land, Scotland.

I put on my CD of Rachmaninov's 'Vigil to the Blessed Virgin' and am listening to it now, as I type this. I shall listen to the sublime music while drinking a cup of coffee, musing about my new adventure.

It's dark now, nearly bedtime. Another Indigo night. I stroked my greying stubble, feeling nothing. 'Fuck it,' I'll shave in the morning, I said to myself. I relaxed, letting the great Orthodox Liturgy envelope me. I almost hear the voice of a grand old Dutch Lady: "Well done, Mynheer."

A tough and pert little blonde Stalinist also, selling 'Soviet Weekly', who kissed me once in Berkley Square. Innocent, Irish Dominic, my Billy Budd. Robin, once a Subaltern in 'The King's Own Dancing Girls'. Gentle and handsome Wes. Bill with his bicycle. Mikhail clanking into Berlin on his T-34. Gungha,'arse-end Charlie' at his 4 Brownings and with his cigs. Lovely Molly, or 'Death-Kiss Kate'; "I was Miss Ramsgate,'39, dontcha know, dear David!" Cavaliers all.

Then a knock at the door and the uncertain buzz of the intercom. I half-stumbled down the stairs, nearly tripping up.

"'Steady the Buffs!" I spluttered.

The blurred shape of a woman behind the glazed front door and a brushstroke of silverish-golden hair. I opened the door and she was standing there. It must have been raining, a spot of it shone on her slightly thickening nose. My heart raced.

"Well, don't just stand there!" she said.

We staggered into each other's arms. She paused at times for breath then blurted out, a Halifax lass again:

"What yer like, Zac?"

My heart was burning and I kissed the small, still rain from her eyes and her funny, sweet nose, then her throat and then our lips at last found each other's and she kissed me as only once I had been kissed before.

Epilogue

Some time into the new year of 2020, I had a strange dream. Nina, my alter-ego's voice seemed to rattle my bedroom window, a gust of accompanying wind fluttered my curtains and then her voice, vatic and commanding:

"GO PINK, girl!'"

I started, fully awake.

I had become lethargic and bored by the Covid lockdown that summer and depressed by the political situation since December of the previous year. Galleries were closing and I was poor at organising online sales.

After living 24/7 as 'Nina' as a part of my NHS transition programme, even taking hormones and gender change consultation, I had ceased the pathway just before leaving Bingley for Keighley. I continued my masquerade as a man, even as a 'gentleman' again. I was cross-dressing more now and flaunting 'Nina' on Facebook, still thinking I was just a harmless old perv.

One of my Fb female friends, being an ex-model herself, suggested that I try some modelling agencies, as, despite my age, I looked nearly convincing as a born woman. By the end of that summer, I received a dozen positive replies to my 'selfies' from modelling agencies. Remarkably, I got one urgent message from a London agency inviting me for an audition and photoshoot. Subsequent telephone conversations were friendly and enthusiastic, for London and they didn't seem to mind my age. They liked what they saw. They were intrigued that I was writing a novel and that I was a professional artist and portrait painter. Maybe I could be a good 'extra', or 'third spear bearer' in some posh TV production or movie?

Eventually, the day came. Thinking wistfully of Julie Christie, I took the 10.45 Kings Cross train from Leeds, my heart beating excitedly. I had been asked to bring four changes of female clothing, shoes, and wigs, no make-up, as their professionals would do it. Thus encumbered and feeling 23 again, I mentally urged the train onwards to the enticing south.

I booked into a hotel in my favourite Bloomsbury area, thinking that I deserved a treat. Despite the slightly war-time ambience, I enjoyed seeing Central London looking deserted. I had taken a few London breaks over the years, some to serve my professional Goddesses, as well as to trawl the galleries and bookshops, wander the ancient streets and attend choral evensong, or even mass, in older churches.

This time, after lugging my suitcase and rucksack down through Fitzrovia and right, along Oxford street towards Belgravia, I found Market Square, just off Soho, and Oxford street. The security on the door boded well and I was ushered down into a swinging basement, echoing and throbbing to hip-hop music and some new and exciting Afro-Caribbean jazz. It was everything I had dreamed of, better even than my first day at Art College.

I was easily the oldest person there and even though I was still in male drab, the mainly black, Asian, Middle-eastern and Latino youngsters treated me like a long-lost friend. This was my England, the one that I thought had died the December before.

"Hey, Nina!" cried a vivid Mexican girl, with jangling, hooped earrings and dancing, jet black curls.

She sat me down to ask me to sign some papers. Four make-up girls turned, lifting their brushes and combs in unison, smiling and nodding their heads towards me in welcome. A super-cool black guy, maybe the boss, waved cheerily at me, mouthing: 'Later?'

I was ushered towards a lovely Sikh girl, from Essex, as it turned out, who invited me with a gracious gesture towards her chair, swinging it around to receive me, from where I faced an array of lights as I had done a few years before on that magical day in Windsor. 'Lights, camera, action!' I mused to myself, as I fancied Nina at my ear: "Think PINK, dear!"

That done, wow! And: "Hi, Nina!" from the gorgeous Kaur, I was introduced to the photographer, a vivid young Caribbean Cockney lass:

"Call me Jade, wontcha, Nina?"

Laughing uproariously, after I had changed into black mini skirt, heels and blouse, clinking 'bling' jewellery, with my favourite silver-white wig, she gave me a couple of indoor shots, writhing on the floor with me camping it up, in a kind of erotic-cum pornographic dance, a hilarious and yet ritualistic drama, subversive and even decadent. Jade writhed and wriggled, clicking her Nikon, a slithering, sleek Salome. Feeling confident and sassy now and safely under Jade's command, I staggered in my heels onto a mini catwalk where we both camped it up and she took more shots, her camera clicking like castanets.

Then she took me out onto Oxford Street and Soho. I imagined the ghost of myself 50 years ago, half-starved and lonely, bone-tired, exhausted, wandering these streets as far as Mayfair, Berkley Square and down to the Embankment, via Trafalgar Square where a strange girl, a feisty young Communist, had kissed me.

After the shoot, Michael, the boss, the black guy who had waved to me, got me to sign a year's non-exclusive contract and flicked through my images on his PC. Saying that he was impressed, he welcomed me aboard and told me how much the team loved me. I felt that I had found my real home. I had joined the Circus at last!

I was given my first job, £3,700 for two days, minus commission, free rail travel and hotel. Not believing my luck, I just felt grateful that I had seen something new and positive. Later, after scrubbing up, I walked on air back through Holborn and Bloomsbury, to my hotel on Southampton Row.

Sadly, Covid put a stop to that, temporarily I hoped, but my contract enabled me to get a loan, enough to buy a second-hand laptop. Many other agencies seemed interested in me and I began to dream that I might have a future and 'Nina' too, of course.

I already had an old and trusted friend, another Jamaican, who promised to be my London agent for my paintings and I started to dream of an exciting future, even in my twilight years, in which I travelled and slept in the best hotels, taking my portfolio with me and earning big money in a job that I loved. I had always fantasised of mincing 'en femme' down the length of the King's Road from Fulham High Street to Sloane Square, Chelsea and maybe to see a Pinter play at the Royal Court Theatre.

Nina could become 'legit' and gradually, with botox, expensive grooming, and electrolysis, I could masquerade successfully as the 'lady' I had always unconsciously yearned to be. I reckoned I could get about 5 years of work, enough to put by and buy proper frames and materials for my painting and to be completely free of debt. I envisioned myself dining at

Harrods, or high tea at Fortnum's, a concert at Wigmore Hall, maybe Brixton Caribbean jazz clubs with Mark, my Jamaican friend; or even, my profound dream, a dominant new wife, myself collared and in a female-led relationship! Another Madame Assumpta?

So, later the following week, I got my laptop, lovely Mark having lent me the money. Booting it up, excitedly, I opened old email accounts that I couldn't access on my smartphone. I opened my email folder, thousands of them appeared as I scrolled down. Then a blast from the past made my heart skip a beat; nothing from the gruesome Glenda that I could see, then, one from 'Fifi'! I squealed with delight, remembering that along with 'Tarty Tina' ' she' had been one of Madame Assumpta's slaves. It was dated 19th December 2019.

"Hya, Nina, some bad news girl!"

Anticipating that Madame A had died, I scrolled down with some trepidation, through her post. The Institute of Correction had closed but Madame A's sister, Annunciata, was making a good recovery from her alcoholism; they had both sold up the Old Hall in Devon and bought a dungeon in Kemptown, Brighton, where Stan and I had bonded so long ago. Madame A, of course, had kept on Fifi and Tarty Tina as slaves; Fifi often chained to the cellar walls in the new Institute's premises on Sussex Square.

In Fifi's next post, she assured me that Madame A had been delighted to hear from me and would shortly be contacting me, with a cordial invitation to visit her at Sussex Square. She added a postscript to Fifi's post:

"Nina, (I could almost hear her voice) *at the least, dear girl, if not here, we can meet at Fortnum's or Harvey-Nicks. I cannot tell you how much I am looking forward to that and I am so glad to hear your good news.*

Goodbye for now, dear gel!" X

Madame A.

Well, well and bloody hell!!! My heart sings.

"Biiiiiaaaitches!!!"

No more shouty men; gone was the Black Douglas, the jackboot and Oliver Cromwell. Sordid as I was, I was free. I was Nina at last.

THE END

Acknowledgements

Abbi and Gemma Hobbs

Maggie Chilvers

Available worldwide from Amazon

---

http://mtp. agency

http://facebook. com/mtp. agency

@mtp_agency

Printed in Great Britain
by Amazon

68296767R00236